Caroline's heart raced at his forbidden touch. Instinctively, her eyelids fluttered closed, and Merrick's lips lowered to brush against hers.

Her ragged breathing warmed his face as the tip of his nose rubbed gently against hers. Bringing her head up to his in a silent plea, he began the consummating kiss with painstaking slowness.

A soft groan of pleasure encouraged him, and he slid the tip of his tongue delicately along Caroline's moist lips, seeking entrance with tantalizing pressure until they parted. As his tongue slipped in, he felt a shudder deep within himself—as though their bodies had joined in the ultimate intimacy, as though this sweet, dewy moistness had welcomed his entire being into her.

Together they felt a burning desire grow, pressing hard against the confines of their clothes, threatening to overwhelm them, no matter how hard they tried to fight against it . . .

RAPTURE'S LEGACY

SUSAN PHILLIPS

ST. MARTIN'S PRESS / NEW YORK

RAPTURE'S LEGACY

Copyright © 1989 by Susan Leslie Phillips.

ISBN: 0-312-91503-9   Can. ISBN: 0-312-91504-7

Printed in the United States of America

First St. Martin's Press mass market edition / March 1989

10 9 8 7 6 5 4 3 2 1

In loving memory
of
my father
FREDERICK SHERMAN LIEPITZ
who gave me the inspiration
of
my German heritage

PROLOGUE

Germany, 1883

Candlelight flickered in the windows of the small stone church nestled beneath a stand of evergreens. From the broad, moss-covered trunks of the black pines to the rustic gray walls laced with flowering vines, there was a feeling of eternal tranquillity. Inside the church, before a gilded altar, a white-haired clergyman sat behind an ornately carved pinewood table and smoothed his gnarled fingers across a parchment document lying before him. His black clerical cassock, with its close-fitting sleeves, was in stark contrast to the ashen pallor of his skin. Watery eyes, pale blue with cataracts, strained to see the words on the tanned sheepskin, and he nodded as if he were reading each letter with perfect clarity.

Across the table, two gentlemen stood in patient silence, facing the white-collared old man. Both were noticeably younger than the clergyman. The older of the formally dressed men displayed grayed temples and a weathered face that reflected more than sixty years. The broad-shouldered second gentleman was easily a head taller and visibly half the age of his companion, his ebony black hair and taut olive skin a testament to his vigorous health.

Crowded into long, wooden pews, the villagers kept reverent silence in respect for the occasion. Watchful eyes of all ages witnessed the momentous ceremony being performed for Herr Johann Hartmann and the young Baron Emmerich von Hayden, a ceremony that would bind together the two most powerful families in this region of the German Empire known as the Black Forest. Like the centuries-old legends of the dark woods, the history of these families was filled with stories of power, both real and mythical. For it was believed they were direct descendants of medieval mystics, people with inexplicable knowledge of things yet to come and other such unusual gifts of the mind.

The words on the parchment spelled out a promise between the Hartmanns and von Haydens, not only for the prosperity of the Church of the Mystics, but also for the rejuvenation of their own unique psychic powers. Since the Thirty Years' War in the seventeenth century, members had been forced to denounce their beliefs and intermarry with the foreign conquerors, a submission that led to diminished powers, as well as the decline of the church. Though some families had tried to remain deep in the Black Forest where their lineage would not be threatened, only two of these families still claimed a small degree of their inherent spiritual gifts.

Now, despite the heavy rains of late spring, no one in the tiny hamlet dared stay away from the single event that was sure to change their lives—if not that day, certainly some day in the years to come.

The seated patriarch of the church lifted his quill pen and solemnly extended it toward the two gentlemen standing respectfully before him. The new Baron von Hayden accepted it with a formal nod, then leaned over the pinewood table and signed the agreement.

In the final act that would seal the covenant, the gentlemen grasped palms in a binding handshake as the clergyman slowly rose and stepped around the narrow table. He gently placed his chalk-white fingers over the two hands gripped firmly together and raised his other palm in a silent blessing. Ageless wisdom shining in his pale blue eyes, the black-robed figure lifted his gaze beyond the men to the gathered crowd.

Although his outer form gave the appearance of frailty and weakness, his deep, resonant voice demonstrated an inner vitality and strength.

"Seven days we have mourned the passing of Baron Friedrich von Hayden, a great man and gifted member of our order," he said. "In the last moments of his life, His Excellency spoke of a dream in which these two special families joined together through marriage of their firstborn children. From this union, a son was born with gifts of prophecy and divine knowledge. In this vision, the boy grew to be a strong and able leader of our people.

"Today," he continued, "we have gathered together to witness the signing of this marital agreement between the Hartmanns and von Haydens. Before us and our omniscient God, Merrick has vowed to honor his beloved father's final wish. Soon he will leave for America where Johann's son now lives. There Merrick will find and marry the firstborn granddaughter, Ilse."

But not every villager welcomed the cultivation of a new leader among them. There was no assurance that the gifted child of this union would be kind and generous to his people. With the signing of the covenant, the seed of dissention had begun to grow.

Hours later, Merrick approached the front of the now-empty church, bowed reverently and stepped over to the first pew. He glanced around the rustic interior of the church, his vision blurring from the tears that threatened to overflow. Deep within, his soul felt torn open again as when he'd sat here years ago, shortly after his mother's death. Tears came easier for a boy of five than for a man of twenty-four. But the searing pain was just as real.

Dropping his face into his hands, he gave way to quiet sobs for the father he would never see again, a reality he still couldn't convince himself was true. Even as his shoulders shook, he half-expected his father's strong, supportive touch on his shoulder.

After several minutes, the cleansing sobs subsided, replaced by an inner peace that glowed with reassuring warmth. Instinctively, Merrick sensed the change had somehow come from his father's spirit, transcending an earthly barrier to comfort him. Though physically exhausted, Merrick's mind cleared of the mists of pain, like an early morning fog dissipated by the heat of the rising sun.

His thoughts focused on pleasant memories, instead of the tragic loss of a great man. His father's forty-seven years had been full and prosperous, filled with many friends. Now the vast land holdings had passed to Merrick, as well as the profitable vineyards, a responsibility he'd earned from countless hours at his father's side.

Yet, unlike his father who had continued to honor his mother's memory, Merrick had never lacked female companionship, a fact he attributed less to his wealth than to his mystical abilities that tantalized the curiosity of Society fräuleins.

Looking back on his casual lifestyle, Merrick sensed somewhere deep in his mind he'd known all along that this day would come, a day when he'd be called upon to put his obligation to family ahead of his selfish pursuits. Despite his independence, Merrick's deep devotion to his father and those who were born under their protective barony compelled him to agree to this preordained marriage.

But winning the granddaughter of Herr Hartmann would prove difficult. Twenty years earlier, Johann's only child, Ernst, had walked away from the old world culture with its myths and legends. He'd found a new life in western Pennsylvania where his friends had accepted him as one of their own kind, not a man of mystical ancestry. Ernst had turned his back on the religion of his forefathers. In a disquieting sort of way, Merrick understood the defiance of this man he'd yet to meet. He also knew that, because of this defiance, his quest to marry Ilse Hartmann would not be an easy one.

The mustiness of the old church building mingled with the scent of pine, then gave way to the light fragrance of lavender, so delicately faint as to almost not exist.

A vision of a young woman standing with an adolescent girl wavered before his eyes—the older one fair and delicate, the younger one dark and robust. Though he knew in his special way that the golden-haired woman was Ilse, it was the large emerald eyes of the young girl that stirred a fleeting response from deep within his soul.

Chapter 1

The sky was cloudless. The Atlantic rippled blue-green, speckled with froth. Gulls cried out as the promenade deck of the White Star liner *Teutonic* teemed with restless passengers bemoaning the effects of their first five hours at sea. As the waves lapped against the armor-plated hull below, Caroline Hartmann slowly made her way beyond first class. Her chaperone, Miss Mathilde Landau, had remained below in their formal stateroom, not quite adjusted to the swaying surroundings.

Baron von Hayden, her brother-in-law of six years, was also in his cabin, but Caroline doubted that his reason was attributable to a poor stomach. The probability of a man with such cold, iron will having the constitution of anything less than an ox seemed highly unlikely. Instead, she envisioned the worldly baron lying in his berth with his hands cupped behind his head of black curls, his long muscular legs crossed at his ankles.

She wondered if he would be snatching a moment of sleep before dinner. Or would those dark, penetrating blue eyes be staring at the ceiling boards above his head, perhaps lost in worried concentration over her sister Ilse and his unborn child in Germany? More likely it would be business matters that concerned him rather than his wife's delicate condition. He hadn't spoken of her once during their entire train trip to Philadelphia unless Caroline broached the subject; even then, his curt replies had discouraged any further discussion.

The steady, biting wind whipped her long chestnut hair against her reddened cheeks. Turning her head into the direction of the strong breeze, she pulled a strand away from her mouth and braced her hands against the wooden railing, locking her elbows as she leaned back and drank in the exhilarating salt air.

Far more than six years seemed to have passed since she had met the black-haired baron on the mountain road outside Sebula, her small hometown in western Pennsylvania. She'd been heading back to her parents' logging camp when a wheel had broken on the supply wagon.

She was only fourteen then, a rowdy, pigtailed tomboy letting loose with a frustrated kick against the broken spokes, following up with a yipe of agony. The scuffed toe of her black shoe did little to shield her from the impact.

A sudden thunder of hoofbeats tore her away from her misery. Bearing down on her, riding hard on a magnificent black horse, was a man she'd never seen before. Afraid for her life, Caroline flattened herself against the wagon box just as the stranger made a swift dismount only a few paces short of her toes.

"Are you hurt?" the man asked in a thick German accent like her father's.

Caroline released the air she'd drawn in when she'd thought it was the last breath she'd ever take. She watched him study her wagon, glance at the broken wheel, then finally look to her sturdy shoes where his gaze slowed and worked its way up to the white hair ribbon tied at the crown of her head. Never before had she feared being alone, whether she was on an isolated road or walking past the mills and lumberyards. But there was something in this man's dark blue eyes that told her to beware.

"No. I'm not hurt," she said belligerently, deciding that spunk was her best defense. She turned and hobbled on her painful foot up to her mare, Becky. "But I think I've just aged five years, thanks to you."

She clicked her tongue to the horse and led it out of the rigging to a pine stump nearby, wishing all the while that this dark-eyed man would leave her be so she could hike up her skirt and climb onto Becky's bare back.

He walked over to her horse, leading his own behind him. "Perhaps you should take my mount. You have to admit that I am better dressed for riding without a saddle." He gestured to her long, full skirt.

Caroline followed his gaze this time, down to where the slightly soiled hem dusted the toes of her catalog-order shoes, then noted the exquisite quality of his boots, planted uncomfortably close to hers. Slowly, her eyes rose as she took in the soft brown trousers that were the color of doeskin and the matching cutaway jacket; at last, she looked directly at his tanned face.

His chin and jawline were sharply defined, as was his fine, straight nose. His ink-black hair was thick and full, rippled with soft curls. But it was his dark blue eyes that captured her attention. They were the color of a moonless midnight— a deep, foreboding blue. Caroline felt her pulse quicken.

I've got to get away, she thought as a shudder swept through her.

His dark blue eyes stared into hers, delving deep inside her, unlocking the odd sensation—though he was a stranger, she felt she had seen him before.

"I mean you no harm," he said with a softness that convinced her he meant what he said.

"I should think not." Caroline broke eye contact and

turned back to her dusty horse, indicating she had no intention of accepting his mount.

In the short distance back to the camp, the stranger rode beside her in silence. It was not until dinner that she learned he was a nobleman, Baron Emmerich von Hayden.

But that was not all of the news: he had come all the way from Germany to claim the hand of her older sister, Ilse, as his bride. This pronouncement infuriated her father as much as it thrilled her ever-scheming sister.

Her father refused to allow the marriage. But before the week was out, Ilse had managed to set the town abuzz by circulating stories of improper behavior with her family's unwelcome guest. While the baron appeared quite unamused with the ruse, he did not object to a quiet ceremony immediately preceding their hasty departure for Europe.

From the moment she'd met him, Caroline recalled, she had felt an uneasiness similar to other feelings she'd experienced over the years—little unexplainable nigglings in the back of her mind that kept her on edge, like those she'd felt upon her Grandfather Hartmann's passing.

As she'd gotten older, she'd learned to expand her precognition at times into shadowy visions, an ability that frightened her. Now, after nearly six years without having heard from her sister and the baron, Caroline had begun to have dark, vivid dreams about them. Something was wrong and she didn't know what.

It wasn't long before Merrick arrived with Ilse's request to bring Caroline back to Germany. His wife was having difficulty carrying their child and had asked to have her sister at her side in the final bedridden months. With a matronly chaperone in tow, he'd arrived never doubting Caroline's willingness to accompany him.

A blustery ocean breeze pressed Caroline's long black skirt against her ankles as she reflected on the present. Aside from her devotion to Ilse, she wasn't quite sure why she had come with the baron and the thin, motherly chaperone, Miss Landau, whom he'd acquired in Philadelphia. An inner voice seemed to be beckoning her to step out in blind faith.

"HO! YOUNG LADY!" A middle-aged seaman hollered from several yards away. "You best get below. Someone's looking for ya!"

Caroline touched the brim of her straw hat as she raised her eyes and waved acknowledgement. She took one last look at the mid-October sun as it sank below the western horizon. Her first day at sea had passed quickly. The excitement of inspecting the newest White Star liner had brought Caroline topside. Long and uncluttered, the *Teutonic* was one of the first steamships to abandon mast-supported sails in favor of short masts that served merely as flagpoles. Consequently, the ship's silhouette was as meticulously modern as her interior refinements.

Merrick stepped outside through a door that opened beneath a set of metal stairs. The wide landing overhead served as a protective overhang from the weather, creating a shadowed alcove from the sun-washed deck. A man's loud voice drew the baron's sweeping gaze toward the bow where he saw Caroline, her head tilted up toward him as she waved.

Folding in the lapels of his outer coat to cut the chill at his throat, Merrick shook his head at the sight of his young sister-in-law. Now a woman of twenty, she wore a plain white blouse and black skirt. He thought she ought to at least have worn a sweater but he was impressed with her indifference to the cold. He wondered if she owned anything besides conventional skirts and amply cut blouses. She was so very different from Ilse.

If young Caroline were to don a crisp, white bonnet that chastely covered her head, she'd fit in perfectly among the Quaker women they'd seen when their train had passed through York County. But her lustrous head of hair ended any similarity to the plain people. It was her crowning glory. While he watched, a cascade of glistening red-brown curls was blown back over her shoulders by the cold sea wind she seemed to defy.

"We were worried that you'd fallen into the sea," he said standing directly behind her.

As Caroline turned toward the sound of his voice, the roll of the ship tipped her against the railing. She grabbed hold for support.

"From the way you snuck up on me, Herr Baron, I might think you were trying to help me overboard." she said tartly. She knew she should try to bury her resentment toward him for taking her sister away and destroying the serenity of her parents' lives. After all, he'd traveled all the way back to Pennsylvania for his wife's sake. Certainly that said something about his character.

He stood stolidly against the stiff breeze. "I think it's best if you learn not to make any sudden moves until you're more sea-oriented. Miss Landau called upon me to find you. She's grown quite concerned. You have been exploring the ship most of the day." He smiled. "Did you find it enjoyable?"

"I was just coming to my cabin," she said, resenting the implication of being a mischievously tardy child. "I didn't realize I had been gone so long." Suddenly aware that her fists were clenched at her sides, giving the baron a perfect picture of a defiant little girl, Caroline brought her arms up and crossed them as casually as possible, only to be unnerved by his now arrogantly amused smile. How she wished she could slap his face.

"For a girl who's not accustomed to the teasing of an older brother, you hold your temper fairly well. I would swear you were about to hit me."

"I would never think of striking you," she lied, wondering if her thoughts were so blatantly obvious or if the baron had somehow read her mind.

"Come, it is time to be getting back to Miss Landau," he said as he stepped aside and motioned with a sweep of his arm for her to lead the way, a gesture that pulled at the coppery buttons of his coat.

His appearance reminded Caroline of a ship's captain from a children's picture book. The baron looked very much like a man of the sea, she thought. Although, to gain command of an enormous vessel such as the *Teutonic* she supposed he'd have to be much older. But all the same, his strong slim body and square shoulders could easily withstand the years of hard sea duty. Those fine lines gathered at the outer edges of his deep blue eyes could have been etched by the salty winds.

Caroline listened to his footsteps behind her on the sea-scrubbed teakwood deck as they walked in silence to her cabin.

When the baron opened the door for Caroline, he saw Miss Landau lying in her berth. "Perhaps I may be of some assistance?" he asked with genuine concern, adding, "We could take her up on deck for some fresh air."

"If you think that would help," Caroline said.

In two long strides Merrick was at Miss Landau's bedside. Gingerly, he helped the pale woman dressed in somber gray to her feet.

"Come, Miss Landau," he coaxed. "It's time we get you up on your feet for a brief tour of the ship's deck." He looked across to Caroline and gave her a jaunty wink.

Prim Miss Landau moaned and expressed her embarrassment, but obliged the rescuers. Shortly thereafter she repeated her apologies after an indelicate performance at the railing. Although Caroline began to feel queasy herself, the baron continued to cajole the chaperone back to her predeparture spirit of adventure.

Once again in the stateroom, Mathilde Landau lay limp against her pillow, holding a cool, damp cloth to her forehead. Although the walk had added some color to her pale cheeks, the motion sickness had left her feeling like a wrung-out old rag.

Though any movement took extra effort, Hilde slowly rolled her head to the side to see what was keeping Caroline so quiet. Sitting cross-legged in a terribly unladylike manner on her mattress, the girl's head was bowed over a small, black leather-bound book. Her dark hair, drawn back and secured at the crown of her head with a black velvet ribbon, swept down over her far shoulder just past the tip of her bodice. Unconsciously, her long, slender fingers twisted and untwisted a thick strand of her hair as she studied the book in her other hand. Hilde thought Caroline was a lovely young woman, made more so by being completely unaware of her natural beauty.

Mindful of the girl's rustic upbringing, Hilde saw beyond the remnants of the rough-edged tomboy to the woman of grace and elegance that lay just beneath the surface. In the days that had passed since they'd met at the Hartmann house, she had often wondered whether Caroline would have discovered the lady within herself had she stayed in that small logging town. Perhaps. More than likely Caroline would have gone on being Caroline and been married in a year. This line of thought always led Hilde to the inevitable question—why did this American girl leave her parents to follow a German baron halfway across the globe?

Hilde doubted that the answer was less complicated than her own reason for accepting the position as chaperone. After twenty years in Philadelphia in the employ of a German immigrant family, the baron's timely offer afforded her the excuse and means to finally return home.

Caroline lowered her book and closed her eyes, tilting her head back to stretch her tense neck muscles.

"Tired?" Hilde asked.

Caroline half smiled just before she opened her eyes and looked across the room. "Just stiff," she said, lifting her head, then tilting it forward. "Feeling any better?"

"A bit, but I couldn't dance a jig."

"Then I wouldn't dream of leaving you again just to stand around all night in the ballroom," Caroline said. Hilde noted the obvious relief in the way the girl settled back against the wall of her berth, opening the book again.

"I find it hard to believe that a pretty thing like you would pass up a chance to dazzle everyone in one of your new gowns." Hilde was curious about Caroline's relationship with the baron. When he'd hired her, he hadn't said much about this trip. He'd needed a matron to chaperone a young girl to his home in Baden, near the town of Karlsruhe. Until the last-minute change in shipboard accommodations put Hilde in the same stateroom with her charge, she had assumed she'd never know the whole story. It wasn't any of her business, and prying was not her way, but there was something about Caroline that made Hilde feel maternally protective. She had learned to curb this emotion in her years as a governess—it was an emotion that too easily blurred her role as a paid servant. But, she told herself, every rule asked for an exception.

"I find it hard to believe that the baron would waste good money on a new wardrobe for me. My clothes serve my needs and my needs don't include ballroom dancing. What am I going to to with those gowns when I get back to Sebula?"

Hilde shifted over to her side to get a better look at Caroline.

"Back to Sebula?" Had Hilde misunderstood the extent of her services? She didn't realize she might be expected to return with Caroline. The baron had never mentioned it.

"Of course. As soon as possible."

"I thought that, maybe, you and . . . I mean . . . I'm not really sure what I thought about you two. But His Excellency only said he'd need me to accompany you on the trip over. I wondered if you were to marry him there."

"Marry?" Caroline looked appalled. "He is married to my

older sister. Ilse asked him to come and get me so I could be
with her when she has her baby."

"Ah, it's beginning to make a little more sense. His formality. Sending us out on that shopping excursion. He just
wanted you to feel more comfortable in his customary surroundings."

Caroline shrugged. "For that I should be grateful, but I
find it hard to feel that way about him." She went on to
explain the events that led to her transatlantic journey, con-
cluding with the parting gift of her mother's small Bible.
Caroline held up the black book she had been reading, its
leather binding frayed from daily use.

"Mama knows I have my own, but she insisted I take this
one. She said to study it hard. So you see, Miss Landau,
before arriving at my sister's, I plan to have this Bible thoroughly studied." Caroline lightly shook the Holy Book with
determination.

After Hilde politely asked Caroline to set aside formality
and call her by her given name, she admired the young
woman's tenacity. "Quite an undertaking, don't you think,
reading the entire Bible in such a short time?"

"I think I've come across something already. Mama underlined some words."

"You mean verses?"

"No, just words. Look." Caroline moved to sit next to
Hilde, then pointed to a yellow-edged page.

The older woman welcomed any diversion from her background nausea and commented, "You might jot them down
as you find them. Perhaps they all mean the same thing, like
'love,' 'kindness,' 'truthfulness.' Those are all virtues your
mother would want you to maintain."

Caroline shrugged. She walked over to a narrow secretary
against the wall, sat down, and copied the words. After a few
quiet moments, she turned excitedly to Hilde who still lay in
her berth.

"It's a poem. Listen . . .

> *'Amid your battles you have fought,*
> *Stand armed with spiritual thought.*
> *While you walk this earthly ground,*
> *In this book your hopes are bound.'* "

"A riddle?" Hilde's forehead creased in thought.

Caroline studied the piece of paper, shaking her head. "I don't think so. It's just like something Mama would say. In spite of her failing health, she's the most devout woman who ever lived. Always saying that fulfillment is found in the Bible."

"Then why did she underline those words?" Hilde countered in an effort to be helpful. "Why didn't she just write the poem inside the front cover?"

"That will take some thought."

A quiet knock sounded at the door.

"Yes?" Caroline called out as she lowered the paper to her lap.

"It's Baron von Hayden."

Caroline unlatched the door and stepped back, admitting him into the cabin while Hilde sat on the edge of her berth. The tall baron dipped slightly as he passed beneath a low beam. He nodded a greeting in Caroline's direction; her pulse leapt at the sight of him in his formal black evening attire.

He addressed Hilde who was self-consciously smoothing her modestly coiled hair. "You look one hundred percent better than when I left you, Miss Landau. Will you two be joining me for dinner and dancing?"

"Thank you, no, Your Excellency. Perhaps Caroline would like to—"

Caroline stepped up, "After this afternoon, I think I owe it to Miss Landau to stay. Perhaps you could send someone down with some beef tea for her."

"And something for you?"

"A small plate—"

"Nonsense, child," Hilde scoffed. "I will not allow you to waste a perfectly beautiful evening playing nursemaid to me.

Baron von Hayden is quite capable of escorting you to dinner, I'm sure." She nodded humbly to Merrick who returned the gesture with an added look of amusement when he turned his gaze on Caroline, all three knowing full well her only course was to agree.

"Very well," she sighed. "I'll be ready in one hour."

"I'll return in half that time. I'm famished." Ignoring her protests, he was out the door the next instant.

The walls of the dining-saloon were upholstered with mellow pictures wrought in tapestry and the ceiling seemed aglow with paintings done in oil.

Merrick pulled the chair out from the captain's table, his hands gripped tight around the turned knobs on the high back. With a rustle of taffeta, Caroline took her seat on the rich burgundy-colored velvet cushion, barely pausing to acknowledge his gentlemanly gesture with only the slightest nod. In less time than seemed imaginable, she had transformed into a breathtakingly beautiful woman, dressed in a royal-blue gown that followed the curve of her breasts, down to her narrow, corseted waist and over the swell of her hips.

He was well aware of the eyes in the dining-saloon, especially those of the men, that were riveted on Caroline with her mahogany curls pinned up off her long, slender neck, set off with a small blue hat. A delicate heart-shaped locket drew admiring attention to her décolletage, a thought Merrick found irritating somehow.

Even without his uncommon perceptiveness, he knew that Caroline's warm, welcoming smile hid a timid awareness of her shapely endowments. All it took was an appreciative stare from the gentleman seated next to Captain Werner for Merrick to feel a surge of anger. With the sweet scent of Caroline's perfume drifting up to his senses, Merrick's reproachful glare crushed the presumptuous younger man across the table, making him nervously turn his attention to the Captain. Caroline noticed the exchange. When he met her puzzled look, he momentarily felt at a loss for words to explain his behavior, especially when her green eyes seemed to dance like emeralds in the evening light. He could only hope that she interpreted his reaction as a protective act of a brotherly nature.

Fighting back the possessiveness toward her that he had no right to claim, Merrick walked around to his chair and seated himself. Almost immediately, two lovely ladies joined him, eagerly introducing themselves.

The elegant squab dinner was wasted on Caroline. Pushing a baby carrot about her Meissen dinner plate, she was preoccupied with playing the role of a sophisticated debutante, while praying no one could see through her charade. Whatever induced her to buy this gown in Philadelphia? The baron, of course. He'd insisted she have a few things so she'd not feel out of place among the first-class passengers. Admittedly, she was a bit excited about owning this exquisite gown, one of four she'd found on such short notice. But in her haste, Caroline allowed herself to be swayed by the dressmaker who swore that the revealing dip of the neckline was relatively conservative.

From the general reaction around the table, the clerk seemed to have been right. Still, she kept wanting to cover herself. Her modesty, she'd concluded, was hers alone. The other two women seemed quite proud of their tantalizing display of flesh. It showed in their delicate gestures, touching their jewels or drawing their fingertips across the swell of their breasts. They seemed delighted to draw the men's attention to that area—especially the golden-haired woman to Merrick's left.

More often than not, Caroline found herself stealing glances at the casual interplay between the baron and his European lady friends. He seemed to enjoy their gaiety immensely, occasionally throwing his head back as he laughed at a comment whispered into his ear. Though he didn't return their bold advances, these highbred women worked hard to keep his attention rapt by constantly touching his hands and his sleeves.

As the blonde teased, pressing the bodice of her white satin gown against his forearm while she cupped her hand to his ear and whispered, Merrick's mirthful eyes met Caroline's and froze there, his amused expression fading. Although she'd resented the baron for taking Ilse away, she no longer felt years of pent-up anger. What she felt now was more of a hurting sort of pain. She told herself it was for her sister, for the fact that he shouldn't be so happy when Ilse lay in bed desperately fighting for the life of his child.

With sudden regret, Merrick sensed Caroline's disapproval and tried to convey in his gaze that all was not as it seemed. His young sister-in-law didn't understand the socially acceptable behavior of his society. How could she? Living in that small Pennsylvania logging town didn't expose her to this kind of living. Thinking back on his wife's introduction to these social games, he remembered how quickly Ilse had assimilated into the peerage. Unlike Caroline, his wife not only approved of the playful repartee between the sexes, she quickly became the queen of double entendres and vampish friskiness. Inevitably, there had been talk about possible infidelity. He knew it was nonsense.

"It appears my sister-in-law needs rescuing from boredom." Merrick placed his white napkin on the linen tablecloth. "If you will excuse me, I will see you ladies in the ballroom."

"You will save me the last dance, Your Excellency," the blonde traced a fingertip down his sleeve to the top of his hand, ending her caress with a light, suggestive squeeze. Merrick smiled recklessly at her decadent tease, pushing his chair back as he stood up.

* * *

"I'd prefer to go back to my room," Caroline told the baron, feigning a smile as he led her from the dining salon.

"Which will give the scandalmongers material regarding the two of us," he playfully whispered in her ear.

"What are you talking about?"

"If I disappear with you now, it's my bet that the entire room will be wagering on our whereabouts."

Flushed with a mixture of anger and embarrassment, Caroline pulled up short of the ballroom entrance and turned to the baron with a rasping whisper. "You are an arrogant, perverted—" His chuckle added to her frustration. "Don't laugh at me!"

"My dearest Carrie, I have so much to teach you." Merrick tucked her hand into the crook of his arm, mildly astonished at his own proclamation, and turned them into the already crowded room. The sea of colorful gowns and dark formal suits parted when the baron and Caroline entered, and a hush fell for a moment before the music started up once more.

His endearment took Caroline by surprise, leaving her with no resistance as he swept her out. His palm grasped hers. His other hand slid to the small of her back, pressing through her blue taffeta. Moving to the music with rigid formality, Caroline couldn't have felt more uncomfortable than if the baron's body were a red-hot branding iron ready to sear her skin. She didn't dare look up into his eyes, the eyes as dark as midnight. He would certainly see her confusion written on her face and there were no words that could explain or question what was taking place. All she knew was that her heart was pounding so hard she thought her chest would burst from the pressure.

"I don't belong here, Your Excellency," she finally said when she found her voice. But she spoke so quietly into the center of his crisp white shirt that she thought he hadn't heard her over the music. Swallowing hard, she tilted her head up and found his deep blue eyes, lined with thick, spiked lashes, gazing down upon her.

"You are extremely perceptive." Merrick felt her tense under his graceful lead, yet he continued to tease. "A princess belongs on a castle balcony overlooking her kingdom on the Rhine."

"You know full well I didn't mean—"

"To sound pompous?"

"I'm not pompous, Your Excellency," she said with emphasis.

"Is that an indication that *I* am?"

"At times."

"And what about these other people who are simply having a good time of it?"

"I would hardly call open solicitations the proper manner in which to 'have a good time of it.' "

Though he obviously tried to hide it, the corners of Merrick's full lips curled into a bemused smile. "I'm sure you wouldn't."

"You're mocking me."

Merrick grew sober. "No, Carrie. It's just that I think your resentment has more to do with *my* conduct than a particular lady's at the captain's table."

Caroline quickly looked out onto the dance floor, avoiding his pointed gaze. "You are married, Your Excellency."

"What if I told you it is in name only?"

She looked back at him sharply. "And in whose name will this child of Ilse's be christened?"

A wide grin split his features. "You have a fast wit, little one. Thankfully, not as caustic as your sister's. She'd have reeled off her favorite epithets and stormed off." He laughed, but Caroline sensed a trace of bitterness. "No, there is no denying that the child is mine. I'm as certain of that as I am that the sun will rise tomorrow."

"Do you love Ilse?" she asked with a bluntness that startled him.

"Yes," he said after a slight hesitation. "But in a way that I'm sure you can't understand." His gaiety vanished.

"Perhaps if you gave me a chance, I could understand. I feel like you still think of me as a pigtailed tomboy. I'm not a child anymore, Your Excellency."

I am only too aware of the fact. Deep within his body, Merrick felt a tingling warmth building, defying his practical reason. To his relief, the music stopped, curtailing their private conversation as they joined in the polite applause.

Now he would have to decide whether to guide her into the den of young wolves who anxiously waited their turn with her, or to escort her out and leave them all curious about his position with her. Caroline deserved to be admired, to be enjoying a taste of this gilded life. Yet, whom would he choose to introduce her to the subtleties of such a decadent style of living?

The thought agitated him. No, it infuriated him. He wanted Caroline to remain fresh and untainted.

Why? For whom?

For him. The idea hit him as sharply as if Caroline had slapped him, and his reaction to his tumultuous thoughts was as if she'd actually done so. He stared incredulously at the young woman in his arms for one long moment, then took her arm and walked her toward a gathering of gentlemen. The possible social harm these men could inflict upon Caroline in the short span of their voyage was minimal compared to the irreparable damage he could do to her if he didn't bring his feelings under control.

"We'll discuss this later," he said.

Caroline's fingers dug into the sleeve of the baron's black evening jacket, feeling the hard muscles of his upper arm as each step drew them nearer to the cluster of young gentlemen who eagerly watched their approach. Her mind raced over the brief exchange on the dance floor. What had she done that angered Merrick so suddenly? Without warning his expression had grown dark, his jaw clenched. Now she was being led over to these men as though His Excellency was ready to toss her into their midst.

After brief introductions, in which Merrick conveniently left out his marital connection to Caroline, he withdrew her gloved hand from his arm and offered it to a pale, red-haired gentleman with a thick Scottish burr. "Please entertain Miss Hartmann while I tend to some business."

"Be more than happy to, sir," Hugh MacKenzie replied.

Despite the baron's abrupt departure, Caroline made the best of the embarrassing situation and returned the gentleman's warm smile, allowing him to lead her in a waltz.

Preoccupied with the manner in which the baron had just rid himself of her, Caroline felt a polite indifference to Hugh MacKenzie's firm but gentle grasp of her hand and waist. Dancing with Hugh was like dancing with any of the lumbermen or local boys back home. Nothing remarkable. Caroline found her attention wandering to the couples around them.

There was a fascinating assortment of first-class travelers: American, German, Danish, French, Russian, Swedish. Some were on business but many were on a holiday.

"Who is that?" Caroline asked when an elegant woman her sister's age danced past in the arms of an equally dashing partner. More than once that evening, Caroline had turned to see the woman's eyes on her, only to quickly glance away.

"Countess Reinhart. She's quite a lovely one, she is," he said, adding, "but not as bonny a lass as y' be."

Caroline gave him a skeptical smile. "You flatter me, Mr. MacKenzie." She turned her attention back to the beautiful woman, drawn by a curious niggling in the back of her mind. "A countess, you say. Is she German or is Reinhart her husband's name?"

"Both. But there is no longer a husband. Rumor has it that he died penniless."

Caroline's eyebrows lifted questioningly. There was no doubt that the woman didn't fit the description of a destitute widow. Besides the cost of the voyage, her gown alone had to have cost a great deal.

The Scotsman shrugged, saying, "It seems her background prior to her marriage is only a bit more mysterious than the name of her . . . benefactor. I've only heard he's a generous sort but not likely to leave his wife for the Countess."

"Leave his wife?"

Mr. MacKenzie studied her with a twinkle in his eye. "I believe that is what I said. Does that shock you, Miss Hartmann?"

"No," she lied, trying not to appear judgmental of such arrangements. Perhaps among the continental elite it was perfectly acceptable for an elegant woman to be kept as a mistress. From the endless line of dancing partners, it appeared that Countess Reinhart didn't want for acceptance, despite her scandalous lifestyle.

Upon the conclusion of their dance together, Caroline's curiosity got the best of her and she asked to be introduced to the Countess. The dark-haired woman, dressed in a plunging gown the color of spun gold, was quite visibly titillated by the mention of Baron von Hayden. Her lips curved into a wistful smile as she sipped a glass of champagne. "The von Haydens are from an old family. Very powerful. Very respected. Though I've never had the pleasure of meeting the Baron, I have met the Baroness on several occasions. Unfortunately, it was always at a time when His Excellency was away on business."

"Then you know my sister—Ilse!" Caroline beamed proudly to the small group of ladies and gentlemen gathered around them. The older woman, however, had simply lowered her glass just enough to study Caroline with a scrutinizing look that confused her. "Is there anything wrong?"

Hugh MacKenzie, standing with Caroline, patted her hand on his arm. "No, Miss Hartmann, I don'na believe we realized ya' to be related to such . . . nobility."

Whispers filtered through the circle, causing Caroline to

wonder about the passengers' reactions and to vow silence on the subject again.

Two hours passed before Merrick appeared to escort Caroline back to her stateroom. The ease of his gait as he crossed the room showed him to be more relaxed than when he'd left her in the hands of Mr. MacKenzie, a fact she attributed to the faint masculine scent of tobacco she smelled on his jacket when he reached her side. While she had danced with almost every eligible male on the ship until her feet were sore, he had apparently been wiling away the time in the gentlemen's smoking lounge.

With a multitude of curious eyes watching, Merrick offered his arm to Caroline. "I believe your chaperone said you had to be back at midnight?"

Though Hilde hadn't imposed a time limit on her evening, Caroline understood the baron intended to clarify publically the existence of a chaperone to the doubters. Too exhausted to retaliate for his earlier desertion, she stepped closer and took his arm.

"Thank you for a lovely evening, Mr. MacKenzie. Remember—tomorrow morning at nine." Caroline gave him a bright smile and wave over her shoulder.

Walking out into the night, away from the noise and lights, Merrick asked, "What are you doing tomorrow morning at nine?"

"He invited me to play a game of shuttleboard," she said proudly.

"*Shuffle*board," Merrick corrected irritably.

Once on the open deck, Caroline stopped and faced him, waiting to speak until a strolling couple was beyond range of hearing her. "What have I done to make you so mad at me?"

Merrick wanted to deny it, but even if he had masked his emotions—as was his wont—Caroline would have seen through it. He sensed—no, he *knew* beyond a doubt that she had some mind-reading capabilities. When he'd met her at fourteen, he'd denied his intuition about her. But six years later, even when she herself didn't seem to acknowledge it, Merrick knew that Caroline had the same abilities as he.

As fate would have it, of the two sisters, it appeared that it was Caroline—not Ilse—who possessed the special gifts. Pre-cognition. Mind reading. Telepathy. *No doubt she denies them,* he thought, *probably even considers them evil.*

Merrick stepped over to a bench, gently pulling Caroline down beside him. "It's time you knew about our families." His dark brows lowered as his expression grew serious and he told the seemingly incredible story of her gifted ancestors, of her own special powers and of a baby yet to be born.

Chapter 2

Eight days later, the night before their arrival in the Dutch port of Rotterdam, Caroline strolled the deck with Miss Landau and the baron, her mind wandering from the polite conversation concerning German politics. The knowledge of her ancestry that Merrick had imparted to her was like a key that unlocked the shackles of condemnation. Better than that, she decided. It was as if he had given her a key to a room full of treasure. But she must never forget, he'd warned her, that everything good has a dark side to guard against. Since she'd learned that her unusual mental abilities were not to be feared, she had thought of little else but the awesomeness of it all. If only she had known that there had been others like her, what anguish it would have saved her—the fear of eternal retribution.

The threesome paused at the starboard rail and gazed at the full moon rising above rolling swells to the east.

"It's like an enormous lighthouse lantern signaling that land is ahead," Caroline noted of the bright yellow moonglow that illuminated the Atlantic, creating opalescent whitecaps.

"It also signals the end of Miss Landau's misery," the baron said.

"It certainly has been a memorable voyage, Your Excellency," Hilde responded. "We appreciate your kindness."

"My pleasure, Miss Landau. Now I must tend to a few details before docking tomorrow. I'll escort you back to your stateroom and be on my way."

Hilde fell in step beside him and called over her shoulder, "Coming, Caroline?"

The young girl had become lost in her thoughts as she watched the rhythmic dance of the iridescent waves amid the slow, shallow roll of the swells. The multitude of small white crescents that appeared and disappeared looked like giddy pixies popping from the dark depths in a private game. *Come play,* Caroline imagined they whispered to her. *Don't go away. Come play.*

A penetrating warmth spread through Caroline at the touch of a hand on her shoulder. She stiffened and an odd sensation swept through her; it was similar to the tormented feelings she experienced the last several nights when she'd had dreams of the baron. For the time it took to breathe one breath, reality seemed entwined with fantasy, and fantasy with reality. What was real? What was an illusion? *But I'm not dreaming now. I'm awake. On deck. Watching the waves— and pixies?*

"Are you all right?" The baron's voice sounded concerned and his hand on Caroline's shoulder slightly shook the girl.

When her head came around, she was transfixed by his dark eyes. Her senses were so acutely attuned to him, she felt completely surrounded by his presence. The subtle masculine fragrance of his cologne filled her. His light touch radiated from where his fingertips lay, kindling a confusion of desires and self-denials.

"I'm fine." She smiled and hid her disorientation of the moment. "Just enjoying the beautiful moonlit ocean."

"With your eyes closed?" The baron cocked his head quizzically. Caroline forced a calm shrug.

"Falling asleep at the rail. That won't do," Hilde Landau chided, making her presence known. "I think it's best if you get to bed."

As Hilde and the baron led the way back to the cabin, Caroline glanced back at the water. *Pixies?* She shook her head and turned her attention ahead of her. Perhaps Hilde was right, she concluded. She was tired.

In their stateroom, Caroline lifted her mother's Bible from the walnut writing desk and walked to her berth. "I think I'll read awhile, if you don't mind."

Hilde gave her a worried look, "After nodding off at the railing, don't you think you should get your rest? Tomorrow is going to be a long day."

"I promise I won't stay up long." Caroline immersed herself in her reading while Hilde changed into nightclothes and slipped into the berth on the opposite wall. Before long, Hilde's slow, even breathing drifted across the room. Coupled with the gentle roll of the ship, the relaxing sound of deep sleep played upon Caroline's heavy eyelids, pulling them lower and lower.

She imagined the moon outside, climbing the night sky, keeping watch over the restless ocean and its seafarers. It was an intoxicating night of shadows and light, of elusive colors defined in shades of gray and white. The allure of one last look beckoned Caroline. She pondered the idea for a brief moment, tangled in the indecision of accepting sleep or pursuing the magnetism of some mystical presence.

Drifting, Caroline's thoughts turned to the baron. Once again his face hovered over hers. His dark blue eyes were the color of the night ocean—the ocean that beckoned her. He moved closer, creating a heart-pounding anxiety she only

knew in her dreams of him. She felt his warm breath upon
her as he slowly lowered his mouth to hers. But when he
reached up to caress her thick curls, she struggled and pulled
back.

"Someday, Carrie," his eyes told her. Then he was gone.

She sat up abruptly. Her breath came in shallow gulps.
Her pulse throbbed within her temples. Perspiration beaded
on her forehead. The strange chill was upon her again, just as
with her other dreams. She felt the walls closing in on her.

Get some fresh air, a voice echoed in her mind. *You'll be fine
after a nice walk on deck. The beautiful moon. The sea air. Don't
be afraid. Remember what the baron said. You're different. You
have powers that can protect you.*

Caroline glanced at Hilde one last time before quietly
closing the door behind her.

Familiar with the boundaries of the passenger area, Caroline was careful to stay within them. But it was late and
dark. In the daylight she hadn't realized the similarity in the
passageways. After their evening walks, Caroline had always
followed the baron and Hilde back to the cabin, too preoccupied with conversation to pay attention. When she turned a
corner, she heard deep voices and laughter behind one of the
doors.

"Where's Bates tonight?" she heard a gruff voice ask.

Another mimicked a woman's shrill voice. "Off hiding
somewheres—drownin' his sorrows." Several masculine
voices cackled at the effeminate gossip.

"Somethin's eating 'im. That sonovabitch ain't fit to live
with."

"I seen him 'round first class at odd hours near that Countess' cabin."

"Naw—didn't ya hear? He's been eyeing that baron's
young plum in first class. Ain't no two ways about it."

The men whooped and stomped their feet.

"Is he crazy?" asked the first voice, sounding somber.

"Capt'n ever hear 'bout this an' Bates'd be chain-whipped. He'll wish he's dead after Capt'n gets through with him."

"Capt'n ain't nothing to what I hears 'bout that baron. He's a warlock, ya know. Cast ya' dead sure as I'm sittin' here."

"Yer daft, man. There's no such a thing as a gawddamn warlock."

"Doesn't matter anyway. Neither of them's gonna find out nothing from me," someone snarled. "Bates's scrawny but I seen 'im fight an' y' won't catch me temptin' his bad side."

With no doubt in her mind that she was the object of the men's discussion, Caroline turned on her heel and retraced her steps, hoping to find her way back to the cabin before being discovered. The voices echoed in her mind as she quickened her pace. Each shadow threatened her. If she couldn't find the stateroom, she could at least get to the bridge and find Captain Werner to help her back to her cabin.

Up on deck, Thatcher Bates squatted low in his secret drinking alcove and pushed a shank of stringy brown hair from his sunken eyes. Obsessive thoughts of the voluptuous dark-haired girl brewed in his liquor-soaked brain. The high, rounded mounds beneath her prim blouses excited him. The full curve of her hips beneath her dowdy skirts teased him. The schoolgirl bows at the crown of her head created a beguilingly innocent image to him. The girl in first class was like a tempting apple, ripe for the picking. He couldn't resist the temptation, no matter what the risk.

He shifted his position to relieve the growing tightness of his trousers. Each night of the cruise, he'd played out the fantasy of overtaking the girl and claiming her virginity as he had done to countless other victims.

A surge of excitement stabbed in his loins and he stifled the chuckle of contentment at his multiple conquests in ports around the world. He raised his near-empty bottle of whis-

key in a smug toast to himself and polished it off, drinking
more than his usual.

He would have her, he thought. He would follow her
from the ship after she left in the morning. And when the
moment was right, somewhere in the streets of Rotterdam,
he would steal her away from her escorts. Until then, he'd
have to wait, not an easy task for a man who was used to
taking whatever he wanted.

Two levels below the drunken sailor, in a first-class stateroom that boasted the finest luxuries that the steamship line
had to offer, Merrick was unaware of the malicious kidnapping plot developing as he slept. Deep in his mind, another
disturbing dream invaded his peaceful rest, one of many he'd
had since leaving Sabula.

In each, he saw his young sister-in-law with realistic intensity: first, as the feisty child he'd met on the road from
town six years earlier; then, as the young woman he'd taken
from the security of her home. But this night the vision he
saw before him was the Caroline he'd come to know every
evening across the table, on the dance floor, and on the
promenade deck.

Her long tresses were pulled up off her slender neck and
secured with diamond-studded pins that reflected twinkling
candlelight. A golden heart-shaped locket rested against her
satiny skin, calling tantalizing attention to the generous rise
of her breasts in the high-waisted, emerald-green gown.

Merrick longed to take the locket in the palm of his hand
and let his knuckles brush casually against her, feeling the
warmth of her silken skin. He wanted to grant himself one
brief touch, a touch that wouldn't threaten her and drive her
farther away than she already seemed, yet that would satisfy,
however momentarily, his deep need to be close to her. But
he knew such liberties were forbidden to him.

For the aristocracy among whom he was raised, Merrick
knew sex was considered nothing more than entertainment.
Marriage was for appearances and prestige. Prior to his own

betrothal, he, too, had taken carnal enjoyment in the arms of a number of beautiful wives who were fully aware of their own husbands' dalliances. But he'd long ago vowed to make a solemn commitment to his marriage, as his father had once done.

Besides which, circumstances warranted a monogamous commitment to Ilse, if not in soul, at least in body. When she'd learned of his formerly rakish reputation, her jealous tirades had indeed tempted him to return to old habits. As their once-promising relationship deteriorated under Ilse's unsubstantiated accusations of infidelity, she'd threatened to have any man of her choice, wherever and whenever she pleased.

As much as Merrick sensed Ilse's declaration was her bitterly pained response to their faltering marriage, he also knew her vengeful tactics would place grave question on the parentage of any child she would bear.

Shackled by the prearranged covenant between their families, Merrick was determined to keep close watch on his spiteful wife. He hadn't come so far, relinquishing his own personal freedom, to fail in his promise to his father and his family to produce the mystical child. If Ilse hadn't become pregnant, he'd never have trusted her to be left behind when he went to America. Then again, if she were not so ill with his child, he'd never have had reason to bring Caroline back to Germany.

For some inexplicable reason, he welcomed the opportunity to bring the young girl into their lives. She was like a piece of a jigsaw puzzle he turned around and around in his hand. There was a place for her. A reason for her to be with him. Or he with her. But, hard as he tried, he couldn't figure out how or where she fit in. Somehow, he sensed, he would know the answers when the time came.

Accepting this rationale, however provisionally, eased the inner turmoil over this vision of Caroline before him. As if she were quietly acknowledging that her presence in his dream was no longer necessary, she turned and walked away from him, disappearing into the dark recesses of his mind.

In her place, another image wavered like a heat mirage, then cleared into sharp focus. A dark silhouette of a man squatted low, watching something . . . someone . . . with beady-eyed intensity. Without diverting his gaze, the figure wiped the palm of his hand across his mouth, then rubbed it against his thigh, dipping inward in a quick, but noticeable gesture to relieve his discomfort.

Experiencing his dream as though it were reality, Merrick felt a black hatred harden inside his chest. His body responded with clenched jaw and labored breaths. Who was this man who skulked in the shadows? What was he eyeing with a perversity that disgusted Merrick? Then he saw her. Caroline. Dressed in her familiar, simple clothes, her tentative steps told him of her fear and indecision.

His heart hammered against his ribs. He could no longer believe this was some hideous nightmare. He knew Caroline was up on deck at that very moment, blindly walking into a trap. He had to stop her. The fear for her safety gripped him, tearing him from his sleep.

His eyelids blinked wildly. The stateroom remained as he'd last seen it—quiet and still. Yet instead of calm, the feeling of peril intensified threefold. Merrick swung his feet onto the floor. Yanking his trousers over his hips, his thoughts turned to one possible way he could help Caroline before it was too late. With her mental capabilities similar to his, there was a slim chance she would be receptive to his telepathic warning.

In theory, it should work. He knew she possessed the gift of mind control; he'd sensed it long ago. That left little doubt that she could be as diverse in her unusual abilities as he.

Grabbing his shirt from the back of a chair, he ran from the room. Despite his excellent physical condition, the hard muscles in his legs seemed leaden as he darted down the passageway. The distance between cabin doors appeared far longer than he remembered. He wouldn't reach Caroline before the man in his dream made his move. Merrick was certain of it now, and the knowledge hit him square in the stomach with a sickening fear that sent nauseating bile to his throat.

CAROLINE! YOU ARE IN DANGER! RUN! He concentrated with all the mental strength he possessed while his limbs pumped harder in their full-out effort, taking the stairs by twos. With his shirt hastily pulled onto his back, the unbuttoned front panels fluttered at his hips with each bounding stride. Already the sweat of exertion and fear had spread across his thick chest muscles which rose and fell with each gasp of air.

Caroline stopped for a moment on the top deck to get her bearings, breathless from her quick retreat after hearing the sailors talk about the man named Bates. A thick layer of fog had rolled in, cloaking the ship in a veil of opaque mist. As far as she could tell, she was still too far toward the back of the ship.

In her mind, the feeling of danger intensified along with a powerful urge to run. *But where do I run? Which way? What if I run right into Bates?*

She couldn't be sure whether the answer came aloud, from some obscure corner, or was inside her mind. But it was clear, just the same. *GET AWAY! NOW!*

A gust of wind churned and lifted her skirt hem above her knees, exposing her legs below her underclothes. She tamed the bedeviled cloth with a quick motion and glanced about to see if anyone was around. Suddenly aware of a distinct odor, Caroline touched her fingertips to her lips. The pungent scent of alcohol followed on the tail of the breeze, mingling with the sea air.

"Does the princess blow a kiss to me?" Bates whispered lecherously, excited by the sight of her bare skin.

With a firm grip on her shawl, Caroline whirled around and faced the direction of the voice. "You are mistaken, sir." She backed away slowly. The conversation she'd overheard was still fresh in her thoughts, telling her this drunken sailor must be the man called Bates. Her mind tried to plot a quick escape. If she turned and ran, the man would surely chase her and, in this thickening fog, a careless stumble could very likely send her over the side.

"Nope, I'm not mis . . . taken. Yer perfect . . . the princess o' my dreams." Bates grunted as he pushed himself up against the metal wall and studied her full, round curves.

In the dim light, Caroline could see the man weaving in drunkenness. She hoped he was too inebriated to give chase.

God, help me, she pleaded in silence as she turned and bolted for safety.

"Oh, no, you don't."

She could hear the man's footsteps pound against the deck behind her.

The ship's foghorn blasted directly overhead, startling Caroline. She glanced up, a mistake which cost her dearly as she tripped over a deck chair that had not been stowed for the night. Collapsing over the obstacle, she tried to gather her feet beneath herself, ignoring the pain in her shin and hands. A large rent in her skirt tangled itself on a loose nail and thwarted Caroline's efforts to stand. The shawl lay forgotten in her desperate attempt to crawl away. She clawed at the deck with her fingers. Ripping the material further, the nail caught her underclothes, tearing both garments high up on her thigh. Damp air chilled her skin but was instantly replaced by the hot, sweaty warmth of a massive hand.

Scream, her frightened mind begged but when her voice obeyed, the blast of the ship's foghorn drowned out her efforts. Left with nothing but her own strength to save herself, she flung her elbow around as she rolled to her back and lashed out at her attacker.

His forearm caught the blow across the bone, sending a

shock up Caroline's arm to her shoulder. Using his one arm as a shield against her fists, he slid his other hand under her torn and twisted garments.

Hoping to scream during the brief silence between the foghorn signals, she drew a deep breath. But the man's hand quickly moved from the folds of her naked thigh to her mouth. The foul stench of sweat and whiskey filled her nostrils.

When the sound returned, his hand dropped from her mouth only to be replaced by the repugnant slime of his saliva as he sought her lips with drunken passion. His body crushed her beneath him while one hand reached down and squeezed her breast tightly.

In pain, she tried violently to squirm free. "Stop! NOW!" she screamed in his ear, forcing her will upon him. Never had she deliberately tried to use her powers of control. Now that she needed them, she prayed Merrick was right about her abilities.

Bates sat bolt upright and stared at her for a moment, his knees straddling her hips, pinning her skirt to the wooden deck. She was startled by his reaction but thankful nonetheless for the respite. She garnered her strength, compelling herself to remain calm in order to channel her energy.

"CAROLINE!" Merrick's faraway voice came between blasts, distracting her efforts to control the attacker's thoughts. Bates blinked, as if shaken back to reality, then immediately pinned Caroline's arms down with his knees. As he rose up and fumbled with his belt, the crotch of his dark blue pants hovered inches above her chin.

He chuckled while Caroline closed her eyes and tried to force herself to concentrate on her power. Somehow she knew her strength lay in a centered calmness. *Go slow. Say it slowly,* she thought. But her heart pounded rapidly and her mind raced, all too aware of Bates's intentions.

She opened her eyes in time to see a shiny black boot embedded in her attacker's ribs. When the slovenly body fell off her with a deafening scream of pain, the girl rolled to her stomach, pushed herself to her knees, and scrambled to safety. Once she was out of the way of the violent fight behind her, she tried to stand and run but her trembling legs wouldn't allow it. In frustration, she slumped onto the damp deck and sobbed convulsively.

The sound of cracking wood broke through her muffled cries. Her head snapped up as she choked back the tears. She strained to see through the fog and made out the shape of what appeared to be Merrick as he wrestled with her attacker. The two men had fallen on the deck chair and shattered it into pieces. Bates raised his fist to finish the baron while Merrick closed his hand around a piece of the broken chaise and swung hard. The piece of wood landed square against Bates's cheek, smashing bone and flesh in a muffled snap.

Except for the blowing foghorn, all was still. Saliva from the drunkard's kiss was sticky on her cheeks. She rubbed her face aggressively with the cuff of her white cotton blouse, trying to scrub away the foul slime.

Merrick stumbled over to Caroline, exhausted from his battle. The sight of her collapsed on the deck filled him with an intense protectiveness mixed with murderous hatred for the bastard who'd done this to her. His sorrowful gaze took in the scratched and battered skin of her lower legs before she tugged her torn skirt to cover herself. Quickly approaching her, he noticed her once-white blouse was soiled with dirt and missed two buttons at the high-necked collar and one just above her breasts. From his quick discernment came a wave of relief; it appeared that he'd saved her from the worst of the attack, though God knew she'd always remember the brief hell she'd just experienced.

He bent low at her side and placed one arm around her back. When he gripped her shoulders to bring her to her feet, she drew away defensively, a reflex he should have expected but one that hurt just the same. Until this night, she had only viewed him as the man who had stolen her sister away, and shattered her close-knit family in the process. Now, after such a terrorizing attack, why should she stop to think that it was he who'd saved her? He longed to tell her how frightened he was when he saw her in his dream, when he knew she was in danger. But he couldn't. Telling her of such visions would only make her more wary of him, if that was possible.

Merrick dropped to both knees. "Carrie," he said, commanding her attention with a quiet firmness. "You're all right now. It's over."

She slowly looked up at him, then silently her gaze turned to her assailant, lying motionless a few feet away. Brownish-red blood dripped from the ragged flesh split over his right eye and cheekbone. She choked back a cry.

Merrick felt his throat contract with emotion, but he held his own tears at bay, pulling Caroline into his arms. Thankful for her willingness, however momentary, to be comforted by him, Merrick held her tight as she let her tears pour out the humiliation of being attacked and the frustration of being unable to stop it. She spoke no words, but he felt all of her fear and pain as surely as if a knife had been plunged into his chest.

After several minutes, Caroline said brokenly, "I tried to stop him. I wasn't strong enough. The noise—"

Another blast of the foghorn filled the air.

Merrick hugged her closer, stroking her silken curls with one hand. His eyes closed tight in anguish. He tried to tell himself that he'd feel no differently if she were just any victim. But the thought of any man touching her intimately sent shards of anger through him.

As her shaking body calmed, he loosened his hold, only to be surprised by her sudden reaction. She immediately grasped the open lapels of his shirt, keeping herself close in the safety of his arms. Merrick dropped his gaze to the look of desperation in Caroline's green tear-filled eyes. He cupped his hands at the curve of her jaw and, with the thick pad of his thumbs, carefully brushed the tears from her cheeks, a gesture that relaxed her, closing her lids. Her long, dark lashes, glistening wet, formed lacy crescents against her flushed cheeks.

Caroline felt her heart-pounding fear slowly ebb. Gradually her thoughts turned toward Merrick. He'd saved her. He'd come just in time—barely. Mentally, she pushed back the horrid scene of what could have happened. Her gratitude toward Merrick suddenly seemed endless. She owed him so much. She owed him her life.

The lulling strokes of his thumbs against her skin made her feel safe and secure, a strange happenstance considering her decisive view of him until now. But for the moment, he was a face she knew and she felt protected. No different, she told herself, than if it had been Captain Werner who'd stumbled onto the heinous attack and come to her aid. He'd have also comforted her. And she'd have grabbed his shirt just the same.

She glanced down to where her hands still gripped the white material. At the bloody sight before her, she gasped and dropped her hands. "You're hurt!"

Crimson stains dotted his shirt where she'd held it; more color smeared his skin. It was only then that she noticed the hard wall of his chest exposed between the blood-marked panels of shirt. Assuming it was he who was hurt and not she, Caroline looked once again, unabashedly pulling back the material to search for a wound. Merrick's defined muscles lay taut beneath his dark skin. A generous mat of wiry, black curls covered the breadth of his upper chest and narrowed down to disappear below his waistband. Not a wound in sight.

Merrick encirled her wrists with his long fingers and firmly pulled her hands from his shirt. "It's you who's hurt, little one."

When she winced, he turned her hands over gently and cradled them in his own. Tiny splinters of wood protruded from her raw fingertips. Her usually neat fingernails were broken and jagged. She looked up into Merrick's face, his thick black eyebrows knit together in a worried look.

"It doesn't look serious, but I'll take you back to your cabin and find the ship's doctor." He lifted her into his arms to carry her, glancing back at the fog-shrouded figure, inert on the deck several feet away.

"Is he—?" Caroline asked, her voice strained from the screams.

"Dead?" Merrick finished her question. "No, but near enough. When he comes around he may wish I finished it."

An hour later, in the stateroom, the ship's doctor concluded his examination and called the baron and Miss Landau in.

"There are no physical injuries except her hands. Use this salve on them when needed." The doctor handed Hilde a stout, white jar. "I've given her a dose of opiate syrum that should take effect soon so she can sleep through the night."

Miss Landau accepted a small brown vial from him, placed it in a drawer, and walked over to Caroline's berth. Sitting awkwardly on the edge of the bed, she held her young friend's bandaged hand.

"Thank you for your services, doctor," Merrick said in a low voice, taking only a moment to shake the man's hand before he looked back to Caroline and gave her an encouraging smile.

"I'll have the purser check by hourly. If there's anything you need, leave a note on the door so he won't have to knock if you're sleeping." The doctor snapped his bag shut, tipped his hat, and let himself out the door.

Hilde nodded and smiled. Turning her attention back to Caroline, she gently brushed a tear from the girl's cheek. "You do as the doctor says and get some sleep. I'll be right here."

Almost envious of Miss Landau's position, Merrick fought

to keep his feet firmly planted where he stood instead of
sending everyone out so he could sit with her himself. Adding an extra gruffness to his voice in an effort to mask his
true emotions, he said, "It appears you'll have to forgo 'shut-
tle'board for a few weeks."

"*Shuffle*board," Caroline corrected, the tease registering on
her face, relaxing it for a moment. As she drifted off to sleep,
her trembling slowly subsided, as did her sniffling sobs.

Before dawn on the ninth day out of Philadelphia, the
Teutonic made port in Rotterdam, but the passengers were
allowed until noon to depart. Hilde had been up early to
pack their trunks, leaving time to attend to Caroline.

A tap on the door startled Caroline's already shattered
nerves.

Hilde patted her hand as she passed to reassure her, "It's
probably the baron."

"Who is it?" Hilde spoke after the second tap.

"Baron von Hayden," the accented voice answered. Hilde
unlocked the door and stepped back to allow him admit-
tance. Caroline, feeling the need to withdraw and garner her
strength, merely watched their exchange.

"How is she?"

"Please see for yourself, Your Excellency." Hilde moved
aside and waved him toward Caroline's berth.

Merrick looked first to Miss Landau as if asking permission and then to Caroline, who could barely muster the
slightest smile. Her coloring was pale, ashen. Her bandaged
white hands lay at her side, useless. How could he tell her
what he'd come to say?

He knelt on one knee and touched her shoulder. "I have
some disturbing news. The doctor said that Bates was as good
as dead. But when the authorities came on board to get him
this morning, he was gone. They're saying that a couple of
his cronies secretly smuggled him off the ship."

Hilde spoke up. "Will it be safe to leave the ship?"

The baron answered, "The doctor said he doubts that Bates will live a week. He can't hurt you. It's just . . . well, we must take every precaution. I'm not sure about his friends."

Merrick turned back to his sister-in-law. "I know you are frightened, Caroline, but Bates is gone. And I honestly doubt that he is still alive. You must put this behind you and act as if nothing has happened. I am sorry if I am being coldhearted, but you'll be with Ilse soon and you must be strong for her."

Caroline knew he was right. She must appear strong and confident for Ilse's sake, even if it meant burying the memory of that last night on the ship. She faced her brother-in-law with new resolve. The attack was frightening, a dark experience she would never forget, but with her fear had come a valuable discovery.

Her unique powers—however frightfully intimidating—were gathering intensity. Caroline found herself wondering just how much more powerful the baron was than she. Could it have been he warning her just seconds before the attack? Perhaps in time her own abilities would equal his . . .

She looked up from her cloth-wrapped hands to the baron, studying his dark eyes and the hidden fire behind them. *But he is married to Ilse,* a voice inside warned. Still, she could not help but wonder what her own mind could accomplish if joined with his.

Shaking herself out of her dark mood, she smiled weakly at him.

"You're right, Your Excellency," she began, unconsciously toying with her bandages, "I must be strong for Ilse and whatever awaits me in Germany."

Chapter 3

The port city of Rotterdam bustled with late-morning excitement, reminding Caroline of Philadelphia and her last view of America a little over a week ago. How she longed to turn back to the safety of those distant shores. Fighting those feelings, she reminded herself that the attack of the night before could have happened anywhere, anytime. She had to be strong. There was no stopping the clock. Ilse was foremost in her mind now. Nothing else mattered. It couldn't.

Aside from the lilt of unfamiliar languages that drifted through the salt-tinged sea air, this foreign city carried the faint ambience of home. Merchants traded everything from large wheels of cheese to clothing. Travelers scurried for carriages or kissed loved ones good-bye before boarding a ship. Longshoremen in sweat-stained clothes muscled heavy cargo to and fro.

A refreshing breeze slipped through a break in the crowd and tugged at Caroline's bonnet. Despite the fact that the green grosgrain ribbon had been tied securely under her chin, she reached to clutch the brim, only to have her bandaged fingers remind her of her fears. She found herself studying each masculine face that even remotely resembled Bates.

Merrick grasped her elbow and spoke close to her ear. "He's not here, Caroline."

She turned her head and looked squarely into his eyes. His words weren't needed to convey the protective reassurance she read in his expression, nor were her words needed to say thank you. It appeared they had drawn an invisible line that neither dared to cross, a line that kept Caroline from completely trusting the baron, though at times she was tempted.

Merrick, too, recognized a barrier, but not one of distrust. It was a crumbling wall of right and wrong, moral and immoral. For what was this odd feeling for his young sister-in-law except a forbidden desire? He was legally married to Ilse, no matter how mismatched the union had been from the start. If it took every ounce of restraint, he was determined to keep the wall from crumbling any more than it already had.

Miss Landau's voice broke Merrick away from his thoughts. "Thank heaven you set our trunks directly to the train station, Your Excellency," she said. "We'll have quite a time just getting ourselves there." Turning her back to the flutter of incoming wind, she followed the baron as he escorted Caroline toward a street teeming with carriages and wagons, each as different as the horses drawing them.

"We won't get there if we don't stay together in this crowd," Hilde gently reminded from behind Caroline's shoulder. The younger woman glanced back apologetically and slowed her pace. Accustomed to keeping up with her father's long strides, Caroline often forgot the role her height played upon such simple tasks as walking. Her long, graceful gait multiplied the shorter steps of most other people.

Within an hour the baron, Caroline and Hilde patiently waited in the midst of another crowd of fellow travelers. In the distance, a massive black steam engine approached. A long, low whistle blew louder and louder with the arrival of the 12:15 train, right on schedule. Slowly, it chugged past the platform, pulling the coach cars into boarding position. Air brakes hissed from beneath the belly of the windowed cars. The waiting crowd shuffled and parted, allowing the arriving passengers to disembark.

For the last leg of their journey, Caroline had worn a forest green poplin dress with a carter's frock. The underskirt was green sateen. Under her high collar was a lace choker, a feminine touch that Merrick noticed with subdued surprise. Hilde wore a polonaise walking suit of wine-colored lightweight wool. Her little bonnet was trimmed with artificial silk flowers.

Standing a head taller than most of the men in the crowd, Baron von Hayden turned heads as much for his distinctive nobility as for his handsome attire—a black morning coat over a blue silk vest and a gray silk tie. His trousers were of gray wool. The admiring gazes went unnoticed by Merrick who had his mind elsewhere.

While the baron was lost in thought, Caroline leaned toward Hilde and asked quietly, "Are these people speaking Dutch? I understand very little."

"That is because the people of the Netherlands are not only of Germanic origins, but also Celtic origins. Their Teutonic language was formed by the expansion of the dialect found in this province of Holland—" Caroline's broad smile stopped Hilde's impulsive recitation. A reservoir of information concerning her heritage, the older woman obviously enjoyed sharing her knowledge with her young friend.

"Please go on. It's wonderful that you know so much."

Hilde shrugged nonchalantly, then turned to follow the boarders. "I've been teaching such things to children for the past twenty-five years. It seems that old habits truly are hard to break."

"I'm thankful you haven't. Father is a proud German but

he's never volunteered information about his country, let alone the Netherlands."

"Just keep asking questions. I hope I'll have the answers."

When the baron interrupted the conversation, his mood had changed noticeably. "It's time to board," he said darkly.

Suddenly anxious to be home, Merrick tried to tell himself that it wasn't an unusual feeling, considering he'd been gone a long time and anything could have happened since his departure. But he'd have received word by cable and—more significantly—he'd have *known*, as was his way. He also tried to convince himself that this growing sense of foreboding could have been spawned by Caroline's attacker escaping custody. The mishap was cause for some concern, but he couldn't shake the feeling that this dark oppression was the warning of something yet to come.

Why couldn't he figure it out? Why must he be taunted by this dread?

After an unexpected delay, the train lurched forward as it started down the tracks. Seated across from the baron, Caroline shifted restlessly on the burnished leather cushion, then glanced over at Hilde sitting next to her.

"Getting anxious so soon?" Hilde asked, pulling her brown traveling gloves from her hands. "We have over five hundred kilometers before we reach Mainz for the night."

Caroline shook her head in puzzlement. "You may as well say we have to go to America and back, I don't understand these kilometers very well. How many miles?"

Merrick answered, "Roughly three hundred. But we won't be stopping over in Mainz." He gave Miss Landau a sharp look to quell any thought of protest on Caroline's behalf. "We will continue straight through to Karlsruhe."

The matronly chaperone deftly opened the small gold watch pinned above her left breast. "With stops, I dare say it will be two or three in the morning when we arrive."

Caroline frowned, partially at the thought of their late

arrival and partially in discomfort at the baron's sudden moodiness. But she had to admit she was anxious to see her sister.

"I have been away far too long as it is," he explained, his agitation mounting with each passing moment. He felt as if he were about to enter a dark cavern where he couldn't see the certain danger that lay ahead.

Caroline shuddered inwardly at the haunted look in the midnight-blue depth of the baron's gaze, then slid her eyes away to look out the window.

Gigantic blazing furnaces and belching factory chimneys populated the endless industrial cities along the Lower Rhine River. Vast deposits of coal in the area had brought the development of iron and steel mills. Factories seeking access to the barge traffic crowded the shoreline like the travelers who'd stood along the Rotterdam railway for the south-bound train.

Eyes focused outside the train window, Caroline studied the symphony of the late-October colors along the wide Rhine River. Brilliant orange and yellow leaves pulsed past to the rhythmic drumming of the iron wheels upon the track. Soft white clouds drifted across the afternoon sky, while full-toned shades of green foliage blended and trans-posed the landscape in an enchanting visual concerto.

Occasionally, the unfamiliar sight of a castle on a lush green hilltop in the distance entranced her, conjuring up im-ages of kings and queens, knights and maidens, dragons and sorcerers. Her mind would wander, playing with vivid scenes of nobler times. But darker thoughts soon invaded her mind, always bringing about unanswered questions about her psychic abilities.

"You look troubled," Merrick said from across the small compartment when Miss Landau had taken a short walk. "And I don't believe it concerns Bates or Ilse."

Turning her attention to the one person she knew had the

ability to read her mind, Caroline spoke softly, "Is it a curse or a blessing to have these gifts?"

"I would be lying if I said it was only a blessing. There are times I consider it more of a curse." *Right this minute being one of those times,* he thought.

"Does it ever frighten you?"

Moved by her innocent questions, Merrick imagined his his child standing before him, awed by his uniqueness. How could he tell her that such powers are frightening at times without making her fearful to use them? "Carrie," he sighed, "if I told you that many times in your life you could—no, you *will* be frightened beyond your worst imaginings, would you lock yourself in a room and never come out again?"

She shook her head.

"Why not?"

"I couldn't live that way," she answered matter-of-factly.

"Even if you knew the dangers?"

Merrick saw the point of his question dawn across Caroline's soft features. Her lashes dipped low, then rose to show the green of her eyes dark as moss in her reflective contemplation. "Everyone must face their fears, Your Excellency. I suppose there is no reason why I should be any different."

"Ah—but you are, Carrie. I don't speak of the gifts when I say that it's true that everyone must face their fears, but not everyone can overcome them."

"Overcome?" Caroline nearly laughed at his preposterous remark. Holding up her sore, bandaged fingers, she said, "I could hardly say that I've overcome the fact that I was a hair's breadth away from—" She bit back her own words before she embarrassed herself with choking emotion.

Merrick quickly moved to her side and cradled her hands in his as he'd done after the attack. "The strength you displayed last night was far beyond what anyone would have expected. I'm speaking of your ability to move forward, put it behind you. Stronger for the experience, not weaker. No gift of foresight or power of mind control created that ability, Carrie. It is who you are."

Confused by his tenderness, Caroline could only deny his praising compliment. "I did it for Ilse. She needs me now."

"And when Ilse no longer needs you?" A sudden dread tore through his soul as the question escaped his lips. The possibility was there. He'd sensed it all along. It *was* Ilse who warranted the ominous cloud of doom in his thoughts.

"What is it, Your Excellency? Something's wrong. It's Ilse, isn't it?"

Further unexpected delays in Mainz and Heidelburg extended their train journey well into the night. It was dawn when the baron's carriage finally crossed the small tributary that marked his property.

Three-quarters of the distance into the heart of the estate, the entrance road, wet from the aftermath of yet another thundershower, curved like a velvety brown ribbon through the lush green countryside, sweeping in a wide arc around a small, tranquil pond. The opaque blue-green water seemed almost motionless, as if caught in a still life. But only the brilliant artistry of nature could capture on the mirrorlike surface the breathtaking reflection of the gray stone Schloss Hayden that stood in the distance. Two stately mansions— one real, one an illusion—perfect duplication matched only by the surrounding oaks in autumn reds and yellows and oranges.

The main house was a three-storied L-shaped dwelling with a steep slate roof that loomed above a brick-lined drive. The forward wing of the "L" displayed four diamond-paned windows—two upper, two lower—which gave a spectacular view of the front lawns and the tiny lake where waterfowl claimed refuge. Green ivy climbed up the stone face of the house, forming intricate lace patterns over the facade. The shadowed entrance was protectively nestled between either end of the house, flanked by more multi-paned windows.

Accepting Merrick's hand to help her down, Caroline stepped from the oversized black carriage onto the brick steps leading into the baron's home. The crisp morning air chilled her, prompting her to tug her woolen coat tight about her full breasts. The navy-blue cloak, designed for her mother's delicate frame, was much too snug. She wished there had been more time on their shopping trip to buy a proper wardrobe for the colder climate.

The coachman barked a command at his pair of high-spirited carriage horses, bringing Caroline's thoughts back to the present. She waved good-bye as the coach carried Hilde around the corner to the servant's entrance.

Knowing that she would soon be with her older sister, Caroline felt her heart pound with anxious anticipation.

As Caroline and the baron approached the enormous pine door, its soft wood weathered into dark ridges, Merrick's steps quickened. "I expected Conrad to meet us after I cabled him about our arrival."

Inside the doorway, Caroline felt dwarfed in the great hall. High overhead, ornately carved wooden beams braced the whitewashed ceiling. Oil paintings of Merrick's ancestors adorned the richly paneled walls. Each somber face of the six life-size portraits stared menacingly down upon Caroline while the ticking of a tall pendulum clock imposed itself on the quiet.

At the end of the stairs hung a portrait of a distinguished young couple and a little boy whose eyes were the dark color of a midnight sky. Merrick couldn't have been older than five in the portrait, yet his eyes held the smoldering soul of a wise man.

Caroline wrinkled her nose at the musty smell of dampness. She loosened the ribbon beneath her chin and pushed the green bonnet off her head, leaving it to hang between her shoulders.

In swift silence, a stone-faced butler rigidly descended the staircase before them.

"Thank God you've come home, Your Excellency," he said in German, the tone of his voice low. "The baroness has taken a turn for the worse. The doctor has been called but—" Merrick's bolt for the staircase silenced the butler.

With painful realization, Caroline understood the baron's servant perfectly. Not only had her father tutored both of his daughters in his native language, but the German liturgy of her Lutheran church had helped Caroline master the written word. Hurrying to keep up with the baron's fast, stair-skipping steps, she ascended the wide, curving staircase.

Merrick's legs pumped harder as they brought him to the landing at the top of the stairs. Nearly knocking over a vase as he rounded the corner where a decorative table stood, his mind screamed, *The baby wasn't due for another month! What did Conrad say? He couldn't get the doctor? I never should have left her.*

When he reached the familiar door adjacent to his room, he paused to prepare himself for the worst. His fingers tightened around the polished-brass doorknob, the metal cool in his warm palm. Hearing footsteps behind him, he glanced back. Caroline's green eyes were wide with fear and uncertainty, emotions he hoped were not mirrored in his own features, though he felt fear twisting a knot deep in his stomach.

Caroline followed him into the room, clasping her hands together at the waist of her mother's blue overcoat and silently praying for her sister. As she cautiously stepped inside, her attention was drawn to a wattle-chinned, wide-hipped maid in a crisp apron. The stout old woman approached and and spoke in hushed whispers to the baron. Then she stepped past them and went out into the hall, eyeing Caroline suspiciously the whole time.

The baron moved across the vast room to the opposite wall where a four-poster bed stood with heavy brocade drapes tied back at each corner. In the center of the down mattress lay Ilse, dozing restlessly. Caroline approached her brother-in-law's side and gazed at the childlike figure of her sister. Ilse was smaller and frailer than she had remembered. Her golden-red wavy hair was damp with perspiration.

Without warning, Ilse's body tightened. Her face tensed and she moaned, a deep guttural sound.

Merrick touched his wife's pale, thin arm. "Be strong, Ilse. The doctor will come soon."

Caroline leaned close to her sister and said softly, "Ilse? I'm here."

"Carrie?" Her voice was a hoarse whisper.

"Yes, Ilse. It's Caroline." But her words went unheeded as her sister fell back into her private world of pain.

Caroline straightened and began fumbling with her bandages as she walked purposefully over to a floral-patterned settee.

"I couldn't hear what the maid was telling you, Your Excellency," she said, dropping the torn strips of white cloth onto the cushion.

"She said Ilse refused to be examined. What are you doing?"

Ignoring his question for the moment, Caroline knew he was coming up behind her by the sound of his boots as he walked across the Persian carpet. Caroline removed her hat, then fumbled with the buttons on her coat as she said, "Is one of your servants experienced in midwifery?"

"Not that I'm aware. Even so, Ilse would refuse."

"As you can plainly see," Caroline said miserably, her injured fingers failing to undo even one button, "she's in no condition to argue."

"You don't remember Ilse very well." Merrick reached up and grabbed his young sister-in-law by her shoulders. Instead of shaking her as she expected him to, he turned her to face him. As soon as he undid the last button of her coat, she quickly shrugged out of it, and it fell behind her, covering the small pile of cast-off bandages.

Looking first at Ilse, whose moans were growing louder,

and then at Caroline, who was now rolling up her left sleeve despite the obvious tenderness of her fingers, Merrick once again stepped in to help her, brushing aside her hand. "You are not a doctor. You don't know any—"

"The mixed blessing of a rural upbringing—we don't have a medical doctor at our beck and call."

"Are you saying you know how to deliver babies?"

"It appears we have no other choice, though God knows, I wish we did. The best I can do is see whether she's ready to deliver."

"If she's not?"

"We wait," she said gravely. "And pray the doctor comes before the baby does."

Turning back to her sister, Caroline gently grasped hold of Ilse's lily-white hand. Its icy chill pierced the warmth of her own skin. "Ilse, can you hear me?"

Slowly, Ilse opened her eyes. "Carrie?" she whispered.

Caroline attempted a brave smile but her sister's tightening grip warned her of the onset of another painful spasm. Ilse's free hand cradled the swollen belly as if to protect it. Eyes closed tightly, Ilse took a deep breath, clamped her pale lips shut and gave herself up to her labor.

"Can't we do something?" Merrick asked.

"There *isn't* anything we can do. It's in the hands of God now."

Pain temporarily released its hold on Ilse. She lay her head back into the sweat-stained pillow.

"God won't help me now," she sighed. Her eyes, once the blue of a summer sky, were dull and reddened. She stared at her younger sister. "You're . . . all grown up . . . Carrie. Your eyes are just like . . . Father's. Does he still . . . hate me . . . for marrying Merrick?"

"No, Ilse. He never hated you. Please rest. Don't worry yourself about such things. Once you have this baby we can talk." Caroline licked her dry lips.

"Carrie, listen to me. I . . . had to go with Merrick. I

loved him. Everything has . . . changed. I . . . have so much to explain—"

As another contraction bore down on Ilse, Caroline pried her sister's fingers from her white-knuckle grip on the wrinkled lace sheet across her belly. With a quick jerk, Caroline flung the covers to the foot of the bed.

"Help me move her to one side," she commanded Merrick. He slipped one arm under Ilse's hips and one arm under her shoulders, then hesitated, looking back up to Caroline. His eyes met hers, and she saw his grave uncertainty.

Caroline broke free of his gaze and turned her attention back to Ilse. Her tiny ankles were thin as a sparrow's. Caroline wrapped her fingers around them and together, in one effortless movement, the baron and Caroline eased Ilse closer to the side of the bed. A scream of pain rang out.

"I'm sorry, Ilse," Caroline fretted. She loved her sister but she wanted desperately to be home, to be a little girl again. Fear churned in her stomach. She swallowed hard and scolded herself for being so childish. Her sister needed her. This was not the time to be wallowing in self-pity.

Discreetly lifting the hem of the pale pink nightgown, which reeked of stale perspiration, Caroline folded the gown over Ilse's belly while Merrick knelt at his wife's side.

"Dear God," Caroline swore quietly in a controlled breath.

Watching Caroline's shoulders sag, Merrick felt a knot bunch up in his stomach. "What is it? What's wrong?"

"The head is crowning," she said, glancing up to his worried face, then to her sister who was wracked with the pain of another contraction.

Merrick looked down on his wife. For the first time in his life, he felt totally helpless. No matter how badly their marriage had deteriorated, she didn't deserve this. If only he'd known . . . if only. . . . He stroked the damp tendrils of hair from her face and her gaunt features relaxed. How she would have carried on about her ghostly appearance if she had been able. Merrick would have given anything at that moment to hear her sharp tongue once again. He would gladly be the victim of her insults if it would mean the end of this terrible pain caused by bearing his child.

Caroline watched her brother-in-law caress Ilse's face with a tenderness that gripped her heart. He truly loved her, a welcome surprise after the thoughts Caroline had been having over the course of her trip.

"Ilse?" she pleaded, hoping to get her sister to respond. Caroline closed her eyes and said softly, "Lord, she's so weak. If she can't push the baby out, we'll have to do it."

Merrick slid his hand to his wife's stomach and massaged the rock-hard muscle. "This child is meant to be born. It is God's will."

Another contraction mounted, arching Ilse's back as she tried to roll to her side in her search for relief from the searing pain. Merrick reached up and gripped her shoulder with one hand and drew her back. *Give her my strength, God. Make her strong. Don't let her die. Save her, Lord. Save the child.*

"No—!" Caroline yelped as her sister relaxed.

"What's wrong?"

"The baby slipped back. It came just so far, then went back up after the contraction. I've seen this happen once before back home."

"What caused it?"

"The cord was around its neck. The baby couldn't come down."

Merrick jumped to his feet and nervously raked his fingers through his hair. "What can we do about it?"

"I don't know. I've only helped our midwife when there weren't complications!"

"Well, what did you do about the baby with the cord around its neck?" He began to pace.

"The baby died," she said, her voice barely audible. The baron stood silently for a long moment until Ilse cried out, breaking the long silence and bringing them back to their desperate situation.

He strode over to the bed and positioned himself to witness the impending birth of his child. Caroline had been right, the head was there.

"Goddamn it!" His frustration mounted as quickly as the contraction ebbed. "There's got to be a way to help her!"

Behind them, the stout maid spoke up; her arrival in the room had gone completely unnoticed. "It's your duty to save the child, Your Excellency."

The baron whirled around. "Is the doctor here yet?"

"*Nein.*"

"Then what are you suggesting?" he asked. His voice rose in anger at the remote possibility that the maid could be thinking of the barbaric ritual of sacrificing the mother to save the baby.

"I have a scullery maid waiting outside with a knife—"

"GET THE HELL OUT OF HERE!" he roared with a swoop of his arm toward the door just as Ilse groaned once again in agony.

His pulse racing, Merrick turned back to his wife. Time was running out.

Caroline said, "If you could press on her belly so the baby can't slip back, maybe I could reach the neck and free the cord."

When they set to action, Merrick couldn't help but fleetingly admire the level-headed calm Caroline displayed, a calm that helped him to regain his own composure.

Positioning his hands on the crest of Ilse's abdomen just below her ribs, he focused his concentration on the translucent blue-white skin beneath his dark brown hands. It was hard to accept that a child—his child—was inside, so close, yet so far away, fighting to be born. When the muscles began to relax, he leaned his weight gently forward to add more pressure, keeping the baby from retreating until Caroline could release the cord.

Ilse screamed and lashed out at the abusive hands of her husband, raking her nails across his forearms. Thin strips of skin curled away as he jumped back in pain.

"Ilse!" Caroline shouted. Her eyes filled with hot tears as she stared in disbelief at her sister's desperate act.

"I'll be all right," Merrick said, turning away for a cloth. His wish had been half-granted. Ilse was her old she-wolf self, but her pain had not let up.

"Leave me alone. I'm damned to hell and you know it as well as I do. Get out of this room and let me die. LEAVE!" Ilse hissed, her eyes slits, like those of an enraged animal; her breathing, deep and fierce.

"Stop it!" Caroline grabbed her sister's shoulders. Ilse broke free of her grasp.

"Keep your hands off me. Is the smell of death sweet, pretty sister?" Ilse hissed between clenched teeth. "Get out!"

Caroline yanked the bedsheet from Ilse's feet and tore it into wide strips. Merrick helped her bind the anguished young baroness to the bedposts. Her rantings turned to fast panting grunts as the final wave of pain rose again to overwhelm her. Instinctively, she drew a deep breath and held it for strength. Her arms quivered as she pulled on the restraints in her attempt to strike at Merrick's hands once again.

Caroline knelt on the bed at Ilse's feet, tears now streaming down her cheeks. Brushing aside a lock of dark brown hair with her forearm, she said a quick prayer and began the insurmountable task before her.

Merrick's face dripped with sweat as he hovered over the critical birthing.

"Press harder," Caroline commanded, wincing in her own pain as her sore fingertips prodded for the cord.

"Please forgive me, Ilse," Merrick whispered.

Ilse screamed.

In an instant, the belly flattened. On the blood-smeared sheet lay a wet blue-tinged infant—a boy. Caroline hurriedly cleared the baby's mouth but no sound came out.

"Come on, little one," she begged, grabbing a cloth and carefully swabbing the lifeless form.

Merrick turned to look at Ilse, afraid his wife would see the hopeless sight. All of the hatred and fight had drained from the new mother. She lay back on the pillow, her eyes closed, her breath shallow. He sensed the worst was not over as it seemed, though he hoped the ominous feeling was wrong.

Caroline worked feverishly trying to find a sign of life in the baby. Finally, there was a slight movement and a faint cry that cleared the air passage. Though obviously relieved, she did not smile, but hastily cleansed him in the wash basin, wrapped him in a blanket, then offered him to the baron so she could tend her sister.

Merrick hesitantly accepted the baby, awed at first by how light the bundle felt in his arms. Gathering the boy close to his chest, he studied the delicate features of his new son. The thick thatch of hair was red-gold, like his mother's. As he felt the tiny body move beneath the blanket, Merrick clutched him closer and cooed softly to him. When his eyes opened, they were a deep shade of blue. Reaching up, Merrick touched the tip of his littlest finger to the delicate rosy lips as if to feel for himself that he was not holding a porcelain doll. The tiny mouth opened instinctively and began to suckle urgently; Merrick's heart swelled with happiness.

After Caroline finished with Ilse, her sister spoke so quietly that Caroline had to lean close to hear her words. "Was it a boy or a girl?"

"It *is* a boy," Caroline reassured with an encouraging smile. "He's alive, Ilse."

The mother moaned. "If only it'd been a girl."

Puzzled, Caroline wasn't sure what to say. "He's very small but if we keep him warm and—"

"Take him away. I don't want to see him," she said weakly.

Merrick was standing behind his sister-in-law when he heard Ilse's request.

Fighting back the emotions that seethed within him, Merrick stepped around Caroline and addressed his wife. "Your son will die without your milk, Ilse."

"Find him a wet nurse," she said flatly.

Her eyes rolled open and she stared at her husband with a hatred the likes of which Caroline had never seen. "You have your . . . precious son, *Your Excellency*. There is no further . . . need for me."

"Hush, Ilse!" Caroline couldn't believe the harsh words coming from her sister's mouth.

Merrick read the painful reason for Ilse's bitterness. It was in her eyes as she spoke. She was dying; he knew that for sure now. So did she. He felt her fear, her pain, her helplessness as surely as if it were a very real part of him. This angry scene was her way of severing her ties, renouncing her claim on him, on the child. But it was not what he wanted for her. Despite their differences, he desperately wanted to let her go in peace, a peace she wouldn't find in the state she was in right now.

Merrick began to concentrate on passing soothing thoughts to his dying wife.

Still cradling the swaddled infant, he sat down on the edge of the bed, his hip pressed against Ilse's. "You are absolutely right that I have my son. But he is yours, too. And he needs you as I do. Look—" Merrick pulled away the draped cloth. "He has your hair." He talked as he unwrapped the fragile infant. "He will have your drive, your confidence."

Caroline stepped back and covered her mouth, holding back the torrent of tears that threatened to spill. She watched the baron's tender patience as he helped place the newborn comfortably in the crook of Ilse's arm. Too weak to help herself, he unfastened the bodice of the gown.

Ilse's tiny son settled into his first feeding while the new mother studied him with awe. She slowly lifted her hand to his tiny one. He gripped her thumb tightly then released it. Both her strength and the baby's were limited. Each tired quickly.

As the infant dozed, Ilse looked up at her husband, then her sister. Caroline had been watching the bond between mother and child being formed. When Ilse's eyes met hers, Caroline knew the bond would be short-lived.

"Give him a good Christian name. Keep him safe."

"Safe?" Caroline glanced from her sister to the baron, confused by the bizarre—yet pleading—nature of the requests.

"He won't be safe here. There are . . . people who don't want him to live. He . . . will always be in danger."

"What are you asking of me?"

Ilse turned her attention to her husband. "You have your son, Merrick . . . Give me one final wish. Let Carrie take him . . . raise him as her own."

"No, Ilse," Caroline protested. "He's your son, not mine. You're going to get well and watch him grow up. I can't take him."

"I'm sorry I said those terrible things, Carrie. Will you forgive me?" Ilse's eyelids closed. She struggled to open them, to come back to consciousness.

"Of course, I forgive you, but—"

"I see a light, Carrie. And lots of people." Ilse stared intently at the wall across the room as though she were focusing on something.

"Where?" Caroline followed her gaze.

"Oh, Carrie. Aunt Evie's there. She's as pretty as the day—" Ilse closed her eyes, then opened them and turned to Caroline. "Promise me that you will take my son and keep him safe. Promise me, Carrie."

Merrick couldn't find it in his heart to protest, not when his wife lay on the threshold of death. She needed the reassurance, as surely as she needed to see those on the other side who beckoned her now. Touching Caroline's elbow to draw her attention to him, Merrick gave the slightest nod.

Understanding his intent, Caroline turned back to her sister. "If that's what you really want, Ilse." She brushed away the steadily flowing tears and took her sister's hand.

"Pray for me, Carrie. I've tried to pray but I don't think God listens to me anymore. I've done so many things wrong. I'm sorry, but I think it's too late . . . too late."

"Shh. Don't say that," Caroline said, in an effort to comfort her tormented, dying sister. "Mama underlined a verse in her Bible that said, 'If we confess our sins, He is faithful and just to forgive our sins and cleanse us from all unrighteousness.' God forgives you, Ilse. It's not too late."

"It's so bright." Ilse's eyes closed tight, then opened, focusing once again on a secret vision. She reached toward it, then slowly lowered her hand, laying it gently on her sleeping son nestled at her side.

Caroline cupped her hand over Ilse's. The fingers were no longer cold, but warm to the touch—and lifeless. "I love you, Il—" Her voice broke just as she felt her brother-in-law's hand on her shoulder. Turning into his arms, she buried her face in his shoulder and let loose the tearful sobs.

Holding Caroline, Merrick stared blankly at his wife's still form on the bed. He was reliving his parents' deaths all over again. The pain was there, as real as ever, wrapped around his chest like a taut rope, lodged in his throat like a stone cutting off his air. He was suspended in time, desperately needing to maintain control of his emotions. Unlike Caroline, he couldn't allow wracking sobs to overcome his defenses. In an odd way, he found himself envying her the ability to release the pain.

Caroline looked up when she heard the faint tapping on the door.

"Come in," Merrick said softly, dropping his hands to his sides. Caroline turned around and lifted the sleeping baby into her arms.

Hilde entered quietly, pulling her black sweater tightly about her shoulders. Her black wool skirt and high-collared white blouse gave her the uniform appearance of another servant.

"I was worried when you didn't come down—" She stopped short at the sight of the baron drawing the sheet over a figure on the four-poster bed.

Next to the bed, Caroline cradled the tiny bundle against her breast. Her mahogany-colored hair cascaded over one shoulder touching the swaddling blanket. She sniffed and lifted her reddened eyes to Hilde. "He's a fighter, but we must find a way to keep him warm."

The older woman stepped up next to her, placed a loving arm around her shoulder and peered down at the baby. "He's tiny but he's beautiful."

"Perfect," Caroline said, reaching for her friend's reassuring hand while she studied the child in her arms.

As the three of them stepped from the room with the baby, they came upon the butler. Merrick hung back and murmured instructions to the dour-faced servant, sending him retreating quickly down the hall, then rejoined Caroline and Miss Landau.

Four maids huddled at the end of the hall, whispering as the butler passed. The burly old nursemaid stepped from among them and approached.

"I'll take the child now, Fräulein, if you please," the woman sneered. Caroline clutched the baby close to her chest, the promise to Ilse still fresh in her mind.

Aware of her apprehension, Merrick touched Caroline's elbow and nodded in the direction of the nursery. "You may have the room next to his," he said with kind understanding.

Still reluctant, she informed the maid, "I will follow you there and bring the child." She felt as if the calm voice with which she spoke belonged to someone else. For within, her own voice screamed in pain.

"If that is your wish." The white bonnet on the maid's head was dwarfed by the old woman's mass of iron gray curls. She bowed, then turned and marched to the nursery.

Several minutes later, after the cradle had been prepared with cloth-wrapped warming stones and moved closer to the nursery hearth, Caroline lay the weak newborn down and touched the red-gold curls, wondering if he would survive, praying he would. Then she thought of Ilse's warning and she turned to look at the baron standing at her side. "Is what Ilse said true? Are there people who want to harm him?"

Merrick indicated with a nod for the nursemaid and Miss Landau to leave the room, then gazed down upon his tiny son, so small he could cup the infant's head in his hand and cradle him with his forearm and still the baby's bottom wouldn't reach the inside of his elbow. Yet, in the seemingly frail body of a newborn was the child of the prophecy, the gifted child. But more importantly, this was Merrick's flesh and blood, his son.

When he lifted his head and looked at Caroline, she searched his eyes for the answer to her question. The deep midnight-blue depths told her what she feared.

"Yes," he finally said, adding, "I've learned recently that there are some who choose to destroy what they do not understand. He does need to be protected. But I can't let you take him."

"Not if it means saving his life?" Her voice rose an octave, realizing the danger that lay ahead for her fragile nephew. "What kind of barbarians would kill an innocent baby?"

"Caroline—"

"I made a promise to my sister, a promise to keep her son safe. How can I go back home knowing her baby might not live to see his first birthday?"

"He will."

"Can you guarantee that?"

"Even if my blood must be spilled to do so, yes."

Caroline threw her arms up in frustration. "What good are these 'powers,' these 'gifts from God' if they put a price on your head? Damn them anyway. Damn you, *Your Excellency*," she spat, then turned away and fought back the angry tears that burned the back of her eyes.

Merrick grabbed her arm and spun her back around. "Don't *ever* curse your gifts. You don't know the strength of your abilities—"

"My strength. Ha! What good did my so-called abilities do me when I needed them? Where were they when I was nearly raped? And why couldn't they have saved my sister?"

"It will take time," he said, his fingers still wrapped tight around her arms.

"Just tell me—what purpose did I serve by coming here? To witness Ilse's death by my own doltish incompetence? To make promises you have no intention of letting me keep? Well, I won't be here to watch your precious son murdered."

"You can't leave."

"Let go of me," she demanded. "I won't stand helplessly by and watch your false pride stand in the way of your son's safety. Let go." Even as she tried to pummel the hard wall of his chest, she felt her body weaken, more from the emotional exhaustion than the physical. Unable to hold back the choking tears, her knees buckled and she sank to the baron's feet, her stained green skirt crumpling around her on the carpet.

Merrick lowered himself to the floor and gathered this woman-child into his arms, offering solace and needing it in return. Ilse was gone. He could never turn back the clock to save her life. In spite of their differences, Merrick mourned the life too quickly taken.

The cozy nursery echoed with Caroline's soft crying while, inside his mind, Merrick's own sobs silently joined hers.

Chapter 4

In the quiet privacy of her room next to the nursery, Caroline rose sluggishly from hot, sudsy bath water and reached for a towel the maid had left on a nearby chair. Unaccustomed to the assistance of a personal maid, Caroline had dismissed the young servant girl and spent the last hour soaking in the luxuriously large porcelain tub. The heat of the lavender-scented water and the lulling crackle of a burning log in the fireplace helped to relax and soothed her mind.

Stepping onto the carpet, she rubbed her freshly washed hair with the towel, then patted her skin dry as she came out from behind the cloth screen in the corner of the room. Though meant to be a governess's room, the high ceiling and expanse of floor was still considerably larger than Caroline was accustomed to in her home in Sebula, Pennsylvania. If the canopied bed and mahogany armoire were removed, along with the scattering of other tastefully matched pieces, the size of the room could match that of the common room in her family's house, an area that encompassed most of the bottom floor where the lumbermen gathered in the evening.

The sudden remembrance of times past washed over her in a strange nostalgia for seemingly unimportant everyday events. Now Ilse was gone and there was a baby to consider. *Oh, to return to the mundane life among the farmers and loggers,* she thought longingly. It was that simple life that Ilse had fought so hard to leave and that Caroline had been so blissfully content to cherish.

You will soon be back. Stop the wistful thinking as if such things are long gone. Vigorously rubbing her head with the towel as if to rub away the melancholy, she padded across the carpet toward the tall armoire.

As she passed the cheval glass, her eyes deliberately avoided her brazenly naked reflection. Then she paused.

A wicked temptation began in the deep recesses of her mind and crept tantalizingly throughout her warm body.

A proper lady does not appraise her nakedness.

But curiosity won out and Caroline stepped cautiously to the mirror, feeling like a naughty child. As hard as she'd tried to deny her wonderment about herself, she'd always miserably failed. And, she had decided, her body had miserably failed, as well.

Her gaze traveled hesitantly up her long, slender legs, over the soft swell of her hips, to the deep curve of her narrow waist. Everything was in satisfactory proportion, she knew, except something of which she was already uncomfortably aware. Caroline had strikingly large breasts.

She cupped her palms beneath the generous low curves, lifting their pendulous weight off her rib cage where dewy drops of water had trickled down from her wet hair. Being so well endowed in a family of nearly flat-chested women made it worse, although Ilse had done her best to convince Caroline that she was very lucky.

Her mother had sympathetically explained that such body structure was the German in her. As proud as Caroline was of her ancestry, she'd have gladly renounced it in favor of a feature that was a little less noticeable, especially to the easily impressed young bucks.

Her mind wandered from innocent self-criticism to sensual curiosity.

What will it feel like to be touched by my husband? What will he look like? She stared at the reflection of her green eyes for an unknown answer. For an instant, an aristocratic face with deep blue eyes reflected back. Merrick.

Appalled, she quickly turned away and hurried to grab her modestly styled nightgown. Yanking it over her body, she felt shamefully unclean, even though the long sleeves and ribbon-gathered neckline concealed her curves in a matronly way. But how could she possibly be so disrespectful as to think of Ilse's husband with her sister just "gone over"? What on God's earth could ever possess her to imagine *him* as her husband?

Possess. A chill shivered down her back at her choice of words.

Caroline walked over to the mahogany dressing table and sat down in front of the oval mirror. She stared blankly at her pale reflection as she lifted the mother-of-pearl hairbrush.

Pulling her damp hair forward, Caroline brushed its full length over her shoulder to below her breast. The stiff bristles slipped easily through her dark tresses, scraping against the soft cotton bodice of her nightgown. The light, foreign touch tingled the tip of her breast beneath the cloth. Caroline gently bit her lower lip as she felt goose flesh raise the downy hair on her arms. Her mind envisioned a six-year-old memory of Merrick kissing Ilse in the garden below Caroline's bedroom window. The thought of one day being caressed in such a manner brought warmth to her cheeks.

Snatching her eyelet-trimmed dressing robe from the hook behind the wardrobe door, Caroline denounced her immoral thoughts and moved over to the window, repeating a silent prayer and ending with a passage from the book of Romans.

". . . put ye on the Lord Jesus Christ, and make not
provision for the flesh, to fulfill the lust thereof."

Over the last year and a half, she had asked forgiveness so
many times for such thoughts that she had the verse memo-
rized.

Pushing away the devil's temptations, Caroline gazed
through one of the diamond panes, beyond the colorful
countryside, to the darkening sky. The sparkle of the first star
on the horizon signaled the coming of night and with it the
close of a long, terrible day, shadowed in a sadness that still
hung in the air.

A knock sounded at the door, taking Caroline's mind off
the disturbing train of thoughts.

"I brought you some dinner," Hilde said in a motherly
fashion, entering with a tray of delicious-smelling food covered with a cloth napkin.

Caroline attempted an appreciative smile at the slender
woman, ever the pristine governess. "I don't feel much like
eating."

"Nonsense, child. You haven't eaten since before—" There
was an uncomfortable moment as Hilde stumbled over the
mention of Ilse's death. After setting the meal on the polished
desk top on the other side of the vast room, the woman
turned to face Caroline, appraising her seriously.

"I was asked to give this to you," Hilde continued, reaching into her skirt pocket and withdrawing a small book.
"That crotchety nursemaid Louise took me aside this afternoon and shoved it in my hands, none too happy about it, I
might add. She said the baroness wanted you to have it . . .
if anything happened."

"Why didn't the maid give it to me herself?" Caroline
asked as she accepted the small olive-green, leather-bound
book.

Hilde studied Caroline as if she held the clue to the meaning behind the secretive exchange. "She said that she'd prefer

to have as little to do with you as possible. Perhaps you intimidate her."

"Why, for heaven's sake?" Caroline asked, enthralled with the cover of the book. Haphazardly, she remarked, "That woman can scare the grin off a gargoyle, which is far more than I could do to her!"

Hilde's sniffling chuckle began to bring Caroline's spirits back up.

"I don't know why she dislikes me so," Caroline stated flatly while Hilde watched her cross the room. The tall girl moved with a regal grace in her long, flowing dressing gown. Pink ribbons were tied into bows at the collar and again at the bodice, leaving the cotton material to drape in generous folds. *If one didn't know the circumstances, a visitor to this house could mistake her tired eyes and generous figure as that of the new mother,* Hilde thought, then wondered where such a peculiar observation had come from. If anything, she looked more like a chaste young bride in white.

Mentally shaking herself, Hilde spoke softly with the wisdom of her years. "Perhaps it is not *you* the old woman dislikes, but your arrival here. I understand that Louise had been the baron's nursemaid. She may feel her role as the baby's caretaker has been usurped, especially if you stay. Either way, I don't think she'll let any harm come to the child. She probably looks upon him as if he were her own grandchild."

"True," Caroline conceded. "But I did make a promise to Ilse that I don't know how to keep. She was so afraid for the baby's safety, she wanted me to take him home with me. Someone had frightened her and I don't know if I can trust anyone here."

"Not even the baron?"

"I . . . honestly can't be certain. Even Ilse wasn't sure she could trust him to protect their son."

"But he's the child's father, for goodness' sake."

"I don't understand it, either," Caroline said with a shake

of her head, asking herself a mental question. *Could these reservations about him be linked to Ilse's concern?* "Ilse *did* say that she had much to explain, that she had done some terrible things."

"Do you think that could be why she wanted you to have this?" Hilde nodded to the book in Caroline's hand.

"Apparently so. It looks to be her diary." She glanced through it. "She started it shortly before she met the baron. The last entry was . . . yesterday." Her hand smoothed over the half-filled page of nearly indecipherable scrawl. "The last line says, 'I pray Carrie will arrive in time to save my baby.' "

Caroline looked at Hilde.

"Whatever in the world——?" Hilde saw concerned determination on her young friend's face, an expression she'd seen there once before. "First your mother's Bible, now your sister's diary."

As Caroline flipped to the first page and began reading her sister's diary, Hilde rose from her seat. "If you'd like, I'll look in on the baby before I go down for dinner. Has His Excellency decided on a name?"

Caroline looked up from the pages. "Not that I know of. Ilse had asked *me* to give him a *Christian* name. But I doubt that the baron will honor her request."

"Why not?"

Caroline shrugged and frowned. "He doesn't plan to honor his promise to let me take the boy home with me. I can't imagine him thinking I should have a say in naming his son."

"Stranger things have been known to happen," Hilde paused at the doorway. "At least eat a little something while you're searching through that diary," she said upon leaving the room.

Book in hand, Caroline crossed the room, already skimming her sister's words, and sat down to the cooling meal of succulent lamb, tiny carrots, and dark rye bread.

Biting off a piece of butter-laden bread, Caroline began to read a descriptive passage that drew her curiosity, despite her better judgment. It was Ilse's account of her secret rendezvous with the baron two nights after his arrival in Sebula.

". . . The warmth of his tongue encircling my breasts brought a sensation such as I have never known. Deep within I ached for more, pulling him closer. As he kissed me tenderly, his hand slipped beneath the cloth of my underclothes. The pleasure overshadowed my embarrassment as I felt a warm wetness."

Caroline gripped the book with cold, clammy hands and read on. —

"I thought Merrick would be repulsed, but his breathing grew heavier, his kisses more urgent. I did not know that there could be a deeper ecstasy than which I felt at that moment. Yet Merrick taught me so much more before the night was over."

Caroline crossed her legs, desperately trying to suppress a feeling that had caught her off guard.

"His nakedness stirred my senses. When I shivered he only smiled and plunged himself deep within me, joining us as one. The pain was only for an instant, the pleasure hurled me into eternity."

Shaken, Caroline slowly closed the book and laid it on the table, staring at it in shameful embarrassment. How ignorant she'd been when her sister had returned that morning. Though she'd seen their impassioned farewell kiss upon their return, it had never occurred to her to consider that Ilse had surrendered herself to the baron.

Mentally, Caroline was taken back to that morning, to memories of being awakened before full light by an ambitious young rooster. When she found Ilse still missing, she'd pulled aside the lace curtains and looked out onto the garden. The full moon had cast long shadows across the yard.

Silently, two figures neared the outer fence on a tall horse. Caroline recognized the fine ebony stallion and its riders immediately. The baron slid down from the saddle and helped her sister down to the ground.

As the moonlit night began to give way to sunrise, Caroline watched Merrick gently grasp Ilse's shoulders and kiss her passionately. Slowly, he slipped one hand to the small of her back and pulled the length of her body to his. Ilse tipped her head back as her lover lowered his mouth to her neck.

Caroline felt a strange uncomfortable feeling surge deep inside. Although embarrassment beckoned her to turn away, an unfamiliar warmth overpowered her senses. She swallowed hard. Her mouth was dry. As she wet her lips with her tongue, perspiration beaded on her back beneath her nightgown.

The sun would soon be above the horizon. She wanted to warn Ilse that time was running out. But she couldn't.

Merrick released Ilse's arm and unfastened the buttons down the front of her blouse. As he pulled her hips tight against him with one hand, he slipped his other hand to her breast. As the baron once again crushed his mouth to hers, Ilse arched her body into him.

Caroline covered her mouth with her hand to stifle her surprised gasp. Her sister allowed the baron to do as he pleased, even if it meant discovery. Caroline felt her strange fascination give way to anger at the arrogance of this man. She clenched her fists, resisting an urge to call her sister to her senses.

Merrick placed one finger under Ilse's chin and lifted her face. Her eyes closed; her lips parted in anticipation. Then the baron turned and looked directly at the second-floor bedroom window. His eyes fixed on Caroline's and the corners of his full lips curved into a faint smile. His knowing stare told Caroline that he had been fully aware of her presence.

Turning back to Ilse, he completed his farewell with a kiss on her forehead. He reached up to her hands clenched behind his neck and lowered them to her sides. A confident smile remained on his face as he turned to his horse, grabbed the saddle horn, and swung his weight onto the large animal. His black stallion snorted and pawed the clay soil with impatience. Without looking back, the baron urged his horse silently into the dawn.

Caroline slipped back under the soft cotton sheets and turned her back to the door. Unwilling to face Ilse, she was certain that her own embarrassment and guilt would be written on her face.

After six years, Caroline hadn't forgotten the vivid details, nor the seductive curve of the baron's knowing smile. She now wondered whether his smile had been one of amusement with the snooping little sister—as she'd long supposed—or was it a victorious smile of contentment, his way of showing that he had irrevocably claimed her sister's virtue? Either way, Caroline had always wondered about his knowledge of her presence overlooking the garden. Only now did she consider that his gift of clairvoyance may have entered into it.

She also realized the scandalous rumors that led to her sister's hasty wedding had been true, though Caroline had always believed it to be a fabrication. Much of the world as she knew it was quickly unraveling, and the cause of it always came back to the baron. Who was he? For years she had seen him as the hated enemy. Part of her still felt that way. But another part of her added a confusing twist, with feelings of empathy and . . . She refused to acknowledge the other strange, inexplicable reaction she had to him.

In an almost trancelike state, she stood and went over to the bed, sorting the hodgepodge of thoughts that confused and tormented her brain. Sitting on the edge of the bed with her hands pressed between her knees, she began a very slight rocking motion as she stared at the muted colors in the Persian rug at her feet.

The marriage had been arranged to create a gifted child of great spiritual strength. But no one knew that it was me, not Ilse, who had the psychic abilities. Could a mistake have been made?

Caroline pulled a pillow to her lap and bunched it against her stomach as she doubled over in the painful realization that gripped her. *If it had been me,* her mind raced, *Ilse would still be alive.* The irony riddled her with guilt. Why wasn't she given this insight when it could have made a difference? Would it have mattered?

Somehow, she knew it wouldn't have changed the course of events. If she had learned nothing else from her mother's Bible, she had at least learned that there was always a greater plan, though one might not understand it at the time.

The knot of pain lessened, though it didn't completely go away. Fatigue wrapped itself around all of the turmoil in Caroline's mind and lulled her into a fitful sleep.

In the deep recesses of her imagination, a dream began with the shadowy images of the garden surrounding her. The back of her tall clapboard house stood behind her. It was a warm summer night with the light of the full moon dusting the surrounding mountainside with a pearly glow. A soft snap of a twig brought her attention around to see the baron standing beneath a far tree. Without a word, he beckoned her to come to him. As she walked closer and closer, her heart pounded with a strange excitement. Leaving the garden, she walked through long cool blades of grass until she stood in front of the baron.

Silently, he stared into her eyes and the midnight blue darkness stirred her soul. His hands touched hers, then slowly moved up her arms, leaving behind a trail of tingling heat. Without dropping his gaze, his hands worked the buttons of her blouse free and pulled the material down off her shoulders. He lowered his mouth to her neck and kissed the soft skin. As if he sensed the weakness in her knees, he caught her with one hand and drew her closer.

In the next moment, Caroline felt the warmth of his hand on her breast and a strange throbbing need arose deep in her being. His lips brushed her nipple, then his tongue swirled around it. When his teeth tugged ever so gently on the erect nipple, she arched and moaned softly.

Only Merrick was a part of her dream now. All else faded away until he had become the center of her desire. He took time to undress her and laid her on her strewn skirt and petticoats. It mattered not that she was naked and unashamed at his feet as he removed his own clothes and lowered himself down to her. She slid her hands over his back and felt the hardened muscles flex beneath his smooth skin.

His lips joined hers as their bodies came together to fill one another with ecstasy.

In his library, Merrick sat in a burgundy leather chair across from his desk. His boots were propped on a matching stool with cabriole legs. His deep blue eyes saw only blurred yellow flames dancing in the fireplace several feet away. Like all of the rooms in this old house, the library was spacious, with high ceilings trimmed in crown molding. The polished dark floor was native pine, logged from the surrounding woods, and protected with years of wax and a large Persian carpet of multicolored designs. The furniture was an eclectic collection of heavy Chippendale pieces and the lighter Hepplewhite designs.

But these appointments were of little interest to Merrick. The house and its furnishings had changed very little since he was a boy and that suited him. His only domestic concern was that everything be modestly clean and pleasant to the eye when he entertained.

He had been somewhat surprised that Ilse, who loved exquisite clothes, made no effort to redecorate to suit her own tastes. But domesticity had certainly not been her forte.

Merrick scoffed at the reminder of his wife's shortcomings. If the circumstances had been reversed, would she be pondering his failings? Quite likely. For she'd never passed an opportunity to verbalize her discontentedness since the baby'd been conceived. It was then that her mood darkened considerably, far more severely that in the first few years of marriage.

She'd begun to accuse him of all sorts of diabolical schemes, but he'd attributed such nonsense to her state of restlessness. Now, looking back, he wondered if there was a more justifiable reason for his wife's paranoia.

Even in Sebula, when he'd brought her back from their night-long tryst, she'd been skittish. He smiled at the memory of making love to her under the oak tree. Then another image came to mind, one of Caroline looking down on the two of them in the garden. Suddenly thoughts of an older Caroline filled his daydreams in front of the fire.

He closed his eyes and, in his wildest imagining, he pictured her coming toward him across the wide expanse of grass that grew behind her home. Her white blouse seemed to glow beneath the moonlight, accenting the fullness of her breasts.

Her large green eyes told of her surrender to her need to be with him. Deep in his loins, a fullness grew, pushing him to take her as he'd taken Ilse. In a quiet reverence, he unfastened her buttons and kissed the delicate skin of her throat, drinking in the subtle scent of lavender. He felt her pulse pounding harder with each touch. As he steadied her against him with one arm, he dipped his head and took her nipple in his mouth, teasing it until it hardened into a flushed red peak.

His body responded with its own hardness, straining against his trousers for release. The task of undressing served only to heighten his anticipation to the point of near-frenzy. As he knelt in the grass, his restraint wore to a bare thread.

Every fiber of his being was raw with a desire that pulsed through his veins like fire.

In the moonlight he let his gaze drift over her pale tempting flesh, from her fully rounded breasts to the soft swell of her belly and down to her deliciously dark patch of forbidden curls. As he lowered himself onto her, his knee parted her long, coltish legs. She raised them instinctively as he lowered his mouth to hers and plunged his manhood deep inside her.

For only a moment, she cried out in pain as his hard shaft tore through her maidenhead, but it soon subsided as he slid in and out of her with a tantalizing rhythm. Ecstasy soon replaced the pain he'd caused as the two of them mounted the summit of pleasure. As Caroline arched in abandon, her body shuddered in fulfillment beneath him. Then his own body welcomed the explosive release that shook his entire being.

Reality suddenly burst upon Merrick as his eyes opened wide. Even though it had been a vivid daydream, his heart thumped hard against his chest. Unquenched desire ached in his loins. He glanced to the ceiling, thinking of the young woman who slept in the bedroom above. He never should have let himself get caught up in the fantasy.

Shaking his head in puzzlement, Merrick let his boots drop to the floor with a muffled thump, then rose from the chair. Absently walking from the warm seclusion of the library, he went to the parlor where Ilse's lifeless form lay in wait. She would be buried the next morning. There would be a crowd of mourners for his wife, for she had successfully charmed his friends. They had known there'd been no great passion between the baron and his baroness, but this was often the case in their set, and a loveless marriage did not prevent their acceptance of her.

Tomorrow, carriages would arrive in droves. The house

would be swarming with well-meaning guests, delivering condolences and inquiring about his son.

His son. He had a son. The boy's arrival should have been joyous. The guests should be arriving for a celebration. The bitter irony pushed Merrick's dark reflections deeper until the familiar pain tightened in his chest. When his father had died and left him this twisted plot to fulfill, had he known the price Merrick would pay for his loyalty?

Standing before the closed pine casket, he braced his hands on the lid panel while his mind repeated the same questions he'd heard earlier from Caroline.

What use were these supernatural powers if Ilse couldn't be saved? Why have the gift of insight if I couldn't foresee her fate in time to send for the doctor?

His fingers tightened around the hard edge of the box as he tilted his head back in anguish. The ceiling was only a watery blur of white through the welcome spill of tears.

"What kind of God are you to snatch her life away, to deny my son the mother he needs?" he asked in a voice wracked with agony. "Why did you give me these powers and then deny them to me when I need them most?"

Undetected in the doorway, Caroline watched the baron, and a strange sensation fluttered in her stomach. She had awakened near midnight by her startlingly realistic dream and looked in on the baby, then felt drawn downstairs to this room. As she had descended the stairs, she'd thought the lateness would afford her the solitude to say a final good-bye to Ilse. Now, instead, she felt compelled to comfort him as he had comforted her. A jumble of feelings warred within her.

From the look of the wrinkled white shirt partially untucked from the narrow waist of his black trousers, Caroline surmised that he had not yet been to bed. He lifted his head and once again she noticed how his ebony hair lay in thick curls at the edge of his collar. When his shoulders rose and fell in a heavy sigh and he turned, she felt her heart race at the thought that he would see her standing there. But her alarm was for naught when she realized he was only reaching for something. His sleeve was rolled above his elbow, exposing the dark skin of his forearm as he withdrew the object and bowed his head over it.

To her bewilderment, he read a short scripture aloud, then continued to speak as if her sister were there in the room with him.

"I wish you could have met my father, Ilse. Maybe then you would have understood why I was faithful to the covenant. There was so much more at stake than our two lives. Perhaps I was blinded by my loyalty to my father, to my heritage. Had I known the cost, I would have laid down my own life for the sake of our child."

His words came haltingly as he read from the Bible another verse from Job. She couldn't bear to remain silent, feeling his pain mix with her own.

"Herr Baron?" she said quietly in the hope that she wouldn't startle him. His head snapped around, revealing the glistening tracks of tears across cheeks faintly shadowed with the day's growth of beard. His jaw was set in a strong, tense line. Was the anger she saw in his eyes his way of hiding his tears? Then again, she couldn't help but wonder if he was putting on a sorrowful charade for her benefit. Not once had he spoken voluntarily—or lovingly—of Ilse on their journey from America. Now he quoted biblical passages?

He turned his back to her. "I thought I was alone," he said with a sharpness that cut away her sympathy. Was this the real baron, a man who turned his emotions on and off to manipulate the naive and vulnerable? Did he let people see only what he wanted them to see as long as it served his purposes?

"Did you honestly think you were alone?"

"What is that supposed to mean?"

"Do you remember the night you brought Ilse back home at dawn?" she asked, visions of his brazen caress clear in her mind. "You . . . kissed her even when you knew that I was there in the window."

"I only saw you at the very last moment," he said with his back still turned. How odd that she would mention that particular night. Had she been thinking of it when he'd had the vivid daydream?

"How did you know? Was it one of your . . . gifts?"

Suddenly his shoulders shook and Caroline thought he had broken down.

"I'm sorry, *Herr Baron.* I didn't mean to bring back memories." She moved across the room and reached for his sleeve, then changed her mind and pulled her hand back.

Merrick looked sideways to her, shaking his head with the slightest smile tipping one corner of his mouth. "Oh, little one. You are a blessing in disguise. I suppose I could lead you on and say that it was some divine knowledge that led me to see you in your bedroom window. But it was only a glint of reflection from the morning sun on the window pane that caught my attention. Nothing more."

Embarrassed, Caroline dropped her gaze, hoping he would be a gentleman and let the delicate subject of her spying pass. She rubbed her arms in the unheated room and shivered, realizing that she should have donned her mother's coat to walk the drafty halls of this old house.

"Come into the library," Merrick said, briefly touching her elbow. "The fire should still be burning."

Escorting Caroline into the book-lined room, he gestured to the hearth as he left her side and walked over to a stout cabinet.

"I would offer you cognac or something equally relaxing. But something tells me that you and Ilse don't . . . share the same tastes." He stuttered over the confusion of past and present.

Caroline started to agree with him, then changed her mind. "I *will* take a glass, Your Excellency, if for no other reason than to help me sleep."

Nodding, he prepared the wine and joined her in front of the hearth. After giving her the glass and placing another log upon the fire, he straightened to his full height and found her watching him. His gaze wandered over her face. Her green eyes were the color of dark moss, a color that beckoned him to look closer, to fall under its magnetic spell. Behind, in the recesses of her mind, dwelled a power that threatened to equal his own, a thought that challenged him in an almost frightening manner. Unlike her sister, Caroline had the means to capture his very soul simply by her quiet naïveté about her abilities, strength and—most endearing—her natural beauty.

His logic reminded him that the changes had not come overnight, as it seemed. And through those changes, Caroline had become a woman of much stronger material than his poor wife.

Thoughts of Ilse returned. She'd been a beautiful woman who had craved the undying love of a devoted husband. If she had visited Europe as an unmarried young lady, there would have been at least a dozen men of high breeding who would have offered themselves to her. She'd deserved that much. Instead, she'd been destined to be a disillusioned wife with a courteously indifferent husband.

Ilse had been a challenge to find, but certainly not to seduce or to marry. Although he'd often recalled the fleeting vision he'd had long before they met, never had he expected such an exquisite beauty to greet him that autumn evening. It seemed as though he'd been blessed for taking up the quest to fulfill the marriage covenant. The same assurance had filled him when he'd made love to her the night Caroline had seen them return.

He lifted his glass in a halfhearted toast. "May you find the happiness that your sister sought," he said.

Caroline wordlessly clinked her glass to his and sipped the liquid. "She *was* happy, Your Excellency. The morning after you—"

Merrick smiled, wondering how much she knew of that night. "Are you still embarrassed that I caught you watching?"

"Yes. No. I mean, yes." She walked over to a long sofa and perched on the edge, drinking down the last of her small amount of cognac in a matter of minutes. The numbing glow that seemed to be seeping into her muscles was far more relaxing than the hot bath had been and she welcomed it.

"May I please have another?"

"I think you will despise me in the morning if I give you one."

"Let me worry about that tomorrow," she said, a bit irritated with being monitored like a child. "If Ilse could enjoy it, so shall I."

"You aren't quite ready to match Ilse, little one."

"Oh, I wouldn't be too quick to judge, *Herr Baron*. Again, you forget that I'm grown now."

"But not grown enough to know the price of overindulgence."

Caroline was tired of the talk, tired of the pain. She rose from the cushion and walked over to the cabinet of bottles. "I can handle anything. Remember? Or have you already forgotten my shipboard incident?" she asked bitterly, reopening the fresh wound of memories as she opened the decanter. The splash of cognac in her glass was like the rush of horrid memories pouring out of her.

Merrick came quickly across the floor but she had already gulped down a generous swallow, then coughed. Grabbing her wrist to stop her from reaching for the bottle again, he tightened his grip as she fought to free herself.

As if shaken back to reality, she stopped and stared at his dark fingers wrapped around her arm, then slowly let her gaze drift up to his shoulder, then his face. His dark eyes covered her in their scrutinizing glare, forcing her to lower her lids.

"Please forgive me, Your Excellency. This isn't like me."

"I know, Carrie. We are both trying to forget, aren't we?"

Her attention was drawn upward and settled on his stubbled chin, then his full lower lip. She reached up and stroked the soft growth of beard covering his cheek. Their eyes met each other's with pain, fear, and uncertainty.

Merrick slid his hands to her waist and lowered his mouth to hers, touching her lips tentatively at first, then closing over them with a tender longing that begged for her response.

In the fog between the numbness and the pain, Caroline felt the unmistakable inner warmth in the touch of his body to hers, a welcoming of a new pleasure that blocked the hurt and the anger.

Wrapping his arms around her, his mouth moved over hers in a stirring swirl of passion, conveying his own need to be taken away from their present reality. The sweet smell of flowers drifted from the soft curls of her hair, mixing with the fragrance of the burning evergreen bough. Pine and lavender. Her body arched into his and he felt the fullness of her breasts press against him. The scent of pine and lavender would never affect him the same way again.

Stimulated by the heady fragrance, he recalled the vision he'd had years before of the two sisters in the rustic church. Remembering Caroline's large emerald eyes that had stirred a deep part of him, he now recognized that it was this lavender perfume that had permeated the air and mixed with the scent of the forest.

All at once he tore his mouth from hers and stepped back.

"What's wrong?" she blurted out, then wished she hadn't. It was wrong of her to allow him to kiss her. And she should have been the one to stop it, not he.

With his breathing ragged, he raked his hand through his hair, putting some distance between them before he turned and spoke. "It is my turn to apologize, Carrie. I never should have overstepped my bounds. Now if you'll excuse me, please." He nodded toward the door as his indication for her to go ahead of him to retire.

Sobered by the sudden turn of events, Caroline quickly escaped from his presence, certain that his polite coolness was simply his gentlemanly way of ending the awkward situation that she'd allowed. He had dismissed her as surely as if she was the child she had earlier claimed not to be.

When the latch of the library door clicked, Merrick let out a pent-up sigh as he stared into the flickering flames. It was going to be an even longer night than he had anticipated. And now he had more on his mind than ever. Through his own selfishness, he had been one step away from taking his sister-in-law to bed on the night of his wife's death.

He lifted the iron poker and jabbed at the log, damning his desires, and fell once again into thoughts of times past.

Ilse had instinctively known how to please him. But afterward, when their spent bodies had lain contentedly together, Merrick had felt terribly, miserably alone. Physically, his body responded to Ilse with an explosive fever. But emotionally, he felt like a thief, stealing the ultimate offer of her love with a coldhearted greed. As days passed into weeks, he grew to hate himself, selfishly pouring his seed into her only for the sake of siring the child of the covenant.

The weeks turned into months without Ilse taking his child into her womb and Merrick was convinced she was barren. Still, they came together again and again. The fitful sleep that followed their lovemaking had become the only time he found rest from his cold, lonely depression.

When Ilse became desperately sick with nausea and fever, he had sensed immediately that she was pregnant. Because of her delicate health, he'd left her to bring back Caroline. And because he'd left her, she'd died. Was this the price of his schemed, prearranged marriage? Had there been a curse placed on the covenant that he was not aware of?

He rose from the hearth and dragged himself up the stairs. As he passed Caroline's room, he saw a shaft of light beneath the door. He paused, shook his head, then continued on to his room at the end of the hall with one thought monotonously repeating itself over and over in his brain: *Pine and lavender. Pine and lavender.*

Chapter 5

"Caroline? Caroline?"

Through a dreadful nauseous haze, Caroline could hear Hilde's concerned voice between gentle but persistent raps on the bedroom door. She rolled to her back and draped her forearm over her eyes.

"Come in," she called out.

"Dear God, child. What's gotten into you?" Hilde asked, seeing the ashen look on her young friend's face.

Caroline's head felt like an old hickory log being chopped from both ends. She didn't dare tell Hilde the cause of her sudden illness, even though she knew the woman would keep it in the strictest confidence. The baron had been right to warn her about the price of overindulgence, if only she'd heeded.

Hilde pulled back the heavy forest-green drapes to let the morning sun light the room while wondering how Caroline could have become sick so quickly, hoping her initial information was incorrect. Ilse's maid Greta had come downstairs all atwitter about the new houseguest lying in bed moaning

about something. The girl had brought up a breakfast tray
since the hour was late but, reported the maid, the fräulein
had run to the basin at her first sight of the fat-fried sausage
and eggs.

The maid turned out to be quite a gossip; Hilde realized
when she'd overheard the conversation with the scullery
maid.

"She's acting just like the way the baroness did when she
was first carrying," Greta had said. "Same way, I tell you.
All pale and sick in the morning like this."

The other girl asked, "Why on earth would she come
clear from America if she was expecting? What would her
husband say?"

"If you ask me, there is no husband. And I bet His Excellency wasn't sent to get her just because the baroness was
wanting family around. I bet she sent him to fetch her sister
so she could have her baby here—away from home as it is."

"So . . . Fräulein Hartmann's in a family way," the dim-
witted cook's helper finally realized.

"Sure as I'm standing here. She's been doing a fine job of
handling it—what with her clothes and all."

"Do you think His Excellency knows?"

"I can't be sure. But did you see how tight her coat fit?
She's filling with milk already, I tell you. You can bet we'll
have two little ones in the nursery before long."

Hilde had no choice but to purposely make a noise at that
point, for there was no other way she could leave the room.
Remaining where she stood, she was sure to be discovered by
either one of them in another minute or so, if not by another
loyal staff member. In this household of strangers, it was
better to come forth and appear bold than to cower in the
corner, fueling their open contempt toward newcomers.

"Excuse me," Hilde said. "Did I hear you say Fräulein
Hartmann seems to be with child?" The two servants looked
at her with disdainful amusement.

Greta answered with haughty airs, "You've traveled with her enough to know as well as I."

Ignoring the slight, Hilde cheerfully addressed both. "Perhaps I should go see if I can be of any help." She pressed her skirt out of the way as she moved past them in the narrow passage between the kitchen and the servants' stairs.

Hilde moved across the sun-filled room and stood at the edge of the mahogany bed where Caroline had curled into a tight ball, clutching her stomach. Was it possible that Caroline was with child? She hadn't been ill like this on the ship but, as Hilde well knew, each pregnancy was as different as each woman.

Hilde bent over and lightly touched the back of her hand to Caroline's forehead, testing for fever. Her pale skin was cool and damp, a sure indication that her body wasn't battling influenza.

Sympathetic emotion gripped Hilde with thoughts of this young girl, whom she'd grown so fond of, facing the ultimate humiliation of bearing a bastard. With the sister lost as a result of childbirth, poor Caroline was destined not only to bear the illegitimate child alone but to do it with memories of a painful example still fresh in her mind.

Though Hilde's obligation had been fulfilled and she was due to leave that afternoon for her aunt's home near Freiburg, she couldn't bring herself to abandon her young friend. The least she could so was to offer her assistance and companionship until the baby was born. First, however, Hilde had to hear from Caroline herself if the suppositions were true.

Gently touching Caroline's shoulder, she asked, "Perhaps if you tell me what is wrong, I might be able to help."

"Mmm?"

"I feel I must ask you a delicate question, dear." Hilde straightened, uncertain of the words to choose. "Caroline, are you . . . with child?"

Caroline's eyes popped open. She stared incredulously at the older woman. Had she heard Hilde correctly?

"Am I what?"

"Pregnant."

"Where ever did that idea come from? I am simply not feeling well."

Hilde realized then that there was a strong chance this girl from a very puritanical upbringing didn't recognize the symptoms. But Hilde dismissed the notion, considering the fact that Caroline had supposedly been sent halfway around the world *because* of her condition. More than likely, she just didn't want Hilde to know. In which case, the older woman had to accept that fact, but not quite yet.

"If you were sick, you would have a fever. If anything, your skin is a bit too cool. Now . . . is there something you are afraid to talk about?

Caroline thought back on her conversation with the baron in the library and the intoxicating cognac. The memory of his mouth moving over hers and his body pressed close brought a flush of shame to her cheeks.

"No. There is nothing to say." Tossing the heavy coverlet to her feet, she rolled away from Hilde and sat up abruptly, a move that sent the room spinning. Her empty stomach reeled at the dizziness and throbbing pain in her head. She half-ran, half-stumbled the short distance to the wash basin, her muscles convulsing but producing nothing.

Afterward, she gripped her hands around the edge of the table top and braced her arms. Her knees felt like they wouldn't support her weight a minute longer.

With uncondemning silence, Hilde came over to the washstand and filled the ornate basin with water from the pitcher. Caroline stared at the beautiful flowers painted along the sloping sides of the bowl in deep, rich shades of pink. Flowers of similar design decorated the rotund base and handle of the the water jug. She welcomed the soothing touch of Hilde's hand on her back, gently rubbing in a wide circle between her hunched shoulder blades. With her other hand, Hilde dipped a small cloth in the water and squeezed.

"Let me see your face," she said quietly.

Bringing her attention up, Caroline's watery eyes blinked and focused on the devoted, caring woman who gently swathed the damp, refreshing cloth across her forehead and cheeks. It wasn't fair to hold back the truth when Hilde was willing to accept an untimely pregnancy and still offer emotional support.

"If this is what it is like to be pregnant, I don't think I ever want to be in a family way," Caroline said with a shaky smile. "I believe this is the quintessential penance for having too much to drink."

Hilde paused. "You got drunk?" she asked with surprise.

"Let's say overindulged. That sounded so much more genteel when His Excellency said it."

"You got drunk with the baron?"

Caroline winced at the awful connotation to the innocent circumstances. *Were* they so innocent? She turned around and walked away from the table, followed closely by Hilde.

Wrapping her hands around the tapered bedpost, Caroline leaned her forehead against the polished wood. "It's not as it seems, Hilde. When I was wakened by a bad dream, I went downstairs and came upon the baron in the mourning room. It was I who asked for the cognac to help me to sleep."

"One glass did . . . this?"

Caroline cocked her head to one side and looked at Hilde with a sheepish lift to her dark eyebrows. The guilty expression told volumes, eliciting a heavy sigh from the compassionate chaperone.

"I'm certain you didn't stop to consider the ramifications of such an innocent encounter. As it stands, your early morning illness has unknowingly triggered scandalous gossip between two of the servants. And, I hate to say, I'm sure it must be common knowledge among the entire staff by now."

Caroline gasped at the horrible thought that the more-

than-friendly kiss had not gone unseen as she'd assumed. If
they were discovered, how little would it take to speculate
on the outcome of her first night in the baron's house . . .
on the night of her sister's . . . his *wife's* . . . passing!

"The way gossip spreads like a fire out of control, I
wouldn't doubt that the rumormonger will point a finger at
His Excellency as the cause of your suspected pregnancy."

"Baron von Hayden? The father?"

"Yes. The two almost had your month figured out by the
time I interrupted their idle gossip. I wouldn't be surprised if
they didn't think the baron himself had taken a fancy to his
younger sister-in-law. It's been known to happen."

"Hilde!"

"Oh—I am sorry, Caroline," the woman took a step toward her. "I don't know what made me go on like that."

"No. I didn't mean to scold you. It's just that you gave me
a wonderful way to solve my problem!" She reached out and
hugged Hilde, then moved away, holding her aching head
while it raced with plots and plans.

"What did I say?"

"The servants think I am expecting a baby. Right?"

"Yes."

"Did they say *anything* that would imply the baron's paternity?"

"No." By now, Hilde was thoroughly mystified by the
change in Caroline's behavior.

"Good." She took Hilde's hand and led her to a settee
similar to the one in Ilse's room. Taking a seat, she patted the
cushion next to her and asked Hilde to be patient for another
moment. Grabbing one of the smaller pillows in the colorful
array at her side, Caroline deftly slipped it under her gown,
then brought her hands out and plumped the tiny mound
into a natural position. For all intents and purposes, the
young girl looked like a glowing young mother blossoming
into her second trimester.

"What do you think? Does it look real enough?"

"Yes. But—"

"I want you to go downstairs and say a few things, as if in the strictest confidence, to verify my pregnancy to one of those maids."

"Why in heaven's name do you want to *appear* to be expecting a baby?"

"Ilse asked me to take her baby back to America where he'd be safe. But everyone who knows about the child of the covenant knows about his birth yesterday, as well as Ilse's death. Anyone who wanted to harm him could easily follow me to America. I wouldn't be able to take him anywhere. I think the baron knew this when he refused to let me take his son."

"At least if the child stayed here with his father, he could be given the ultimate in protection."

Caroline shook her head. "Don't you see? I promised Ilse. We aren't speaking of little things. We are speaking of her flesh and blood. She feared for his safety. I must do what I can to keep my promise, at least until I can be certain that the danger has passed."

"Certainly you cannot be suggesting that you are going to smuggle him out of the country under your clothing. He'll suffocate within minutes beneath the layers of cotton and wool!"

"No," Caroline said. "Hear me out."

She worked through the details with Hilde's added suggestions. The tiny newborn would need time to develop enough strength to travel, allowing Caroline three or four months to masquerade her developing pregnancy. When her own delivery approached, she would insist upon returning to America, claiming that the death of her sister augured ill for the safe birth of her own baby. Though it would be difficult, she would then find a way to have the baby stolen for her and meet the kidnapper on her way to Rotterdam. En route, she would falsify a death certificate for the baron's son, discard her padding, and claim the infant as her own.

Hilde asked soberly, "What about the baron? Will you tell him of your plan?"

"I hadn't thought that far yet." She paused thoughtfully. "I think not."

"But you would be stealing his son from him."

Caroline sat back against a cushion and closed her eyes, squeezing them tight as if to shut out the frustrating moral flaw in her plan. Lacing her fingers over the soft swell beneath her gown, she slowly lifted her lids and stared blankly at the floral patterned wallpaper.

"Yes," she finally said. "I suppose it looks like I'm stealing the baron's son. But until I can be absolutely certain he is not somehow a part of the danger, I can't take the risk."

Hilde observed the natural pose of Caroline's hands on her belly. If she could maintain this maternal casualness regarding her figure, and Hilde instructed her in the other nuances of pregnancy, there was no doubt that the charade could be carried off. That was, until it came time to kidnap the baby. Hilde wasn't entirely convinced that such an intricate plot could be executed without detection. Then again, could she bring herself to leave, now, and never know if the baby had been saved? There was no other answer in her mind to such a question. She would stay and help Caroline.

"Did you ever find anything in Ilse's diary?" she asked.

"At first, Ilse was very . . . happy in her marriage," Caroline said. "Shortly after she came here, she had a few encounters with a woman who warned her that her first-born son would have a strife-torn destiny, marred with death. After that, Ilse was terribly afraid of becoming pregnant by Merrick . . . the baron."

Caroline purposefully didn't mention that her sister's visitor had also claimed Merrick to be the devil himself. If Hilde were the type to fear such things and then learned of Caroline's unusual mystical abilities, what would she think then? Would she denounce their friendship and label Caroline an evil witch?

In further reading, Caroline had learned far more about her defiant older sister than she cared to know. Though Ilse had publicly played the young lady to Caroline's tomboy, secretly Ilse had all but relinquished her maidenhood to a married head of the community. She'd openly confessed in her writings that, if Merrick hadn't arrived, she would have given herself to her married suitor in hopes of winning him away from his wife.

Little had Merrick realized how timely his presentation of the prearranged marital agreement had been. Another week and his virginal Ilse might not have been the inexperienced, yet receptive, enchantress. On the other hand, Caroline thought, he would have had a clearer indication of the vixen that he would take back to Germany with him.

Hilde touched Caroline's arm, drawing her back. "Didn't you say they had been married quite a long time? Yet it was only in the last year that she conceived. How odd. I mean, if the baron wanted a child, certainly she didn't deny him his conjugal rights."

"She obtained a . . . 'Dutch cap' to keep from conceiving," Caroline explained, completely unaware of the function of the device. Though she was aware of most aspects of procreation, it seemed strange to her that one would wear a hat, cap, or any other kind of head covering to prevent an unwanted pregnancy.

A bemused smile on Hilde's face told Caroline that the older woman obviously knew the term and its use.

Hilde patted the young girl's fingers spread over the makeshift padding. "I suppose if this doesn't work out as we planned, you could always dispose of the pillow and say that you lost the baby." Caroline's face brightened at the first positive sign that Hilde would help. "While I go down and ingratiate myself with the servant girls, I would advise you to find a way to secure your padding. That pillow is enough for now, but I think we'll have to stitch something together that can be altered easily as the weeks pass. You'll need to learn how to walk differently, too."

Caroline nodded, grinning from ear to ear like a school child who'd just gotten the best part in the Christmas pageant.

"And you absolutely must eat like there is no tomorrow. Do you think you could put on ten or twenty pounds very easily?"

"Too easily," Caroline laughed.

"Good." Hilde rose and smoothed her hair back into the tight bun as was her nervous habit. "I'll let you know how it goes downstairs."

After Hilde left the room, Caroline repositioned the pillow into her underclothing and went to the mirror to inspect her handiwork. Turning to one side, she viewed the long white gown that hid her little secret, then she slid one hand just below her breasts to hold the fabric in place while the other smoothed over the slight bulge. The sudden skip of her heart at the sight of her maternal silhouette surprised and delighted her. A small pang of longing welled up inside, a feeling she had never known in all the many years of playing with her dolls and daydreaming of knights in shining armor. She was a full-grown woman of twenty now, embarking on a ruse that she hoped would one day be a beautiful reality for her.

She looked down, but the bodice of her gown obstructed her view of her padded pregnancy. For the first time in her life, she viewed her generous endowment as something other than a cross to bear. Under the circumstances, her body was well suited to take on the appearance of an expectant mother. The corners of her mouth curled into an appreciative smile.

The morning had dragged on endlessly for Merrick, as had the long line of carriages that had brought countless numbers of mourners. The cold October wind kept the windows closed and the fireplaces burning cords of aromatic cedar and pine. All of the servants were busy, seeing to the needs of each guest. Some would stay the night and had to be settled in various rooms of the house. Each way he turned, Merrick was being given tearful kisses by the ladies or firm handshakes by the stony-faced men.

The entire house seemed to be bursting at the seams with well-meaning visitors. Though it was customary to accept condolences in the mourning room with the open casket, Merrick was never one to follow tradition, especially now. As with his father, he would honor Ilse in his own way and he would remember her as he saw her last, resting peacefully with their son at her breast.

His thoughts fell back to Caroline's compassion and strength during the painful birth. Again, he found himself comparing her to Ilse who, he was certain, would have fled the room at the first whimper of another's suffering. Caroline filled his mind, with her silken mahogany curls and soft moss-green eyes that could change to the color of brilliant emeralds. In his memory of the night before, he recalled overstepping his bounds and taking her into his arms, an advance that he'd soon regretted yet had played over and over in dreams. She was so alluring in the white dressing gown. Despite the fact that it covered her nightgown, he couldn't help but notice the translucence of the layered, cotton material as she stood before the light of the fire. Just enough shadow and light revealed a tantalizing glimpse of her long, coltish legs and the swell of her hips.

Dammit, man. Get a hold of yourself. You have the mind of a hedonist, his senses reeled.

"Your Excellency?" the butler beckoned quietly.

"Yes, Conrad. What is it?" Merrick asked, expecting yet another announcement of another arriving dignitary.

"Pastor Oppenheimer has just arrived and wishes to speak to you in private."

Merrick scoffed. "Where in the hell do you think that would be in this god-forsaken house—the broom closet?"

Despite the extenuating circumstances, Conrad stiffened at this unusual display of angry emotion from the generally reserved baron. "Might I suggest the nursery, Your Excellency. The reverend did indicate an interest in seeing the child."

"Fine. I'll be there in five minutes. And tell Louise to expect us." Merrick didn't want to get up there to find the minister had stumbled upon the wet nurse feeding his son. He wouldn't have been so aware of his new employee if he hadn't hired her the previous day, a formality the nursemaid could have done. He was so afraid for his son's life, he'd taken to suspecting a distraught widow who'd lost her baby and husband only two days earlier. Frau Haun was a pathetic sight. Even so, he ordered Louise to accompany her at all times, at least until he could be certain she was not sent by his enemies.

Merrick walked into the nursery with a purposeful stride and offered his hand to the uncommonly young Lutheran minister. *"Guten tag, Geistliche Oppenheimer.*

"Guss' Gott, Baron von Hayden," he greeted, giving God's blessing.

Merrick turned to the curious old maid who had raised him. "Please leave us alone, Louise, and be sure that we're not disturbed. I will send for you in one hour."

"As you wish, Your Excellency," the woman said as she nodded and left.

"I will come right to the point," the clergyman said. "It is simply out of the question to hold the baroness's funeral service today."

"May I ask why?"

"A number of parishioners have pointed out to me that perhaps, in your grief, you have forgotten the custom of waiting three days for interment."

"No, I have not forgotten. The burial will take place today at four o'clock. There is no need to prolong this."

"But, Your Excellency, I beg to differ with you. Considering the circumstances, wouldn't tomorrow at least be more suitable?"

When Merrick's dark eyes leveled on the minister in an impatient glare, the young man quickly added, "Today is *Walpugisnacht*— the witches' Sabbath. They will damn her soul if you insist upon burying her today."

Merrick felt a chuckle rise in his chest, followed by hearty laughter that spilled out unchecked for several moments, to the horrified astonishment of Pastor Oppenheimer.

Small grunts and peeps halted the near-hysterical laughs, reminding Merrick that his delicate little son had been wakened. Crossing to the cradle near the warm hearth, he talked over his shoulder.

"You mistakenly think of me a pagan, yet it's you who keep the ancient Druid's rites alive and honor their holidays. It doesn't matter to me in the least whether today is of any particular interest to anyone." He looked down on the baby who'd been bundled so that only the tiny head, with its red-blond hair and little red face could be seen. His voice was barely more than a faint squeak.

"Does he have a name?" The pastor stepped up and joined Merrick in appreciating the baby's mere existence, considering the struggle of his birth.

Merrick thought of the second promise he'd assented to with Ilse's dying words. "No. Not yet. My sister-in-law has agreed to help choose."

"Is she available right now to attend an informal baptism?"

"What?!" Merrick asked heatedly. "Do I understand that it is acceptable to baptize my son on *Walpugisnacht* but not bury my wife?"

The minister's complexion paled from the confrontation. "Baptism is best administered as soon as possible to save his soul, in case—"

"In case *what*? He dies? He is *not* going to die," Merrick vowed. He touched his fingertips to his son's wispy curls, certain of his own words, yet angered by the clergyman's. The baby quieted, as if he felt his father's tender love. Despite his disagreement for immediate baptism, Merrick saw no valid reason for sending the man away. Perhaps it was as easy to perform the ceremony now as later.

Pastor Oppenheimer said, "Ilse would have wanted him baptized."

"I do not deny my son that right. I simply question the basis for your reasoning. But since you're already here, I'll get my sister-in-law and we can get this over with."

"Wouldn't you like other witnesses?"

Merrick glanced around the room, then at the clergyman. "This room will not accommodate all of my guests and my son cannot risk exposure to the cold drafts in the halls. No. It will only be the three of us. Now, if you'll excuse me."

Caroline nervously took one last look at herself before facing the throng of mourners downstairs. The new gowns were not suitable for the somber occasion, or her new figure. Instead, she settled on an understated, brown-checked wool dress. Although the tight basque jacket molded over her fully rounded bodice, the matching skirt held her pillow secure while the wraparound overskirt lay in soft folds in an effort to seemingly disguise her "condition." It was an excellent choice, she decided before turning toward the door.

Just as she reached for the knob, a hard rap from the other side startled her.

"Your Excellency?" she said with mild surprise as she swung open the door, suddenly very much aware of his midnight-blue gaze. Would he notice the change in her?

Merrick spoke, but his words seemed to belong to someone else as he took in Caroline's beauty. Her long mahogany tresses were tied back in a brown ribbon at the nape of her neck. Her pale coloring, not her normal flush of peach, served to remind him of her low spirits this morning—news that had quickly reached him.

"You are finally up and about, little one?" he asked in a low voice for only her ears.

Caroline tipped her chin to avoid his eyes, knowing her overindulgence was not the only memory that they shared.

"I was not quite up to receiving anyone this morning," she said, avoiding the topic that was really on their minds.

Merrick swallowed hard, forcing his heart to calm its pounding race at the sight of her thick, sooty lashes that nearly brushed her cheeks when she dipped her head. Her rose-colored lips were full and inviting, he noticed, letting his appraising gaze follow the curve of her neck to her collar.

The color of her dress was drab and matronly and the style at least ten years old, but it didn't alter the physical effect it had on his body. Though the long, tapered sleeves of the jacket looked to be suitable, the seams strained against her large breasts, and he was certain she had to be uncomfortable. The layers of light wool accented her curves, reminding him of how she had looked silhouetted by firelight the night before in the library.

Caroline forced her hands to remain at her sides when he inspected her. *Does he notice? How will I explain?*

"Do you want something, Your Excellency?"

Merrick's eyes shot upward, his inner voice chastising him for the rude departure from his usual facade of indifference to his beautiful young sister-in-law. "Pastor Oppenheimer wants to baptize the child today. My first thought was to wait until the baby's stronger. Perhaps next month. Then it could be held in the church and a proper celebration could be given to welcome him instead of this . . ." He indicated the houseful of guests with a cock of his thumb over his shoulder.

"No," Caroline replied, having quickly calculated that the size of her padded stomach in her progressive charade would be too noticeable in a month's time. She could pretend to be pregnant up to a certain extent, but to stand as a "fallen woman" before God in His House to witness the Sacrament of Holy Baptism was more than she dared. She wasn't sure which was more condemning—to be shamed as an unmarried mother or to be a deceitful, scheming kidnapper. In the eyes of the church, she'd probably be worse off if they knew of her psychic tendencies.

"If the pastor is here," she continued, "we should do it today before the funeral."

"For the superstitious reason that today happens to be some sort of pagan holiday, he refuses to perform the services for Ilse until tomorrow."

Caroline opened her mouth but, seeing the baron's irritation with the matter, clamped it shut and stepped past him out the door.

"I understand that you are to choose the child's name," the minister said to Caroline after being introduced.

Her gaze snapped around to the baron who simply nodded approval. Searching the depths of his eyes for an answer to her confusion, she spoke after a prolonged silence.

"Peter," she said. "Peter Emmerich."

For one quick instant, she thought she saw a smile of acknowledgement turning up the corners of his mouth, but it was gone as quickly as it came.

Behind her, the minister conceded, "Ah—yes. Peter is a fine name. Fine name, indeed. Now if you'll step over here and take the child, we may start."

Merrick watched Caroline bend over the cradle and lift the baby into her arms with a maternal grace that suited her well. While the minister withdrew a small vial from inside his waistcoat, Merrick noticed the way Caroline's hips slowly swayed in a gentle movement to rock his son. Studying her quiet tenderness, he couldn't help thinking that she could have been the boy's mother.

And well she should have been, a voice mocked him from the dark corners of his mind.

"Let's get on with this," he said gruffly, angered with the conflict of emotions that raged within.

The three stepped into a tight circle and reverently bowed their heads as the minister began with a prayer.

The ceremony had taken but a few minutes, after which Pastor Oppenheimer had congratulated the baron before departing, promising to see him at noon the following day.

Merrick closed the nursery door and turned around to see Caroline kneeling at the cradle, a picture of serenity framed by the vast brick fireplace beyond. Merrick walked over and watched as she adjusted the tight folds of the blanket.

"Must he be bound so tightly?" he asked with fatherly concern.

Caroline smoothed the wet, red-gold hair where Peter had been annointed by the Holy Water from the vial. "He needs to feel the security of being restrained. It keeps him warm and makes him think he is still in the confines of his mother's womb."

"He is a quiet one."

"He's a good baby. I'm glad you had him baptized."

"So am I," Merrick said, somewhat amazed at the truth as well as at his willingness to admit it. "I like the name Peter Emmerich."

She paused. "I know."

"Thank you."

"You're welcome, Your Excellency."

Aware that she was feigning concern with the baby's needs, Merrick reached down and grasped her elbows, assisting her to her feet. "I would like you to call me Merrick," he said.

Caroline had read enough to know that formal address was the rule of aristocracy unless one was given a personal request otherwise. But the invitation was commonly limited to the most intimate of relatives, usually the immediate family. Caroline had never considered herself such in his eyes. True, he was her sister's husband, but that no longer applied.

"I beg your pardon, Your Excellency. But I would not feel proper calling you by your given name."

"It is a request and I expect you to honor it." He still gripped her elbows, holding her before him, though she seemed as uneasy standing close as she did with the order to call him by his Christian name.

"Very well," he relented. "I shall be 'Your Excellency' except—" He tilted her chin up with the curve of his forefinger. "Except when we are alone."

She lifted her long lashes and searched his clean-shaven face. He was a truly handsome man. She admired the fine, straight line of his nose. And his blue eyes. Focusing on their almost mystical darkness, Caroline felt locked in time. Her body ceased to be a part of her and yet every sense seemed to be heightened beyond reality. His touch heated her skin. His masculine scent of spices and pine swirled through her nostrils.

I feel ashamed for feeling these things, her mind said.

His eyes seemed to convey an answer. *Then I should be shamed, as well. Because I can no more stop my feelings for you than I could hold back the wind.*

Had they spoken or had she only imagined his response? It soon didn't matter. Nothing in the world seemed to matter as his fingers slid from her chin and cupped the nape of her neck. As he slowly stroked the curve of her throat with the pad of his thumb, she felt no one else existed at that very moment except the two of them.

Her heart raced at his forbidden touch. This time she had no excuse for allowing this exquisite luxury. But all the reasoning in the world couldn't drag her away from the mounting excitement he created in the depths of her soul.

Instinctively, her lids fluttered closed and his lips lowered to brush against hers.

Merrick felt her pulse throb beneath his touch, forcing his own to race with anticipation. Lowering his mouth to hers, he tasted the slight saltiness of her skin and slowly peppered her with kisses as light as butterfly wings. Her ragged breathing warmed his face as the tip of his nose gently rubbed against hers. Bringing her head up to his in a silent plea, he began the final consummating kiss with painstaking slowness.

A soft groan of pleasure encouraged him and Merrick slid the tip of his tongue delicately along her moist lips, seeking entrance with tantalizing pressure until they parted. As his tongue slipped in, he felt a shudder deep within himself as though their bodies had joined in carnal intimacy, as though this sweet, dewy moistness had welcomed his entire length into her.

He felt burning desire grow in his loins, pressing hard against the confines of his clothes, and he knew that Carrie was, and always should have been, the only woman to take him in her arms, to bring him ecstasy, to be filled with his seed.

But for now, perhaps for always, he could only imagine that shuddering fulfillment through a kiss, this kiss. Deep in his throat, a moan emerged and he could keep his distance no longer. He wanted to feel her soft curves next to his hardness. He needed to feel alive again.

Her tongue tentatively moved over his, then swirled around and joined in the seductive dance, driving him to mad, abandoned thoughts of taking her right there on the floor of the nursery.

He knew that his orders for privacy would not be disobeyed and he also knew that his intentions were reprehensible. But above all, he wanted Carrie beneath him as he tenderly introduced her to the full meaning of womanhood.

Slowly, he moved his hand below the curve of her back, their kiss growing feverish, their breathing rapid. He pushed her closer and closer to the brink of complete surrender. But once he'd penetrated her, he would soothe her with slow, steady strokes, teaching her ways of lovemaking that he was sure she would quickly learn.

Thoughts of her body arching into his peaked his need until he could stand it no longer. He dropped his other hand to her hip and drew her tightly against him.

"No!" Caroline broke out of his embrace. Without thought to her actions, her hands flew to her stomach as she stumbled back.

Merrick's eyes quickly glanced from her horror-stricken face to her fingers splayed protectively across the folds of the checkered fabric where there was an unmistakable roundness to her belly.

He wanted to deny what he saw. He fought back the sting of betrayal. But there was no denying the look in her eyes. There was no question of the guilt he saw there.

No wonder she was so receptive to this trip. She had *used* him to escape the shame of telling her parents, the public humiliation among her friends. And here he was playing right into her manipulative hands in her effort to snare a father for her bastard. She and Ilse were cut from the same cloth.

He'd be damned if he was going to give her the satisfaction of seeing his seething anger, his insane jealousy of the man who'd taken what should have been his all along.

Merrick took one lazy stride, closing the short distance between them. As he placed his hand over her rounded stomach, he allowed a leer to curl one corner of his mouth. "How very convenient. Now I can pleasure myself with your body and no one will be the wiser."

Her hand flew up and smacked hard against his left cheek just as the door opened.

Greta gasped, dropping an armful of towels, while Louise barged past, nearly knocking the young girl down.

"I'm sorry, Your Excellency. I didn't catch up to her in time—" She stopped short at the frozen scene before her. The young maid gawked. Towels were scattered at her feet.

The American girl had one hand cupped to her mouth and one over her curved belly. The baron's face showed a red handprint, darkening to a brighter red even as he stood there.

Caroline watched in muted silence, waiting to see if Merrick would strike her in front of the servants or wait to dole out her punishment later. In an unspoken answer, he turned his eyes on her, commanding her attention as if to say he would not let the matter drop, then marched from the room.

It took all her strength and then some to hold back the tears of humiliation that begged for release. But she didn't dare flee from the room like a wounded bird. Uncertain of her next move, she turned back to Peter, asleep through the best and worst five minutes of her life.

The gruff nursemaid stomped up from behind and snapped, "He'll be needing to eat."

Caroline jerked her hand out of the cradle. "Yes. Of course," she said, her quavering voice defying the visual calm she was trying hard to display. She cleared her throat and spoke with stronger conviction. "I'll be on my way."

Greta kept her head down, picking up the towels when Caroline passed.

"By the way," Caroline said as she reached the open door. "His name is Peter." The old woman only grunted and continued with her back turned.

Though Greta had paused to stare at the foreigner, as soon as Caroline's eyes met hers, she immediately dropped her gaze to her chore at hand.

Feeling miserable with her unintentional—albeit successful—revelation of her "pregnancy," Caroline walked back to her own room next door.

Chapter 6

Hilde sat at a table in the warm kitchen with a pen and paper. During the day, she had endeared herself to the cook by offering to copy several new recipes for her. Over the twenty years in America, Hilde had kept up her German writing skills through letters to her aunt in Freiburg, as well as through teaching the children under her charge.

The cook, Frau Krumhauer, was a kindly woman whose husband was the primary groundskeeper of the baron's estate. They had raised one daughter and one son while in the employment of the von Haydens. The son worked in the stables and was a fine horseman in his own right, often accompanying the baron on his daily ride. The daughter had long since married the cobbler and moved into the township where she kept busy mothering nine children.

Hilde delighted in the stories of the village during happier days. It reminded her of her own childhood growing up in the Black Forest, so unlike the city of Philadelphia.

"Some folks say that they wouldn't work for someone like the baron, but they just don't know him like we do,"

Frau Krumhauer said, finally opening up onto a topic of great interest to Hilde. "What with the covenant and all—and a dark one it is—they think he's an evil one."

"A dark covenant?" Hilde asked, curious about the woman's comment. "Are you speaking of the baron's prearranged marriage?"

The cook nodded. "It began a long time ago." She pressed her elbows against the table as she leaned forward with her hands clenched around a coffee cup. "People say there was a race of people who had supernatural powers. They could read minds like the Gypsies. They could *control* minds." The woman's gray eyes widened. "The legend says they were a goodly sort, never doing anything bad to anyone."

The wooden chair creaked as Frau Krumhauer settled back heavily into it, repositioning her cup atop her great stomach. "Years went by. A lot of years. Centuries. These peaceful people slowly married outside their village and that's how they lost their powers—maybe. No one's sure."

She sipped her coffee while Hilde sat fascinated. "What they *are* sure of is that some of the first ones kept their lines pure, or leastwise close as possible. So there's supposed to be some descendents who still have these supernatural powers—the baron being one of 'em."

"He is?" Hilde gasped, shocked with the news. Then she smiled, "You're teasing."

The cook shrugged casually. "Can't say I've ever *seen* anything to convince me in all the forty years I've been here. But sometimes I get to wondering about things being too coincidental—then I laugh it off. It's just my friends' gossip getting to me, is all."

"What sort of things?"

"Oh—like me knowing what he wants for Sunday supper right before he tells me, like he's already told me only he hasn't."

"It sounds to me like *you* are the one with the powers."

Frau Krumhauer swallowed a sip of coffee, calmly shaking

her head. "No, no, no. If it's anyone, it's him. His father was the same way, like he's telling you with his *mind.*"

"Is that all he does? What about moving objects or controlling another person's thoughts."

Again the cook shook her head. "I've never seen it. Probably never will. His Excellency is not the type to do showy things, let alone something as . . . different . . . as lifting things without his hands. No, he draws enough attention without effort on his part. He certainly would never display such . . . talents." Hilde felt the cook was reluctant to use a more suggestive word. "You know, there is another thing about him I've always been curious about over the years . . ."

Hilde prompted, "Yes?"

"My son, Wil, who works in the stables?" She paused to see Hilde's nod of understanding. "He's about the same age as His Excellency. They grew up like brothers, those two— what with the baron being an only child and all. Wil says the baron has an unusual rapport with the animals in the stables. Says he can climb on the most untamable mount and ride it like it was a child's pony. Wil says His Excellency has a humble respect for these creatures. And they seem to know it. It's the strangest thing I ever heard."

Frau Krumhauer quickly straightened at the sound of footsteps descending the servants' stairs.

Hilde turned her head to see who was coming, then felt fingertips on her hand and looked back to the cook.

"Keep all this to yourself," Frau Krumhauer whispered. "Some folks around could see it for a good excuse to say the baron's possessed by the devil."

Hilde nodded as the two servants entered, arguing.

"Mark my word," the cranky nursemaid Louise warned. "That foreigner will be gone by week's end."

"He's sweet on her, I tell you. And I bet that bundle she's carryin' is his."

"That's quite enough, Greta. His Excellency would

never—" Louise snapped her mouth shut when she realized that two more servants knew what she'd hoped to shield.

The cook lifted her white eyebrows in interest. Because of their similarity in size and coloring, the cook and the nursemaid could have been sisters, Hilde thought, for all that their personalities were completely opposite.

"What's this I hear?" Frau Krumhauer asked. "The baron and his sister-in-law? I find that hard to believe!"

Greta's eyes twinkled above the heavy load of soiled laundry she'd brought down with her. She glanced between the two graying servants, then, when Louise departed, the girl hurriedly dropped the clothes aside and dragged up another chair. Paying no mind to Hilde, she described the heated scene in great detail to her captive audience.

Hilde kept her enthusiasm well-hidden. Though proud of Caroline's masterful acting, she wondered if it had been wise to have let the servants observe the spat, leading them to the wrongful conclusion of an affair. If the plan came to fruition, it would not do to have people believing that the baron was the father. There could be a great deal of skepticism regarding Caroline's insistence on leaving and having the baby elsewhere.

Greta rambled on, "Isn't it odd the way fate happens to folks? Lottie Haun's lost her husband and her baby in that wagon accident, then comes here to nurse a baby who's lost his own mother. And now this—a girl who's got no husband and not wanting for a child."

Frau Krumhauer, upon hearing the news, got a sad, faraway look in her eyes. "It's a shame—one woman bearing an unwanted child while another pines over the death of her only one."

"Sadder still," Greta offered, "is that the widow nurses a motherless baby. Wouldn't it be a good turn of her luck if she could have the boy to replace her own?"

"Bite your tongue, girl!" The cook jumped to her feet

with one hand to her heart. "The baron would dismiss you straight away if he heard such talk."

"I was only saying—"

"You know full well that there's a price on that innocent baby's head," she scolded.

Hilde could hold her tongue no longer. "A *price?*"

Frau Krumhauer's pudgy fingers clenched her cook's apron, wrinkling the white material in her worrisome fiddling.

"You don't know?" the chatty Greta asked, ever happy to share the tidbits, even if it was with the newcomer.

"I understood there to be some additional worry other than about his weakened state. But a price? You mean someone has actually place a reward on a newborn?"

"Not exactly," offered the cook.

"Yes, exactly," Greta argued. "The baron is a direct descendant from the founder of the Church of the Mystics down in the glen. There's a prophecy that his son will be their new patriarch. But the church has split right down the middle over it. Half of them have become followers of the Prince of Darkness." The young maid suddenly looked fearful. "I've heard rumors that they want to kill the baron's son. They're afraid his supernatural powers will destroy them."

"Greta, you are frightening the daylights out of Hilde," Frau Krumhauer declared. "Now go see to that pile of dirty laundry." She shooed the girl from the room.

Hilde sat dumbfounded over the cache of information she'd been handed.

The cook turned to her. "Please believe me. The baron is a *good* man. He is *not* one of the rebellious devil-worshippers."

"Supernatural powers? This man is a part of something that all of my life I have been taught to fear."

"Only because we fear that which we do not understand."

"I understand enough." Hilde stood, smoothing her dark hair back into its chignon.

"Perhaps we can talk more about this later."

Hilde realized from the hopeful look on the cook's face that she may have slighted her new friend with her staunch opinion. Offering an apologetic smile, she patted Frau Krumhauer's arm. "I would like that. Right now I think it's best if I go up and see how Caroline is fairing."

"May I ask you a question before you go?"

"Yes."

"How well do you know Fräulein Hartmann? That is . . . I mean to say . . . Have you known her long enough to know if she is carrying the baron's child as Greta says?"

"I can only tell you what I know to be truth," Hilde said. "The baron secured my services in Philadelphia and escorted me to Sebula, a small town in western Pennsylvania, for the purpose of chaperoning Fräulein Hartmann on the journey here to be with her sister. As I understood it, the baron had not set foot in Sebula since he married his wife. He'd left behind extremely ill feelings toward him, which Caroline carried with her well into our travels. No, I would be inclined to say that the baby is not his."

"But she *is* in a family way?"

"Yes. It appears so."

"She hasn't spoken to you about it?"

"Only just this morning did she seem to be showing the . . . signs, which reminds me—the hour is late and she hasn't had much in the way of food yet today."

Caroline forced herself to eat the hearty slab of beefsteak with its trimmings that Hilde had brought on a tray. Her appetite had not returned, but she was mindful of the necessity for a substantial weight gain if her scheme was to succeed, and swallowed each bite with difficulty.

"So you received a full account of my . . . confrontation with the baron," she said to Hilde as she sliced the meat. Her knife and fork clinked against the plate.

"Blow by blow."

Caroline stopped and tipped the knife point into the air. "Only *one* blow," she corrected sardonically.

"How did he discover your condition?"

As Caroline's teeth ground needlessly on the tender beef, she recalled the scene that had led up to her violent reaction. She swallowed. "Let's just say," she said bitterly, "the baron is a vile, disreputable human being, and leave it at that."

Hilde chose to heed her words and sat in silence for several minutes, studying Caroline, unable to decipher the basis of the girl's vehement anger.

Did she know of the baron's unusual background and had she confronted him with it? Could that have been the cause of the argument between them?

The questions reminded Hilde of the disturbing information she'd learned downstairs. "Something else was said that I think you should know about. Greta spoke of a church in the glen, a group of people who believe in mysticism."

Caroline swallowed hard, mentally forcing back a defensiveness that had immediately set her on edge. Her own abilities must not be revealed. Anxious to hear more, she motioned for Hilde to continue as she concentrated on her dinner. All the while, she hoped that she did not appear as nervous as she felt inside.

"Apparently the baron is a descendant of these people who have . . . supernatural gifts," Hilde went on. Caroline's palms turned clammy against the metal utensils. "The prearranged marriage was a covenant to bring forth a son who is supposed to be their spiritual leader someday."

Caroline's mind recalled an entry in the dairy that she'd seen shortly before Hilde had come in. Ilse had mentioned that the baron had much to lose if the baby lived to take over the church. Until then, she'd only known that the child of the covenant was to have strong powers. Now it appeared he had an even greater destiny. Was this leadership to be the strifetorn life?

Hilde hurried on, interrupting Caroline's effort to make

sense of the puzzle. "But many of the members have broken away. They've chosen to follow an evil path with the Lord of Darkness. They're devil worshippers!"

Caroline coughed, nearly choking on a mouthful of food. Ilse's short entry about a woman visitor came to mind, a woman who'd claimed the baron to be the Devil himself. Again she recalled the recently-read concern that if the son took over, the baron would suffer a great loss. If one were good and the other evil, the two would surely be at odds, even to the point of losing one's life. What greater loss was there?

"Did Greta say that the baron is among those who have broken away from the church?" Caroline asked, silently adding, *Or worse—is he the Devil incarnate?* A chill ran down her spine.

Hilde shook her head. "No. Although the cook said some people think he's evil because it's thought that he possesses supernatural gifts. She, on the other hand, is of the strong opinion that he is a good man."

"Did the cook or Greta say that he actually *has* some kind of power?"

"Frau Krumhauer, the cook, believes he's special in that way but she's never seen anything with her own eyes to prove it."

"And Greta?"

"She'd left the kitchen by then," Hilde answered. "Do you still intend to keep your kidnapping a secret from the baron?"

Again Caroline thought of the claim of which her sister had written. "Just because His Excellency seems on the side of good doesn't mean he can be trusted."

"But from what you've told me, he wanted a child."

"Yes—to fulfill the covenant. But what if he'd learned after Ilse conceived that his own son would pose a threat?"

"Did you learn something from the diary?"

"Enough to suspect that the baron didn't know the extent

of the far-reaching effects of the covenant until after it was too late to avoid the birth. I still must get Peter to safety."

"Then I think we may have just the person we need to do the kidnapping."

Caroline looked up. "Who?"

"Lottie Haun, the wet nurse. Two days ago, she and her husband and baby were in their wagon when it overturned. She had only some cuts and bruises but the other two were killed. That's where the doctor was when your sister was delivering."

"And now to be feeding another's baby so soon . . ." Caroline's words drifted off. In her reaction to the tragedy, she'd forgotten Hilde's reference to using Lottie as their kidnapper. A lump formed in her throat but she forced it back. Setting her fork down, she pushed the near-empty plate away and closed her eyes.

When would it all stop—the sadness and the pain? She opened her eyes and silently walked over to the window. A pent-up sigh escaped her lips as she looked out upon the peacefully beautiful landscape. Then she reminded herself of baby Peter and her heart warmed.

"Do you think it will snow?" she asked, her back still to Hilde.

"About Lottie—"

Caroline wearily waved her off. "Oh, Hilde. I'm sorry but I don't want to hear any more. I'm tired of it all. I can't even cry for her. I want to but I can't. The tears won't come."

"In time, the wounds from your loss of Ilse will heal."

Caroline turned away from the colorful splendor of the outdoors and looked at Hilde. "So much has happened. Do you know how helpless I feel? I can't bring Ilse back. I can't bring back Lottie's husband or child. I'm not even certain I can get Peter to safety before harm comes to him. It's as though I have no control. Do you know what that feels like?"

"Yes," Hilde responded quietly.

Gazing out of the diamond-shaped panes, Caroline watched a squirrel scurry up a nearby pine and disappear high among the dark green boughs that were silhouetted against the low, gray sky. She touched her fingertips to the glass to feel the chill from the outside on her warm skin.

Hilde's words broke through the silence. "You have more control over your life than you realize."

The irony of the statement gave Caroline an inwardly bitter chuckle. *If only Hilde knew the truth to those words.*

"You have a strong faith, a stronger will, and the power to face the most insurmountable challenges."

Looking back on the shipboard attack, as well as on Ilse's death, Caroline chided herself for not realizing all that she had successfully endured. She reached up to her neck and kneaded the tight muscles. Seeing it for the first time from Hilde's point of view, she had made it through trials that some never faced in a lifetime. And yet, thinking of Lottie, she had not suffered nearly as much as others.

"You wanted to tell me something else about Lottie."

"I think she would be the perfect one to kidnap the baby," Hilde said from the seat she'd taken on the settee. "She has no relatives to take her in, so there would be no means with which to trace her whereabouts before you met up with her to get the baby from her."

Caroline walked over and sat next to Hilde. "What would happen to her after she handed Peter over to me? Where would she go? Karlsruhe is her only home."

Hilde's thin brows knit together in contemplation for a moment, then she answered, "She *could* come back, telling them that the baby died of exposure. You'll have filed the falsified death certificate with the proper authorities, so it could easily be verified by the baron. Caroline! Don't you see? Any woman who has been through her ordeal would be the first suspect in the kidnapping simply from her delicate mental state."

"I won't do it."

"You may not get a better chance than this."

"I don't care. I'll find another way . . . somehow. Using that poor woman's misfortune and misery is wrong." Her expression was solemn as she gazed down upon her arms folded over the padding. "To send her back to God-only-knows what kind of fate? She'd no doubt be tried and executed for murder. No, that is a terrible idea."

Another thought suddenly occurred to Caroline, and she felt her hopes surge. "Instead of sending her back, Lottie could come with me to America. If she went on her own accord, there's no reason why it wouldn't work."

"Of course it will all hinge on convincing her that taking the baby away from his father is a wise decision."

"I'm sure I can handle Lottie," Caroline said, thinking of the mind control she had exercised a few times over the course of her lifetime, though it was only recently that she'd fully understood her gift. Lottie would be easy to sway, especially after she had nursed the baby for three or four months. Such a strong bond would be likely to influence the woman to the point of sacrificing her own safety if it meant saving the child.

Saving the child from whom? If only she knew the face of the enemy, she could feel more sure of her convictions, especially now, when her emotions clashed over Merrick's role in all of this.

The leather saddle squeaked beneath Merrick as he shifted his weight on the sorrel gelding, one of the dozen fine horses from his stables. He felt the movement of the animal's muscles beneath his thighs as it walked slowly toward the pond near the entrance road. Far beyond the other side of the water stood the only true home he'd ever known, a cherished feeling he did not have when he stayed at his estates in Switzerland or England or Italy. Those were simply properties he used for business and, in times past, pleasure. Growing up under the loving tutelage of his father, Merrick had learned to carry on the von Hayden tradition of being a renowned vintner, as well as a participant in the industrial revolution. Both continued to be successful ventures.

Reaching the water's edge, Merrick swung his leg over the broad rump of the horse and lowered his feet to the moist, moss-covered shoreline. The first winter snow would fall soon, evidenced by the fading grass, most of which had turned to a pale yellow from the early morning frosts. Merrick led the sorrel to a place on the bank where the animal could drink, then dropped the reins, confident that the horse would stay near. In his nineteenth year he'd claimed the roman-nosed sorrel for himself, naming him Ghebellino after a medieval Italian sympathizer of the German emperor. Since then, the two had shared a mutual affection that defied explanation. Ghebellino would no more leave Merrick's side than Merrick would leave Ghebellino lame in the forest.

Merrick walked up the easy grass-covered slope of the embankment, taking long strides to stretch his stiff legs. After two hours in the saddle, having not been on a horse in months, he was sore from lack of riding. The dull pain was almost a welcome discomfort, blending with the tortured feelings he harbored inside.

He had ridden over a great deal of his wooded estate without touching the half that was covered with vineyards. Still, his mind seemed no less clouded than when he had marched down the hill from the main house to the stables with the red handprint marking his cheek.

He cursed himself for becoming a slave to his emotions. Never before would he have been tormented by the past of one of his paramours. Were he to have taken any other delectable female into his arms and found her to be pregnant by another, he'd have simply walked away without a care. Most would expect such behavior from him, considering his reputation for being heartlessly self-centered.

If he'd kept his emotions in check as he usually did, he would not have felt the pain of her indiscretion. Reaching to his face, he rubbed his still-tender cheek. The sting of her slap was nothing compared to the sting of jealousy he felt inside. Who could have done this? Who was the father of her child? Perhaps it was one of the boys in town she'd grown up with. A school-girl crush that had gotten out of hand. Then again, she could have been caught unaware by a lumberman while on her way home. Not only did these thoughts bring back the anger he felt toward Bates, her attacker on board ship, but they also put into question his presumptuously high opinion of her morals. Each time he began this line of thinking, he reminded himself that Ilse had to have been in on the scheme to bring Caroline to Germany. He'd somehow been duped by Ilse into retrieving the lying vixen. He should have known. Somehow, with all his abilities, he should have known.

The harder he tried to get Caroline off his mind, the more he thought of her. No matter how much he hated her, he was attracted to her. He told himself it was wrong, that she was still his wife's sister—more importantly, his *recently departed* wife's sister. Any indication now of an involvement with Caroline was certain to arouse suspicion on the cause of Ilse's death, as well as the paternity of Caroline's child.

Though he didn't mind in the least what others thought of him—or Caroline, for that matter—he didn't want Peter to carry that burden of shameful speculation. Merrick's father would never have done such a thing to Merrick, and he was not about to do it to his own son. He sighed. Recalling the scene in the nursery earlier and the look on the faces of his servants, he had to face the fact that the damage might have already been done.

Ghebellino jerked his massive head up and looked about, his flared nostrils twitching as he sniffed the breeze. Someone was upwind. The animal stared raptly at a sudden rustling in the thicket.

Somehow, as was his way, Merrick knew before he

reached the bushes and pulled back a large branch that he would find Caroline.

"What are you doing here?" he demanded impatiently, reminding himself to control his eyes from dropping to her belly. She was still dressed in the same drab attire, he noticed, but her cheeks were flushed pink from the chill of the late afternoon. If it were not for the slight redness of her eyes, she would appear to be the epitome of health for an expectant mother. The sun would soon set, however, and he found himself worrying that walking back in the cold air after sundown could easily threaten her delicate condition with an unwelcome fever. Inwardly, Merrick chastised himself for his concern and shook himself back to reality.

Caroline took a hesitant step backward, snapping a twig under her heel. It made her jump, amusing Merrick, though he refused to show it. She was obviously afraid of him and what he was going to do to her now that they were alone.

"I thought a brisk walk would . . . clear my mind," Caroline stammered.

"Then why would you be hiding behind a bush?"

"I saw you riding and I didn't want to draw your attention over here."

"Where there are no witnesses if I decided to . . . discipline you for your earlier impertinence?" He stepped toward her with growing intentions of taking her there in the thicket. She'd been quite ready to give herself in the nursery before he'd discovered her secret. Perhaps now would be a good time to chasten her after all. He would let her think he was going to take her. If she fought him relentlessly, which he doubted, he'd free her with a stern warning. If she gave in willingly to his subtle caresses, her punishment would be in her shameless submission.

Her biting words lashed out against him. "Discipline? Impertinence?" She stood firm. "It was not *I* who could have been called *impertinent.*"

Merrick watched her green eyes flash like emeralds and

swore he wouldn't fall under their spell again. He'd have her, but on his cold, hard terms. She was a scheming wench that he couldn't wait to be rid of once he was through with her. Let her go back to America. He would help her pack her trunks.

He moved closer, then dropped his gaze momentarily to the swell of fabric below her waist. The wasted time and money to retrieve her from the states angered him deeply, causing him to want to hurt her in return.

"I believe I have every right to speak my mind, considering your devious little charade. How long did you think it would take me to find out?" He was close enough to reach up and unfasten the buttons of her jacket.

Caroline's blood froze at the prospect of being caught so soon in her plot. Forcing her chin up in defiance, she clenched her fists and glared into his dark eyes. "I'm sure I have no idea what you are talking about. Now if you'll move out of my way, I'll be going back to the house."

He blocked her only exit from the thick tangle of branches and leaves. "It was not Ilse who needed you, but you who needed her. The two of you plotted to have me swoop in as the daring rescuer, thinking it was my wife I was saving from torment. If truth be known, I could guess that your parents were as much in the dark about your sibling scheme as I. Tell me," he demanded, his body towering over her. "Did the father refuse to marry you or is he even aware of his bastard?"

She opened her mouth, hoping a cutting remark would be forthcoming, but nothing came to mind to downgrade his arrogance.

"Just as I thought, you are more like your sister than I ever could have realized. Grown on the same bitter vine, both of you."

Her innocent silence weakened his resolve to chasten her. Her sweet perfume aroused him. Her full lower lip thrust

out in a rebellious pout drew his attention. Instead of seduc-
ing her as he'd planned, he was playing right into her hands.

"I'll be damned if I'll fall into your trap. You're just like
Ilse." He abruptly turned around and walked away from her
in hopes of gaining some semblance of dignity, for the
longer he stood so close to her the more his body defied his
reason.

"How can you compare me to Ilse?" she called out from
where she stood as Merrick approached Ghebellino near the
water. Gathering the reins in one hand, he reached up with
the other and scratched the horse's forehead.

"You have no right to say that I am trying to trap you.
I'm not my sister. I'm not capable of . . . of the things she
did," she said with a desperate fury while he continued to
stroke the light chestnut-color coat of the gelding.

"Are you denying the nature of your expectancy? At least
Ilse came to me a virgin, though from my understanding,
that wasn't saying much about other aspects of her wanton
behavior."

Ghebellino lowered his head and impatiently nudged Merrick in the chest, drawing the man's attention away from the
heated argument as Caroline closed the distance between
them, unnoticed.

"How dare you!"

His arm was grabbed and yanked back before he realized
what had happened. The back of his hand smacked the
horse's tender muzzle as it came around, shocking the animal.
Ghebellino took several staccato steps back, his velvet black
eyes wide with panic.

"Get back," Merrick barked at Caroline, knowing all too
well the vengeance of his horse when angered. Years before,
he'd seen a man crippled and nearly killed trying to break
Ghebellino's mean spirit.

Needing no warning, Caroline had hurriedly backed away
the moment she saw the results of her foolish move. Like
Merrick, she, too, had been around horses when they had

gone wild, their hooves trampling a man's body as if it were a pile of tinder-dry twigs.

The horse pranced frantically, his hooves digging up tufts of dried grass. Ghebellino carried the aristocratic airs of his namesake as well as the spirited nature of a knight from those medieval times.

Merrick lowered his voice to a calm tone and spoke in German to the horse, *"Schtil,* Ghebellino."

He cautiously stepped closer. For several heart-pounding minutes, he tried to soothe the distraught animal, but Ghebellino had been bought from a brutal owner and it had left a permanent scar. There was no prediction as to how he could react.

His hooves pounded the ground in nervous steps. His snowy mane fluttered as his neck arched, then bobbed.

Then Merrick, in a strange change of attitude, moved aside and allowed the horse freedom to run. Ghebellino bolted up the embankment, tearing deep chunks from the soil, sending bits of dirt and grass flying.

Shocked, but mildly impressed, Caroline apologized, commenting, "Now you don't have a ride back to the house."

"Sometimes it's better to let go and allow him his freedom so he can see he won't be harmed. His mean spirit only shows itself when he feels trapped."

Her voice softened. "Strange you can see that in a horse, yet you failed to see that same characteristic in Ilse."

"What makes you so certain I was not aware of the reasons behind my wife's shrewish nature?" he snapped.

"I'm not certain. It seems as though, were she as miserable as she appeared, you would have gladly stepped aside as you just did with that horse, and given her the freedom she desired."

"Ilse didn't desire freedom, as you say. She didn't know what she wanted." His pride kept him from telling Caroline that Ilse had, on many occasions, playfully lured him to her bed, only to later accuse him of taking her against her will.

"Ghebellino, on the other hand, wants trust and, once given, he gives it in return. A quality your sister never had."

The sorrel reappeared on the rise of the embankment and stared down on the two of them. Merrick pointed.

Caroline's eyes followed the length of his sleeve, to his brown hand, then to the majestic sight of Ghebellino, tossing his head in a playful manner. The sheen of the horse's light chestnut coat was brilliant in the light of the setting sun.

"He's back!" She turned to Merrick, subduing her enthusiasm. "You knew he'd come back, didn't you!"

"I hoped." Looking down into her dancing eyes, a voice inside his head told him, *She's a vixen. She'll trick you into believing that she's as innocent and lovely as her beauty makes her seem.*

Ghebellino trotted down the embankment and came up to Merrick as if the earlier incident had never happened.

Caroline reached tentatively up to touch the white mane. When the horse didn't shy away, she ran her hand firmly over its neck and shoulder.

"He's beautiful," she said in an effort to converse on a neutral subject.

Merrick accepted the compliment begrudgingly, adding, "You should be getting back before it gets too cold."

The chirps of birds were more prevalent than before, and Caroline wondered if the creatures had been there all along or had just come home to their nests for the night. Accepting the baron's arm, she gathered a bit of her skirt and walked up the hill to the road she'd followed earlier. Merrick's easy gait as they walked together, and the way in which his horse followed, reminded her of the first time she'd met him on the road in Sebula.

So much had changed since then. She had changed since then. But the baron seemed the same. Somehow, she knew he would never change. His handsome good looks would always be attractive to women. His aloof arrogance would always infuriate her. That was to say, his manners *might* aggravate her if there was ever a time when she would see him again after she left with Peter.

A cold, hard knot suddenly formed in her stomach. God help her if he caught up to her before she found refuge with her parents. She hated to think what the baron would do to her if she foiled any plans he might have made for the child. Despite his coldheartedness, she still found it hard to believe that he would bring harm to his own son. But she remembered how Ilse's diary claimed that he had much to lose if Peter lived to take over the Church of the Mystics.

They walked in silence, passing beneath a natural arbor of trees whose bare branches meshed like fingers entwined in prayer. When Merrick described them that way, Caroline turned and gazed at him with the most puzzled look. He returned the expression when his eyes caught her arms folded across her stomach and she winced in pain.

"Come here," he said, walking back to the saddle. Caroline turned around and saw him waiting for her to heed his command. "Please," he added.

Still confused, she went back to where he stood next to the tall horse.

"Is there something wrong with Ghebellino?"

"No. Let me help you up. You can ride sideways if we go slow."

"I can walk."

"Obviously you've walked too much today."

It finally occurred to Caroline that he had mistaken her expression as something to do with her "condition." Allowing herself the luxury of riding wasn't such a bad idea. Besides, her feet were terribly sore from shoes that had yet to be broken in for such things as long walks in the woods or along estate roads. Next time, she would remember to wear her old shoes.

They had walked a short distance when Ghebellino pricked up his ears. Merrick saw it, too—a horseman in the distance, riding hard over the open field from the house.

There was only one man and one horse who could clear hedges like that. And Merrick wondered what would bring Wil out at a full run with the prized jumper, Vindicator.

"Something's wrong," said Merrick, surprised at the loudness of his voice.

Shading her eyes, Caroline looked out onto the field where the horse and rider deftly jumped another obstacle.

"He's coming to get me," said Merrick.

"How does he know where to look?"

"He's knows if I am not back, I am at the pond."

They both knew they were passing the moments with idle talk, afraid to voice what was really on their minds.

Wil slid from his mount at almost the same moment he brought the black jumper to a halt. His German came at a fast clip. "Louise sent me to get you. It's the baby. Someone climbed the trellis. Broke into the nursery—"

"Oh, dear God, no!" Caroline pleaded, her words bringing Wil's blond head up to address her.

"He's safe, Fräulein."

But his reassurance had not been enough to quell the fear, nor waylay her own chastisement for leaving the baby. She had to get back. Now.

Before the baron or Wil could stop her, she swung her leg over to straddle Ghebellino's back. Leaning forward, she rapped her heels against his flanks in just the spot that would take him into a full run, if he'd do it. He responded as if she were Merrick on his back and not a strange woman; he raced toward the house.

"Caroline!" Merrick shouted after her, then tried to summon his horse back with a whistle, but to no avail. He had never known Ghebellino to accept another rider. Yet there was no denying what he saw, and if he didn't move fast, the horse might suddenly realize that it was not his master on his back and toss her into the nearest ditch. Images of Caroline lying on the ground sent his mind spinning. He had to catch up to her.

"I'll send someone back," he said to Wil as he grabbed the reins from his friend and leaped onto the black jumper. Within a short distance, he'd brought the frothing animal back to a run, but he was hard-pressed to match Ghebellino, especially when the sorrel was not only rested but carrying a lighter load.

What a foolish chit. If the horse doesn't kill her, certainly the ride will send her into labor. True, it wasn't her child he was worried about. But another fatal delivery was not what he wanted on his hands, especially if it was Caroline's.

Peter was safe, of that he had been assured. Now, if only he could be so certain of Caroline as she wove around the trees and obstacles. She was an excellent horsewoman, he had to give her that. No other woman, and very few men, could match her skill. But Merrick had the advantage of a jumper beneath him. Clearing a fallen log, he finally gained much needed ground. Another like opportunity and he'd be even with her.

In his pursuit, he was dangerously oblivious to the peril he had placed his prized jumper in. Pushing the exhausted horse was foolish. Not knowing the terrain was another error that could easily cause a disastrous stumble after a jump. As they cleared the final hedge that would put him with Caroline, Merrick saw the deep stream of water. The horse would land in it, there was no doubt. But if a rock should be in the wrong place or the soil too muddy, they'd both go down.

Land solid, Vindicator, he pleaded.

Muddy water splashed. The horse's powerful legs buckled, taking the brunt of the landing. It all seemed to happen so fast, yet Merrick felt every splatter of mud, every trickle of cold water seeping into his clothes. For a frozen moment, he was certain his mount had fallen chest deep in the water, its legs snapped from the sudden resistance of the water and mud.

But it had all been a deceiving lapse of seconds, not minutes. The horse came out of the jump like the champion he was, no worse for the gallant effort. Merrick felt a wave of relief wash over his senses, grateful for the reprieve yet determined as ever to catch up to Caroline.

When he brought the two horses neck and neck, he gave a short shrill whistle at Ghebellino, who immediately slowed, allowing Merrick to lean over and take the reins.

"Why didn't you do that before?" he mumbled half to himself and half to his horse.

"Please—I beg you, Your Excellency. Don't stop me. I need to get back."

"Wil said Peter was unharmed. But I'm not so certain about *your* baby."

Caroline gasped and looked down.

Chapter 7

In her feverish race to get back to the baby Peter, Caroline had ridden recklessly, without thought to her feigned pregnancy. If Merrick hadn't mentioned her delicate state, she'd have dismounted in the manner she was accustomed: sliding on her belly and landing hard on her feet.

Think, Caroline, her mind commanded of her as she faced the baron while both were still astride their sweat-soaked horses. *What would I do if I were truly expectant?*

With quick use of her wits, she closed her eyes in an attempt to appear overcome by the moment, her hand gripping around the padding as if a spasm of pain shot through her. Distracting him with her little act, she felt to see if the tiny pillow had slipped.

"What have I done, Merrick?" she whimpered, purposely using his given name for the first time. "How could I have been . . . so foolish?"

"Don't move, little one," he murmured, genuine concern etched across his face. Merrick was off the black horse in an instant. Caroline suddenly hated herself for deceiving him so.

But even if she wanted to tell him the truth of her charade, she could not do it now without angering him to his limit.

The tall sorrel held himself stock-still as Merrick stood close to his shoulder, reaching for Caroline. She leaned cautiously forward until his strong hands caught her securely beneath her arms where the outer swell of her breasts felt touched by his fire. Tightening her quivering fingers around the taut muscle of his arms, she dragged her leg over the horse's rump.

"I have you," Merrick reassured her as his elbows bent to bring her down. Before her feet had been on the ground for more than a moment, he slid one hand to her waist, the other to her knees, and lifted her into his arms. As his fingers unknowingly came within a hair's breadth of discovering her false padding, he called over his shoulder to a groom who'd run up from the stables upon their arrival. "See to it that Wil gets back and that these two get extra attention."

Leaving the silent young man with the winded horses, Merrick strode toward the back steps of the house.

"Thank you," were the only words Caroline dared to whisper as she settled her head onto his shoulder, dropping her face from his view. It was nearly impossible to be in his arms, so close to him, and yet continue to lie convincingly.

She stiffened her muscles again as though another contraction had begun. "Perhaps if I walk, the pain will ease," she suggested, adding a small groan for effect.

Merrick's deep voice rumbled through her ear that lay against his black wool jacket. "You need to be in bed and that's exactly where I'm taking you."

He marched up to the back door, ready to kick it in with his riding boot. Frau Krumhauer had been nervously watching for the two, and swung the door open before the noise could rattle the entire kitchen.

"Your Excellency!" She spoke in German with shock registering in her voice. "What has happened to the Fräulein?"

"She is not feeling well. Where's my son? Where's Peter?"

He continued past the servants' stairs which were too narrow to allow him to carry Caroline up its steep treads.

"The boy is safe and warm here near the oven, Your Excellency. Until the window in the nursery is repaired, it is too cold up there for the little one."

Though her eyes were closed so as to seem in pain, Caroline knew by Merrick's movement that he had turned around, no doubt to see his son. When he spoke, his mood had turned dark. "Get someone to guard that door immediately. Another attempt could be made on his life if it is learned of his close proximity to an easy escape."

"Yes, Your Excellency."

Caroline hated to be disruptive but thought it best to keep up her pretense or Merrick would wonder why she was too quiet. Careful to keep her arm protectively draped across her belly, she worried her lower lip and whimpered.

The cook stepped forward. "Is it her baby she carries?"

Merrick didn't answer. Instead he turned and left the kitchen through the passage that led to the great hall, the clump of his boots echoing authoritatively. Though she kept her lids squeezed tight in her deceptive pain, the loud buzz of voices and the moist warmth told Caroline that the hall was filled with guests.

"Step aside," Merrick ordered and the din gradually quieted into silence. She was certain the sea of mourners had parted, their mouths open in astonishment at the sight before their eyes.

Playing her role, Caroline pushed her face into the fabric of his coat and stiffened just enough for Merrick to sense her discomfort. Careful not to overdo the charade, she wanted to be able to show a full recovery by next morning. Too many moans and he might summon the doctor, a possibility which hadn't struck her until now. She made a mental note to assure Merrick that medical advice wouldn't be necessary, then set about wondering how she'd accomplish it.

As they passed one woman, Caroline heard in German the

question that was on everyone's mind, *"Was ist los mit Ihre Schwiegerschwester?"* What is wrong with your sister-in-law?

But Merrick's long gait continued uninterruptedly when he tossed out a gruff response. "The circumstances have taken their toll on all of us, Frau Brubaker. Now, if you'll excuse us."

The lift of his thigh taking the first step up the curved staircase made Caroline's heart slow its thunderous beat. Still, her mortification lingered at the prospect of the seedy gossip that their entrance had undoubtedly caused.

Keeping her head tilted down, she opened her eyes slightly before they passed the nursery. "I would very much like to see for myself that Peter is doing well. Could he be brought up to my room?" She forced her voice to sound strained.

Again Merrick spoke without breaking his stride. "For the time being, you are going straight to bed. I'll send Greta up with a tray, and to help you . . . other ways. After I take care of several matters, I'll see if you are feeling up to seeing Peter for a few minutes."

Caroline feigned another spasm, a lighter one this time, then looked up weakly and thanked him.

"That one didn't seem as bad as the others," he commented, gazing down on her as he crossed her room to the four-poster bed. The closeness of his mouth and the warmth of his breath brought back memories of his kiss.

"No," her voice croaked. "It wasn't. I should be able to attend Ilse's services tomorrow."

He lowered Caroline onto the bed. For a moment, her back pinned his arm against her pillows, unknowingly holding him captive. Leaning over her, his face close to hers, he hesitated as they both became very much aware of the intimacy of the moment. His midnight-blue eyes locked with hers, creating the familiar flutter deep within her.

"We will hold off the service until we see what the doctor has to say."

"No, Merrick. Please." She grasped his lapels in desperation. "I could never bring myself to . . . to . . ."

His dark gaze wandered over her face and a realization of her modesty dawned into a rakish smile. "Come now, little one. It is not as though you have never undressed before a man."

Shoving him away in anger, she knew his tenderness was too good to have been true. Determined to turn the cards in her favor, she hissed at him. "You are vile, depraved and . . . and . . . immoral. I hate you and I hate to be called 'little one.' I . . . oh—" She rolled away from him and drew her knees up toward her chest.

Cursing his own bullheaded arrogance for pushing her too far, Merrick knelt at her side and touched her shoulder. "Carrie?"

"Go away and leave me be," she tried to sob, finding it not as difficult as she'd thought. His hand slid away and with it the warmth she had felt through the light wool dress. For a fleeting moment, it had been sweet to hear his worry. All too quickly she regretted the loss of his gentle caress, the concern in calling her name. Though her mind told her to play this game to the end, her heart wanted her to call it off, to be honest with Merrick, despite the likelihood of his righteous anger.

"I'll have the doctor here by nine," he said coldly.

"He'll be met with a locked door."

"I would advise against it, *little one*," Merrick warned, then marched out.

The moment the door closed, Caroline looked back, waiting to see if he would barge back in to issue another order. When he didn't, she hurried over and turned the lock, then went to the wall that separated her room from the nursery and leaned close. She wanted to know what had happened earlier. Did the intruder get away? How close had Peter been to being harmed or killed?

The thick plaster muffled the voices on the other side.

One, she was certain, was Merrick's. There was no mistaking his deep imposing tone, even if the words were indecipherable. After what seemed like only a few minutes, she was startled by a rap on her door.

"I'll be right there," she called out with a feebleness that supported her guarded condition. When she approached the door and reached to unlock it, her posture slumped to simulate her discomfort.

With some relief, she found Hilde had accompanied Greta on her task of readying Caroline for the night.

And the doctor's visit, no doubt, she thought. *At least with Hilde to lean on, there should be some way to stave off disaster.*

"Caroline!" Hilde rushed in and took her young accomplice by the elbow, guiding her over to the bed. "Why on earth did you take off on that horse in your condition?"

Ignoring the double-edged reprimand in order to seek much-needed answers of her own, Caroline asked, "How is Peter? Tell me exactly what went on when I was gone."

Greta deposited the cloth-covered tray on the table and went about silently preparing the bath, clearly frustrated that the language barrier prevented her from reporting back to the downstairs staff.

Hilde gently helped Caroline lie down, then drew a chair up to the side of the bed. "Peter was down in the kitchen when it all happened. Frau Krumhauer insisted that the best place for him was in a shoebox near the oven, where he'd get the constant warmth he needs."

"What was wrong with the nursery?"

"Louise had said that the nursery's chimney flue had not been working properly. So they arranged to move Peter into a warm place, since the nursery was so cold."

"Is that when the . . . kidnapper came in?" Caroline could not bring herself to admit that the intruder may have had macabre plans for her nephew other than kidnapping.

"He wasn't a smart one to break the window. The man working on the flue tried to give chase but he wasn't about to scramble down that trellis. Says the intruder was a small man, and wiry, too."

"He'd have to be to scale the side of the house like he did."

Greta piped in. *"Das Bad ist fertig."*—The bath is ready.

Caroline's eyes darted to the maid, then to the fabric screen that had been moved aside to reveal the generous dimensions of the porcelain tub with ribbons of steam curling into the air toward the ceiling. Returning her attention to Hilde, she winced in supposed pain.

"I am not altogether sure I should take such a hot bath."

Hilde stroked Caroline's forehead, brushing a strand of hair away. "Perhaps you should rest a bit longer." Turning to Greta, "Why don't you let me sit with her until she feels up to bathing. I'll be more than happy to assist."

"Oh, no, madame. I mustn't shirk my duties." Greta's protests were followed by a very effective groan from Caroline. "Although—your help would speed my supper time. Thank you."

After the girl fled, Hilde playfully swatted Caroline's arm and chuckled. "You're incorrigible. Now get out of those clothes so we can refit that padding. You're fortunate you didn't lose that pillow in the ditch from what I heard about your high jinks on that horse."

Caroline's cheerful smile faded quickly as she sat up and dangled her feet over the side. "Oh, Hilde," she sighed. "I'm not very good at all these lies. I'm afraid I've woven quite a web of deception and it's getting more and more tangled. When that stable man told us about Peter, all I could think of was getting back. I'd completely forgotten about the way I needed to behave."

She threw up her hands and continued. "Then I think myself clever to pretend that I am in distress, which only served to make matters worse because Merrick insisted upon carrying me up here through that crowd of Ilse's friends. What they must think!" Her agitation grew. She leaped to her feet, spouting. "And that's not the worst of it. He's sent for a *doctor* to examine me!"

She went to the armoire, unfastening the buttons of the tight brown jacket while talking over her shoulder. "I told him that my door would be locked. I think I'll pretend to be asleep."

"The doctor's already here."

Caroline whirled around, clutching the open jacket bodice as if the man had entered the room without her knowledge.

"He came to look in on the baby's health again," Hilde explained with an apologetic lift of her thin eyebrows.

"What am I to do?"

"Perhaps you could play upon his sympathies."

"If he's under Merrick's orders, I doubt he'll want to bow to my plea and face the baron's wrath."

Hilde noted the familiarity with which Caroline bandied about the baron's name. "There is one thing that is inevitable —the doctor won't respect your modesty if he should assume your condition is due to a foolish mistake."

Hurrying through her bath and meal, Caroline worked through yet another ruse with Hilde's help. By the time Merrick escorted the doctor in, Caroline had been securely padded beneath her nightgown, though the layers of bed-clothes concealed her secret.

While Caroline pretended to be dozing, Hilde welcomed the men into the room with a book in her hand and reading glasses perched on her nose.

"She's doing fine now, Your Excellency," she said in a soft tone. "I think the warm bath did her a world of good."

Caroline heard the doctor speak next. "Did she have any bleeding?"

"No. None," Hilde answered.

From behind her closed lids, Caroline wondered if the older-sounding gentleman was watching her as they spoke. Could they see through her act of sleep?

The heavy sound of Merrick's boots on the carpet grew

louder as he approached the bed. "Open your eyes, Caroline," he commanded. "You can't hide behind the governess's skirts any longer."

Her lids blinked open and she found him standing over her. He was taller than most men but his height seemed even greater as she lay trembling on her back. Her hands slid up and clutched the blankets to her bosom.

"Please, Your Excellency. I ask again that you spare me this humiliation. I know you refuse to believe me but I told you the truth when I said that I have not undressed before any man."

The doctor glanced at Merrick and the two shared a knowing look between them. Before the baron started for the door, he made his final statement. "I will return when the examination is finished."

"Don't go," Caroline called out, distraught.

Merrick stopped and slightly turned his head, only enough to take in the little vixen's act. Her dark locks had been brushed out into a shimmering cascade over her pillow, a picture of innocence set off by large green eyes that begged for his understanding. The beautiful child-woman perched in the center of the bed was an inviting sight to his senses, but the deception of her visit still angered him. This little display only fueled his temper further.

She sniffed. He rolled his eyes.

"I want you to stay and hear what I am about to say to the doctor. Perhaps then you will not treat me so cruelly."

One dark eyebrow lifted in a skeptical tilt as he swung around, planted his feet firmly and folded his arms across his chest.

Caroline poured her heart and soul into her performance. Focusing on the doctor's soft hazel eyes was far easier than Merrick's piercing midnight-blue gaze. The older gentleman was a head shorter than the baron, with a slight roundness beneath his brocade vest. His hair was black, not the shiny ebony of Merrick's, but a dull color, and thinning.

"Fräulein Landau and the baron can attest to an attack made upon me the night before our ship made port in Rotterdam."

She paused to allow the doctor to glance at Hilde and Merrick for their confirmation. His expression was one of quiet perplexity. Hilde's head bobbed vigorously to verify Caroline's statement. The baron watched through hooded eyes, giving one simple nod.

"What they do not know—" Caroline continued, her voice cracking with emotion. "—is that Thatcher Bates had followed me from my hometown. Three months ago, he attacked me outside of Sebula, on the road home." She released her sobs, hoping her fabrication was convincing the baron as much as the doctor. "There was . . . no one to help me . . . I was all alone . . ."

Hilde rushed over to the bed and cradled Caroline in her arms. "It's all right, child. You don't have to say anymore."

"I never told . . . I didn't want anyone to know I'd been . . ." Caught up in a wave of emotion, she gave a performance that could best the most famous actresses of the day. But instead of pride, she felt a tremendous shame as if, through her own doing, she had stripped herself of her dignity.

It took a few moments to gather her wits about her, to remind herself that what she had done—and would continue to do—was for Peter's sake, and Ilse's. For family.

Merrick stood for a while and studied the crumpled figure of a girl in the older woman's arms, determined not to let his emotions show. A vengeful streak wanted to applaud her marvelous display of melodrama. But this cynical side was quelled by another part of him, the part that warmed to her nearness, that stirred from the scent of her. He wanted to be the one to hold her and comfort her.

What was it about her? What was this effect she had on him? Until now, he'd always been perceptive of others' motives, and profoundly decisive under such pressure.

"Do what you think best," he grumbled to the doctor and stormed out.

The hour was late when the clock in the foyer chimed throughout the great hall. Merrick pulled his door closed and walked toward the stairs to join his guests for dinner. Over a blue silk vest, he wore a black jacket with a gray silk tie, the color of which matched the gray in his wool trousers.

Stepping into the nursery as he passed, he saw the window had been covered temporarily with a scrap of wooden crating and a fire burned in the hearth, but the cradle lay empty.

"Louise?"

She was nowhere in sight, as he could plainly see, but he called just the same. His heart pounded wildly with the thought of the narrowly averted kidnapping earlier. Was this the kind of life he would now lead, constantly on edge about his son's well-being? The boy would hardly live a normal life if he had to be continually watched.

Perhaps his son was still in the kitchen. He would look there first before setting up another panic throughout the house. Turning to use the servants' stairs, a common practice since his youth to shorten the distance, Merrick came upon Hilde leaving Caroline's room.

"Have you seen Louise?" he asked brusquely.

"Yes, Your Excellency. She was here not five minutes ago to leave off your son for a brief visit with his aunt. I believe she said she'll be back shortly." Hilde regarded the baron with a wary eye. His dark mood didn't detract from his handsomeness. On the contrary, it added a touch of something captivating. There was a polish to his mannerisms that showed even more so in his return to the estate, perhaps due to the command he held over the multitude of servants under his employ. No, she decided, from the tidbits she'd learned from his cook, his mystique went beyond being the master of all this grandeur—a thought that sent a shiver down her spine.

He glared at the door as if he tried to see through the hand-rubbed wood. Could he, she wondered?

Her question was answered when he asked, "Is anyone in there with the two of them?"

"No, Your Excellency. Lottie had some chores to tend to, and I was about to go down for a cup of tea. Caroline asked for some time alone."

"Why isn't someone guarding the door?"

"Are you suggesting that Caroline might harm the child, Your Excellency?"

"I am not suggesting anything of the kind. But she is hardly in any condition to fend off anyone who might!" He brushed past Hilde and let himself into the room without knocking, ready to do battle with the willful girl who'd taken it upon herself to decide the fate of his delicate day-old son. But when he entered the room his heart leaped to his throat. In the center of her bed, with her dark brown hair flowing over one shoulder, Caroline cradled the baby in the crook of her arm.

"Oh—look, Hilde," she gushed without looking up, assuming her friend had forgotten something. "He's trying to suckle me. No, Peter." She chuckled, reaching up and stroking his cheek. He turned his tiny head away from the bodice of the gown toward the distraction of her touch. "Oh, now look what you've done to me." His vain attempt to find a nourishing teat had left a pronounced wet circle on the cloth over her peaked nipple.

Merrick swallowed hard, his soul warmed by Caroline's motherly tenderness, his manhood stirred by her body's womanly response. How he wanted to drop to his knees and cherish the son in her arms, and the woman who held him. But beneath Peter, she grew another man's child in her womb and the green serpent of jealousy raised its ugly head. He blocked out the tantalizing, sweet vision in white before him and cleared his throat quite obviously.

"Merrick! I . . . I didn't know it was you." She shifted

the baby gently until the embarrassing dark spot was concealed, but not before her face grew pink at the knowledge
of his interested gaze. The man didn't have a decent, respect-
ful bone in his entire body.

"Did you come to see Peter?" she asked, mentally adding,
I'm sure it wasn't me you came to ogle.

He walked over and growled, "You have no business
whatsoever in deciding the fate of my son."

Forever on her guard, Caroline forced herself to remain
calm against his accusing remark. She turned her eyes onto
tiny Peter, away from Merrick's piercing gaze. He couldn't
possibly know of her kidnapping plan, yet every time he
spoke she found her mind twisting and turning his words
into threatening statements. And every time, her fears had
been unfounded. The mental anguish was driving her mad.
For three months she must tolerate this nerve-racking anxiety
in his presence.

She spoke in her defense. "I only wished to see the baby.
He's quite warm in my bed and I meant no harm to his
welfare. If you distrust my treatment of him, take him back
to his nursemaid." She carefully lifted the small bundle from
her and offered Merrick his son.

The baron stepped back, hesitancy clearly written in his
features. When he'd held Peter shortly after the birth, his
thoughts had been on Ilse. Now he was more acutely aware
of the baby's fragile state. "I don't doubt your abilities," he
said, noticing the fullness of her unrestrained breasts beneath
the gown as she leaned toward him with the baby. "It is your
carelessness about my son's safety that I question. You know
the danger, yet you send away all who should be near in the
event that another attempt is made upon his life."

Caroline blanched under his harsh reprimand. He had every right to be angry with her stupidity. Still, the manner in
which he rebuffed his son certainly wasn't the behavior of a
doting father, a thought which made contempt boil up in her
veins.

She drew Peter close to her bosom and lifted her chin boldly to match Merrick's cutting remarks. "You bluster in here as though you truly care about this baby's welfare, yet you refuse to so much as touch him. You can see for yourself that I love Peter as if he were my own. And I will stand between him and anyone who tries to harm him." *Including you!* she vowed to herself.

His eyes became narrow slits as he moved toward her, ready to snatch his son out of her protective grasp. But he thought better of it when she suddenly cowered beneath his bent frame. Hovering over her, Merrick's attention was drawn to his son's tiny face. The closed-eyed babe had once again found Caroline's erect nipple and struggled to close his mouth over the thin fabric of her gown. His rosebud lips parted when he couldn't take hold and he rooted with his open mouth and began to fuss. Merrick was spellbound by his newborn, completely forgetting himself in the midst of the argument.

Caroline sat transfixed by the view of the baron's face close to hers. While Merrick's gaze was intent upon his son, she was free to drink in his familiar masculine scent, a heady combination of his own body mingled with a woods and spice smell. The hard, pinched lines at the corners of his eyes softened, joined by the beginning of a crooked grin. She was vaguely aware of the babe nuzzling her breast, creating a fluttering deep inside, beginning very low and growing with intensity. Merrick's profile was perfectly silhouetted before her, his deep-set eyes, long tapered nose, full lips, and strong chin. She had a sudden urge to reach up and trace the arch of his cheek bone as she might run her fingers over a river stone worn smooth by raging waters. She could almost feel the rocklike hardness of his bone beneath the smooth skin, and imagined his stark, handsome features carved by the same universal power that had shaped the stone.

The baby's fussing soon turned to angry squalls, breaking

the moment of awe for them both, each with different reasons for drifting back into their silent thoughts.

Merrick straightened to his full height and yanked at the cuffs of his shirt, paying uncommon attention to his appearance. Though he was the type of man who dressed meticulously, he then went about his business without further thought to his natural attractiveness. It wasn't in his nature to mince about, constantly primping. And so, Caroline surmised with an inward chuckle, it had to be his discomfort with the circumstances that warranted his preoccupation with his cuffs while she readjusted her gown.

Avoiding his gaze, she bent her knees up under the coverlet and lay her nephew on her lap so she could look at him. He had his mother's red-gold hair, but the color of his eyes appeared as though it might settle into the dark midnight-blue of his father's.

"I promise to be more attentive to his safety, Your Excellency," she murmured, choosing to focus on little Peter, who had settled down only slightly in his new position.

A timid knock came. The door pushed open hesitantly and a mouse of a girl stepped into the room. "I beg your pardon, Your Excellency."

Merrick recognized the wet nurse and nodded. "I believe my son is in need of you, Frau Haun," he blustered, thinking as he did when he hired her that she was far too young to be any kind of wife, much less a childless widow.

Her head was bowed, her words barely audible in her shyness. "I heard him and thought it was time."

"Yes, well—" Momentarily at a loss, he glanced between the two young women and his son. The whole scene was so unreal as to seem absurd. Before him stood the wet nurse, still a bud of a girl herself. Then there was Peter, a babe without a mother to call his own. As if knowing that fact, he was fretting in the arms of one who was carrying yet another new life that was sure to become one more lost innocent. Somehow, he felt responsible for the whole lot of them, their lives tied to his like stringed puppets to the puppeteer. Mindful of the scheme that had brought Caroline pregnant into his house, Merrick altered his assumption, resentfully seeing himself more as the manipulated toy.

He muttered something about dinner being held up by his delay and stalked out, bellowing down the hall. "Get someone to guard that door immediately."

Caroline spoke in German as she offered Peter. "I wish you didn't have to take him."

"I'm sorry for interrupting, but his cries bring on such an ache," the girl explained, taking the babe into her arms. Then she saw the sympathy in Caroline's eyes and hurriedly clarified her remark. "I'm speaking of my milk, ma'am, though I won't deny that I'm thinking of my own when I'm full like this. I'm grateful that there's a little one to take away the fullness." She started for the door when Caroline called after her.

"I'd like you to stay and talk to me while you're nursing him . . . if you don't mind."

The girl shrugged. *"Gar nicht,"*—not at all, she said and sat down on the brocade settee. Peter fussed and fumed while she deftly untied the gathered neckline of her plain brown blouse. Caroline was surprised that such small breasts could produce enough milk, or any milk for that matter. Envious not of the girl's scant endowments, but for her ability to nourish Peter, Caroline sat for just a moment and watched the baby greedily latch on to the milk-moistened nipple.

The girl smiled down at the little boy, touching his curls while she settled back. "He's a beautiful baby."

"Yes, he is."

"My Barrett was, too."

"That was your son?"

"Mmm. He'd been a year next month."

Caroline conveyed her sympathies, which the girl quietly accepted. Then in her effort to change the subject, she asked Lottie's age.

"Thirteen last August," she made an attempt to square her shoulders. "Pastor Oppenheimer told me I'm still plenty young enough to get married again and have more. But I don't know who'd have me now."

"Why ever would you say that?"

"They took one look at John and me and turned their backs on us. That's okay. We managed fine before we came here, we managed fine after."

"Do you know what caused them to act that way?"

The baby's eager lips smacked in the silence that followed. Finally Lottie said, "John was just older, is all. They saw him and me together and said it wasn't right, him being way up there like he was."

"He was of a . . . higher station?"

"Oh—no. Nothing like that. John took me out of an orphanage when I was eleven and he was . . . fifty-one, I think. He put a ring on my finger soon as he walked me out those iron gates and told me that now I was his." She lifted her chin proudly, innocent of the cruel travesty played upon her. Caroline had little doubt that he'd paid a price for his child bride, nor that he wasted much time on asserting his husbandly rights to the girl. It was not too surprising that Lottie hardly knew enough to mourn her loss to any great extent.

Caroline tried to imagine being taken advantage of by a man at such a tender age, bearing his child, then losing both before turning fourteen. She was just that old when Merrick had arrived in Sebula. Remembering her reaction to seeing the kiss in the garden, she realized that she'd only begun to feel the stirrings of nature, and yet this girl had experienced everything by then. Her envy rapidly dwindled, replaced by a heartfelt sorrow that went beyond the tragedy of the husband's and baby's deaths. With no one to turn to, Lottie trusted everyone, with the mind of a simpleton.

"Where will you go after the baron's son no longer needs you?"

The girl looked up, her brown eyes large in her small face. "I can't say I know. Probably find servant's work. I learned quite a bit at the orphanage."

Caroline saw her plan falling into place like pieces in a puzzle.

The cold night passed quickly, leaving behind a light covering of snow on the ground. The final leaves had yet to fall from the oaks, their bright oranges and reds glistening in crystalline sparkles. White powder dusted the boughs of the evergreens. As far as the eye could see, the baron's estate was a serene display of shimmering white, broken only occasionally by the contrast of dark foliage peeking out from beneath its new winter coat.

In the nursery, Merrick inspected the windowpane, drawing his finger along the new wood muntin that held the beveled glass in place. Below the frost-covered window, remnants of the trellis and its vines lay in the barren flowerbed, chopped down by the baron's orders and waiting to be cleared away. The wet nurse had finished feeding his son prior to Merrick's arrival; now he waited for Louise to finish dressing the boy.

"Here he is, Your Excellency," Louise said from behind him. He spun around as if he'd just been told he had a gun at his head.

"No need to be so skittish. Now, you two get acquainted while I see to some things. I'll be back before you know it. Come on, take him. He won't break."

Merrick glanced at the old woman, the corners of her eyes crinkled in amusement. She'd been around longer than he could remember and been ornery just as long, but he often saw her good-heartedness. In spite of the wariness Louise had felt for Ilse, she took care of Peter in the same way she'd taken care of Merrick as a boy, and it made him appreciate her all the more.

"Are you sure he won't break?"

"Absolutely. Now put your arms out."

Merrick would never have allowed anyone to speak to him in such a way, let alone see him so unsure of himself. But Louise wasn't just anyone, so he complied.

"Not so stiff," she scolded.

With a bit more instruction, he was soon comfortably rocking Peter. Immersed in silent communication with his son, he gazed upon the miracle wrapped tight in his arms, while Louise slipped from the nursery unnoticed.

In the warmth of the room, Merrick carefully unwrapped Peter from the layers of neatly tucked blankets. Louise would post a fit for uncovering the boy, but after his hesitancy last night in front of Caroline, Merrick decided it was time he got to know his newborn son.

With the wrappings draped across his knees, Merrick lay Peter in his lap, recalling the position from watching Caroline. The baby's head was cradled up near his knees so he could look down at his son. Merrick took the minute hands and uncurled the long fingers, studying the intricacies of the little blue veins that showed through his translucent skin. The baby's forearms were hardly bigger than the base of Merrick's thumbs, he noticed with awe. Peter's small chest rose and fell like a miniature bellows. When Merrick drew his finger across his ribs, Peter drew his knobby knees up.

Merrick chuckled. "Does that mean you're ticklish?" he asked, then took hold of the baby feet presented to him. He leaned down and pressed his lips to the soft pink soles, a smile tugging at the corners of his mouth.

"You like that, hmm?" he cooed in soft German, and the little one seemed, for an instant, to have returned his father's joyous expression.

The pale gray clouds hung low in the sky and threatened to release another snowfall on the crowd of mourners who filed out of the main house several hours later. Caroline stood next to Merrick, bidding somber good-byes to the seemingly endless line of grim faces. Fear of another storm sent them off in their carriages, foregoing the interment.

Without proper mourning clothes, Caroline had made due with a borrowed black shawl which she draped over a high-collared white blouse. In addition, she wore her black wool skirt, satisfied that it was the best she could do.

Merrick was more suitably dressed, Caroline noted, in his black suit. It was quite clear that he spared no expense with his finely made clothes. She supposed that was one of the first things that Ilse had noticed when the baron was introduced to her. No doubt her sister's wardrobe had quickly grown to equal the size and quality of the baron's. After all, she was the Baroness von Hayden. *Was.*

Caroline felt her throat tighten as it had a dozen times during the service. It was so painfully sad to have lived such a short, empty life, then to be laid to rest in a strange land on such a cold, blustery day. In addition, the funeral was held at the estate as a safety measure and not in the Lutheran church in the town.

Upon learning of the change earlier in the day, Caroline'd confronted Merrick in his library. Had Ilse known the change in funeral arrangements, she'd have blamed the twist of fate on her own professed damnation, saying it was God's way of punishing her. Caroline had thought differently, accusing the baron of denying her sister a proper church service because of his own religious beliefs.

Merrick had laughed in her face, then slammed down an empty glass. "If it were the middle of July, little one," he'd said stormily, "I'd have gladly seen that Ilse was honored properly. As it is, I have a two-day-old son who can't be taken far from his bed, let alone dragged out in this god-forsaken cold. And after what happened yesterday, I am not about to leave him behind with one or two men guarding his door. The service will be performed here, and anyone who wishes to face the weather can join me at the interment in the estate's cemetery."

* * *

Caroline recalled his words once more as she joined the small group huddled around the grave after the casket had been lowered into the ground.

As Pastor Oppenheimer began to open his Bible with his hands quaking from the cold, Merrick stepped forward and offered him another. When the reverend stared at it questioningly, the baron placed the book in his hand, saying, "this was Ilse's Bible. Even though you may hate what the von Hayden name stands for, I ask you to honor her by reading from it."

Without further incident, the ceremony was over. But when the clergyman returned the Bible to Merrick's hand, the baron knelt down and dropped the book onto the flat lid of the coffin.

Unable to keep her peace, Caroline spoke up before Pastor Oppenheimer could do so. She jerked Merrick's arm back, a move that brought gasps to the scattering of other guests and few servants. "How dare you desecrate the Holy Book by tossing it into her open grave? You speak of honoring my dead sister, yet you choose to defile her Bible? I demand you take it out at once!"

Pastor Oppenheimer joined in Caroline's protests, though not nearly as vehemently. "Yes, Your Excellency. I must insist that you not do this. It is most unorthodox."

Merrick stared at the clergyman for what seemed like an unusually long time before he spoke. "The baroness's Bible will be buried with her and that is my final word." With that he motioned for two shabbily dressed men standing by a snow-covered pine to come forward. They picked up shovels that were leaning against the fence and hurried toward the graveside.

Caroline sensed that she had just witnessed the baron wielding his mystical power of suggestion on the reverend, for the man seemed as though he'd been struck mute. He stood in silent approval while the first shovelful of soil hit the wood with a muffled thump. Furious with Merrick for blatantly showing his disrespect, she glared at him across the mouth of the grave. He could never prove to her that his actions were paying homage to his wife. Far from it, she decided.

Her thoughts were directed at him, though she dared not voice them. *I'd begun to believe that Ilse had been crazed in her suspicions that you were the devil incarnate. And I am shamed to say that you had me fooled with your occasional kind words. But no more will I fall into your trap, Herr Baron. I will keep my promise to Ilse. Peter won't learn your ways. I will protect him from you, your temper, your . . . powers. I swear I will.*

Merrick felt an unusual pull to lift his eyes from their focus on his wife's casket. He knew the others didn't understand his need to bury the Bible with Ilse. But something inside told him it was the right thing to do. He knew they were staring at him and it didn't matter. But this was a strange feeling that enveloped him, commanding his attention. His gaze rose and settled on Caroline, seeing the anger and bitterness there.

I will keep my promise . . . protect him . . . I will. He didn't question whether he heard her mind speak to his, any more than he questioned his own voices that often echoed within. What mattered was that he sensed her strong bond to his son, her vow to protect him. Despite his regard toward her condition, he sensed his need for her to join in his battle to save Peter. Did he dare trust her to help him save his son?

Caroline locked her gaze with his and suddenly the color drained from her face. *Oh my god, he knows what I am thinking.*

Chapter 8

The four-pedestaled mahogany dining table had been set for three, upon Caroline's request to include Hilde. It was their first meal together since arriving at the baron's estate, though Caroline hardly thought it could be considered eating together. The baron was seated at one end of the fourteen-foot table and she at the other, which suited her. Hilde was midway, necessitating a loud voice to carry on any semblance of conversation.

Caroline lifted her coffee cup and eyed the reflection of the silver candelabra in the richly waxed wood, thinking of a much happier dinner scene back home. There, the pine table was half as long and worn smooth from years of use. Ravenous lumbermen crowded its perimeter, jammed elbow-to-elbow. Though they could be a rowdy bunch, her father ruled with an iron authority, demanding proper behavior in the main house when ladies were about. Caroline had helped serve up the meals, along with her mother, the cook, and Ilse; now her hands lay idle in her lap while others waited on her.

Politely waving off an offer of more coffee, she watched

the maid fill the baron's cup and was reminded of Ilse's eagerness to lean between the men to pour their cups full. Caroline had willingly relinquished the close encounters to her less endowed sister, noticing how the men had eyed Ilse's bosom when she'd brushed their shoulders or wore a recklessly low neckline.

Merrick's voice cut through the undercurrent of tension that seemed to fill the elegant dining room. "When will you be leaving us, Miss Landau?" he asked in his accented, yet perfect, English. Considering his knowledge of Caroline's bilingual abilities, she knew his intention was to be clearly understood by both women.

Caroline and Hilde exchanged glances, then Hilde spoke. "I am considering offering my companionship to Caroline during her delicate time."

"Did I understand correctly that you have not been back to Freiburg since you left twenty years ago?"

"Yes, Your Excellency."

"I'm surprised you are not eager to return."

"Oh, I am," she quickly replied. She switched her attention back and forth between the baron and Caroline. "But considering my parents are gone now . . . well . . . I thought Caroline may want to have someone near whom she is comfortable with."

"So, Caroline—" Merrick's deep voice carried easily. "Is it my understanding that you plan to stay until your child is born?"

"I . . . I'm not sure of my plans, Your Excellency." Her mind scrambled for an acceptable excuse to remain until Peter was capable of travel. "If you wouldn't mind the imposition, I'd rather not go home until . . . after . . ."

"And how do you think your parents will regard your extended visit in light of Ilse's passing?"

"I don't know," she said quietly, envisioning the toll such news would take on her weak mother, a woman whose health had always been fragile.

"You'll have to speak up, I can't hear you," he said with a gruffness. He was tired of her meek little game. She had every intention of staying until her bastard was born, and now she was going to play the forlorn outcast for his pity. Any other man would have given in to her fabrication of an attack, as he'd almost done. But his dependable intuition told him otherwise. Caroline was not being truthful, beyond that he could only surmise that she was lying to protect her family from the shame.

Merrick's head snapped up at the sound of Caroline's empty coffee cup hitting its saucer with a force that nearly shattered the china. She rose and slammed her napkin to the table where it slid off the polished surface and onto the floor at her feet.

When she spoke, it was with a strained politeness. "I *said,* Your Excellency, I don't know how my parents will regard my plans. They do not know of my current situation. Nor do I intend to inform them. My sister's death may prove more than my mother's health can handle. I have no intention on pushing her beyond that which she can bear."

Her caustic tone softened as she realized her boldness would not help her anymore than swatting at an angry bear. "I ask your permission to remain until I may find other accommodations."

Merrick took his time, first wiping his napkin across his mouth, then calmly placing it next to his dessert plate. He pushed back his chair and walked up to Caroline. She thought he was going to leave the room without another word, but then he stopped just as he was about to pass her by, his shoulder even with hers.

"You may stay as long as you need. And so may Miss Landau. But it isn't necessary for her to hold off her return to Freiburg. If her concerns are for your welfare, I assure you I do not pose a threat to your health."

"I would think not, Your Excellency." She glared at his crooked, mocking smile.

"Very well. Then let her go for a few weeks. She may return whenever she wishes."

"You make it sound as though it is I who hold her here."

"Don't you?"

"Not in the least. She offered to stay."

"Then let her do as she pleases. But I still say it is not necessary to watch you day and night." Merrick let his gaze wander to her squared shoulders and back to her face. *No, it is no longer necessary to keep you out of trouble, is it, little one? You have already seen to that with the bundle you carry.*

"I will convey your concern," Caroline said, aware of his insinuation. She hated him. She hated this shame she must bear for a crime she did not commit. Once again she had to remind herself of the duty she performed, and the red flush dissipated from her cheeks.

"Perhaps it is better that I go," Hilde said later in Caroline's room. Seeing the apprehension in her young friend's eyes, she patted her hand as they sat side by side on the settee. "You'll be fine without me here. You can stitch a seam as well as I, so altering the padding won't be difficult. I don't think I could instruct you any better on how to act maternal. You have a talent for it."

"You would call riding a horse at a full run maternal talent?"

Hilde chuckled. "That isn't exactly what I had in mind. I've watched you put your hand to your belly as you're doing now." Caroline's cheeks flushed as she moved to drop her hand. "No, don't stop. It's good. It's . . . unconscious. Just like a mother would do . . . touching her baby within her. You must have grown up seeing it. I'll write down some things to remember to do before I go. Yes, I think you'll do fine."

Caroline smoothed her hands across the pillow beneath her dress and sighed. "It's not as if I *need* a chaperone anymore, is it? My moral status couldn't possibly be questioned farther than it already is." She looked up at her older friend. "But I'll be desolate without you to talk to, Hilde. How long will you be gone?"

"Two weeks?"

"That should be long enough to please the baron."

Hilde nodded. "It will be nice to see my aunt after all these years."

She fiddled with her fingers in contemplation. "I don't understand him, Hilde. He's thoughtful one moment, moody the next, then arrogant. He's . . . different."

"Yes, dear, he is different. You be mindful of that. I don't think His Excellency is one you could second-guess. Or should try to. Why, I wouldn't be the least surprised if he knew exactly what you're plotting and he's just biding his time until he figures out what he's going to do next."

Caroline's eyes shot up to meet Hilde's, knowing that she was talking about Merrick's unusual gifts. Yet there was no indication in the older woman's manner that connected Caroline to the same powers, a realization that gave her a moment of relief.

"I have to have faith that I'm doing the right thing for Peter. I won't back out now, not after that scene at the graveside. He's—"

"Wicked?" Hilde prompted.

"No. Yes. I don't think so. Oh, Hilde. I hate him for the cruel, heartless things he says and does. But I can't prove that Ilse's accusations are true. I'm not sure anymore. He frightens me, but I don't know if I'm afraid of him for what Ilse claimed or if I'm afraid for the deception he may see in my eyes."

"Did Ilse say anything more in her diary?"

Caroline clamped her mouth shut, then her shoulders slumped in resignation. "You may as well know the rest. Ilse had learned that Merrick would one day be pitted against 'his own' in a struggle for all he possessed. She was told he would win this battle, which meant his opponent would certainly lose—most likely his life."

"And Ilse was told that 'his own' meant his son?"

"Yes . . . in so many words. She thought she could forestall her son's fate. When she found herself in a family way, she was positive it was a boy. That's when she sent Merrick to get me, hoping I could help her save the baby."

"Didn't she mention names of anyone she may have suspected?"

Caroline rose to her feet and paced, trying to summon any recollection. "There was one name." She went to her bureau and opened the bottom drawer. After digging through the array of clothes, she snatched the diary from the folds of color and flipped the ink-filled pages.

Caroline read from the book.

. . . Elena and I had tea together today. As always, she visited when Merrick was away on business. It's odd how the woman is quite skittish whenever I invite her to come to one of our parties. Just the mention of my husband causes a reaction. I can't help but wonder if she had been Merrick's paramour—perhaps still is. No one could say she was too homely to catch his eye. In truth, her beauty is too exquisite to be ignored. I will not trust her. She's up to no good, visiting me as she does."

"So your sister was a jealous wife. Do you think Elena meant her harm?"

Caroline pondered, resuming her pacing steps, her green eyes dark with inner concentration. The open diary was clutched to her bosom.

"She could have been one of the rebels who'd vowed to prevent the new patriarch from rising to his place in the church. Merrick could have been unaware of the friendship, unaware that Ilse was in danger." A chill skittered down

Caroline's spine. Though she knew so little of her mystical powers, she knew enough to fear the evil prospects by one bent on destruction.

Caroline released a groan of frustration. "It's all speculation, Hilde. Merrick has shown no interest in the church but he could be hiding his ties. How do I find out the truth? I can't ask anyone around here."

"When I visit my aunt in Freiburg, I'll see what I can do . . . away from this center of attention. There could be some way to help you."

Five days passed, then ten. Intermittent snowfall had gradually built up a thick blanket on the landscape, creating a look and sound of quiet reverence. Each morning seemed markedly colder than the previous one.

While Hilde was gone, Caroline had little to do but read. Her life had fallen into a steady routine. Avoiding the baron was her foremost concern, which was not difficult in the large house. It had been disturbing to think he might have read her mind at the gravesite. But his behavior since had put her fears to rest, at least temporarily. If he'd truly known her thoughts, he'd certainly have confronted her by now. Since he hadn't spoken of the incident, she assumed her secret was still safe . . . for the time being.

To satisfy her duty as his guest, she attended dinner each evening, but otherwise stayed on the second floor. Visiting Peter was the only joyful point of her day. It was clear her presence was not welcome by Louise in the nursery so she made an effort to confine her time with him to the early afternoon. From the sounds overheard through her wall and footsteps passing her door, she calculated Merrick's visits with his son to be early in the morning before breakfast and early in the evening before dinner, but always after Peter had been fed.

Caroline pulled a needle and thread from the small sewing kit next to her feet, then sat back in the chair by the window. She snipped a seam of the muslin padding she'd fashioned before Hilde had left. Each day she added a tiny bit more kapok from the pillows in her room. When bunched, the silky fibers were heavier than down and kept a firm shape. Soon she would have to find a way to refill the cushions on the settee before the maid grew curious.

In the dim light of the late afternoon, her fingers worked nimbly over the small opening. The task took but a few minutes but they were anxious minutes, for a knock at the door would mean a hurried attempt to replace the padding and explain her dressing gown at this unreasonable hour. It would be so much easier when Hilde returned. The older woman could act as a buffer against any intrusions.

She wondered, as she snipped the knotted thread, whether Hilde was enjoying her visit, then thought of her own home. Caroline missed her mother and longed to be back with her. She rose and went to the mirror, parting her robe. The false padding had ribbons attached to each side which she tied behind her back, then brought her knee-high drawers up and over, tying those about the front of her. Over this went the corset, its strings loosened to accommodate her wider girth. She caught each hook until the stiff garment was closed all the way up to her breast bone. Finally, she pulled her soft, knit corset cover down to complete the disguise. Surveying her work in the mirror, she looked pleasingly plump, and almost wished Greta would knock at the door with an armful of towels. The maid would have her tongue wagging before her toes hit the bottom step of the servants' stairs.

Caroline chuckled, smoothing her hand across the rise of her belly, a continuous habit she'd come to enjoy. What she would give to have Hilde here to tell her all the tidbits of information from the servants' quarters. Caroline's smile faded. Had her chaperone learned anything helpful on her trip as they'd hoped? For the last ten days she'd read Ilse's diary and her mother's Bible. Yet nothing seemed to explain the mess she'd floundered into, especially whether Merrick was involved with the rebellion or, in the least, still committed to the original Church of the Mystics.

Her thoughts darted back to Ilse's hateful accusations, then further back to her sister's descriptive passage of the tender love scene in Merrick's arms. A light draft touched her, drawing gooseflesh to her bare arms. She felt her body respond to the memory of the dream she'd had of the baron and her heartbeat quickened. A faint fluttering began low inside her.

Stop it, her mind scolded. *He was Ilse's husband. Now Ilse's dead. She's gone.* Caroline worried her lower lip at the reality of losing Ilse. The sadness rushed back unexpectedly, as it had many times over the last two weeks, often vanishing as quickly as it had come.

Hearing a knock at the door, Caroline hurriedly tied her dressing gown and wiped her wet cheeks as she moved across the room.

She opened the door to find Greta standing on the other side, yet it was not the maid whom she saw but the baron as he passed behind. His blue eyes fixed on hers, his lips drawn tight in disgust until he noticed the tears, then his expression changed to one of guarded question.

Caroline pulled her attention back to the maid, sniffing back the remnant of tears. "I was taking a nap," she explained in regard to her gown, then realized the tears would be a sure sign she'd not been sleeping. "What is it?"

The girl held out a letter. *"Ich habe einen Brief fur Sie,"* she answered but Caroline's eyes had wandered once again to the baron's.

Merrick paused at the door of his son's nursery, watching as she turned away and took the letter. It was hard to stoke his anger when her reddened eyes caught him off guard like this. Was she still mourning Ilse? Or was she upset about the humiliation of carrying the child? Both would be perfectly natural. The maid looked at him and he shook off his musings and entered the nursery. He didn't need to be clairvoyant to know Greta's thoughts. Louise had informed him that, despite indications otherwise, the little maid presumed he was the father of Caroline's baby.

He wished to God he was.

In the privacy of her room, Caroline tore open the envelope.

"Dearest Caroline," the letter read. "I hate to inform you of this but my aging aunt needs my care for the time being. I feel terrible to desert you in this way. Perhaps you should come here for a few months. It would make me feel better, knowing you are not under the baron's scrutiny every day . . ."

The rest of the letter gave an effort to be more cheerful but the words blurred under Caroline's efforts to finish it. She didn't blame Hilde. Fate had brought them together and fate had pulled them apart. She wished to go to Freiburg but couldn't risk leaving Peter at the estate. Reading the letter again, she wondered if perhaps Hilde was trying to tell her something that she was afraid to convey openly for fear of the letter falling into the wrong hands. But she found no clue to such. Even if she had, Caroline would not have left Peter. Another intruder had been seen on the estate grounds two days earlier but again had slipped away. No one could persuade her to leave now.

At the dinner table that evening, Caroline waited for Merrick to join her. As was her routine, she made certain to be seated well before he arrived. Her dislike of parading past him in her disguise was more than enough reason to slip downstairs as soon as she heard him in the nursery with Peter, even though it often led to almost an hour of sitting alone in the dining room.

As he entered the room, Caroline noticed he'd worn his brown jacket and trousers that were the color of dark chocolate. His ebony hair was brushed back, the ends curling slightly over his collar. He looked tall and trim, Caroline thought, and exceedingly handsome. She, on the other hand, felt fat and dowdy. In her opinion, the extra servings to broaden her hips had already begun to show. When Merrick cast an appraising eye upon her, she sensed her expanding waistline only added to his continuous disapproval.

Merrick nodded to her with his usual expression of contempt. "Good evening, Caroline."

"Good evening, Your Excellency," she said before bowing her head, cutting off further conversation.

The baron started for his place at the opposite end of the table, then turned and came toward her. She looked up when he stopped at the first chair to her right.

"Would you care for some company tonight?"

Her incredulous stare centered on him for a long moment, then she answered, "If it is your wish, Your Excellency."

Merrick stiffened at her austere response but forced himself to quell the urge to march to his usual seat. He sensed pain behind her biting tongue, something he never felt with Ilse, and followed his instincts.

As he sat down, a servant entered the room and noted the change in the baron's position. Without a word, she continued over to His Excellency to deliver a glass of his vineyard's Reisling, after which she moved his napkin and utensils to his new place.

Lifting the stemmed glass, he offered, "Would you care for something?" Immediately correcting himself, "Oh, I forgot. You only drink occasionally . . . to aid your sleep. We wouldn't want you to nod off before you eat, would we?" He meant his comment to be light and noncommittal, yet he saw a spark of embarrassment in Caroline's eyes, then indignation. What, for god's sake, had he done now?

"If I have offended you, little one, I beg your pardon." She was not half as surprised with his kind apology as he was with the slip in his facade. For almost two weeks, her ploy had rankled him. Every time she was out of his sight, however, he'd found his thoughts dwelling on her incessantly. If she was to be under his roof, he supposed they could be civil, if nothing else. Yet his attempts at such had appeared to be for naught.

In a mannerly tone, she said, "It is quite all right." But he knew the reverse was more the truth.

Moving on to a safer subject, he inquired about Miss Landau. "Have you heard from her?"

"The letter Greta delivered was from Hilde . . . Miss Landau. She's been kept due to her aunt's health."

"Did she say when she would return?"

Caroline shook her head, taking her napkin to her lap. "I don't believe she is. But she's invited me to come stay with her for a few months."

His gut suddenly tightened as if he'd taken a blow from a beefy fist. She'd be off his hands, it was true, but she'd be gone for good, and that realization sent a wave of regret through him. How could he feel such confusion over her? She'd proven herself to be a scheming liar. Wasn't that enough to make him glad she was leaving?

Steaming plates were brought out and placed before them. Caroline fairly salivated over the *Bauernschmaus,* a hearty combination of smoked ham, sausages, pork, and dumplings with sauerkraut. Adding a few extra pounds would take little effort with the heavy foods the German cook produced for them on a regular basis. It amazed her that the baron had not developed a paunch about his middle from such exorbitant eating. Yet unlike her, he led an active life. Every morning as he rode off upon his horse, Ghebellino, she watched from her window. When they returned hours later, she anxiously looked upon the fine animal and rider, telling herself that the magnificent sorrel was cause for her interest.

Merrick noticed from the corner of his eye the manner in which Caroline toyed with her food and found himself wondering if she were ill again, though her features denied it.

From her radiant skin to her softening curves it seemed that childbearing immensely suited her, at least physically. How different from Ilse's first months of carrying Peter.

He poked his fork into a bite-size piece of sausage and took it into his mouth. How different, too, was his own regard for the two sisters. With Ilse, he almost welcomed his trip to America as an escape from her constant whining and complaining. Now, he fought the odd desire to hold Caroline back, finding that he enjoyed her beauty even though it was only for a brief time each day at dinner, even though it was another man's child that created her glow. His good sense reminded him of her sharp tongue, but another part of him argued that it was like sweet honey compared to Ilse's and Caroline had understandable cause, considering her circumstances.

Why was he defending her? If he wasn't more careful, this game his mind and body played against one another would be his emotional downfall, for his weakness for Caroline could well become his Achilles' heel.

Merrick continued his meal in silence, remembering her on the ship, before he knew of her condition. He'd had to force himself to leave her side, to push her into the pack of young men who eagerly courted her. Her beauty was beyond compare and it was almost more than he could stand to see other men look upon her with hope in their eyes. He'd realized then that he'd wanted her for his own. Yet now he'd come to distrust her. Questions constantly battered at the front of his brain, one conclusion always followed—surely his sensitive powers would have revealed her pregnancy long before that afternoon in the nursery. Most certainly, he'd have sensed her deception the night before, in his study. He recalled the vision of her before the fire, the translucent veil of her gowns revealing her long legs. It was a scene he'd run through his mind at least a hundred times, each as vivid as the last. Yet, as hard as he tried, he could only see her silhouette facing him, never the profile of the soft swell of her belly.

The fact that he'd never suspected her deception haunted him. His instincts were seldom, if ever, wrong, And on the ship his instinct was to desire her as a beautiful, innocent young woman, not the cunning viper he'd discovered.

In the course of his inward contemplation, Caroline had apparently found her appetite. He was somewhat surprised to see her plate nearly empty when he glanced over at her.

"I must have been hungrier than I thought," she said in answer to his look of mild astonishment.

His dark eyes slowly rose up from her dish until they met with hers, commanding her full attention. There, in those moss-green depths, he read the soul of a frightened young girl. Whatever secrets she hid from him he'd discover soon enough, knowing if she were confronted now, Caroline would probably run scared.

"Are you going to accept the offer to stay with Miss Landau?" he asked, straining to keep his voice or expression from giving Caroline a hint of his thoughts.

"I have considered it." She told herself that her words were not completely true nor were they false. She *had* considered it for the blink of an eye. The next move was up to the baron. Did he want her out? If so, she'd have a hard time finding an excuse to stay, only to come up with another reason to leave after she had Peter kidnapped.

Merrick kept his gaze locked with Caroline's, wanting to see the emerald sparkle in those eyes again. He wanted to take her back to the ship and erase the last two weeks, no . . . the last six years. He broke his visual hold on her and turned his eyes to his glass of wine, shaking off the dark cloud of could-have-been's that hung over him of late.

"I've told you that you are welcome to stay here until your baby is born. But if you feel a need to be out from under Ilse's shadow, I understand. Perhaps you would want me to arrange a suitable place for you in Munich near a good hospital," he offered, hoping to allay her fears of childbirth.

He does want me gone, Caroline realized dejectedly. *He can't stand the sight of me and how can I blame him? I've settled in as if I belong here. I've abused his hospitality. What's more— my pregnancy must cause him a deal of embarrassment and appre- hension. He doesn't believe my story about Bates anymore than I would.* But it was painful to think he presumed her to be the sort of girl who was bedded willingly.

"No, thank you, Your Excellency." She hastened to add, "You've done enough for me already. I couldn't impose fur- ther."

"It's no imposition, Carrie." His voice softened. Caroline felt as though she were cloistered in a tiny room with him instead of the vast dining salon. "I want you to feel safe and secure during this difficult time for you."

Why was he so concerned for her welfare? Or was he? Maybe this was his way of getting her out of his life without feeling guilty about casting her out in the cold of winter to seek shelter in a stranger's house.

"I appreciate your offer, Your Excellency." She noticed the slightest frown of his disapproval at her formality. "But after all our . . . differences, I must ask why you are being so generous?"

His broad shoulders lifted in a noncommittal shrug, cover- ing up his surprise at the unexpected question. The girl was not only stubborn, but also bold, traits he admired until they opposed him. "It's the least I can do," he said.

"The least you can do?"

"For Ilse's sister."

He'd done it again. In sidestepping her inquiry, as well as his own reasons for wanting her to stay, which were vague to him, he'd succeeded once again in raising her ire.

The servant girl stepped through the door with dessert, tempering the escalating heat of the conversation. She carefully set a slice of *Sachertorte* in front of Caroline, and another in front of the baron.

After the girl left, Merrick cut through the rich chocolate cake with the edge of his fork. "You do what you want," he said without looking over to Caroline. "But you needn't run from here because you resent me or my obligation to you. I don't care for the manner in which you and Ilse plotted behind my back to bring you here so you could be saved public humiliation. If Ilse had told me the circumstances, I'd have consented to helping you. As it stands, I don't trust you. And I will no longer tolerate being manipulated. My patience has been worn down by the lies and trickery. To add to this mess, I must be on constant guard against whomever is trying to harm my son."

Caroline sat stunned like a child duly chastised. She wanted to deny his accusations but what could she possibly say—that she had not plotted with Ilse to come here? That she was not involved with the lies and trickery? How much could she say without giving away her real reason for this charade of maternity? Yes, it appeared Ilse had an ulterior motive when she sent Merrick to America. Though Caroline's plight had not been a part of it, it was best to let him think so. But the thought of having already lost his trust startled her. The realization was like the shock of suddenly being plunged into ice-cold water. If she didn't gain it back, she would undoubtedly be the first person he'd suspect in the kidnapping of Peter. She had to find a way to win his favor before that time.

Resolved to keep her temper despite his rising agitation, she pushed her plate aside. "If you wouldn't mind, I would like to be here for Peter's first Christmas," she said humbly, eyes downcast. "After the New Year, I'll leave for Munich, but I don't expect you to pay my expenses. I have enough money to keep me until . . . the baby arrives."

"What will you do then?"

Her mind grasped any idea that seemed remotely logical.

"I'll make arrangements to find him a good home. Then
. . . I suppose I'll go home."

"Have you changed your mind about telling your parents
about your situation?"

She shook her head vigorously, somewhat relieved to be
able to answer truthfully, if only to one minor detail.

"Don't you think they'd want to see their grandchild?" he
asked with neither concern nor anger. It seemed to Caroline
that he could have just as easily been asking her about the
depth of the snow outside.

"Oh, yes. Especially my Mother. I mean . . . once she
gets over the initial shock of losing Ilse . . . she'll dote on
the baby like—" She caught a glimpse Merrick's pensive
gaze. He was thinking of Peter, it was plain to see, just as she
was. Had he realized her intention or was he too caught up
in his own reflections?

His dark eyes slowly blinked, then turned to her. "I'm
sorry. You were saying?"

"I . . . was talking about my mother . . . how much
she'd love to see her grandchild." She studied his features,
wishing for solutions. If she tried, if she really wanted to,
could she read his mind? "Do you think she'll ever see Peter?"

"I hope so."

Her heart tripped a beat at his quiet affirmation and compassionate look. Merrick was so hard to understand. It
seemed to make her life all the more dangerous to be stirring
up these unreasonable feelings for him when she conspired
against him. Where was her anger for his defiling Ilse's Bible? Her condemnation of his questionable beliefs? Drawn
into his gaze, Caroline felt warm and comforted, tempting
her to relax for a moment and try to envision Merrick, not as
the culprit of evil, but as the target of it.

A slender thread of doubt wove back into her crumbling
rationale. In all that she'd attempted with her special gifts,

couldn't she have just glimpsed beyond his cold exterior into his true, innocent identity?

She felt like a defenseless child tossed into a frightening world of inexplicable phenomena. She vowed she would escape. She must.

Pushing back her chair, she said in a rush, "I'm quite tired, Your Excellency. Excuse me."

"Wait!" She half turned. "Why are you afraid of me?"

She feigned a light chuckle and lied. "I'm not afraid of you, Your Excellency." *I'm afraid of what you may do to me if you ever discover my charade.*

As two more weeks went by, Peter grew by small but significant measures. Merrick proudly noticed his son's progress in his daily visits. The baby seemed to be the only one contented in the house of Baron von Hayden. Caroline spent all but a few brief periods shut in her room, obviously avoiding further contact with all other members of the household except for her nephew. Even Louise had voiced her prejudice against the American girl countless times to the baron when he visited the nursery.

On one such occasion, the nursemaid had muttered in German, "Fräulein Hartmann doesn't belong here, I tell you."

"Now, Louise," Merrick had soothed while holding his son. "Caroline poses no threat to your position as Peter's primary caretaker."

"Hmph. You are blind if you think she is harmless. That girl is devious. She *knows* something. Heed my words, Your Excellency. If times were different, she'd be burned at the—"

"That's enough!" Merrick barked, his harsh tone startling Peter into a startled wail. "I won't have you speak of my guest in such a manner. And if I hear of it again—in my presence or not—there'll be hell to pay." He handed Peter into the nursemaid's arms and marched out.

The bitter recollection faded as Merrick closed the ledger

on his desktop and leaned his head into his hands. His properties and businesses had done well while he was away, but
now his inattention was beginning to show. He couldn't
stand guard over Peter and take care of his other extensive
responsibilities. While this weighed heavy on his mind, the
clock in the foyer chimed midnight.

He ran his palms over his face, then lay them flat on the
green felt pad on his desk. Though he'd retired earlier, his
restlessness brought him down to the library to catch up on
figures and letters. Concentration had been difficult, to say
the least, due to other thoughts that pursued him. The religious rebels. Peter. Caroline. Ilse.

His long legs stretched out beneath the massive Chippendale desk as he slouched back against the chair, letting his
hands fall to his robe-clad thighs. The wine-colored velvet
material shifted but Merrick ignored the chill on his bare
legs. The fire had died to embers long ago, leaving the drafti-
ness to work through the warmth of the thick weave. With
his head resting against the leather chair, he peered at the
ornate ceiling as if he could see beyond it into Caroline's
second floor bedroom. In spite of his mind's powers, not even
he could accomplish such a feat. The musing, however, led to
another, more serious thought: Caroline was full-grown now
with abilities that could easily match his. Yet she continued
to resist exploring her gifts, to hone them into something
useful. He wasn't really surprised by her reluctance. As he'd
told her on the train from Rotterdam, the gifts she'd been
given could either be a blessing or curse. He was certain that
her religious upbringing made her consider them the worst
of all possible evils.

He stared at a curlique pattern in the molded white cor-
nice, blocking out all else. The taut muscles in his shoulders
and neck eased. His breathing slowed. Colorful, serene images flitted through his mind's eye: remembrances from
childhood to the present. A glimpse here, a lingering view
there. The pond in spring. His stone Schloss Hayden beyond.

His youthful romps across the fields with his pet Newfoundland, long since gone. Then there was a majestic vision of Ghebellino standing tall and proud on the rise of the embankment. A hand came into view—Caroline's hand. With girlish enthusiasm, she pointed out his fine sorrel, then checked her excitement.

Caroline.

Letting his gaze drift down the length of her, he observed an ethereal transformation take place. Her brown-checked dress evolved into a formless gossamer gown that seemed to shimmer with stardust, revealing the full curves of her breasts, her narrow waist and the swell of her hips. As if wishing it to be so, her belly was flat, firm, taut—prompting his loins to stir with renewed awakening.

Her soft green eyes drew him closer. The corners of her pink lips slowly tipped up with an invitation to taste her sweetness. Taking her in his arms, his mouth moved over hers with a hunger that couldn't be sated. She allowed him to slip the gown from her body. He lowered her onto a soft carpet of grass, then unbuckled his belt. As he shed his clothes, she tantilized him with her ready pose. Eagerly, she took him into her with a fever that quickly carried them both to the peak.

As they laid together afterward, her attention was drawn past him. Whatever she saw changed her alluring gaze to one of wide-eyed panic.

What was it? What frightened her? Merrick tried to turn his focus behind him but found he was unable. When he turned back to Caroline and moved toward her, the clear, crisp image of her began to fade. Her arms reached out to him. Her mouth opened as if pleading for help.

Merrick willfully broke himself out of his dreamlike trance. Pushing himself from his desk with his palms, he jumped to his feet and made for Caroline's room as quickly and quietly as possible. The vision was a strong warning. And after the shipboard dream, he didn't waste a minute wondering at the timeliness of the precognition. He had to be sure she was safe. The lingering notion in the back of his mind was too much like the ominous feelings he'd had coming back on the train about Ilse.

As he approached her room in the darkened hallway, he saw no light peeping from beneath her door. No doubt at this late hour she was asleep. His fingers gently wrapped around the knob and turned. The door was unlocked.

Why would anyone want to do her harm? It was Peter who was in real danger. Yet his sixth sense told him otherwise.

He wanted to knock quietly, but quickly decided against it. If an intruder was lurking, why give him an advantage. Merrick moved silently.

Please let her be safe, he prayed.

Chapter 9

In the darkness of her room, Caroline had awakened suddenly gripped with a terrible sense of dread. Curled up in the center of the bed, her eyes opened, trying to focus on something familiar in the dark. A foreboding chill prompted her to burrow deeper beneath the quilts, but instinct told her to not to move.

"Carrie?" She heard Merrick whisper. Releasing her grip on the covers, she relaxed and settled back into the soft mattress. Her pounding heart was another matter. A threat of a different sort remained with her—what had brought Merrick into her room in the middle of the night?

Her courage faltered as she felt the mattress shift beneath her and heard the faintest creak of protest from the bed boards. Then a hand cupped her shoulder.

"Carrie, I must talk to you," Merrick said quietly. His soft-spoken words were close to her ear, creating an air of intimacy that she hoped he'd not consciously intended. Conflicting emotions ran through her. His touch burned through the yoke of her flannel gown, warming her to the core, begging for a response. Yet, at the same time she realized if she turned toward him without her padding, he might discover that she wasn't really pregnant and her ruse would be over.

He shook her gently.

Feigning sleepiness, she turned only her head toward the sound of his voice. "What . . .

"I came to see if you were all right. Did you have a dream?"

His question puzzled her, especially since she couldn't recall making any sound that would bring this attention from him. Her voice raised, "Can't this wait?"

"Shh—" he admonished, tugging her onto her back. As he moved to sit closer, Caroline felt his weight settle next to her. She gripped the coverlet and pulled it to her chin, knowing full well that it held no protection against him. "Please answer me. It's important."

Something brushed against her thighs and she held her breath, realizing he'd dropped his hands to either side of her, only inches from her smooth, firm belly. If he moved awkwardly in the dark he'd immediately learn the truth.

Slowly, so as not to draw attention to her distress, Caroline pulled herself back against the headboard while drawing her knees to her chest so the covers bunched high over her stomach. Without the aid of light, she could only assume that his hands were now firmly planted on either side of her feet.

"I had several dreams," she said with a quiet tone that carried only to his ears. "But I don't know why that should concern you in the middle of the night."

In the darkness he appeared to her as no more than a vague black shadow. His pleasant manly scent mingled with the familiar aroma of spice and evergreen, stirring more than just her heightened sense of smell.

"Do you remember having a nightmare shortly before I woke you?"

Whatever information Merrick sought from her, it was clear that he wouldn't leave until he was satisfied with the answers—or lack of them.

"I dreamt of falling off your horse Ghebellino," she offered. She refrained from mentioning that Merrick had rushed to her side and carried her upstairs once again.

"You're not telling me all. I can feel it. You're holding back. Dammit, girl. I wouldn't be waking you from a sound sleep out of idle curiosity. You must trust me. Did you have a vision in which you felt threatened—frightened by someone or something?"

"No. I swear. That's all."

As he muttered another curse, Caroline felt his fist punch the mattress at her hip, punctuating the frustration she heard in his voice. She started to move to the opposite side of the bed when his hand fumbled and grabbed her forearm.

"Where are you going?"

"To light a lamp. I'm tired of whispering in the shadows."

"No!" His order was raspy and firm, squelching her plan to drag the small goosedown pillow with her and slip behind the dressing screen. There, she'd have quickly donned a heavy wrapper, securing the makeshift padding with the robe's sash before bringing up the light in the oil lamp. His tight grip thwarted her effort immediately, chafing her skin as well as her already agitated mood.

"What is wrong with you?" she asked, growing louder with this latest abuse. "Why are you here?"

Merrick could feel Caroline's pulse throbbing beneath his fingertips. Her wrist was like a delicate twig in his grasp, yet beneath her silken skin lay a spirit as unyielding as a solid oak. He had hoped to learn that Caroline had had a dream similar to his own. But the only thing he knew for sure now was that she was definitely hiding something.

Yet another possibility gnawed at him. Perhaps the fear he'd seen on Caroline's face in the vision had been because of *him.*

"Why are you afraid of me?" he asked. "I've seen it in your eyes. I've seen the way you avoid being in the same room with me."

Caroline wrested her wrist from his grasp and wrapped both arms about her legs, aware of how close the baron's face was to hers. She wasn't quite sure whether to anger him into leaving or behave innocently so he would make his departing apologies.

She kept her voice down but let it lash out through cutting breaths. "Six years ago you marched into our quiet lives and laid claim to my sister with some fool document, saying you had a right. All this time I thought the rumors flying around about the two of you were just that—rumors. Now I've learned that you'd made certain Ilse couldn't have been denied to you. Though from the way Ilse's diary tells it, there was question as to who was the wolf and who the lamb." The dam had finally burst, spilling out all the accusations, all the bitterness. "You two had the perfect marriage, didn't you? That is—until Ilse discovered your involvement with the Church of the Mystics."

"You forget, little one," he reminded her, "that I told you about such beliefs on the ship . . . when I explained about our common ancestry."

"Yet you failed to mention that the sole purpose of the marriage was to *use* Ilse for the son she could give you."

His anger projected through his low growl. "You make it sound like I tied her down and bred her like a prized mare."

"Well—didn't you?"

"Watch your tongue, little one. The words you say will come back to you tenfold."

"Then we share the same fate, Your Excellency. Only your fate looks to be much harsher than mine. For what but eternal damnation can befall a man who plots to murder his own son?" Caroline suddenly cringed at her slip.

Merrick leaned close—too close. His warm breath upon her face gave her warning that he was only inches from her, forcing Caroline's head back against the headboard. If there had been light, she'd have seen the seething anger in the depths of his dark blue eyes and the revealing twitch in his jaw. "Murder my son? My god, girl. Are you as mad as your sister?"

She had no recourse but to continue her words, hoping to retreat from his towering body. "Ilse wasn't insane. She was frightened of you, of your church, and the plan to dispose of the child who'd someday rule over all of you."

"She *told* you that?"

"Not exactly," she offered defiantly. "It was in her diary."

"Where the hell is this diary?"

"Do you think I am foolish enough to produce it so you can throw it in the fire and claim that it never existed?"

"Caroline, give me that diary." His low, threatening voice gripped her as surely as if he'd taken her arms in his hands and squeezed them like a vise.

"No. I won't," she answered. She closed her eyes and swallowed hard, awaiting punishment for her defiance. After a long silence he finally spoke with renewed composure.

"You have my word that I have no intention of destroying your sister's diary."

Her frayed nerves only allowed for an indignant grunt of disbelief while she shifted her knees higher and pressed her back harder against the headboard. The discomfort of the wood was nothing compared to the torture of his interrogation. At any moment, she expected him to discover her charade against him and then she would certainly be defenseless under his tirade.

"How can I make you understand that I am not what you think me? I am not to blame for Ilse's death, any more than you are, though we both carry needless guilt for letting her die."

Caroline stiffened under the prick of truth in his confession of remorse.

"The marriage covenant," he continued, "was not meant

as a license to *use* Ilse, as you think. At least that wasn't my intention. I only wanted to honor my father's final wish. It was an obligation no different than other marriages arranged by families for generations. Can't you see the *simple* reason instead of some contrived rubbish you read in that diary? I may have thought that I loved her at first. But I may have talked myself into it because I knew I had to bring her back here."

Her sympathies lodged a stone of emotion in her throat. Indeed, she understood all too well the strong bond of family, for she displayed it herself in this desperate need to rescue her nephew from the clutches of evil that threatened. Still, she couldn't let the similarity of their motivations mask the differences in their deeds.

"And you brought her back to what?" Caroline asked angrily. "A living hell?"

He sighed. "The only living hell Ilse experienced was the thought that she'd married a man who didn't worship her."

"Well, what about your strange powers? As far as my own go, I've often wondered if I was cursed or possessed by the devil."

"Listen to me, Carrie. I am *not* cursed and neither are you. Our unique talents are special gifts from God. But like everything else, it is our choice how we use them. If we abuse them then we could cause harm against ourselves and others. But as long as our focus is on good—we'll be safe."

Merrick found her shoulder in the darkness and let his touch travel down her arm. "You must understand the true danger, Carrie. There are evil ones among the members of my church who fear my son's rise in power over them. And they'll do anything to stop him—even kill him."

"But Ilse wrote in her diary that *you* would struggle against your own son," Caroline studied him curiously.

"Those were her exact words?"

"You would 'struggle against your own,' was what she wrote."

"Perhaps it pointed to the dissension in the church. I am struggling against my own. All of us are descendants of the first members, even those who follow a darker path."

"Could Ilse have become involved with them? Right before she died she'd said that God would never forgive her for the sins she'd committed."

Merrick shook his head, convinced that Ilse would never have denounced her strong Lutheran beliefs. "She'd said time and again in one of her dramatic rantings that she was condemned for loving a man who didn't love her. And I think she was vain enough to actually believe herself." Merrick let out an indignant grunt. "While a part of her loved me because I never yielded to her strong will, another part of her hated me for that very same reason. In a strange way, she hated herself too—for shamelessly allowing me into her bed. No matter how angry she'd get with me, she never denied me.

"I don't suppose you've ever longed so deeply to be intimate with someone that you would humiliate yourself for the momentary pleasure?" The question escaped his lips before he realized his *faux pas*.

Finding his way in the dark, Merrick slid his hand up to hers, then noticed how rigidly they clung to the quilt over her raised knees. How could he have been so tactless? The expectant girl was quite obviously living the day-to-day humiliation of giving herself to a man who hadn't loved her. This growing reminder was the punishment for her moment of indiscretion.

Caroline remembered that early morning long ago when she'd watched Merrick kiss Ilse seductively. The memory brought back Caroline's own feelings—the warm sensation that had been awakened that night in the study. After taking a deep breath, she released the air, unable to answer him.

His voice was like a soft caress when he broke the silence. "I've said too much and I'm deeply sorry." The trembling of her fingers beneath his moved him. While his mind still denounced her, his body wanted her as a lover. But it was his soul that confused him most of all. For deep inside, he knew one thing—if she were to leave him, his lifeblood would go with her.

"Forgive me for waking you, Carrie. Go back to sleep and know that I won't bother you in this way again—I promise." He rose to leave but her hand took his wrist and she whispered to him through the black shroud of night.

"You never said why you came in here."

"I—was passing your door and thought I heard you call out in your sleep."

His excuse was a weak one, but Caroline was not about to argue with him. As long as he kept his promise and didn't visit her again, she would keep her doubts to herself.

Caroline had released her hold when she heard muffled voices coming from the other side of her closed door. Her first thought was for the embarrassing scandal of being caught with the baron in her room. The second was, why on earth were people congregating in her midst in the middle of the night?

Merrick knew, however. Without hesitation, he silently flipped back the covers and slid in beside her.

It was all she could do to keep her voice to a whisper. "What do you think you're doing?"

"Get behind the screen as quickly and quietly as you can."

"But—"

"Now!" he rasped, propelling her toward the edge of the mattress with an impatient shove. She made it without a noise just as the latch clicked. Though the room was pitch-black, she was momentarily thankful for the cloth partition between her and the latest intruders. She waited in anxious silence. Her palms itched from prickly, cold sweat. She longed to scratch but dared not move the tiniest muscle.

Her mind raced. *Why are they here? What do they plan to do?* The possibilities were endless and frightening. Yet Merrick knew. *But how? His powers—of course. But there were two voices . . . two people. Merrick will suffer a fate meant for me. He'll never be able to ward off two interlopers.*

Merrick waited until he was certain the intruders were near to the bed, hoping his calculations were correct. At the last possible moment, a slight squeak of a floorboard revealed the intruders' location.

In one powerful movement, he launched his body out of the bed, throwing the quilt in an attempt to cover and disorient the assailants.

"Get the light, Caroline!" He yelled, throwing her into action.

After what seemed like an eternity, she finally located the oil lamp. Her fingers shook uncontrollably as she heard the muffled thumps and grunts, then a tearing of cloth coming from the middle of the room. The room was suddenly illuminated, giving shapes to the grotesque sounds of bodies being brutally beaten. To her shock, the first sight that caught her attention was Merrick's bare backside. His torn burgundy robe was lying on the floor near the foot of the bed. Then she saw beyond his naked form there was only one man—not two—with whom Merrick fought. Where had the second voice come from? The intruder was nearly the same size as the baron, and appeared to be older by at least ten years, maybe fifteen. While Caroline backed into the corner, the memory of another such fight rushed into her mind with renewed horror.

The bodies slammed into her bureau, sending a trinket crashing to the floor. Though Merrick now struggled with a different assailant than the drunken Bates, his skill was no less a match. With his right fist, he caught the man in the gut, sending him staggering back against the cheval glass. The wall directly behind stopped the intruder from falling backward and held him suspended for an instant, just long enough for Merrick to send his left fist in for the final blow.

Caroline covered her eyes before she could witness the blood that was certain to fly from the man's face. Glass shattered. And the anguished scream that followed came from a voice that was all too familiar. Merrick. She glanced up to see sparkling shards scattered at his feet. He cradled his bloodied hand, momentarily dazed, while his attacker skittered past then turned back to finish his job.

"He's got a knife!" she warned, her scream startling the dark-clad intruder into glancing behind him.

Merrick swung around, dipping down to send a well-placed disabling blow to the groin. The man yelped in pain and dropped to his knees. Doubling over, he gagged, then rolled to his side. Merrick leaned down and picked up the knife, staring at the shiny six-inch blade as he sat on the floor and fell back against the footboard of the bed. Exhaustion overwhelmed his body. Then a throbbing pain in his hand set in.

Coming out of her own shock, Caroline snatched her robe and pillow and made quick work to create her disguise, keeping a watchful eye on the ebony head of hair she could see over the end of the bed. By now, someone was pounding at the door. Evidently the intruder had locked the door behind him. What had he intended? To rape her? Kill her?

Crossing the room, she picked up Merrick's robe and offered it to him, diverting her gaze from his nakedness. The manner in which his hand dropped away caused her to look down. His exhausted breathing told her the rest. While the shouts and hammering on the door grew more frantic, she awkwardly helped him slip his arms into his robe. His bloody hand made her wince and look away, dropping her gaze unexpectedly upon his manhood. Quickly pulling the robe about him, she felt the heat of her embarrassment rise up her cheeks. Tying it closed, she stole a quick look to see if those deep midnight-blue eyes were upon her. Thankfully, they were half-closed, still gathering the strength needed to face the next onslaught of problems.

Conrad was the first through the doorway, with a gun in his hand. He pulled up short at the sight before him. A stranger dressed in dark workman's clothing lay limp on the floor a few feet from His Excellency. The baron appeared the victor but his attire left much to be desired. It was clear from the disarray of his robe that he wore nothing underneath. Though it was beyond Conrad to pass judgment, it was a matter of easy speculation as to the nocturnal dalliances of the master of the house and the young woman looking on, especially considering the door had been secured for privacy.

"It's too late for heroics, Conrad, but thanks for the effort," Merrick said wryly in German. "Give me the gun."

The intruder heard the command and tried to scramble, though he was not yet in any condition to do anything more than grope awkwardly at the rug. "Don't kill me. Please don't kill me. It was her idea. Not mine. She paid me, she did. You ask her."

While Caroline watched from a few feet away, Merrick took the pistol in his good hand and set the hammer with a click. *"Wer?"*

The intruder winced at the threatening sound and confessed, "The old maid."

"You're a liar," Merrick ground out, struggling to his feet. He moved over to the man and tucked the muzzle behind his ear.

"No—please—I swear to God. She paid me. Look! My pockets." He nodded frantically toward his hip. Merrick indicated for Conrad to make the inspection, which he did quickly but not without a disdainful look upon his face. The man had proved correct on the point of having a great deal of money.

"This only proves that you did not come to rob Miss Hartmann. It doesn't prove who sent you here."

The intruder babbled on in his native German. "It was her I tell you. She brought me right up to this door and let me in! She's big and old and she takes care of that baby."

By now several servants had gathered just inside the door, Louise being one of them. "The man's a lunatic," she accused.

"That's her. She's the one."

"Begging your pardon, Your Excellency," she said, a hint of practiced incredulity in her tone. "What would possess me to do such a thing in the first place? And where ever would I get that kind of money?"

"You hard-hearted bitch!" The man raved, his face purple with rage. "If you think I'm gonna die for this, you're out of your mind! Tell him—tell him how you want to get rid of this one just like you did the first baroness. It was to 'set thing right,' you said."

"Shut up!" she said, stepping toward him with fists raised.

Merrick couldn't believe the absurdity of the man's claim, or worse—Louise's harsh reprimand, a slip that proved her guilt. For in all the thirty years he'd known the woman, it was not in her character to let her ire flare if she'd been truly innocent of the charge.

The throb of pain coming from his battered hand worsened. But the matter at hand was far too important to see to his injuries, so he focused his mind away from the agony, blocking out all feeling except for the twisted knot in his stomach. The man's words echoed in Merrick's mind. *Get rid of this one just like you did the last. It was to 'set things right,' you said.*

The stableman, Wil Krumhauer, pushed his way through the robed servants and burst into the room clad in his hastily donned work clothes.

"I saw the light in the window. What's the trouble?"

"We're trying to find out, Wil," Merrick answered, straightening back to his full height while offering the pistol to Wil. "Take him down to the stables and tie him up. I'll deal with him in the morning." Then he glanced to the curious onlookers, settling his gaze upon Frau Krumhauer. "Alfreda, I want you to take over with Peter tonight. The rest of you go back to bed."

As Caroline remained rooted just beyond the confrontation, Merrick turned and leveled his dark blue glare on the nursemaid. Without taking his eyes from the old woman, he called out once more. "Conrad! Wait outside until I need you."

"But your hand, Your Excellency," the head servant reminded him. Merrick had cradled it protectively in the crook of his other arm, unmindful of the droplets of blood that had soaked into his sleeve. "I'll bring up some fresh water and bandages," the butler offered before stepping beyond the portal and closing the door behind him.

"Why, Louise?"

Her white eyebrows arched as she lifted her chin and answered, "I believe there's been a mistake."

"Yes, there has." Merrick marched up to the stout woman and Caroline was quite surprised that the nursemaid stood her ground, puffing her buxom chest out and meeting his gaze full on.

"Don't be thinking you can throw your weight around with me, young man. I won't be having it."

A flicker of a smile dusted across Merrick's lips at the servant's defiance, but disappeared so quickly Caroline wondered if she'd imagined it. Then his features sobered, his dark eyes stared. A chill ran down her spine at the thought of what Merrick was undoubtedly doing. Did he forget that he was not alone with Louise, that Caroline stood near the corner?

"I want answers, Louise. You know I will not harm you. But you—of all people—know I will learn the truth in my own way." Silence engulfed the room for a long stretch of time. Merrick and the woman remained, facing each other in a match of iron wills. Finally, it was Merrick who spoke again. "Since my mother died, I grew to care for you in place of her. You've been like a mother to me."

Those final words cracked the old woman's facade, breaking down her defenses. "You didn't even know your mother. That woman who died when you were six was a harlot. A weasel. Just like your first wife and just like this one." She pointed to Caroline standing in the corner. "They're blood-thirsty witches, all of them."

"Stop it, Louise," Merrick commanded angrily, chiding himself for letting his intense focus on the current problem completely block Caroline's presence from his conscious mind. "I can understand your hatred for Ilse, and . . . maybe your uncertainty about Caroline. But my mother has nothing to do with this."

"She has everything to do with this. If it hadn't been for her, your father would not have made me send my little girl away. She did it to punish me. She said one bastard under her roof was enough, even if my baby wasn't the baron's own flesh as you were."

"My God, woman, what are you saying?" The full impact of her statement hit him solidly, like a blow.

Caroline threw her hand to her mouth. This couldn't be true. This woman was claiming Merrick was a bastard? She glanced over at him. Merrick squared his shoulders, but his hesitation told of his crumbling composure. Caroline went to his side, hoping somehow her own unique powers could strengthen him, if only by her closeness. The world as he knew it was slowly collapsing, like a castle whose foundations had been set in sand.

Merrick glanced down at Caroline, mystified by her supportive stance. Her green eyes sparkled like emeralds in the soft light from the lamp, offering him a grim-faced determination. Something passed between them—a communication of sorts—that told Merrick she was there to help in any and all ways she could.

Turning back to Louise, he took her elbow and led her to the settee. It had been shoved aside in the earlier scuffle so he dragged it back to its former place and sat her down, commanding the full story from her.

"Shortly before I came to *Schloss Hayden,*" Louise began, as she stared spellbound by Merrick, "the baron had fathered a child by one of the maids. This child was you, Your Excellency. Since the baron's wife refused to risk her life in child-birth, he insisted that she raise you as her own. She agreed but vowed never to do so again."

"What happened to that maid?" he asked. Caroline watched in awe as Louise gave Merrick her answers without hesitation.

"She stayed on for a time until you were weaned, then she was sent away. I don't know where, and I didn't ask because I was the baron's mistress by then."

Merrick raked his hands through his hair and paced the room. "It seems my father had quite a brothel among his servants."

"Your father was nothing like the man he seemed. Why, he even joined me in devil-worship, at least for a short time. But the baroness convinced him to denounce my evil influence. Though he agreed to do so, he refused to dismiss me. That was when she sought vengeance by insisting my little girl be sent away." Her eyes moistened as she dropped the proud lift to her chin. "I loved him so much I gave up my baby rather than leave."

When Merrick didn't reply to the silence, Caroline spoke up to clarify a question in her mind. "But you first talked as though the baron was not the father of your little girl."

"I wish he were. Perhaps he wouldn't have let her go. Then she would have shared in this wealth. Her father was only a village boy who enjoyed my . . . company. I saw no more of him after the baron took an interest in me."

"And you stayed on after the baroness found out," Caroline reiterated.

Louise gave a pathetic laugh. "In spite of his wife's protests, he kept me on staff, claiming to her that I serviced his needs that the baroness had long denied. I accepted those terms because I'd have done anything to be near him."

"Even kill his wife?" Merrick asked angrily. "How did she die, if not from influenza?"

"Poison," she said nonchalantly. "I simply helped the

deadly virus that would have eventually taken her life. Your father never knew of my revenge. After a proper mourning, I wanted him to marry me. But His Excellency was determined to continue his charade as a father who pined for his dead wife. He somehow thought you would not think of him as a man with staunch morals if you'd learned of our affair. I saw no choice but to remain his secret mistress."

Louise went on to explain that when her beloved baron died years later, long-denied resentment pushed her to seek the daughter she'd given away, to right the wrong that had been done against her and her child. After all her years of devotion, she'd deserved more. If she couldn't win it by marriage, then her daughter would. But the covenant had ruined it all. Merrick had wed by the time she'd finally located the girl.

Louise shook her head with bitterness. "She faired much better than me. At least she married herself into a title. But that's all Elena got. Count Reinhart died a pauper."

Caroline gasped at the name. "Elena and Countess Reinhart are the same woman?! *She's* the one who told Ilse all those horrible things that would happen to the child of the covenant! *Why?*"

Merrick listened intently while Louise spoke to him. "Because Elena should have been the baroness! She deserved to be the mother of that baby. Elena did everything to destroy your marriage so that she could conveniently be available for your attention afterwards."

"But why did you send someone to kill me?" Caroline asked. "I am no threat to you!"

"You are more of a threat than your sister. There is . . . something . . . about you. I sense a mystical way about you." Caroline forced herself to remain calm, despite the fear that gripped her.

"Is that why you've gone to great length to avoid me?"

"Yes," Louise said. "I was afraid you could read my thoughts and learn of my plan to get rid of you."

Merrick reasoned skeptically, "And once Caroline was gone, I would be free to take Elena's hand in marriage. How utterly ridiculous. Did you ever consider that perhaps my father had seen my marriage to Ilse as a way to escape a marriage to your daughter? After all, Elena wouldn't have been a descendant of the ancient mystics. We have always tried to keep our line as pure as possible."

"Then you should never have married Ilse. Your father tricked both of us. He said that the firstborn daughter would bring a gifted child. But I never sensed a difference in Ilse as I did in you . . . or Caroline. I don't believe Peter *is* the gifted one."

"How would you know these things?" Merrick asked.

"When one's eyes are open to the truth, one sees many things. Your father taught me that."

"And the truth is that you expect me to marry your daughter so she will finally get what you could not—the von Hayden name. That should prove difficult now that I'm aware of your plan."

"There are other ways to satisfy your father's debt to me for my years of love . . . and service. A share of your wealth will do. Then, for my own pleasure, I will see to it that the Church of the Mystics is finally united under one deity—the Prince of Darkness."

"And how will you do that from a prison cell?" the baron asked.

"Elena. She'd kill the two of you as well as the boy if that's what it takes to gain your fortune. And as a member of the church now, she has many who would gladly help her do it."

An hour had passed after Conrad had delivered the bandages and liquor for the pain. Caroline went to the door and summoned him back in.

Merrick stood at the window, his back to the three of them, staring out into the void of blackness. "Take Louise to her old room and lock her in for the night," he ordered, then threw back his head with another gulp of cognac. When the nursemaid gasped, he remained motionless, adding, "I can't trust you, Louise. Even you should be able to understand that much."

After the two servants had gone, Caroline turned to Merrick. "Let me see to that hand."

His tall figure moved slowly to the settee where he allowed her to minister to his wounds. Caroline knew from his stoic response to the stinging medicine that the cognac had numbed more than his hand. She tore the cloth into thin strips and carefully bound the wounds while he silently drained another glass.

So much had transpired in the time since she had retired for the night. If she'd been told as she prepared for bed that her opinion of the baron would make a complete turnabout by morning, she'd have laughed. Yet here she sat, full of nothing but compassion for a man who had defended her honor not once, but twice. For all intents and purposes, he was not the scoundrel or villain she'd been led to believe. His behavior had been triggered by schemes in which he was the pawn and victim. It was no longer any wonder to Caroline that he was distrustful. Now, after learning of his illegitimacy, he had all the more reason to turn his back on everyone.

With his thigh casually leaning against her knee, Caroline secured the last strip while a decision formed in her mind. Merrick would no longer be alone. She would confess her sin against him, tell him of her charade. Then she prayed he would understand her explanation, that she'd done it to save his son.

He'd been unaware of the finished work to his hand until she gently moved it back onto his lap, gaining his attention. "Merrick, I want you to know that no matter what . . . misunderstandings we've had, I'm here to be your friend. But in order to set things right, I want you to know something—"

"I'm leaving here," Merrick said blankly, his immediate attention fogged by the enormity of the deception that had been revealed to him.

"Here?"

"Schloss Hayden. It's nothing but a fabrication . . . all of it. You heard Louise. My mother was some forgotten servant. My so-called saintly father . . . took what he wanted from whatever maidservant was available. When I think of the pedestal I put that man on . . . I honestly believed he pined for my dead mother all those years. No wonder he didn't have affairs with the women of his class, his barbaric tastes were met by his own private brothel. I'm no more than an illegitimate bastard of the one woman who was lucky enough to bear my father a son.

"If only I'd known, I could've forced myself on any one of the females in this household." Merrick's acerbic tone tore at Caroline's heart. "But dear father had such scruples. 'Son,' he'd said, 'when you have certain needs, be sure to satisfy them elsewhere and not with any of the domestics. It could pose a problem.' " Merrick scoffed. "How naive of me not to understand his meaning."

"You couldn't have known, Merrick."

"And so sits the thorn in my side. For as long as I live under this roof, I will feel the barb of deceit. This is no place to raise Peter. I want a fresh start for him."

"Where will you go?" Caroline held her breath in anxious anticipation of the words she longed to hear. But they didn't come.

"Schloss Hayden should go to Peter—my father owes him that much. Besides, selling it now would send warning to those who've tried to harm my son, alerting them to our move. I don't know where there is a safe place." He rose and went to refill his glass for a fourth time.

"May I make a suggestion?" Caroline asked to his velvet-robed back. Despite the events that had transpired, his broad, muscled shoulders were still squared and aristocratic. The truth of his tarnished lineage couldn't change the refined gentleman that stood before her.

"What is that, little one?" he asked, turning to come back to her side. Her nickname suddenly took on new meaning, stirring her with its endearment.

"Would you consider going back with me to Sebula, Pennsylvania? Or if that doesn't suit you—" she hurriedly added, hoping to persuade him, "—perhaps you could purchase vineyards near the south shore of Lake Erie."

"Go back to Sebula?" His midnight-blue gaze penetrated her for one long moment, awakening her senses to his nearness. It seemed as though every pore in her body poured out an intense energy, tingling her skin into a state of awareness unlike any she had ever experienced. "If I choose to leave tomorrow, would you willingly return before your baby is due and risk the embarrassment?"

Caroline looked down upon the swell of the pillow beneath the tie of her robe. "I was trying to tell you about that."

"That Bates is the father? I suppose I should have believed you, but then—"

She glanced up and laid her her hand on his left sleeve. The burgundy fabric of his robe caressed her palm. "You were right in doubting me. Bates is not the father. Please listen to me, Merrick." She felt the muscles tense beneath her fingers. "Promise me that you will not interrupt until I've finished with what I have to say." His dark eyes bore into her. *God help me,* she prayed fervently in silence, then begged aloud, "Promise me."

His face was emotionless as he braced himself for yet another onslaught to his already tortured being. How could it get any worse? His mind ran through the scandalous facts he'd learned. And now he wondered—had his father tricked him into believing that the prearranged marriage would create a gifted patriarch? Could it all have been simply to keep Elena from becoming the baroness?

* * *

Caroline's pleading voice brought him back to the present. He slowly focused once again on her serious green eyes, deepened to the color of moss. Her beauty captivated his soul, revealing to him that which he'd known all along— Caroline was his intended.

"Merrick? Will you promise to listen?"

"Yes," he said. Though a small, still voice in the back of his mind whispered an inexplicable warning, he settled against the tufted back of the settee.

Caroline straightened her spine for courage and drew a deep breath. The lamp behind her on the far wall created a striking silhouette of her face, displaying the fine lines of her forehead, nose, and mouth. How could he have ever thought she was like Ilse? Caroline's soft, natural beauty far outshone her sister's and he found his loins stirring to this new insight as he listened to her words.

"When I came here," she began, "I knew no more about you than I did when you first came to Sebula six years ago. I had no way of knowing—or understanding—all of the things that motivated you to be as you were. When Ilse carried on during her delivery, I wasn't certain whether it was delirium or truth that she spoke. All I knew was that she was my sister, my flesh and blood."

Caroline turned to Merrick, tears stinging the back of her eyes. Worrying her lower lip, she shook her head then confessed. "I swear to you that I only meant to fulfill my promise to Ilse. I didn't mean to hurt you, Merrick. Believe me, I didn't. You were there. You nodded your approval when Ilse asked me to make my promise to her. But later when I broached the subject of taking Peter to the safety of America, you rescinded! I had no choice but to go behind your back. I didn't want to, but you left me no choice . . ." She gave up her efforts to hold the tears at bay and dissolved into choking sobs. "After you threw Ilse's Bible into her grave, how could I not think of you as the worst of enemies?"

Merrick stood up and paced the floor, waiting for the full impact of her confession as her crying abated. "Just exactly what are you trying to tell me?"

Caroline rose to her feet, gathering every ounce of courage she could muster to face him. "I laid out a plan to disguise myself in the various stages of pregnancy until I could have Peter kidnapped. Then I'd planned to leave here before my time was due, giving the excuse that I felt superstitious about Ilse's death. After I was safely away, I was going to meet with the kidnapper, discard my padding, and claim Peter was mine, born after the imaginary attack by Bates in Sebula."

Her long-winded confession was finally out, but Caroline still held her breath, waiting for Merrick's response. If luck was on her side, his liquored state would serve her well, further numbing his mind to the harsh reality of her truth.

Silence filled the room for a seemingly endless passage of time. Slowly she began to hope that her prayer had been heard. But then her eyes saw the twitch in his jaw. Her senses felt his anger begin to boil. Like all the others, she had betrayed him. But they were not alone with him at this moment to know the full extent of his wrath. It was only she who stood before him to suffer his revenge.

Like a violent storm, Merrick's scorn struck viciously. With a quickness that belied his slightly inebriated state, he reached across to her sash and yanked it free. The pillow fell to the floor as his hands grabbed at the front panels of her yellow flannel gown and ripped it wide, sending buttons flying. He shoved the material off her shoulders, leaving it there to imprison her arms so she couldn't cover her nakedness as he appraised her firm, flat belly.

Shamed more for her lie than her nudity, Caroline hung her head, her mahogany curls veiling the tears that came of their own accord. But a moment later, her sobs were cut off by his hands once again upon her. He stripped her gown away, drawing her attention up. In the time that she'd dropped her gaze, he'd shed his own robe. As he gripped her arms, the spark of rage in those midnight-blue depths told her his intentions. With the bed only a few feet behind her, he marched her backwards two steps and dropped her onto the downy mattress.

Caroline felt the heat of his body against her as panic seized her. His knee crashed between her thighs with a painful blow and spread her legs wide.

She closed her eyes tight and pleaded, "Don't Merrick. Please, dear God, stop. I'm sorry, Merrick. I'm so sorry." Her sobs broke her words. "I didn't want it to turn out like this. Don't do something we'll both regret." His hands held her wrists near her head, pinning her hair against the quilt so that every movement sent stabs of pain through her scalp. But she knew that the agony could not equal that yet to come if Merrick had his way. Her body writhed beneath him in an effort to escape his hardened manhood as it prodded for entrance.

"Can't you see—I told you because I didn't want to lie to you anymore. I didn't want to take Peter from you. I couldn't go through with it."

But her babbling pleas fell on deaf ears as Merrick's blind rage sought to extract the ultimate price for her treason. Her most valuable possession would be his.

Disregarding the houseful of servants, Caroline let out a desperate scream. "Please—Merrick. No—"

Chapter 10

As Caroline's pleas slowly found their way into his sodden, tortured brain, Merrick felt his whole being teetering on the edge of a black abyss of damnation. His carnal desire fought violently to drive him over, to plunge his flesh into her full ripe body. He hovered over her, his arousal poised at her moist entrance. Suddenly, her distraught scream jolted his senses, yanking him back as the very fires of hell flared up from the bottomless pit.

Realizing his repulsive mistake, he rolled off Caroline and leapt from the bed, leaving her to snatch the sheet to cover her nakedness. Raking his fingers through his dark thatch of hair, he turned away from the sight of her only to have her convulsive sobs brand his soul for the bastard he was.

"Mein Gott," he swore under his ragged breath. "What have I done?"

Frantic knocks hammered on the other side of the closed door, followed by Frau Krumhauer's loud, anxious voice asking, *"Fräulein, was ist los?"*

Merrick bellowed back, *"Gehen Sie weg!"*—Go away! His

command was followed only by the relentless sound of Caroline's crying. It seared through him as if the inferno he'd narrowly escaped had come back to engulf him, and well it should. She'd tried to tell him that she couldn't go through with the kidnapping. Her charade had worked thus far, he reasoned, there was no reason for her to come forward other than the one she had claimed—she honestly did not want to hurt him. His mind chastised his barbarous revenge when she had only meant to set things right. Now it was his turn to do the same, to correct his mistake—if she would let him.

After he slipped back into the torn robe, Merrick slowly moved around the end of the bed, making his way to the side where Caroline lay curled in a tight ball. Her fists were clenched tight around the edge of the sheet as she held it to her collarbone. Shutting out the world around her, she'd buried her face into the pillow. Her creamy white shoulders jerked with the motion of her sobs.

Condemning himself all the more, Merrick knotted the velvet sash with a firm yank, eliciting a sharp pain from his bandaged hand. He almost welcomed the self-inflicted punishment as he knelt on one knee next to the bed and drew the quilt up to protect her from the chill in the room.

"Please forgive me, Carrie," he asked of her, remorse filling his gentle plea. "So much has happened tonight. The lies. The deceit. In times past, I've stood strong against my share of adversity, to the point that I thought I could endure anything—until now. I was confused and hurt and angry. I suppose the cognac didn't help . . . Still—there is no excuse for what I've done to you."

Caroline grew quiet, listening to his apology. Yet she still kept her face turned away, unable to bring herself to look up into his eyes, afraid of what she might see. For she already knew from the sound of his voice that he hated himself for his fierce revenge. If she were to gaze into those midnight-blue depths and find a reflection of the pain in her own heart, she'd surely draw him into her arms and finish what had begun in violence. Though her tears of humiliation stemmed from his angry form of punishment, she bore just as much guilt for the words that had escaped her lips, now echoing in her mind.

I didn't want it to turn out like this, she'd cried, admitting to herself that she truly wanted him but not in this cruel, heartless way. She wanted to be able to freely give herself to him, to be loved completely and tenderly.

If he had come to her bed in any other way, she knew without a doubt that she'd have shamelessly welcomed him, despite the consequences of losing herself to a man who'd never declared his love. Had Merrick understood the full meaning behind her words? Had his pain-wracked brain comprehended her desire for him?

The touch of his hand on her head startled her, causing her to instinctively back away. He moved into the narrow strip of space she'd vacated, sitting next to her much like he'd done when he'd first come into her room. When he stroked her tousled hair away from her face, she opened her eyes and gave him a furtive glance.

His own ebony locks were somewhat disheveled, but in a way that added to the lost and pained expression that lined his face. Just as she expected, his deep blue eyes were dulled with anguish and her heart went out to him. She slowly turned onto her back and looked up at him, fighting the urge to reach up and touch his beard-darkened chin with her fingertips. He was so like Ghebellino after the sorrel had lashed out in anger and then returned to the one who had hurt him.

New tears flowed at her memory of the majestic animal standing proud on the rise of the embankment. For here was Merrick, calmed yet nowhere close to proud as his head hung over hers.

"Please don't cry, little one," he said, stroking her mahogany curls. "What happened here tonight will never happen again. As long as you remain in my company, I promise that your future husband will not be cheated from his rightful due. I swear I will not threaten you again."

Caroline could only nod, realizing that he'd not only misread the meaning of her words but that he'd clearly declared his lack of interest in her. His shame was merely in his attempt to steal her virginity from some man she'd yet to meet, some husband who'd claim her as his property in order to take what would then be his rightful due. How naive of her to think that this man of German aristocracy, this man ten years her senior could possibly have wanted her! It was obvious from his statement that to him she was still the little backwoods girl in pigtails, a fact that stung her deeply.

Merrick gazed down into Caroline's face, his usual keen perception dulled by the cognac as well as by the countless mind-jarring facts he was forced to accept. In his present state, he attributed the hurt look darkening her green eyes to his brutal introduction to what should have been a gentle coupling of two lovers. With this memory to haunt her, he knew he'd ruined her, albeit not in the tangible sense. But he'd shattered something in her that was far more more fragile—that delicate emotion of intimate yearning. After what he'd done, it was unlikely that she'd look upon her marital bed with anything but dread and fear.

Perhaps she would someday find it in her heart to forgive him, but he doubted that he'd ever forgive himself. Suddenly the pain of deceit from all those he loved and trusted couldn't compare to the emptiness created by his own vengeance. He was the one who had taken all but the physical evidence of Caroline's innocence and now he wanted—no, he *needed* to be the one to restore it.

Silently, Merrick made a solemn pledge. *I will make it up to you, little one. But solely on your terms. I will treat you as you should be treated. And I will keep my promise to stay away until there shall be a day that you would come to me of your own accord. If that day should never come, then I will accept your choice as my punishment and pray that someone you so well deserve will show you the tenderness that you need.*

If he stayed any longer, Merrick knew he'd reveal more than Caroline was ready to accept, further alienating her before he had an opportunity to win her trust. He sensed from her limited knowledge of the gifts that his vow could be misunderstood as a threat to manipulate her mind for his own satisfaction. She had yet to learn that her strong spirit could never be coerced into doing anything against her will. He rose from the bed and turned toward the door.

"Merrick?"

His heart caught at the tentative, non-condemning tone of her voice. "Yes?" he said, looking back upon her. Gone was the boyishly tough adolescent of yesteryear. In her place was a fully rounded woman whose generous curves created a stirring deep in his loins. He let his eyes rest upon hers and fought without success to take his mind off the silken body that lay hidden beneath the quilts. His self-imposed promise would be hard to keep if he continued to entertain the thoughts taunting the more primitive, carnal reaches of his soul.

Caroline spoke and Merrick noticed for the first time the seductively low pitch to her voice. It had a quiet, almost musical quality about it. "When you came in," she began, "and asked about my dreams, you already knew about the man, didn't you?"

"I had sensed you were in trouble. But I'd hoped it was only from a nightmare." Her brows drew together as she looked at him with a curious gaze. There was more she had to learn but now was not the time. Merrick shrugged. "Unfortunately, I was wrong."

"Thank you for . . . coming to my aid."

His chin lifted in a nonverbal acceptance, masking his surprise at her open appreciation. Caroline's remarkable ability to look beyond herself was a gift divinely bestowed.

As Merrick started to leave, his attention was drawn to the

damaged yellow gown at his feet. He slowly leaned over and gathered up the garment, then reverently laid it at the foot of her bed. His fingers hesitated on the soft flannel.

"I will replace the gown," he said, without looking up.

"There's really no need. It'll take but a few minutes to sew the buttons back on. I haven't much else to do except to replace the pillow stuffing now that I no longer need it."

Merrick glanced at the colorful array of limp throw cushions on the settee and a half-smile tilted one corner of his mouth. "You're very clever."

"Thank you . . . Your Excellency."

Inwardly, he flinched at the return to formality, yet he deserved the distance it created. "But don't be so eager to repair the pillows. Come down to breakfast as you always have."

"With the padding?"

"I'm willing to continue your charade if you are. It's quite ingenious and I think it's the best chance we have of smuggling Peter out of Germany." Merrick wished there was a way to convince the entire church that Peter was not a gifted child to be exalted or feared. But doing so would take an act of God. For they would never believe the truth, calling it a weak attempt to save the little boy. And now there was Countess Reinhart with greed as her motivation to stalk them.

"Where will we . . . you . . . go?"

Merrick shook his head, the smile now gone. "I haven't thought that far yet. After tonight I'd just as soon pack my bags and leave for South Africa if it were not for Peter." *And you,* his mind added as he bid her good night and left her room.

The next day, Caroline slipped shyly into her dining chair well after Merrick had given up waiting for her and had begun his morning meal of bratwurst and eggs. In the light of day, her lowered lids and pink cheeks disclosed a remnant of her embarrassment from their shared intimacy—however unsatisfying it'd been.

In flagrant disregard for her own code of duties, Frau Krumhauer herself emerged from the kitchen and waited on the young fräulein with a display of protective clucking that was meant to indirectly shame Merrick. It was clear that the cook assumed the master of the house had taken advantage of the poor unwed mother.

The baron spoke impatiently to the portly woman. "Your duties do not extend to pampering my guest, Alfreda. Shouldn't you be taking care of my son?"

"Lottie's feeding him in the kitchen and there's a guard outside the door," she explained with a stretch of her politeness. As she passed by him, her glower spoke volumes, but he wasn't about to clarify the events that had transpired between him and Caroline, who sat quietly observing his irritation.

He met her gaze, thinking of how lovely she looked with the rosy glow of her blush. Her dark curls were gathered away from her face and caught up with a ribbon that matched her maternity gown of royal blue, leaving the rest of her shining hair to cascade over the broad lace collar that graced her neckline. Merrick couldn't help but imagine for just one moment that she was actually carrying a child—his child—and that the night before held a sweeter memory for both him as her husband and her as his wife.

Across the long expanse of the dining table, Merrick and Caroline remained locked in their study of one another for several long moments. Conrad's entrance broke the curious spell when he came to ask about clearing up the matter of Louise and the intruder. Merrick was visibly disturbed—as much from the interruption as from the reason for it.

"Fräulein Hartmann and I have some . . . business to discuss in my study, then I will see them separately. Bring Louise first, in say—" Merrick withdrew his watch from his pocket and flipped it open. "—one hour," he said, snapping the timepiece shut and pocketing it.

"Yes, Your Excellency."

Caroline carefully sipped her steaming coffee, eyeing the baron over the gold-leafed rim as the butler clicked his heels and departed. The entire staff was behaving strangely and, regretfully, she knew why. Once again she was the subject of humiliation for something she hadn't done, only now it seemed that a generous dose of pity had been thrown in. Merrick, on the other hand, appeared to have slipped a notch. She refused to believe that his servants would disrespect him for his newly revealed lack of blue blood. The baron was too much the essence of a true gentleman to lose such honor. It was more than likely her cry in the night that had brought their scorn, especially when the logical assumption would have been that he'd had his drunken way with her.

Merrick fumbled to cut the sausage, but the thick bandages around his injured hand thwarted his efforts and the knife clattered to the plate, drawing Caroline's startled attention. As he sighed in disgust, she waited for a maid to come hurrying in from the kitchen. But when no one came, she pushed her chair back.

Merrick's eyes looked up questioningly as she came to his side and took the utensils in hand. Without a word, she set about cutting the meat into bite-size pieces while he settled back and watched her in awe.

When she'd finished, she put down the knife and fork and started to return to her place, but Merrick caught her wrist before she took a step. He followed her gaze as she looked down to his dark fingers wrapped lightly around her white lace cuff, then those moss-green eyes lifted and his heart sank. Like an abused puppy that dared not rile her master's ire for fear of further cruelty, Caroline's humble manner disquieted his nerves more than if she'd angrily presented herself as an embittered victim of his wrath. At least with Ilse he'd had practice dealing with haughty, screaming epithets, but this display of humility left him shamefaced and speechless.

"Thank you," he finally managed to murmur.

Her melodious voice held only the gentlest of meanings. "You're quite welcome, Your Excellency."

The middle of December grew colder, though not as frigid as Caroline had thought it would be. Although this region of the German Empire was much farther north than Pennsylvania, the Black Forest—with its woods and ravines and quiet nooks in the mountain slopes—was known for its mild winters. Her ever-growing knowledge of her father's homeland, however, did little to warm her in the centuries-old stone house. The snow still fell and the drafts still chilled her to the bone.

Rarely had Caroline ventured out, except on *Totensonntag* —Remembrance Day—a few weeks earlier. At Ilse's grave, which had been covered with evergreen twigs to protect the new ivy from the winter frosts, Caroline had stood by while Merrick placed a wreath of evergreens and flowers. During the whole of the somber outing, snowflakes had drifted down from the heavens and Merrick had spoken not one word of his mission, choosing instead to keep their conversation to a minimum of polite exchanges. But when he had assisted Caroline into the carriage and tucked the heavy blankets around her, she'd seen his red-rimmed eyes and felt his pain.

When they had returned that day, Merrick had escorted Caroline into his study where he kept the room well heated for his long hours at his desk. Though he was accustomed to the cold drafts of his childhood home, he knew she was not. It was then he'd insisted that she consider his study open to her to use as a comfortable sitting room.

With Louise banished, under guard, to the baron's estate in England and the hired thug marshalled off to prison on a variety of long-standing warrants, Caroline had free reign of the house, especially the nursery. It was there she could often be found, relieving Frau Krumhauer—however reluctantly —of her duties. Though still small, Peter was growing quickly under the affectionate care of the many who adored him, not the least of whom was Lottie.

The fire crackled in the nursery's hearth while the wet nurse rocked the babe at her breast and Caroline worked diligently over a tiny yellow gown, embroidering an intricate white pattern around the neckline. Hearing the greedy sucking, she paused and watched the child. A faint envy tugged deep in her belly, prompting her to unconsciously smooth her hand across the thick padding that simulated her fifth month.

Though she'd intended to stay until Peter had reached a safe traveling age of twelve weeks, when Merrick had broached the topic in his study a month ago, he'd suggested she wait for a longer period of time. Together, they'd worked out more details—including the need for Lottie's unsuspecting cooperation.

Merrick had been receptive to the idea of Lottie being the likely kidnapper, but not so to the idea of making America their destination. It had taken Caroline's stubborn persuasiveness to convince him that settling among the primarily German population of Pennsylvania would not only provide opportunity for Peter to learn the German way but would also provide the security of being far removed from the Continent. The rationale was sound. Merrick knew he'd be forced to leave everything behind—at least for several years until Peter was grown—so their journey's end would have to prove lucrative for their livelihood, as well. Thus it had finally been settled. For the culmination of their kidnapping scheme, Merrick would buy a parcel of land near the south shore of Lake Erie to cultivate into vineyards.

Because he had needed a fair amount of time to procure the needed funds without attracting suspicion, Caroline had agreed to stay an extra two months. The extension, she now knew while watching Peter nurse, was good for all of them. The baby would be stronger in the warmer weather. Lottie would be more attached to him and thus more cooperative.

And Caroline, with her kidnapping secret no longer a cause of tension between her and Merrick, was content to let their plan unfold. Even Merrick's dark mood had lifted.

True to his word, he hadn't threatened her in any way over the last several weeks. In fact, he had behaved faultlessly as a gentleman of high breeding, with kind compliments and eager offerings of assistance. His attentiveness had not gone unnoticed by his staff, either. Their scorn had turned to profound confusion, then slowly transformed into a lighter amusement.

If it hadn't been for the charade she and Merrick shared, Caroline might have toyed with the thought that she was being courted. But when her eyes looked disdainfully upon the rounding figure she was getting from her forced appetite, she saw nothing attractive about her present condition.

When Peter had had his fill, Caroline put down her work. "May I hold him?" she asked, then glimpsed a flicker of reluctance as the girl passed the warm bundle into Caroline's arms. Her smile spread wide when she cast her eyes upon his tiny face. No longer did he have Ilse's golden-red curls. In eight short weeks, the downy hair had gradually turned to a soft chestnut brown. The change hadn't surprised Caroline—though it had Merrick—for she'd often heard her mother tell of Ilse's jet-black hair at birth that had turned blond by the time she was six months old.

Peter's eyes had darkened considerably as well. There was no question of Merrick's fatherhood in those deep blue depths. Caroline cooed and played with the little boy, all the while wishing she could remain with him in America yet knowing her dreams were futile.

"If you don't mind, I'll go to my room now," Lottie said with a tinge of curtness from jealousy, pulling Caroline back from her musing. The wet nurse had moved into a room down the hall shortly after Merrick had approved of the scheme to include Lottie in their plot, though the servant still knew nothing of it.

"That'll be fine, Lottie. As soon as I change him I think I'll take him down to the study."

The younger girl nodded, forcing a smile. "I'm sure his papa would like a visit," she offered, then turned to leave.

"Lottie?"

"*Ja?*"

"I know you love Peter very much but . . . if you become too attached to him . . . it'll only make it difficult for you . . ."

"*Ja,*" Lottie responded dejectedly, continuing in her native tongue. "Once he is weaned, he won't need me anymore. It'll be hard to say good-bye. He needs a good mother."

"Don't you think Frau Krumhauer is doing well by him?"

The diminutive wet nurse cocked one eyebrow as she leaned over the cooing baby. "She's the cook. And she's old. I'm still young enough to raise Peter *and* give His Excellency several more."

While Caroline fought to control her shock from the girl's casual solution to Peter's motherlessness, she struggled to deny yet another set of feelings. She had expected—in fact, anticipated—Lottie's strong bonding to the infant. But she'd never dreamed the adolescent would wish to lay claim to the baron himself! The idea of Merrick taking the wet nurse as his wife, or simply as a lover was absurd. However, Caroline couldn't ward off the intense possessiveness that gripped her. Could she actually convince Lottie to kidnap Peter, then escape with them to America, only to discover herself back in Sebula while the wet nurse took up residence with Merrick? As always, the answer fell back on her loyalty to Ilse, to her family . . . and to Peter. She would do anything to ensure her nephew's safety.

When Merrick heard the door of his study open, he looked up from his ledgers, then dismissed his secretary—a wiry, bespectacled man of about the baron's own age. The two had been deep in their work for hours but Merrick was suddenly refreshed as he took in the sight before him. Caroline held his son to her shoulder, cradling his dark head with one hand while his bulky diapered bottom perched on her other forearm. A multicolored crib quilt was tucked about him, which Caroline dropped onto a chair as she passed it. Merrick glanced at her padded belly and smiled wide, as much at the wiggling baby toes as at her expanding disguise. His gaze drifted down to where her blue velvet skirt swirled about her ankles, hiding her long legs from view but not from his imagination. Though he eagerly took Peter from her, Merrick was hard pressed to know whose company he enjoyed more—his son's or Caroline's.

The last few weeks had been a true test of restraint. Each night as he passed her door he was tempted almost beyond endurance to enter and profess love for her. And each night he fought the battle with a measured amount of wine to bring on sleep, only to dream of holding her in his arms. Yet he never again dared to drink too heartily, as the night he'd let the cognac undermine his self-control was still painfully vivid.

Until he could sway her heart, until Caroline came to him willingly, he had to suffice with these unexpected visits on safer ground than her bed chambers.

"How is my boy doing today?" Merrick asked Peter in his accented English. It was only in Caroline's presence that he refrained from his native tongue, in deference to her as well as to teach Peter the language as he grew. "Would you like Caroline to play for you?"

Merrick winked at Caroline's puzzled look.

"Oh, look, *Pay-ter*," he said, using the German form of the boy's name as he was accustomed. Merrick stood and headed for the far end of the room. "Papa's bought you *another* toy. How shameless of me. But you're too young to use it yet. So maybe *Tante* Carrie could entertain us instead."

There on the other side of the enormous study, to Caroline's delighted surprise, stood a magnificent grand piano.

"How could I have not seen it when I came in?" she asked herself aloud. But she knew. Even if the door hadn't blocked her view of that side of the room, Caroline wouldn't have paid any notice. With Merrick's mesmerizing eyes fixed on his son in her arms, she wouldn't have noticed if an elephant had been standing behind her.

She raced over to the elegant instrument and glided her hand over the dark, rich walnut. Once when she'd mentioned that this corner of his study seemed bare, Merrick had told her that Ilse hated the grand piano that had always stood there, and she'd ordered it removed to the attic.

"It's so beautiful. Ours at home was . . . is an upright."

"I know." Merrick sat on one end of the bench with Peter in his arms and, with a nod, motioned her to sit also.

"But why did you do this?" She lowered her voice in conspiracy. "Especially when we'll be leaving in such a short time."

"Because it was time my son learned to appreciate music," he answered with a boyish cockiness tilting the corners of his full lips. The deep midnight-blue of his eyes seemed to twinkle with starlight.

Perched on the edge of the bench, Caroline lifted the fallboard to reveal a glistening line of ivory keys. Overcome with awe, she pressed her palms to her cheeks. She wasn't certain which delighted her more—the splendid beauty of the piano or its unexpected appearance.

In the past few weeks, Merrick had been full of surprises, this being the greatest of many. His first had been a flat box tied with a lavender satin ribbon that she'd found on her bed shortly after that fateful night in her room. When she'd lifted the lid and drawn back the white tissue, her heart leapt at the sight of the pale pink gown, its silk luxurious to the touch. His attentiveness went on to range from hothouse roses that had mysteriously appeared on her bedside table one morning, to a gift of sweets, to each of the maternity dresses that she'd discovered time and again hanging in her ward-robe.

"Aren't you going to enchant us?" Merrick asked, draw-ing Caroline out of her thoughtfulness. He shifted Peter to the crook of one elbow as he leaned his other forearm on the ledge above the keyboard, a move that afforded him a pleas-ingly full view of her beautiful face.

"Yes, of course." Caroline dropped her hands to her lap and vigorously rubbed them until her palms were warm. She raised her fingers to the keys, then flexed them several times to relax the muscles that hadn't been used in such a way for several long months. With a strong set to her chin, she glanced at tiny contented Peter, then at Merrick. Her twin-kling green eyes teased his patience unmercifully until he was ready to march playfully away in disinterest. Yet he knew he could never pull his gaze away from the dancing emerald-green eyes, a sight he cherished more each time he watched her face light up with joy at his gifts.

"Well—I hope my lack of practice doesn't show too much," she said, then began a Schumann concerto she had committed to memory years before, sending the clear reso-nant notes throughout the study.

It only took a moment for her soul to be caught up in the music and her lids drifted closed as she allowed the muse within her to take control.

Merrick watched in awe, overcome with a wondrous rev-erence for her talent and for the way in which her entire body seemed to transform, becoming one with the melody that flowed through her.

Even little Peter was affected. When his wiggling fingers caught Merrick's attention, his father smiled down on him. With eyes open wide in fascination, Peter listened to the delightfully moving sound of music for the first time in his young life.

And so began the afternoon sessions per Merrick's polite request—"for the baby's education." Silly as it seemed to perform for an infant, Caroline enjoyed the music as much as Peter and his father. Oftentimes, in the evening after dinner, Merrick lightheartedly coaxed her to play, even though he knew she didn't need to be asked. In reality, he'd have to lock the door to keep her from playing.

With Christmas approaching quickly, Caroline ushered in the season with spirit-filled Yuletide carols, warming the hearts of all the residents of Schloss Hayden. Yet, despite the gay atmosphere, she felt a gnawing pang of homesickness descend upon her as Christmas grew near. Even Merrick's efforts to cajole her had little effect, though his sincere attempts hadn't gone unnoticed—as on the morning of December sixth. Caroline had come down for breakfast to find on the cushion of her chair a pair of her slippers filled with candies, nuts, and many other good things to eat. Merrick had remembered the sixth as the traditional red-letter day for German children. When she was a little girl, Caroline had also eagerly set out her shoes the evening before and awakened to find them as overflowing as her slippers. But her childhood memory of the delectable chocolates held no comparison to the ones from Merrick, perhaps because she was old enough to appreciate the rare gift, or perhaps because of the gift-bearer. She couldn't be sure.

Shaking off the thoughts of childhood, Caroline refolded a letter from her mother and placed it atop the others, retying them with the slender lavender ribbon she'd saved from Merrick's first gift box. She rose from the tufted settee and placed the small bundle in the top bureau drawer next to her mother's Bible. Ilse's diary lay alongside, no longer buried away from sight, though yet to be seen by Merrick's eyes. Caroline still vacillated between giving it to him—which served no purpose other than to torment him with more of Ilse's accusations—or to keep it, which lent to an illusion of distrust. Either way, she couldn't avoid hurting Merrick all the more. She fingered the ribbon around the letters, her feelings for Merrick clouded for the moment by the despair of missing her parents.

Slowly, she closed the drawer and smoothed the lush red nap of velvet that hung in folds over her padding. Merrick seemed taken with this choice of warm fabric; he'd had five different gowns made of the material—a fact that made Caroline immensely grateful during the cold winter, though she chided him privately for wasting his money on clothes she'd wear but a few months only to discard when their ruse was over.

Making her way along the second floor to join Merrick downstairs for the holiday evening dinner, Caroline could no longer see her toes over the awkward swell of her false belly. Forever mindful of her feigned condition, she purposely took longer to descend the stairs, all the while thinking of her parents and how they'd have disapproved of her plot and the same of her misshapen figure.

Thoughts of her mother's last letter added more loneliness. Again, her mother had lamented the mysterious reasons behind Caroline's extended stay in Germany. And again she'd begged her daughter to come home in time for Christmas. Caroline envisioned the few lumbermen without families to visit gathered around their upright piano, bellowing the rafters down around everyone's ears. Her mind wandered to them sitting down at the pine table for oyster stew—their traditional Christmas Eve meal. Then she remembered that it would be several more hours before night would come to their part of the world.

Their part of the world. Caroline had been gone nearly three months and already she'd begun to slip with little words that divided her past from her present as if she was no longer a part of Sebula. The thought brought a catch to her throat that she quickly swallowed back as she saw Merrick emerge from his study, shrugging into his black, high-buttoned frock coat. Contrasted against the formal white shirt, his forest-green brocade vest lent itself well to the gaiety of the season, though it was the closely tailored fit against his lean, muscular frame that set Caroline's heart thumping beneath her breast.

At that moment, Merrick caught a glimpse of her and faltered, an unconscious move that made Caroline drop her gaze, though she wasn't certain why. To save him embarrassment? To save her own? In the condition she presented, she could never be sure if his occasional lapse into awkwardness was due to her startlingly bloated appearance or his possible misgivings about the charade. No, Merrick would never let such a thing disturb his cool facade. Yet, there was no denying the times she felt his eyes upon her, then heard him swear under his breath as he burned his finger lighting a lamp or bungled something equally as simple.

He stepped forward to the base of the stairway, blocking her path before her slippered foot could touch the polished floor. She paused on the first tread as he perused his latest purchase for the holiday festivities. His dark eyes took in the simple lines of the red velvet dress all the way to the hem, then back to her belly, lingering for a moment before wandering up to meet her gaze.

"Do you approve of your acquisition, Your Excellency?"

He reached up and gently touched one of several wisps of hair she'd curled about her face and neck. The rest of her mahogany curls were looped and coiled atop the crown of her head, maturing her soft features. "Most wholeheartedly, little one," he murmured affectionately for only her to hear as he stepped aside and held up one elbow to escort her to dinner.

Slipping her fingers around his arm, she took in his elegant handsomeness in the silk shirt and black coat and trousers. Then came a familiar flutter deep inside, stirring her senses, and suddenly the drafty entrance hall was overly warm.

Merrick cupped his hand over hers, drawing her eyes to meet his as they walked the short distance to the dining salon. "I am sorry you feel so all alone this Christmas."

Although Caroline was no longer surprised that he could read her moods, she still insisted upon denying their mutual ability. Her own gift seemed specially tuned to Merrick. She had come to know the moment she awoke what sort of day it would be before she even set eyes on him over the morning meal.

Raising her voice in conjured cheerfulness, Caroline replied to Merrick's statement of fact with a quick denial. "I am not alone. I have Peter and Lottie and Frau Krumhauer and—" She glanced at the expectant look in his dark eyes.

"I was hoping that my name was in there."

"Oh—it is. Somewhere," she teased. "Down in some dark cave . . . lost."

He directed his eyes straight ahead, his strong chin jutting out in a mocking gesture. Then, just as they reached the double oak doors, he looked at her askance and spoke with a seriousness that sent a tingle down her spine. "I fear it is not just my name which has been lost to you, little one," he said, and opened the door.

The voices of a room full of people happily shouted, "Merry Christmas, Fräulein Hartmann!" Caroline gasped in surprise. Around the table stood most of those she'd come to know beyond the forbidden barriers of station, her only friends in this foreign country—Frau Krumhauer and her husband, son, and daughter. The daughter's large family had come as well, though Caroline could only count four youthful faces. Perhaps the smaller ones had been kept quiet out in the kitchen until after the surprise. Lottie had conveniently positioned herself next to the baron's chair. Even Conrad had taken a place at the table. All of them were dressed in their best clothes—quite new from their appearance, prompting Caroline to wonder if Merrick had secured a private clothier full time to fill this tall order.

Merrick nodded for them to sit down, and led Caroline over to her chair. After pulling it out, he watched her lower herself to the cushion, noticing how she added a bit of awk-

wardness to her movement. His taut jaw muscle did little to
hide the smile he fought to hold at bay. When he looked up,
he found most of the staff observing his interested appraisal
of the young mother, and he became slightly annoyed. Never
had he felt under so much scrutiny but then, never had he
invited his servants to join him. This was a breach of protocol, but he'd hoped the crowded table and chatter of friends
would ease Caroline's longing to be with her family.

Ignoring their amused stares, Merrick scanned the faces
and asked nonchalantly in German, "Where is Peter?"

"Right here," Frau Krumhauer piped up, gesturing behind
her. Merrick walked around the side of the table nearest the
wall and found his tiny son in a small basket behind the
cook's chair. "He's a good boy. All our noise and he doesn't
cry. He's more like his papa every day."

Merrick bent his tall frame over and scooped Peter into his
large hands. "This is his first Christmas and you leave him
down on the floor to stare at flocked wallpaper? Shame,
Alfreda. He should be allowed to enjoy it with the rest of
us." Following his teasing reprimand, he took his seat and
positioned the cooing Peter in the crook of his arm so his son
could look out upon the heavily laden table.

Two large white porcelain tureens of oyster stew anchored
each end of the fourteen foot white linen cloth. Between and
around the tureens sat assorted other platters, dishes of roast
beef and vegetables. Baskets of golden-brown rolls were covered with festive red cloths to hold their freshly-baked
warmth. On the sideboard, plates were piled high with the
customary dessert of soft and tempting *Pfefferkuchen,* with its
spicy gingerbread scent, and *Lebkuchen.* From both, stars,
hearts, and clover leaves had been cut and coated with chocolate or sugar icing. The children were not the only ones who
glanced longingly over to the sweets.

Protocol aside, Merrick decided, as he watched Caroline
accept a steaming bowl of the creamy stew, that he preferred
her acknowledging smile across the crowded table far more

than the quiet solemnity that would have surely prevailed if they'd eaten alone this night. *One day,* he said silently, *I will be happy when that smile is shared only between the two of us.*

Two months passed slowly but when the first day of March arrived, Caroline stood at the window, watching the deep black of the night sky lighten with the coming of dawn, and decided the time had slipped by in the wink of an eye. She'd hardly slept due to anxious anticipation of the events yet to unfold. With her trunks packed and waiting, the final stage of their kidnapping ploy was about to begin. In the next few hours, Caroline would have to give the most convincing performance of her life. Shortly thereafter, she would board a rented coach and leave Merrick's home forever.

Rivulets of spring rain traced paths down the beveled glass panes, distorting the view of the muddied, melting snow that still hung on as the last gasp of winter. The wet, rich soil and fresh-washed evergreens created a strong, heady scent that seemed to carry on the drafts circulating along the ancient stone walls. In the air, there was a feeling of beginning . . . rebirth.

Caroline sighed at the obvious focus of her train of thought—birth. This masquerade of pregnancy had become more than a donning of over-stuffed padding. It had become her very existence over the last four months, augmenting a maternal desire that had grown stronger with each passing day. How she wished that this bundle beneath her clothing was a real part of her! *And a part of Merrick.*

Her taunting inner voice infuriated her. She threw her palms to her forehead and whirled from the window. *Stop it! Stop pining for a man whom you cannot have. He's your sister's widower, for heaven's sake.* But the sharp edge of such reasoning had long since dulled, no longer torturing her with guilt for being drawn to the man once married to Ilse. Now that she'd lived in his midst, all of her hateful assumptions had lost most of their bitter sting.

Weighted down by the cumbersome disguise, Caroline walked awkwardly over to the bedside table and picked up Ilse's diary. Smoothing her fingertips over the gold-leaf letters, she remembered a time when she'd wondered if the accusations within were truth.

No more did she doubt Merrick's denial of those lies.

For the sake of their kidnapping scheme, the two of them had settled into an amicable truce, a truce that—for Caroline —had developed into something more than a strong friendship. Her hidden feelings ran deeper, rooted in some mysterious recesses of her soul. Realizing this made it all the more difficult to go down to breakfast and face Merrick, for they both knew it would be the last time she would take her place at his table.

Caroline lowered the diary to the polished tabletop, then hesitated, her hand still touching the worn leather. Minutes passed while fleeting images of times long gone darted through her mind—dancing with Merrick on the ship, sharing his grief when they'd lost Ilse, feeling his emptiness at the shock of Louise's confession. After all they'd been through together, keeping the diary from Merrick now seemed wrong somehow. Although Ilse's slanderous statements were simply more of a long line of deceptions, withholding them created another secret to further taunt him.

"There will be no more secrets," Caroline vowed as she snatched the book back and pressed it to her breast. Closing her eyes, she muttered a quick prayer for strength, then blinked wide.

The diary in one hand, Caroline checked her padding with the other, shifting the bulky kapok pad up slightly to alleviate a dull ache from the binding straps. Mindful of her off-balance stature, she thought for a second that perhaps she would be happy to be rid of the ponderous weight. But another thought immediately followed—too soon she would lose Peter, as well. She would be back home in Sebula without her nephew . . . and without Merrick.

Her heart twisted with regret as she nervously adjusted the blue wool draped over her voluminous belly, then moved slowly across the room to the door. Her fingers wrapped around the cold brass knob as she squared her shoulders and set her mind for the task at hand. Her wants . . . her desires . . . mattered not. What she was about to do was for Peter's sake. And absolutely nothing would stand in her way.

After stepping into the empty hallway, Caroline glanced down one last time and tightened her grip on her sister's diary, then drew the door closed behind her. The click of the latch falling into place seemed to echo with loud finality.

There was no turning back.

Chapter 11

"I don't give a damn anymore whose child you carry," Merrick said tersely. "You can't leave."

"I can and I will," Caroline countered in perfect German with well-rehearsed venom. Their feigned argument erupted just as one of the younger maids poured Merrick's coffee and the quiet girl's eyes darted back and forth between her master and his guest. She scurried off, but not before a quick whisper at the door to another maidservant carrying the breakfast tray.

Merrick noted the exchange, knowing their act would soon have at least half the staff listening beyond the portal that led to the kitchen's passageway. He sipped the scalding brew, then drew back with a curse and pursed his stinging lips. When his eyes came back upon Caroline at the far end of the table, he caught a glimpse of an amused look in her eyes. *The vixen,* he thought affectionately, *She dares to spoil our scene by laughing at me with those eyes.*

"You are too far along to risk traveling at this time, Caroline . . . especially alone. It's too dangerous and I won't permit it." He forced himself to appear angry, narrowing his eyes. If he hadn't known differently, he'd swear Caroline shuddered involuntarily.

"I beg to differ with you, Herr Baron," she spat. "But you do not own me." She dramatically thrust her left hand out in front of her, causing the servant to jump back. "Do you see a wedding band on this finger, Your Excellency? No—Neither you nor any other man speaks for me. I speak for myself. And I will not stay now that the highways are passable."

The servant stepped forward and quickly placed a plate in front of the fuming woman, fearful that the argument would intensify and bring on the young mother's labor.

The baron skidded back his chair and marched toward the two women. Although the maid retreated, Caroline remained stoically erect in her chair, her chin tilted high to meet his gaze.

Before he could reach the far end of the table, Frau Krumhauer burst into the dining room, having watched the baron's angry approach through the discreetly ajar door. Her rotund, aproned frame protectively blocked Caroline from Merrick's view. "If you wish to raise a hand to this girl once more, you will have to strike down this old woman first. I stood outside her room and wept the first time I heard the screams and I have been haunted by my weak-willed silence ever since. I won't stand by and let you abuse her again."

Merrick did his best not to smile openly at this maternal tirade.

"All these many years, Herr Baron," she continued in her caustic tone, yet with a sadness in her eyes, "I watched you grow up with Wil and prayed you'd not be the same as your father and mother."

"Hmph," he scoffed. "And which mother would that be?"

Frau Krumhauer gasped, taken aback at His Excellency's confrontational attitude.

"Ah—but it must be my honesty that startles you, for

which I apologize, Alfreda," he said sarcastically. "You knew my mother was one of the maids, didn't you?"

"The entire town knows," she snipped.

"Of course the entire town knows—now. But you knew all along."

Silence prevailed while Merrick and the old woman stared at one another. He should have ordered her out of the dining room the moment she'd boldly intervened. Why had he let his boiling caldron of bitterness rise up now?

Alfreda's pinched lips relaxed. "You were never anything less than a gentleman in my eyes, Your Excellency. There was a time when I'd hoped you'd become my son-in-law."

Merrick frowned at the touching confession, disarmed by the cook's sudden change. As with Caroline, who sat entranced by the unexpected confrontation, Merrick took in Alfreda's softened tone.

She shook her head solemnly. "Now—I don't know what's become of the young man I once knew. Never would I have believed you could purposefully hurt another, let alone strike a woman."

Merrick decided to put a stop to the cook's maudlin rambling, and—for the sake of the charade—he had to force himself to be brusque about it, despite her need for his compassion.

"Contrary to what you and the rest of the staff may assume, I did not bed this poor girl . . . neither before *or* after I brought her here. The scream you heard at her door was the result of my intoxicated anger that I unleashed upon her—with utmost regret, I assure you." He wanted to clear Caroline's name, even if he had to lie to do so. "I'd mistakenly accused her of trying to snare me as a husband in order to hide her . . . indiscretion from her parents and her child's father." It wasn't a complete fabrication. After all, his mind had come to that conclusion at one time.

Merrick turned aside and braced his hands on the high-backed chair adjacent to Caroline, hanging his head in dejection. Then he looked over one outstretched arm to gaze upon her silently. Her green eyes anxiously watched him unfold their story in a manner they hadn't planned.

Though his words were directed to Alfreda, his attention remained fixed on Caroline as he laid his confession before her, purging himself of his sins. "Yes, I hurt her . . . deeply. And humiliated her. I wish to God there was a way to rescind the damage I've done. But I did not bed her. Her condition is the result . . . of an attack. She is but an innocent victim. That is exactly why—" He straightened and faced Frau Krumhauer. "—I *refuse to let her leave.*"

Alerted by the underlying cue in Merrick's final, emphatic words, Caroline picked up his signal and launched them once again into the heated argument that would lead her out the door. "You will have to tie me down to stop me. I have enough time to reach Sebula before . . . before . . ."

Wisely, Frau Krumhauer stepped aside as Merrick cut off Caroline's stammering. "Before what?" he asked in German. "You can't bring yourself to *talk* about your baby. How do you think you'll fare when you show up on your parents' doorstep looking like this?" He gestured wildly toward the pronounced roundness of her belly, then turned to the two servants who cowered silently next to the sideboard. "Both of you may leave now." To Alfreda, he curtly added, "Rest assured I'll not strike her."

The cook pursed her lips and gave him a scrutinizing glare before glancing to Caroline to receive a nod from her. After the plump woman departed in a huff, Merrick and Caroline faced off in the dramatic climax of their final encounter.

"I'd much rather face my father's wrath than give birth to another bastard in this house," Caroline said loudly in German for the servants' listening ears. In spite of the fact that Merrick had insisted she say this for the benefit of all to hear, she knew it must have hurt. She wanted to tell him she was sorry but knew she couldn't back out now.

Merrick took her arm and pulled her up out of the chair. "You'll be lucky if your father lets you whelp in a stable."

She pulled away. "Anything would be better than here."

"See here, how do you know exactly when that baby will arrive? Look at what happened to Ilse!"

"Yes. *Look.*" As if overcome by another power greater than both of them, an unleashed anger sprang forth. She leaned awkwardly around the corner of the table, reaching to the chair on her left. "Here. *Read* what Ilse wrote." She flung her hand out, presenting him with the diary. "Then you tell *me* what happened to my sister!"

Accepting it with disinterest, Merrick dropped his arm back to his side, studying the confusing, volatile transformation in Caroline as she raged on, now in English.

"I wouldn't say Ilse was sweet and innocent but she wasn't the same after she came here."

She fumbled out from behind the table and pushed past him, lost in thought. Her voice rose. "She became so . . . vicious and spiteful and—afraid."

"Caroline—" Merrick followed a step, trying to draw her back but her green eyes were glazed. A warning formed in his mind. *Let her speak. Listen to her.*

"Louise was right," she went on. "If I stay here, the countess will get to me somehow . . . I don't know how. But she'll find a way.

"And if the *servants* assumed this baby was yours," she said, gesturing to her swollen stomach, "then Elena and the rest of the devil-worshipers may come to that conclusion as well."

"But Peter is the one they think of as the gifted child . . . the child of the covenant."

"Not if Louise let her suspicions be known. She sensed there was a difference about me . . . that I have gifts like you. You heard her say that Peter is *not* that child, that Ilse was not the right daughter? She even implied that it was supposed to have been me. I am the one you should have taken into your marriage bed. I should borne the child!"

"Quiet, Caroline."

She laughed, near hysteria. "Why? So your servants won't hear? They don't understand English."

"We can't be certain."

"*I* am certain of something."

"What is that?"

"That you are driven—just as you were six years ago—to fulfill that covenant, to produce your heir for your people—your church. How foolish you must think I am! You flattered me with these gifts so I'd give myself willingly to you and take your child into my womb."

The diary dropped from Merrick's hand to the floor with a muffled thump as he snatched her against his chest so hard her head snapped back and she let out a startled cry. The bulky padding pressed into her ribs, pinching her tender skin.

"How quickly you've forgotten, little one," he ground out with a renewed vengeance, "Had I wanted only a child from you, I'd have finished what I'd started that night. I'd have poured my seed into you, then sat back to watch your body blossom with a real baby instead of this godforsaken disguise." His gaze darted down to her padding and back. "Believe me, I was tempted."

"After all that I've read in Ilse's diary and after seeing you discard her Bible like trash into her grave, do you expect me to believe you gave me a last-second reprieve because of a sudden sense of morality?"

"Would you have rather had it differently? We can rectify that right here and now, if you wish. The table would serve well. Or perhaps the floor."

"You heathen bas—"

Merrick's mouth crushed against hers, cutting off the blasphemous insult. She struggled violently against him until she broke free. Her emerald eyes flashed. Determined to rid herself of the burning effect of his kiss, she swiped the back of her hand across her mouth, then yanked her arm up to slap him. But he caught her wrist before she hit her mark.

"You'll never strike me again, Carrie."

"Only if I never face you again, *Herr Baron*."

Caroline remembered her parting words with painful clarity as she leaned against a weathered post in the old barn. It'd been two weeks since she traveled to Freiburg as part of the plan to stay with Hilde—two weeks since she'd left the baron's estate with an ache in her heart after their strangely unraveling scene. Her behavior that morning defied explanation, no matter how many times she'd pondered the confrontation that had gone awry. They'd done what they'd set out to do—to alert the servants of her embittered departure, but they'd gone beyond, both she in her inexplicable anger and he in his cruel suggestion to take her.

Yet something else still bothered her—that Caroline could possibly be sought by the countess and her friends among the devil worshippers. In reality, there was no tangible way for them to learn that she, not Ilse, was the intended mother of a child bearing psychic powers. But Caroline had already learned to expect the unexpected and believe the unbelievable. If Merrick and she possessed a certain clairvoyance, wouldn't Countess Reinhart? If she learned of Caroline's supposed involvement with Merrick, would the countess let the others murder them all? Certainly the woman couldn't go that far.

Caroline closed her eyes and dropped her head back against the post. The endless hours spent in the deserted barn, waiting for Lottie to arrive had given her mind too much time to fret.

"Still no sign," Hilde said, coming up on Caroline in the shadows. Like Caroline, she'd worn a black dress and outer coat in order to sneak through the outskirts of town in the dark. With dawn upon them, they would have to find another route back. "Do you think she'll change her mind?"

Caroline shook her head and pushed herself off the post to return to the path she'd worn on the packed dirt floor. "No —I'm just worried that she may have been followed. As long as she's not caught, she'll come here. She really doesn't know where to go. From the map in your letters, I showed her that this barn would be the safest hiding place until word of her kidnapping Peter dies down."

"*If* it dies down. I still don't understand how she trusted you."

Caroline shrugged. "Lottie was far too attached to Peter. It clouded her reasoning. After I told her that Merrick refused to believe his son could be killed, she was determined to save the baby. What is there for her here? In America she gets a second chance. I had no problem convincing her that coming with me was best."

"How do you think she'll feel when she learns that the baron will be joining you?"

"I don't think it will bother her as long as it was in Peter's best interest."

Hilde perched on an old stool and watched Caroline pace, observing the young woman's prominent maternal silhouette in her dark wool overcoat. Concealing the kidnapping scheme from her sick aunt had been difficult. Yet, surprisingly, the aunt had welcomed Caroline.

"Could the baron have changed his mind?" Hilde asked with quiet hesitation. "Is it possible that he let this charade go on simply to get you out of the house?"

Caroline sighed. "Anything is possible at this point."

The grating squeak of rusty hinges brought their attention to the wooden door where a weak ray of early-morning light cut through the crack. Caroline froze, holding her breath until the diminutive frame of the wet nurse stood silhouetted in the narrow opening. She released the air with a long sigh. The second step of the plan had been a success.

* * *

"He was born three weeks ago. But I have been too ill to come into town to have his birth registered." Caroline explained the next morning, holding the tiny bundle close to her breast so the *burgomeister* couldn't see Peter's features. Although her nephew wasn't as large as most babies his age, he didn't look as young as she claimed him to be, either.

The stout, bearded gentleman nodded disinterestedly behind an oak desk, the size of which reminded Caroline of Merrick's desk. A picture formed in her mind of the handsome baron as he spent many hours leaning over his ledgers. Holding his son closer, she became very much aware that Merrick would soon join her and her heart fluttered.

As in days past, visions of his dark blue eyes and coal-black hair filled her mind. When a hand gently touched her shoulder, she half expected to look up and see Merrick's face above her. It was Hilde, however, who'd stepped forward to offer her assistance.

"Hmm?" Caroline glanced to her friend, then the gruff gentleman, realizing she'd been asked a question.

"Please excuse her, Herr Burgomeister," Hilde said in German. "The fräulein has had great difficulty with her . . . situation." The man lifted his eyes from his paperwork with a disdainful look at the indication of Caroline's lack of husband.

"Fräulein, is it?"

"*Ja,*" Caroline answered.

"And the father. Where is he?"

"Dead, presumably," Caroline blurted out to the shock of the official. "His name was Bates . . . Thatcher Bates. He . . . attacked me near my home . . . in Pennsylvania," she stammered with convincing humiliation, adding a few emotional chokes. "When I learned I was with child, I ran away. I didn't know he'd followed me onto the ship until . . . that last night when he . . ."

Hilde continued for her. "He attacked her again but another man stopped him. There was a terrible fight. Bates was hurt badly, but before he could be taken into custody in port, his friends helped him escape. The ship's captain told us that the man was near death and not expected to live more than a few days, especially since he was not likely to seek medical help."

"You two were together?"

"*Ja*, I brought her to my aunt's home here in Freiburg—Frau Landau."

The *burgomeister* nodded. "So you became friends on the ship?"

"*Nein, Mein Herr,*" Hilde lied. "We are cousins . . . Our fathers were brothers. They were my only family while I was in America."

"Well—neither of you have resided here for very long." He rubbed his beard in contemplation. "Perhaps your aunt could come in and sign the certificate of birth."

"My aunt's quite ill, *Mein Herr.*"

He clicked his tongue and spoke to the older woman. "You've really had your hands full, what with two to care for."

Caroline studied the man across from them, wondering if he was being unduly hesitant or if she was overly anxious to get the procedure behind her.

"We've managed. Now—about the baby's registration . . . Is it absolutely necessary to obtain my aunt's signature?"

"You realize that it is highly irregular that two unknown fräuleins should come into town alone to declare a child's birth." He gestured toward the bundle clutched to the younger one's full breasts, and frowned. "You have no one to verify you are who you say to be and no father to lay claim to that child. I feel it is my duty to verify the man's death before I issue a certificate."

"If you insist," Caroline said, trying to appear unaffected

by the delay. "The captain of the *Teutonic* should give you the information you need."

Hilde added, "It is a ship in the White Star line. His name is Captain Werner."

After the *burgomeister* scratched out the information on a scrap of paper, his chair creaked in protest as he rose to a height that seemed to only slightly surpass his girth. He escorted the two women to the door of his office. "Return in a week. I should have the documents in order by then."

Caroline felt an uneasiness with the official. If she didn't think she would need the birth certificate to enter the United States, she'd never have risked surfacing before Merrick arrived. As it stood, she had no choice. As she and Hilde walked casually away, a niggling apprehension in the back of her mind prompted her to send up a fervent prayer that the coming week would pass quickly—and without incident.

The *burgomeister* watched through the window, making certain his visitors were far down the cobbled street before he returned to his desk and withdrew a clean sheet of paper.

"Dearest Countess Reinhart,

In answer to your discreet request to inform you of any knowledge pertaining to a young expectant woman traveling alone, I believe I have the information you seek.

As per your stipulation on your previous visit, I anxiously await your personal gratitude in this matter. As for the monetary reward . . ."

Merrick wearily slid from Ghebellino's back and lowered himself to the thick carpet of spring grass that edged the pond. In the distance, *Schloss Hayden* no longer seemed the majestic castle of his childhood. Though its physical appearance remained unchanged, it now appeared more like an enormous Pandora's box, harboring pain and grief, deceit and anger.

The sorrel nibbled on long tender shoots of grass while Merrick walked silently along the bank. His black riding boots left imprints in the moist earth. By now, Caroline and Peter waited for him near Freiburg and he was anxious to be on his way. It had been hard to let Lottie slip away with his son, then to lead his men on a wild chase across the countryside in an attempt to appear frantic. His drawn features had not been a false display. Sleep had evaded him these past three weeks since Caroline had left—even more so over the last week since Peter had been taken—and he missed them terribly.

The entire household had grown melancholy with the sad twist of fate that seemed to have shaken the very foundation of the old stone manor. Just that morning, Merrick had dismissed all but a skeleton staff to take care of *Schloss Hayden*. The Krumhauers and Conrad remained, of course, as did Greta and one other young local girl to keep the rooms tidy.

"I'm going to find Peter," Merrick had explained to those left, whom he'd gathered in his study. The scant staff of servants bowed their heads wordlessly. "As usual, my secretary will see to the details in my absence. Attend to your duties and expect me back in less than a month."

Frau Krumhauer had asked, "Do you think you'll find Peter by then, Your Excellency?"

"If I don't, I'll keep looking until I do. Conrad, have my valise packed with the essentials. I'll be leaving for Munich late this afternoon. That will be all." As they'd vacated the room one by one, Merrick had called out to the stableman. "Wil? I'd like you to meet me at the pond near the entrance road before I go."

"Yes—of course," Wil had said.

Looking out over the vibrant splashes of spring flowers dotting the deep green carpet, Merrick pulled his thoughts back to the present. He had taken care of all the details with only one remaining. As he watched Wil approach on the black long-legged Vindicator, he knew this last task would give him at least a modicum of pleasure—though it still couldn't compensate for the tense anxiety that beleaguered his tired soul.

Wil gravely dismounted and faced his lifelong friend.

"Thank you for meeting me out here, Wil."

The stableman stuffed his massive hands in his pockets and nodded uncomfortably. Although he was a quiet man, the silence only added to the awkward parting of the two friends. Merrick's tense behavior in the last four months had put distance between them. But as they stood facing one another, Merrick hoped that his words would change the situation.

"In a way, you and your parents are the only family I know. I want you to oversee *Schloss Hayden* while I'm gone." Merrick withdrew a folded sheaf of papers from the inside of his black frock coat and handed them to Wil. "It's all been legally drawn up. You will act on my behalf, live as I have. Consider it yours for the time I'm away. If I should come back, you may choose to stay or you may have a house of your own where I will set you up in like manner."

Wil's pale blue eyes scanned the pages, then looked up and studied Merrick with profound confusion. Finally he spoke, his voice deep and filled with restrained emotion. "You won't be coming back with Peter, will you?"

Merrick raked his fingers through his hair, shaking his head. "When I find Peter, I won't bring him back to this living hell." *Living hell*— those words that had been Caroline's description echoed in his mind.

"Once you find your son, what will you do with Lottie?"

Merrick hesitated a moment. "Nothing. She's but a child and her past weighs heavy on her actions. She loves Peter. She meant him no harm."

Though uncomfortable conversation had opened their meeting, the familiar banter reminiscent of their childhood now returned. "Fräulein Hartmann is your next conquest, am I right?"

"Conquest?" Merrick laughed. "I haven't considered her quite in that light. She's not like the women I've sought in my past."

"No. You're right on that point. She is . . . gifted like you." Wil smiled knowingly when Merrick glanced at him with suspicion. "Do you think I could grow up as close as this to you—" he held up two crossed fingers, "—and not know what is in your heart. You love her. It doesn't take an extraordinary talent to know that."

"How can I love her when we seemed destined to be at odds except where Peter was concerned?"

"She was merely protecting herself, as mother says."

Merrick winced. "Alfreda said that?"

"She's been watching the change in you since the day you carried the fräulein into the house after that horse race. Unfortunately, she made the grave mistake of confiding to Louise that Caroline was more suited for you than Ilse had been, but that you were too stubborn to realize it."

The warnings from Louise came back to Merrick. *You are blind to think she is harmless,* she'd said. *Heed my words . . . if it were earlier days, she'd be burned . . .*

Louise had been right about Caroline bringing about changes in Merrick, for it was she who helped him decide upon a new life, in Pennsylvania, beyond the borders of his previous existence. Outwardly, it may have appeared the wheels of destruction had started to turn on the day of Caroline's arrival. But in his own mind, Merrick knew he wouldn't have overcome the odds without her presence near to strengthen him. He remembered once again how she'd come to stand beside him when he'd faced Louise.

Shaking himself, Merrick broke out of his pensive mood.

In a friendly gesture, he reached up with both hands and squeezed his friend's massive upper arms. "You're fortunate, Wil, to have a mother as good as Alfreda."

"I'll be sure to tell her that," Wil promised.

The Landau farmhouse was nestled in a narrow green valley at the end of a long, winding road that clung to the hillside. Like others in the Black Forest, the picturesque home provided shelter for the farm animals on the ground floor, while Hilde's Aunt, Frau Landau, lived on the spacious second floor where windows opened to a balcony spanning the front of the house. Directly beneath the high-pitched thatched roof, ample space served as winter storage for the hay supply.

Caroline thought it was an enchanting home from the moment she first saw it, much more warm and cozy than the baron's aristocratic estate, yet each had its own memorable ambience. With the low-hanging eaves of its huge gray thatched roof, Hilde's aunt's home reminded Caroline of a slumbering woolly sheepdog. Whereas, *Schloss Hayden* had the character of a muscular German Shepherd guarding his territory.

While Hilde tended her aunt in the old woman's room, Caroline and Lottie were alone with Peter in the large room that constituted the main living area. The two sat on the floor on either side of the baby who lay a safe distance from the warm crackling fire.

"He's so strong," Lottie boasted as if he were her own, watching him lift his wobbly head to look around. Though the large braided rug served as a barrier from the hard, wood planks, a doubled blanket had been spread out to protect from the occasions when Peter awkwardly dropped his face to the floor.

"Do you still believe that you could be the best mother

for him?" Caroline asked in German, sensing a difference in Lottie since she'd arrived with the baby.

"Vielleicht."—Perhaps. The adolescent wet nurse stroked Peter's back gently. He responded by lowering his tired head and resting his cheek on the cream-colored blanket.

Peter squirmed and bunched his tiny knees under him, making little noises of discomfort.

Caroline lifted the boy into her arms to sooth his quiet fussing. "Do you want *Tante* Carrie to rock you, *Pay-ter?*" Her reference to herself as *Tante* Carrie brought back memories of Merrick's deep rich voice, warming her as deeply as this soft bundle against her breast.

She focused her thoughts back on Lottie who had moved up to a stool by the hearth. "Are you having second thought about America?"

"Some."

"Are you thinking of staying here in Germany?" she asked, hoping the girl wasn't changing her mind. For the care Lottie had given Peter and the risks she'd taken to keep him safe, the girl deserved more than a harsh life of uncertainty.

"Ja."

"But what would you do?"

"The baron would see to it that I'd have enough to keep me from starving." Lottie turned and looked at Peter lying contentedly against Caroline's shoulder, her long fingers curled protectively behind his dark head. His deep blue eyes returned Lottie's gaze as if he spoke aloud of his choice, though she knew it was her vivid imagination. "It looks to me as if you will fill his needs. Maybe you should be Peter's mother." She scanned the slimming lines of Caroline's plum-colored dress that'd been brought out from the trunks after the disguise was no longer necessary. "His Excellency may take to you once he sees you're not carrying anymore."

Caroline smiled weakly at the backward compliment for the good intent with which it was meant. "Thank you, Lottie. But I'm afraid *Baron von Hayden* and I have far too many differences."

The *burgomeister* nodded his head toward the wall adjoining two upstairs rooms at the roadside tavern. "I still don't see why you brought that scum along with you," he muttered, buttoning his gold silk waistcoat with great difficulty. "Don't you care what people may think, seeing you with that filthy scarred beggar?"

"He's but a pawn in my plan," the female voice purred, drawing the attention of the sated official. He looked back at the lovely woman reclining on the rented bed and grinned at his good fortune. Her dark chestnut tresses flowed in disarray down her creamy shoulders and over the white sheet draped tantalizingly over her peaked nipples. When the countess let a seductive smile slowly curve the corners of her red lips, his discomfort began anew. She moved her body across the bed, stretching to reach for a glass of champagne, and the sheet fell away.

The *burgomeister* mentally moved back all prior appointments and began to reverse his order of dress. "Tell me how you knew that the girl would come to Freiburg," he said casually as he climbed onto the creaking bed and accepted a glass from the countess.

Elena watched him swig the expensive sparkling wine noting with a sly look that he ignored its slightly clouded appearance. Her tapered fingernail traced a line along the folds of his chin, then dropped to his heaving chest as one thin eyebrow arched. "I was fairly certain the naive Hartmann girl would either seek out her friend here or pass through Rotterdam on her way home. To be safe, I offered my undying gratitude to several . . . friends . . . along her route if they should come up with the information I wanted."

He dropped the glass haphazardly onto the bedside table and drew her close. "You may have *offered* your undying gratitude to several, but only *I* have the honor to collect on that promise."

Countess Reinhart smiled noncommittally, waiting for the lethal powder she'd put into his glass to take effect. Hopefully it would be quick. Once beneath this bumbling fool had been enough.

The aroused *burgomeister* toyed with her hair while she thought over the botched scheme from the night before the *Teutonic* had made port. For days she had sneaked Bates into her cabin, plying him with liquor and her favors, all to convince him that the Hartmann girl wanted him. The countess subtly enflamed his desire for the fräulein until he was obsessed.

Thoughts of her mission occupied Elena far more than amorous gropings of the lethargic man who attempted with increasing difficulty to move his heavy weight onto her.

With bored indifference, she went through the necessary motions in response to his passionate advance. All the while, she recalled her quest to extract from the von Haydens the riches that were rightfully hers. Becoming a member of her mother's Church of the Mystics had been a means to that end. Ultimately, she had wanted to lure the baroness into the rebellion, as well, then convince her to divorce the baron. Caroline's intended murder on her way over from America had been part of that scheme. The baroness would've taken the blame for the tragedy, becoming vulnerable to the countess's suggestion that she was under a curse. The trap would have been set to win her to the dark side, but when the baron intervened and saved Caroline, the plan had been foiled.

Her anger, however, had been short-lived. After spiriting Bates off the ship and nursing him back to health to aid her in yet another scheme, she'd heard of Ilse's death. Though she'd thought the Prince of Darkness had smiled on her, all of her attempts to kidnap the child were for naught—until now.

At the very moment she braced herself to submit a second time to his disgusting embraces, the obese *burgomeister* gasped and shuddered convulsively. Rolling him onto his back, the countess, relieved, sighed with pleasure at being spared yet another bone-crushing interlude. She slid from his side, donned her dressing robe and tapped the wall to signal Bates to summon the owner of the tavern.

Moments later, she heard a discreet knock. Leaving the man's naked body exposed, she flung open the door and launched herself into a convincing state of hysteria, falling into the tavern keeper's arms.

"It happened so suddenly," she sobbed. "It was horrible." She leaned back, well aware of her untied robe. "Please—I'll do anything you want as long as you keep me out of this. If my husband discovers that the *burgomeister* died in my bed, he will have me murdered. I swear."

Elena pointedly ignored the grumbling Bates as he shuffled back to his own room. For the time being, her pathetic pleas and her visually inviting attributes were about to secure the silence of her latest victim.

As the week passed, an oppressive cloud still hovered all around Caroline. Each morning she awoke more drained than the day before, hoping that this would be the day that Merrick would arrive. She knew she'd feel relieved of most of her worries once he was there to share the anxious burden of their attempt to escape.

The morning of the return trip into Freiburg was gray and drizzly, too disagreeable to take Peter along. Since it was unwise for Lottie to be seen with Caroline and Hilde, the baby stayed with the wet nurse at the house, along with Hilde's failing aunt.

While Caroline sat on her side of the worn black leather seat brooding silently, Hilde steered the hooded carriage slowly through the lightly muddied road.

Everything will be fine after I get those papers, Caroline told herself, but her strong determination wavered in the mounting breeze. As they reached the midway marker into town, the slate-gray clouds overhead darkened with her mood.

Hilde spoke with some reservation. "I hope the *burgomeister* has everything in order so we can hurry back. I wouldn't want to spend the night away from *Tante*."

Caroline nodded, her wary eyes watching the churning storm on the horizon. Back home, she'd studied the weather with her father, noting the changes and learning the signs—important knowledge for lumbering and farming. She glanced sideways at Hilde.

"How will you manage that big place, Hilde?" she asked, seeking a respite from the inexplicable heaviness that weighed on her mind.

"For a while, I'll keep the hired man that *Tante*'s been paying," Hilde answered almost apologetically. "I'm far too old to be finding a husband to run it. When the time comes, I suppose a growing family could put it to better use than a single woman like myself."

"I think Lottie wants to stay here—in Germany, I mean. Do you think she could be of any help with your aunt until she decided where she wanted to go, what she wanted to do?"

Hilde shrugged. "She's a nice enough child . . . very capable with chores . . . she could use a bit more tutoring in her social skills." She clucked her tongue in sad disgust. "Imagine being married off at her young age, not to mention bearing a child and losing him along with the husband—though I loathe to call him that for robbing the cradle like he did."

The older woman's rambling assessment of Lottie's good and bad points lifted Caroline's spirits, however little. Not only did it appear that Lottie might have found a home, complete with an attentive guardian, but also that Hilde might have found the channel for her maternal talents in the spirited young Lottie.

Lottie! The name burst into Caroline's mind as if someone had screamed it in her ear. Struck with the final insight into the threatening chill, Caroline gripped the edge of the leather seat.

"Caroline, you're white as a ghost. What's the matter?" Hilde's voice rose in panic.

"Turn the carriage around. Fast. Something's terribly wrong."

"But the road's too narrow . . . and the mud."

"Let me take it," Caroline quickly offered, snatching the reins from her friend. The wheels slid in the ruts as she forced herself to be patient with the painstaking effort to jockey the horse and carriage. Hilde gasped when the frustrated animal stumbled at the slick precipice that could send them over the steep embankment. But he deftly regained his footing, then started back the way they'd come.

Though the drizzle had intensified somewhat, it was their speed that brought the slashing diagonal sheet of raindrops in under the protective black canopy. Hilde held on with one hand while gripping the throat of her coat with the other. Huddling into the wind, her eyes were glued to the precarious road ahead.

"Pray that everyone will be all right," Caroline shouted over the racket of the complaining old carriage, a needless request considering Hilde's moving lips. The woman was obviously doing her share of bargaining with the powers that be.

Deep in the pit of her stomach, Caroline already knew the dreaded answer.

Chapter 12

Merrick kept a watchful eye on the cathedral steeple rising high above the city of Freiburg. Each step his horse took brought the masterpiece of open rock lacework closer and closer into view, but the miles seemed to crawl by. He couldn't get to Caroline fast enough. He cursed the extra days he'd taken as an added precaution against being followed. After heading for Munich on Ghebellino, he'd doubled back toward Freiburg. Anxious anticipation tensed every muscle as his thoughts remained fixed on Caroline and Peter.

The damnable clouds seemed tied to his coattail, following him in like a smothering blanket of gloom. When the light showers began, he turned his collar up and braved the miserable chill.

Veering off the heavily traveled highway was not only a necessary safeguard but a shorter route around the largest city in the Black Forest, thus cutting the distance to the farmhouse. After checking the knots that secured his valise Merrick gave the sorrel a free rein to cut a path through the beech trees, occasionally trampling a low branch that swept the ground.

The horse and rider emerged from the natural screen of glossy green leaves and came upon a small meadow edged with bramble and pink flowering hawthorn where a herd of deer grazed peacefully. Not wanting to disturb them, Merrick gave a light tug on the reins to stop his mount from entering the glade. But the horse's final step landed on a brittle branch, snapping it with a loud crack. The deer glanced up and froze, their large ears pricked, their tapered faces turned toward the frightful sound. Only a moment passed before the herd bounded into the thicket—all but one young doe. Her large brown eyes stared back at Merrick. Was she too afraid to move, he wondered? Or too proud to run? She reminded him of Caroline.

Go, little one, he coaxed in silent communication.

As if the sleek young animal heard his thoughts, she turned and headed for the low, thorny bramble that bordered the far side of the clearing, effortlessly sailing over it with a strong leap.

Merrick leaned slightly forward and squeezed his legs against his horse's sides. The two quickly cut across the trampled new growth, exiting the meadow through a break in the hawthorns. Thoughts of Caroline and the doe stayed fresh in his mind. It seemed every flower . . . every living thing served as a reminder of the young woman. He pushed his horse up to a faster gait. The sooner he found the Landau farmhouse, the sooner he could put a stop to these mindless comparisons and finally behold the real Caroline with his own eyes.

Water ran off the brim of his hat and onto the wet shoulders of his black traveling greatcoat. Soaked clear through his wool trousers, he wouldn't have been surprised if the rain had found its way down into the toes of his riding boots. He'd come this far without sleep and he was bone-tired. If it weren't for the short distance remaining, he'd take the time to rent a room to dry out his clothes and rest up before greeting Caroline. But a strange urgency pushed him on.

The sensible side of Merrick's mind tried to dismiss this growing need to complete his journey as nothing more than his obsession with Caroline. His paternal instinct for Peter was yet another practical reason to be driven to his physical limit. But with each rhythmic stride of the muscled beast beneath him, Merrick felt a growing fretfulness awakening his senses.

Like the rain pelting his body, the feeling intensified until he gathered the horse and leaned forward, urging Ghebellino into a quick-paced trot. His heart pounded. Still he wasn't going fast enough. Finally, with subtle pressure from his knees, Merrick put his mount into a gallop.

Despite his efforts otherwise, his mind formed a mental image of his most feared nightmare.

No. Not now. Not after all these weeks. Not when we were so close.

Caroline nearly ran the carriage horse right up the outer stairs leading to the second level of the farmhouse. A voice deep inside her chanted to the beat of her racing pulse, . . . *not after all these weeks. Not when we were so close* . . . Hiking her full skirt to her knees, she took the rain-slick steps without thought of the hazard.

"Be careful, Caroline!" Hilde puffed at the base of the stairs. "If there *is* someone up there, he might be armed!"

"I'll be careful," she answered over her shoulder. Fearful intuition hit her square in the stomach. The threat of danger within the house was gone—but so was Peter.

Slamming her shoulder into the heavy oak door that was warped with age, she shoved it wide and hollered, "Lottie!"

Only silence met her.

Caroline bounded into the large main room, her eyes frantically scanning every conceivable nook for any sign of the wet nurse or the baby. Convinced there was none, she dashed to the long hall leading to the back rooms. Hilde was fast on her heels.

"Lottie?!" Caroline called out beseechingly as she checked the girl's room. The bedcovers were a mess and the drawer used as Peter's bed had been flipped over on top of a pile of clothes scattered on the wood floor. Hoping against hope, Caroline picked up the baby's makeshift bed while Hilde checked the wardrobe. There was no sign of her nephew; even his crib quilt was missing. God only knew what terror the girl had lived through—if she was still alive. There was no blood, but that held little meaning to the two women as they scrambled to the other rooms.

Passing their own sleeping quarters, they found them neither occupied or disturbed in any way. Hilde's aunt's room at the very end of the hall was the last to be checked. Pausing for the briefest moment at the old woman's door, the two glanced at one another, each dreading what would be revealed to them on the other side.

As Caroline turned and faced the door, Hilde stepped in behind her, placing her hand on the younger woman's shoulder for support. Caroline felt the warmth of her friend's touch and smiled back with a courage she wished ran deeper than it appeared.

Once the door was opened, they looked beyond the portal to the bed. Hilde's frail aunt lay motionless on her back, one bony arm draped across the patchwork quilt that covered her. The blink of her watery eyes seemed like the only sign of life but then the exposed arm slowly reached toward the other side of the bed. The strain was evident on the woman's gray, lined face. It was only then that Caroline saw the huddled form of Lottie curled into a ball beneath the covers, her head pressed against the old woman's shoulder.

Spurred into action at the same instant, Hilde and Caroline rushed to the bed, one to each side.

"Lottie?" Caroline's hands gently tried to draw the girl out of her hiding.

Hilde leaned over and kissed the soft, crepelike cheek. *"Gott sei Dank!"*—Thank God, she said quietly, continuing in her native tongue. "My prayers for your safekeeping were answered."

The old woman licked her dry lips and forced herself to speak. "They . . . hurt . . . Lottie."

"Yes, we assumed . . ." Hilde's voice trailed off without finishing the thought. "Can you tell us if they took Peter?"

"I . . . don't . . . know. I . . . heard . . . a . . . woman. Then . . . a . . . man. Lottie . . . screamed—"

"Dear Lord," Caroline said in a horrified whisper as she finally coaxed Lottie to roll toward her. The girl's delicate face was red and swollen from several blows. Already her tender skin had begun to turn purplish blue around one puffed eye. Her bottom lip was twice its normal size with drying blood smeared about a nasty cut.

Torn between consoling Lottie and searching further for Peter, Caroline was spared the decision when the battered adolescent spoke between broken sobs.

Her grotesque lower lip hindered her efforts. "They took . . . 'ee-ter. H-hine 'im."

"Find him, yes. But can you tell me anything that will *help* me find him?"

"A . . . woo-nan."

"A woman?"

Lottie nodded. " 'oo-ti-ful . . ." Caroline's puzzlement frustrated the girl. She closed her eyes tight and tried again. *"oo-tee-ful* . . . Ni-ce loo-king . . . Wanna talk t' yoo. I . . . as-t 'er in. Then ugly n-an cane. Stunk." She opened her eyes to see if her words had made sense.

Caroline repeated the garbled story to be sure she understood. "A *beautiful,* nice-looking woman came to see me. You asked her to come in but then an ugly . . . man? . . . came." When the words she'd deciphered appeared correct, she went on. "You mean the man wasn't handsome? What was it about him that made him ugly?"

"Scar. R-ight eye an' cheek an' h-he stunk o' liquor," she said dissolving into tearful memories.

The sobbing made it more difficult for Caroline to hear the description. "A scar over his right eye and cheek and he stunk of liquor?" she asked.

Another nod.

Her final question was painfully quiet. "Did they say that they'd come to take the baby?" Yet another nod confirmed her fear. She had to look away a moment and fight back the burst of silent tears. With no time for self-indulgence, she quickly wiped at her eyes with her open palm and turned back to Lottie for some clue of where they might have gone.

"They foun' 'ee-ter in 'y roo—" The split lip couldn't form the word.

"Room, yes," Caroline prompted. "Come on, Lottie. Find a way to tell me. Think of other words."

"The woo-nan jus' ask m-me q-estions an' ordered the m-an 'round." She winced at the pain of making her mouth work. "Then she took 'ee-ter an' say they need to—take mm-ilk for the b-aby. He to-ok me down to mm-ilk the goat, then he—"

Her tortured sobs cut off the last of a scene that needed no explanation. The intruder had beaten her badly before leaving with Peter.

"You don't have to go on," Caroline soothed, seeing no purpose in letting the girl torture herself. It was obvious that there was no clue to where the two had taken Peter.

A thunderous noise on the steps outside froze them all with a unanimous gasp of terror. Caroline's mind filled with images of the kidnappers returning after having second thoughts about leaving a witness.

"Caroline!" Merrick's voice rang through the house like pealing bells. She was on her feet and out the bedroom door in an instant.

"We're back here!" Caroline shouted, running down the hall. As she rounded the corner, she collided with Merrick, hitting the solid wall of his chest with such force that the wind was knocked out of her. Just as she stumbled back in a momentary daze, he scooped her into his arms and held her tight.

"Thank God, you're safe," he whispered with a profoundly husky strain in his voice. His cold, wet coat dampened the front of her white blouse and sleeves, but she was only aware of the feeling of relief that swept through her.

"Peter's gone, Merrick." She pulled back and saw that the shocking news affected him much the same way as it had her. His tired eyes showed no surprise, only a deep, gripping sadness. "After Hilde and I had left for town, I knew something was wrong so we turned around and came back. But it was too late. We've been trying to find out what happened from Lottie but she's been hurt . . ."

"Where is she?"

"In the room at the end of the hall," she said, stepping aside to let him pass. She followed behind his long strides, pulling up short when he stopped at the open doorway.

The only person that Merrick recognized was Hilde Landau, to whom he nodded as he stepped farther into the room. Assuming the gaunt old woman on the bed to be Hilde's aunt, he gave a polite, but somber greeting, then looked to the form next to her. His gut twisted at the sight of the girl's bloated features, but his serious demeanor hid his revulsion.

With no time to waste and no inclination to further disturb the frail aunt, he walked around the bed and knelt on one knee. His deep, rich voice was placating as he smoothed his fingertips across her temple. "Let's get you into your own bed," he suggested, slowly drawing back the covers.

Shaking her head in mute refusal, Lottie blindly groped for the protection of the quilt and threw it back over her, burrowing closer to the old woman. But the darkening bruises on the exposed parts of the young girl's body hadn't gone unnoticed. Merrick's eyes narrowed in rage. Only an animal could have done this to a woman. And that animal now had his son.

He snatched a crocheted lap robe from the seat of a nearby chair and shook out the folds. Though Lottie whimpered in protest, he tossed it over the girl, modestly covering the tattered dress, then discreetly withdrew the quilt and gathered her feather-light body to his chest. Once in the hall, he turned to Caroline. "Which room is hers?"

"The first one but—"

His boot heels struck the hard wood planks with a resounding echo as he carried Lottie the short distance. Pausing at the doorway, he surveyed the rumpled bedclothes, then caught sight of the overturned drawer that had been Peter's cradle. He glanced down at the small trembling body in his arms, then turned and took her into the next room.

While he waited a moment for Caroline to slip past him and yank the quilt back from her bed, she filled him in on the little she'd already learned.

"It's hard for her to talk," she concluded.

"What can you get for her lip?" He lowered the girl onto the clean sheet and pulled the covers over her without bothering to take away the small blanket.

"I'll see what I can find," Caroline answered over her shoulder as she hurried from the room.

Merrick smoothed a strand of hair off of Lottie's forehead. "I know it's difficult to talk, but I must know if you heard the man and woman talk about going anywhere. Can you think back? Maybe some mention of a town . . . or a direction they were heading as they left?"

Lottie struggled to keep her swelling eye open. "When I . . . mm-ilked the goat . . . the mm-an . . . talked . . . that . . . they're gonna get lots o' mm-oney selling . . . the boy." The painful effort to talk had reopened the wound on her lip. Merrick pulled out his damp handkerchief and dabbed at the corner of her mouth, receiving an attempt at an appreciative smile from Lottie.

"Careful now," he said, striving to be cheerful. "Save up those smiles until you've had a chance to heal."

In the few minutes that it had taken Caroline to return, Merrick had learned what he needed to know.

As she entered the room with a pan of water, he was getting up from the kneeling position he'd assumed to talk closely with Lottie. "I'm going after them," he said, more as a general statement of fact than to either one of them in particular, then walked from the room.

Water sloshed over the edge of the pan as Caroline quickly placed it on the bureau and raced after Merrick. "How do you know which way they went? Did Lottie remember something?"

"No," he answered, marching down the hall to the old woman's room. "But you told me that you'd just come back on the only road leading into town. And I cut through the woods from that direction, following the stream." He ducked his head around the door frame. "Hilde—?"

Caroline heard her voice answer, "Yes—I'll be right out."

When she emerged from the room, he asked, "Other than the road and the stream that comes off the mountain behind this house, is there any other way out of this valley?"

Hilde nodded as Caroline took in Merrick's drenched appearance. Droplets of water still fell from the black curls that looked longer now. He'd shed his outer coat somewhere during the time he'd been there, but she certainly couldn't remember when or where. The jacket and trousers clung to him like a second skin and she swore she saw an involuntary shiver. He couldn't go back out in the pouring rain, but she knew she couldn't stop him, either.

"There's an old trail that winds through the west side of the valley and up through a pass," Hilde offered.

"Does it lead to the river?"

She nodded.

"Damn!" As his open palm slammed against the door frame in frustration, he spun around and headed back down the hall toward the main room. "That has to mean they're looking to cross the Rhine into France."

Caroline caught up to him and tugged at his wet sleeve, making him face her. "How can you be sure?"

"Because that would be the safest route to escape the German authorities in the north who are looking for a baby. And Paris is the perfect place to find someone who would pay a price for Peter without asking questions."

"Lottie told you they're going to *sell* him?"

"Herr Baron?" Hilde interrupted from where they'd left her standing. The two of them stopped and looked back. "There's an old cabin at the summit. With the rain and all . . . they might wait out the night up there."

Caroline practically shrieked, "That's it! It has to be!"

Caught up in Caroline's enthusiasm, Merrick took several long strides and scooped Hilde into a big hug. "Fräulein, when I get back with Peter, I promise you anything your heart desires."

She laughed self-consciously when he released her. "And what if I were to say I wanted to wed a certain young Baron von Hayden?"

"Anything but that," he said with a wink before he headed back out to find Peter. As he reached Caroline, he hooked an arm around her waist and snatched her close, then glanced back at Hilde. "I'm afraid my heart has already been claimed." He returned the older woman's broad grin just as she disappeared through the nearby doorway, then he turned to Caroline.

"If my heart *hasn't* been claimed, I've surely lost it forever," he said, his dark gaze studying every inch of her face, a frivolous use of precious time since he'd long been haunted by those emerald-green eyes and that smile. "I'll be back as soon as I can."

He smiled at the startled expression in Caroline's eyes, so like the doe in the meadow. *Is she too afraid to move?* he now wondered. *Or too proud to run?* A soft chuckle escaped his lips as he lowered his mouth to hers and tasted her sweetness for one brief moment before he left. As her arms encircled his neck, he plyed her lips with his, pressing tenderly with the longing for more. Slowly, the tip of his tongue sought entrance until her lips parted tentatively and it slipped inside, tantalizing him with dreams of a deeper intimacy upon his return.

When he reluctantly broke away, Caroline's hands remained at the nape of his neck. "I don't want you to go out there alone, Merrick," she said, her breathing still ragged from the effect of the kiss. "Please let me go with you."

"No," he said adamantly, shaking his head.

"But you know I can ride that trail as well as you and—"

He reached up and dragged her hands down to her sides, then pointedly led her several steps out into the main room away from the hall. "Don't you realize who that man is who did *that* to Lottie?" He jerked his head in the direction of the room where the girl lay bruised and beaten. "The ugly scar over the right side of his face? It's Thatcher Bates, Caroline. That beating he gave Lottie is what he'd almost done to you on the ship. Lottie was purely a victim of circumstance—you were gone, so he took his revenge on her instead."

Caroline shuddered at the revelation, then marshaled her strength and stood her ground. "It's different this time."

"Hell, yes, it's different this time. *This* time you'll be safely out of harm's way when I kill the sonova—"

"Merrick, listen to me—"

"Stay here and see to Lottie's needs."

"But Hilde can—" His mouth clamped to hers in a harsh, grinding kiss, then pulled away. "Every second we stand here and argue this, Peter's slipping farther out of my grasp. I've got to go, Carrie—*alone.*" He ran back and ducked into her room and came out with the wet overcoat, then bolted out the door, leaving her dumbstruck in the middle of the great room.

* * *

Though the prayers of the women were for clear weather to ease Merrick's travel, the rain continued. If anything, it had worsened in the last hour since he'd gone.

As Hilde passed down the hall, Caroline emerged from her room with a full bowl of vegetable soup. The older woman looked quizzically at the younger, but Caroline shook her head.

"She won't touch it."

"It'll take a long time for this to pass," Hilde said, slipping her arm around Caroline's back and giving her an encouraging squeeze. "Her bruises will fade but the painful memory may last—" She shrugged. "—forever."

Caroline walked with her friend into the kitchen and placed the bowl on the table where she sat down dejectedly. "I want to help her. I want to help Merrick. But I seem to just stand on the outside, watching."

"Sometimes knowing that a person has someone praying for them and supporting them is just what it takes to get through an ordeal such as Lottie's . . . and the baron's."

"That's like saying it's perfectly acceptable to stand on shore and watch someone drown when you know you can do something to save them."

"No—" Hilde quickly took a seat and cupped her hand over Caroline's. "Your *presence* is important. You have a healing gift."

Caroline glanced warily at her. *Does she know?*

Hilde smiled. "I'm not accusing you of being some kind of sorceress or witch. I'm talking about your inner strength. You have an unconscious ability to bring out the best in others. Look at your sister—"

"I couldn't say that anything I did brought out the best in Ilse."

"You helped her have that baby! And you eased her passing just by being there, not to mention by promising to take Peter. Then there was Lottie," she pressed on, "she arrived just days after losing her husband and child. It's a wonder she could function at all. But she told me how warmly you welcomed her and helped her through, letting her talk openly about herself. Don't you see? You give of yourself more than you realize. Perhaps not acknowledging that fact is commendable. There are far too many of us who are boastful bores. But when you begin to think that you have nothing substantial to offer, you *need* to recognize your good."

The corners of Caroline's lips lifted into a sly smile. "You must have been a wonderful governess. With your insight, I'm sure those children became fine adults well worth knowing."

"You turn a clever phrase for one so young."

Pushing back her chair, Caroline picked up the soup bowl and took it to the long bench near the cast-iron stove. "Have you thought any more of Lottie staying on with you? Considering what's happened, she may want to come with us to America, after all. That's if—" The recurring dread of possibly losing Peter to those kidnappers made her cringe. She remembered Hilde's words and garnered that inner strength like a suit of armor. With a strike of her fist against the wooden bench top, she declared as much for Hilde's sake as her own, "Merrick *will* come back with Peter. I know it."

"Yes. I'm sure he will."

With his valise still tied on his saddle, Merrick pressed Ghebellino to the safest gait possible on the treacherous switchback trail, fairly certain he'd find Peter and the two kidnappers at the cabin on the ridge. From the evidence of the deep, mud-strewn hoof prints that had led west from the farmhouse, the two riders had left in a hurry. But the latest tracks told Merrick they'd slowed their mounts to a less-hurried pace. No doubt they were confident that they'd not been followed. With such a relaxed outlook, they would probably see no reason to continue their descent down the other side in the slippery mud.

A trickle of icy water dribbled under his collar, giving him another shiver. He hoped Peter had been sheltered from the cold rain. If they were determined to sell the boy, perhaps they'd had sense enough to protect their investment.

It was approaching mid-afternoon when Merrick spotted the thin curl of pale gray smoke rising above the evergreen peaks. Cautiously, he slipped closer on foot, bringing his horse along behind. The log structure was perched on the edge of the only flat land in the mountain pass. Although Merrick had planned to move in from behind, the absence of trees beyond the rooftop was not a good indication of the terrain. Either there was a sheer cliff or there was too much rock to sustain any growth. Both possibilities necessitated his direct approach—not a favorable choice for a surprise entrance.

Retracing his steps to the uphill trail, Merrick tethered his mount a short distance off the path, then untied the valise and took it to the sheltering boughs of nearby pine. On a bed of fragrant needles, he opened the leather case and withdrew his side arm. After readying the weapon, he made his way back to the cabin.

Careful to keep hidden behind the dense foliage of trees and bushes, he slowly worked round the half-circle clearing that edged the cliff, surveying all possible angles. Against the southern wall of the cabin, a large roof made of rough-hewn lodge poles kept the rain off of the two horses. It looked as if a small supply of quartered logs was stacked near the animals' forelegs. His only choice was to get in near enough to the firewood so that he could catch Bates when he came out for a fresh supply. The trick would be to sneak in there without startling the horses, then hope they didn't put up a fuss about the extra company while he waited.

Not surprisingly, his memory conjured up an image of Caroline putting up a fuss earlier. He would've liked to believe that he could handle those animals as well as he'd handled Caroline. But in a flash of intuition he saw he was

surely fooling himself about Caroline. She was too stubborn
to let him walk out of there without her. Even now he
expected to smell her lavender perfume mingled with this
scent of wet pine. But she hadn't come—not yet—which
was all the more reason he had to get in there and get Peter.
Caroline would be here any minute, he was sure of it, and he
wanted this matter over and done with before she stumbled
into a deadly situation.

A muscle in his left thigh bunched into a spasm from
squatting on his heels too long. Gritting his teeth from the
sudden pain, he stood up and straightened his legs, keeping
his waist bent and shoulders down.

Calculating the distance once more, Merrick flexed his
legs to relax the cramp and warm the chilled muscles. With a
final hope that no one would come out for wood until he
was there and ready, Merrick dashed for the crude canopy.
When he came within the last few feet of the horses, he felt
assured of a clean run and slowed up so as not to startle the
animals. Though winded, he made a wide arc around the
hindquarters of the horse farthest from the corner of the
cabin, then slowly approached the massive white-starred
forehead and gained eye contact. Standing silent, he let his
touch speak softly for him and smoothed his palm down the
broad chestnut cheek. As was his way, he got both horses to
remain calm in his presence, allowing him to move freely
between them.

Eyeing the low stack of aged logs, he wondered how long
he would have to wait until the supply inside was depleted.
Then he decided on a plan that might speed things up.

Swiftly unwinding the leather reins that had been looped
around the iron rings pounded into the wall, he moved the
horses out from under their shelter and sent them into the
clearing. Merrick figured that, if the animals took off without being noticed, at least the kidnappers would have lost
their means of further escape. But he hoped that the animals

would draw the couple's attention, which might distract
them enough to do him some good.

Standing back beneath the cover, Merrick leaned a shoulder against the outer wall and watched each horse slowly
amble across the rain-ravaged mud. Fortunately, the horses
were in no hurry to go anywhere. Like him, they seemed to
be waiting for someone to look out the single window that
served as the only source of light for the small one-room
cabin. At least for now, the plan was unfolding well. He
extracted his watch, checked the time and pocketed it with a
frown.

He'd made the summit in two hours. If Caroline were
taking it at the same pace, she'd be coming in any minute. Of
course, that was only considering she'd saddled a horse as
soon as he'd left.

His eyes strained as he studied the play of light and dark
shadows in the stand of trees. *If you show yourself now, little
one, I'll wring your pretty little neck.*

At that moment, the cabin door swung open and slammed
against something metal. *Maybe a bucket,* Merrick thought.

"You drunken fool," a shrill voice chided in German.
"You told me you tied them up. Get off your back and go
get them."

Merrick prepared his mind to take on Bates yet another
time. He'd have to be quick about it—and silent. A piece of
firewood would serve him well as a club. He'd catch him off
guard as soon as Bates stepped past the corner. The rain was
coming harder, so there was no worry that the woman
would stand at an open doorway, thereby hearing any distur-
bance.

Though he couldn't see her, Merrick surmised that the
woman was still watching the indifferent horses. A muffled
complaint came from somewhere within. Bates was obviously not in the mood to face the foul weather. The female
voice harped again, loud enough to bring the animals' heads
around in curiosity.

"I am *not* going out in that mud and ruin my skirt and shoes, you lazy fool. Now get out there before they take off!"

Another moment passed before Merrick heard the man's slurred voice at the door. "You keep up your screamin' an' I'll keep your half of what that baby of mine'll bring!"

"If it weren't for me, you wouldn't have even known about that certificate of birth with your name on it as the father. You were so drunk the night you left my cabin, you don't even remember fathering that Hartmann girl's child! *I* was the one who tracked her down with the help of *my* friends. If anyone deserves all the money, it's me. All you're good for is beating up women and having your way with them."

"You of all those women should know best." In the next instant Bates stumbled backward out of the house, landing on his backside in the shallow mud. The two horses skittered aside, though they were far enough away not to be threatened.

Merrick jumped back and flattened himself against the log wall to keep from being seen. Bates came up sputtering and screaming obscenities. A satisfied smile crept over Merrick's lips as he envisioned the red-brown muck coating the man's clothes. He reached for a good, solid piece of wood, palming the weight for balance. He'd have to make the first blow count, he might not get another chance to save his son.

Caroline leaned close to the horse, trying without luck to keep warm despite her sodden clothes. Hilde's words echoed in her mind, . . . *knowing that a person has someone . . . supporting them . . . just what it takes to get through an ordeal such as . . . the baron's.* She'd set her mind to go before Hilde had left the kitchen. After dashing off a quick note, she'd silently slipped out with the sparse protection of a shawl over her head, and a sweater. It would have been too much of a risk to retrieve her coat and sturdy black traveling bonnet from her room, where Lottie was settled.

What lay ahead for her at the top of the mountain, she could only guess. But she knew her place was with Merrick. Something told her that he knew it, too. Their bond now surpassed their promise to Ilse. Perhaps it had always been meant to be this way, she thought, looking back on the odd sensual visions as well as on the strange feelings she'd had in his presence. Yet, it wasn't until she'd been left to wait out his fate that she'd realized her need for him. Facing the unknown danger with him was far better than feeling helpless and completely alone.

The climb was exhausting as much for her as for the farm horse. When she spotted the sorrel off the trail, Caroline slid down and led her mount over, uselessly clutching her sweater to her chest. The higher altitude was much colder than down in the valley, even though it was already April.

After checking through the small traveling bag she'd found under a tree, she was satisfied the valise was Merrick's, and left her horse there while she walked the rest of the way up the trail. The cabin couldn't be too far.

Merrick crept low along the front of the cabin, then straightened near the door and flattened himself against the weather-beaten wall. It would only take a short time before the woman would open the door looking for Bates, not knowing her scarred companion lay in a heap next to the woodpile. Even though Bates was barely breathing, Merrick would've felt more comfortable if there'd been a way to tie him up. If all went well, however, Merrick would get his son and be gone long before the man came around.

The door rattled from within. Merrick tensed, ready to spring.

"Bates, what's keeping you?"

With his side arm poised in one hand, he swung his body around and faced the dark-haired beauty who gasped and stumbled back into the cabin. Her fingertips flew to her cheeks in shock. Then, in an instantaneous change, her smile was appealing and her voice sickeningly ingratiating.

"Oh, thank heavens, you've come," she wailed. "You've saved me from that horrid, brutal rapist!"

Merrick's dark eyes gave her a scrutinizing appraisal. This was Countess Reinhart—Louise's daughter, Elena.

"You may stop the poor acting, countess. It won't work."

"Whatever are you talking about?" she said with a dramatic display of wiping away tears.

"You know full well what I'm talking about," he growled. His jaw twitched. "You've been plotting against my family long before Peter was born."

"Are you mad?"

"Just mad enough to point a loaded gun at an unarmed woman. Where's Peter."

"I don't have . . . 'Peter.' "

"Quit playing games."

"Yes, Herr Baron," she said with a cocky, self-assured air. "Shall we talk about games? Let's see—didn't you bring home an American girl who was a notorious 'game player'? Tell me, did you ever wonder in whose bed she played best in those six so-called blissful years of your marriage? Although you may not have known the others, I'm truly amazed that you didn't have the slightest idea about Ilse's involvement with your lifelong friend—the stableboy."

Merrick stepped closer, but she hedged away and continued, ignoring his daggerlike glare, as well as the gun barrel aimed at her. "Oh, I see you never questioned her on how it was that she suddenly became pregnant when you two had worked at it for so long. She told me, you know. It was obvious that you couldn't father a child."

"Your lies are poorly disguised, countess. I knew of Ilse's methods to refrain from conceiving," he said, though he'd only learned in his reading of the diary, a fact that still boiled his blood. "And, even if you could convince me that the boy is not mine, I would still not walk out of here without him."

"Well, then—if she used a method as you say, why in heavens did she let herself get caught with child by Wil Krumhauer? I know!" She clapped her hands together and answered her own question with dripping sarcasm. "She loved you so much that she couldn't stand hearing the gossip about your lack of . . . virility. So, she took it upon herself to find a man who could, shall we say, take your place in that department and father a baby for you."

"Your idle prattle bores me. Give me my son so I may leave before my good sense gives way to violence."

"Which son, Herr Baron? The child you assume is yours by Ilse, or the bastard you fathered by the young sister? When we went to the farmhouse, we expected to find Caroline with her baby. Yet who should we stumble across but the wet nurse who's been sought in connection with Peter's disappearance. This is where I am quite confused, I'm afraid," she lied dramatically.

"It's very simple. You were obviously ill-informed about who was in that house. Caroline left three weeks ago for America. When I was told about a young mother near Freiburg, I came to see if it could be the wet nurse."

Time was running out. Merrick kept one eye on the countess and the gun well aimed as he silently moved around the perimeter of the bare, rustic cabin, looking for a sign of Peter. He found him in a dilapidated crate. A rusty nail stuck up out of the splintering gray wood just inches from his son's head.

"You'll never be at peace, Herr Baron. I am determined to get what's mine and to see your line severed. If it hadn't been for me, the others would never have gotten so stirred up about this so-called gifted child. Even those rebellious members of the church were my pawns," she said, watching him.

Keeping his firearm pointed at her, he awkwardly tried to pick up the sleeping baby with one hand. But tiny wood slivers caught in his fingertips as he cautiously scooped his hand beneath Peter. Finally, he settled on taking a handful of the crib quilt that had been wrapped around the baby, hoping to lift the bundle high enough to gather him to his chest. Slowly he brought it up two inches, then four, then six. Peter's slight weight was just enough to burden the loosely folded quilt. The material slipped. He lost his grip and the baby fell.

"Peter!" Merrick gasped, reaching to protect his son's tender head from a deadly puncture.

At that same horrifying moment, the door crashed open, sending chunks of rotted, splintered wood flying over Merrick's head.

"Take your hands out of the box or the girl dies."

Chapter 13

Merrick froze, unable to turn from the sight of his motionless son in the bottom of the crate. He knew even before the door had crashed open that there was no human way possible to stop Peter's fall in time. The crib quilt lay strewn beneath the small, still form, leaving him exposed. The minute fingers were peacefully relaxed. The thick lashes formed dark crescents across his chubby cheeks. Merrick's chest tightened to the point of physical pain. He would give his life to see Peter's blue eyes gazing brightly again.

"Lay your gun down. Then step back. Slow."

The second command confirmed Merrick's initial conclusion that it was Bates. Without turning, he knew also that Caroline was the threatened hostage. Blocking out the biting sting in the back of his eyes, Merrick forced himself to be clear-headed and ready to make a lethal move the moment the opportunity presented itself. He did as he was told.

Elena scrambled for his weapon the moment he was safely out of range and lifted the gun with both hands until she held it pointed at him.

"Turn around," Bates ordered.

Again, Merrick followed orders. Caroline stood rigid, despite the slightest shivering from the wet clothes. With her back up against Bates, her arms were pinned to her sides by one of his. The once-white blouse clung to her skin, smeared with mud from her captor's filthy sleeve. Her chin was tilted high in a valiant effort to avoid the blade lying flat against her throat. One quick avenging slash and Bates would have taken away the only reason left for Merrick to live.

His gaze settled on her green eyes. Unrestrained fear flashed within. *Be strong, Carrie. We'll get through this alive, I promise you.* He sensed her trust in him with a glimmer of hope.

Merrick turned his attention on Bates. The stringy-haired animal had to have a head of steel, considering the blow he'd taken to the back of it. But the ragged scar that puckered his eye lid and cheek were strong evidence that it would take more than a wooden club to put him six feet under.

The countess whined, once more in the tone she was more at home with. "Well? What are you waiting for? Get it over with. Then we can use him to dig the graves, before we do him in."

Bates looked at the woman incredulously.

"What's the matter?"

He tightened his grip and moved Caroline ahead of him, the twitch in his bad eye telling of the pain that was still fresh.

"That wench at the farmhouse sent them up here. If we kill them, they'll know we did it. Besides, I'm not done with this one yet. I was sorta disappointed that I missed out on having her this afternoon," he said, inching her closer to the paper-thin ticking lying on a rope bed.

Caroline whimpered. Merrick took a step.

"I wouldn't if I were you, baron. I have a feelin' it'd be a lot harder on you to see her choke on her own blood than to watch us have some fun."

Elena shrieked. "If you think I'm going to stand here and witness your little act of self-gratification, you're out of your mind!"

Inwardly Merrick smiled, if he could fight his own rage and keep his mouth shut, the woman would keep Bates from fulfilling his craving. Though she'd probably revel in making both Merrick and the girl suffer intensely, the countess was still enough of a lady to be repulsed by being forced to witness such barbaric coupling.

"Then take a walk." Bates turned Caroline around to face him, moving the sharp edge of the knife to rest just below her earlobe. "Undress for me, sweetheart." She slowly raised her hands to the top of her blouse. The buttons gave way one by one.

As Merrick watched her glance apologetically at him, he swallowed back his frustration and turned to the countess. Studying her features, it was clear she was more than a little upset with Bates's intentions. She'd gone so far as to turn her shoulder away to spare herself the embarrassing sight.

"Has he ever done this in front of you before?" Merrick asked.

"Shut up." She waved the mouth of the heavy pistol at him.

"I didn't think so. Maybe you should go over there and tie her hands like he did that girl's in the farmhouse. At least that way he won't have to call you over to help restrain her. After all, your arms are already tired from holding that heavy piece of iron for so long. Look . . . you're already letting it drop."

"I said shut up!" she screamed, shaking the weapon threateningly. "I know what you're trying to do and it won't work."

Merrick heard Caroline whimper and it was all he could do to keep his eyes locked on the countess, focusing all his energy into securing her as an unwitting ally. "You can't even keep the muzzle still. How do you think you'll hold down a struggling woman who's half your age and twice as strong."

"I . . . I could do it . . . but by then you won't be alive to see me prove you wrong."

"I'm impressed with your strength of character. Not many . . . ladies could restrain a beautiful adversary while their lover pleasures himself—perhaps beyond previous . . . experiences?"

"Ah," Bates sighed, delighted. "It's good that I'm not too drunk this time. Now I'll be able to remember this lovely body till the end of my days. Put yourself down there, sweetheart and ready yourself for the first of many."

Merrick steadied his breathing, staring intently into the eyes of the countess. What would it take to push her over the edge? Time had run out.

The bed's worn cross ropes squeaked.

Then came a metallic click. Merrick contained his relief as he watched the countess turn her head away from him to the corner. He followed her gaze.

Stripped to his waist, Bates had his back to them, leaning over the partially obscured form of Caroline huddled beneath a drab green blanket in the hollow of the threadbare mattress. "You give me a hard time and we'll have to shoot your baron friend over there."

"I'll be as cooperative as you please," Caroline said, shaken yet proud. "But not until you let him take the baby and leave."

"You're in no position to deal, ladylove."

The open wound of losing his son tore wide in Merrick's heart as he thought of carrying his lifeless child home.

Be strong, his mind commanded. Though his primary objective was to bolster the countess's strength so she'd stand up to Bates, Merrick also hoped to serve Caroline . . . and perhaps even himself.

Be strong, he repeated.

Bates glanced around as if looking for a place to lay the

knife when he caught a look at the two other adults in the room. His smug lips curled up. "Keep him right there. I wanna get a gander of his face every so often, specially when I get her callin' out for more." His chuckle was hideously vile. For dramatic effect, he flicked his knife-wielding hand and sent the blade flying into the wall above Caroline's head, where it stuck just out of reach.

With his back again turned, his hands worked the buttons of his muddy, brown trousers, then his thumbs hooked the waistband. The bed protested as Caroline squirmed to her side, turning away from the impending attack.

Merrick's palms were cold with the sweat of fury and revenge. *Be strong.*

"That's enough, Thatcher," the countess purred with the claws of a lioness ready to strike. With a jerk of her head, she motioned Merrick around toward the bed, keeping him well guarded.

Bates scoffed. "You really are afraid of losin' me, aren't you. Too good to pass up. Don't worry. There's enough of me to go——" He stopped when he caught sight of the baron cautiously moving up, then he twisted his head around.

The gun was now aimed dead at him. Even if she wavered, a shot at such close range would penetrate some vital part of his torso. She spoke with biting sarcasm. "You've succeeded in making me a jealous lover, if that's what you wanted." Merrick noted the woman's twitching response. "Get dressed. We're leaving."

"Over my dead body."

"If that's what it takes," she said, squeezing the trigger. Bates dove as a deafening report shook the rafters. Caroline screamed and Merrick started for her, but the sound of the hammer once again being cocked warned him back. "She makes a better target, Herr Baron. She can't dodge like Bates."

"Jesus, you shot me! You didn't have to shoot me!" Bates complained, writhing on the dirt floor and holding his arm.

Blood ran over his fingers and down to soak into his filthy pants. The earlier beating had slowed his response just enough for him to catch a bullet through his upper arm. Coming out the other side, the bullet had deflected and dropped its angle, embedding itself less than a foot above the rope frame.

Elena glanced down on the dazed man then back up. "Maybe you'll learn not to test me again. Now get up. We're taking that baby and getting out of here."

Though Merrick was relieved that Caroline had been spared the final act of her humiliation, he wondered what more would happen when the two realized Peter was . . . Merrick's head jerked toward the crate. His mind had to be playing tricks on him. He swore he heard a soft whimper.

"Where's that whiskey you were putting away like water?" the woman asked.

"It's in my bag."

"Here . . . get up and sit in that chair and hold this on the girl while I get it." She handed the gun to Bates who took it in his free hand. "Don't even think of turning it on me or the baron will no doubt kill you in a second for what you tried to do to the girl."

The man's glassy eyes enlarged at the threat. As long as he kept aim on the girl, he'd be safe. The countess he'd deal with later.

As she went over to the bag, she reminded, "If *he* moves, shoot her."

"Shoot her? Aren't we takin' her with us?"

"No—we aren't taking her with us," she said with a sardonic tone, poking through an old leather saddlebag. She extracted the bottle and held it up to the light, then walked toward Bates while Peter's cries grew louder, a reassuring sign to Merrick's glad heart.

When the woman passed on by, Bates became annoyed. "Where you goin' with that?"

"I'm going to give some to that wailing brat. A half of a capful did pretty good last time."

Merrick was furious. "You've been giving him liquor?"

"You've been giving him *my* liquor?" Bates chimed in.

"Keeps him quiet, especially when he's hungry. I've got to make the goat's milk last." She shrugged off their disapproval and turned her attention to the girl.

Caroline had remained on the bed, afraid to even ask if she could dress herself, despite the fact that the attack had been halted. After she'd screamed from the frightful sound of the gunshot, she'd flipped back over to see what'd happened, scared beyond belief that she might find Merrick mortally wounded. When she saw it was Bates who suffered on the floor, she looked over to Merrick. His head was turned toward an almost inaudible sound coming from the small wood crate near the rock fireplace. For a moment his eyes closed and his whole body seemed to sigh in relief. From his response, the noises must have been from his son.

Though Caroline was keenly aware of Bates's leer as he held the gun on her, she tried to keep her mind focused on the woman who looked so familiar to her. Until now, Caroline had been too scared to pay attention to the appearance of anyone in the room except Merrick. She'd never forget the anguished pain in his eyes as he was forced to stand idly by.

"Get dressed," the woman barked, glaring at Caroline.

Clutching the blanket to her bare breasts, she climbed out of the sunken mattress and huddled over the pile of clothes. Her white undergarments were soiled from Bates rolling over them in his muddied trousers. Both the blouse and black skirt beneath were cold and wet. She glanced up to Bates, then Merrick.

"It seems Bates hasn't quite had his fill of the young fräulein, countess," Merrick pointed out. "Perhaps you should hold the blanket for her privacy."

The countess! Caroline's head whipped around as the

other woman looked up from tending the baby and eyed her, then Bates, and finally Merrick.

"Be my guest," she offered with an acerbic tongue. "But don't try anything. Remember who is at stake." He knew her meaning included Peter.

Several minutes later, while Elena finished wrapping Bates's wound, he ordered Caroline to take a seat on a rickety stool and Merrick to stand behind. "That way I can hit both of you on the first try."

"Ah—but could you *kill* me is the question, Bates," Merrick posed to him confidently. "If you don't, yours will be the next life claimed." The other man seemed visibly shaken by the threat, though he tried hard to mask it.

Caroline felt Merrick's hand on her shoulder and assumed he'd placed it there to bolster her courage. For as his fingers pressed into the hollow of her tender skin, his baby Peter was being lifted out of the crude bed to be whisked away once more.

Elena gathered the now-groggy child to her breast, her fingers cradling the silken hair that had continued to darken with each passing week.

Merrick asked, "Are you sure it's only the liquor that makes him sleep so. Perhaps he's ill. He won't bring a fair price if he's sickly."

The countess smiled. "Some . . . interested parties will pay anything for a baby." Her implication met with his glare of comprehension. It was an easy enough ploy. Blackmail could bring much higher profit than selling the boy for some unknown amount in Paris.

"We've got to get going," she said to Bates, then leaned over for the quilt. When the blanket appeared snagged on a nail, she juggled the listless infant and tugged impatiently, ripping the cloth free. As she covered Peter, she straightened and muttered about the rusty nail as she walked past Merrick and Caroline on her way over to the bed. The rent left a gaping three-corner tear, exposing the thick kapok batting that had prevented the nail from penetrating the thickness of the quilt.

When Merrick's grip relaxed, Caroline reached up and took his fingers in hers and squeezed lightly. Though she was thankful he was there to support her, she sensed a tension that stemmed from watching his beloved son slip through his grasp.

"Take the baron out to get those horses and bring them up to the door. He won't do anything as long as I have her," the countess ordered as she rummaged around in her own bag and withdrew a small one-shot pocket pistol. After the two men went out, she laid the derringer on the mattress above the baby, folding and wrapping the warm quilt, then securing the bundle with a length of rope similar to that which Caroline had found in Lottie's room.

The woman was ready and waiting at the door when Bates returned with Merrick and motioned to Caroline. "Get up."

"What are you doing now?" the dark-haired countess asked.

"She can ride with me."

"I told you—she's not coming with us!"

"She's our only way out of here."

"We don't need her. We have the baby."

"That's not good enough. He's probably happy to have my bastard outta his house."

"You really are an idiot. I told you this brat was yours just to get you to help me. There is no feasible way for you to be the father—unless you knew her before she boarded the *Teutonic*, which I highly doubt."

"He's not mine?" The incredulous tone rose to an angry high pitch.

"Of course not. How ignorant are you? Even if you'd gotten to her on the ship, it's only been five months. God, you were easy to fool—if only I'd known how simple-minded you really are—" She turned and marched out.

The kidnappers were no sooner out the door than Merrick ran to the window with Caroline close behind. He rubbed away the grime and watched as Bates struggled to help the countess onto her horse, then hand Peter up to her. It took even further struggle for him to mount the star-faced chestnut, which was very nearly impossible.

"Come on," Merrick said, bolting for the door after the other two had left the clearing.

"Why aren't you leaving me here?" she gasped, following.

"Would you have stayed?"

"No."

"Then I wasn't going to waste my time trying. Hurry! We have to catch them before they make the river." He reached back and grabbed her hand to keep her steady as they ran through the mud. The rain had stopped, at least temporarily. A small blessing.

"Do you think we'll lose them if they get across?"

"I'm more concerned about the flood level from the early thaw this year. It only takes a day's *Foehn* in the Alps to melt enough snow to bring the water up. Neither of those two know the far-reaching effects of that south wind. They'd take their horses right up next to those weakened banks and the weight of those animals will take them right in—and Peter along with them."

Within minutes, they reached their two horses, untied them and headed up the hill, leaving the valise behind. They rode hard and fast, equalling one another in their riding skill on the perilous mountain. It didn't take long for them to spot the slower riders on the switchback trail below. Merrick motioned with his hand and slowed Ghebellino. Close behind, Caroline followed suit. If their presence was known too early, the kidnappers would try to run for the river, a dangerous mistake on the narrow, muddy path.

At the next turn, Merrick paused to let Caroline come alongside. He nodded to the fairly steep slope. "Do you think you could handle that farm horse down a hill like that?"

She surveyed it. The slippery wet leaves and pine needles would make it a challenge that she'd never have attempted back home, even on her own horse Becky. "Sounds like I may not have a choice."

Merrick reached over and brushed a gentle but fleeting kiss against her lips. "Such confidence," he teased, then quickly sobered. "We must get to them before the river."

"How are we going to stop them?" she asked.

"I'll hold back until you can cut down the hillside and get ahead of them. If they chance to spot me, they'll think I left you at the cabin. Besides, they wouldn't think for a minute that a woman could ride so well as to beat them through the woods."

"But what'll I do once I face them? I don't have any way to keep them from going right by—they have Peter," she countered, amazed that she had to point out that minor detail.

"Using your horse to block the path will be enough to hold them until I can jump Bates. I don't think the countess would be foolish enough to think she could go on in this wilderness without him. She may finally have to barter with Peter but she won't kill him. If necessary, she knows I'll pay her what she asks."

Caroline's fast, harrowing descent on the old horse was an endless barrage of seemingly insurmountable obstacles. The soggy ground cover muffled the thunderous hoofbeats, only to add to the unsteady terrain. Repeatedly, the horse's hooves slid, then caught. Her heart banged against her ribs as Caroline ducked beneath limbs. Giving the horse free rein, she let him decide when to weave and dodge. Hopefully, his survival instinct would save them from a fatal spill.

She made it to the first turn and checked the trail. Bates and the countess were nearly out of sight far ahead, though not yet at the jackknife turn. She plowed on with a mixture of trepidation and confidence. If she'd made it through once, she'd make it through to the next turn.

Again branches switched her full skirt. At times, needles scratched her tender skin beneath. She struggled to miss limbs. On flat land she'd have leaned down close to the horse's neck but such a shift of weight could very well send them headlong into a deadly tumble. Finally, she reached the trail. And from the looks of it, just in time. The path continued only another forty or fifty yards to its end.

As Caroline drew a deep breath and waited, she could hear the churning waters of the Rhine. Leaning over, she stroked her palm against the frothing shoulders of her mount. She wanted to praise its effort but dared not speak for fear of ruining Merrick's plans.

Then she heard them. Their loud arguing voices filtered down through the screen of trees and underbrush.

"Can't you hurry it up?" Bates called out.

"Why don't you carry this brat awhile and see if you find it any easier."

"I didn't carry him when he was *mine,* I sure as hell ain't carryin' him now. Specially with the bullet hole in my arm."

"Quit drinking that stuff," the countess chided. "All I need now is for you to fall off that horse and break your neck."

"At least you'd get to keep my share of the money."

Suddenly the woman's voice rose in panic. "Oh, my god! The baron's behind us. Hurry up!"

"Give me that brat so we can get outta here," Bates yelled.

"Be careful, for God's sake!"

"You got him tied up so tight, he wouldn't even know if I dropped him."

Caroline braced herself. In the next moment, they sped around the corner and faced her, pulling up just before the horses collided. Caroline's mount snorted and shuffled back in fright but she quickly regained control.

After the initial shock, Bates roared, "Get outta our way!"

She held her ground. "It seems the trail's too narrow to pass. Maybe you should back up."

Bates pushed his mount toward her until his smaller horse's nostrils nearly touched her knees. "If you don't find a way to move that nag, I'll shove this precious bundle of yours right down between these two animals. We can see which one crushes him first." The beasts were already agitated from the strange closeness of the other. Their hooves shifted nervously.

Caroline studied his watery eyes, reddened from the drinking. He reeked of whiskey, a stomach-churning reminder of his attack on the ship. When she remembered Lottie's battered body, she didn't doubt that his present state would lend easily to another heartless travesty.

Peter was so close she could reach out and touch his sleeping face. He looked like a photograph she'd seen in a book of a tightly bundled dark-haired Indian baby. Caroline sent up a silent prayer, hoping Merrick would realize before he made his move against Bates that the man now held Peter.

Elena craned her neck around to check the trail behind but missed the flicker of movement Caroline had seen beyond Bates. It was the first and only sign of Merrick before he broke through bushes on the upper bank and grabbed the woman. She screamed in surprise as he dragged her down and overpowered her.

"The child, Bates," Merrick demanded, holding the livid yet subdued countess.

"Or what? You don't have a gun anymore."

Merrick locked an elbow around Elena's neck and tightened. The muscles flexed, straining against the black sleeve of his jacket. The woman's eyes grew wide as she gasped for air.

"She can go slow or I can snap her neck. Which do you prefer to watch?"

A shudder went through Caroline from the icy sound of Merrick's threat. She wasn't altogether certain he wouldn't do whatever it took to win back his son. She looked at Bates, then at Merrick.

"How far do you think you can make it with that baby without the countess here to take care of it? Remember— he's no good to you sick. Think of the money, Bates."

Caroline mentally pleaded with the drunk kidnapper. *Give me the baby, Bates. Give him to me.*

Whether he'd sensed her eyes on him or he simply wanted to size up his options didn't matter. For whatever reason, Bates turned and stared at Caroline. She focused her gaze on him until his nervous blinking slowed.

Give . . . me . . . the . . . baby, Bates. Give . . . him . . . to . . . me.

His shoulders gradually relaxed and his arm started to move.

That's—right . . . Give . . . me . . . the . . . baby.

His hands lifted the bundle, then paused.

You want me to have him, Bates. Caroline directed all her energy on the man's mind, her eyes fixed on his.

Just as he began to extend his arms, his horse jerked its head up in a challenging show of intolerance. Knowing the moment was lost, Caroline lunged for Peter. Her fingers grasped the quilt as the dazed man realized her intent. He tightened his hold, drawing the bundle back. But her fingers snagged the rough rope.

"Give him to me before you hurt him!" she pleaded brokenly as the baby began to fuss from his jostling.

"Bates!" Merrick bellowed. "I swear I'll kill her!"

"Do it!" Bates yanked the bundle free and Caroline's horse pranced backward, bobbing its head angrily. Roughly shoving Peter under his wounded arm, he struck Caroline with his knuckles. Her head snapped sideways as she reeled back.

Bates gathered the reins and landed a hard kick to his horse's flanks. The mount lurched forward, pushing Caroline aside. The farm horse faltered on the slippery edge, desperately seeking solid footing in the mud.

"Merrick!" Caroline felt the massive body teeter. One back leg went over first, turning the beast so the other slid off.

"Jump, Carrie!"

She only vaguely realized Merrick had released the countess and was coming toward her, skidding down the incline.

The belly of the horse slammed against the steep bank. His forelegs caught the edge, slipping over it fast. Her foot dragged the ground, gouging out a blackened trough in the wet soil. If she didn't jump now, her leg would surely snap. She pushed off, leaping from the helpless animal, then stumbling to her knees. Merrick reached her as she scrambled to get up.

She looked back to see the farm horse struggle to gain his footing now that it was free of the extra weight. In an effort to help, Caroline reached for the reins.

Merrick pulled her hand back and ordered, "Don't hinder him," then tugged her up the hill as she watched the wild-eyed horse finally manage to gather his legs beneath him.

"Come on! You can make it!" she encouraged. The animal fought to climb the weakened embankment. Waning strength hampered its effort. As she coaxed the animal the last few steps, Merrick abruptly dropped her hand.

"No—!" he yelled, reaching the trail a moment too late to stop the countess from sailing past on her mount.

Merrick felt the power of blind rage send new strength to his limbs. He ran back beyond the turn and found Ghebellino. By the time he'd reached Caroline again, she'd led the exhausted mount up to the bend so he'd have room to pass. From the manner in which she'd tucked her skirt, he knew she stood ready to ride with him.

Against his better judgement, he put out a hand. If she'd been any other woman, he'd probably have lost her in the mud. But she made the lift in one swift movement and squared herself on the wide rump. The ride was no less difficult with her arms around his waist than if he'd gone alone.

At the bottom of the hill, the trail emptied onto another that followed the wide, turbulent river. They spotted the countess racing north after Bates, both riding at a fast clip. Merrick pressed his knees into the sorrel's sides and went in pursuit. The gray-brown water churned and boiled along the rocky shore. Small stones tumbled and clicked against one another, knocking out more rubble in their wake.

Merrick noted points where the path snaked close to the precarious bank. Slowing his horse, he guided it far away from the unstable shore. This precaution dropped them back considerably, though they could still see the two riders ahead.

Their luck changed when the winding trail veered away in several yards through a low-lying meadow. Merrick pushed Ghebellino to a run, halving the distance to the countess who, like Bates, had slowed considerably. Then Merrick saw the reason. The raging river had chewed away the existing trail. Bates worked hard to hold the baby and guide his horse among the large rocks—all that was left of the narrowed ledge between the water and a ten-foot-high embankment. Although his drunkenness and battered body made it difficult for Bates, the countess had equal difficulty. Yet she'd managed to keep pace only a few lengths behind her cohort.

When Merrick and Caroline had almost caught up, Bates repeatedly kicked his horse until he reached the end of the washout. It looked as if he'd succeeded in escaping once more. When he turned with the child tucked partially under the bad arm, he grinned at them, his mount mincing around the rocks as horseshoes clacked against stone. The hideous scar seemed to mock them.

The man's horse pranced impatiently but he continued to gloat. The countess raised her fist and shouted curses at the man for leaving her trailing behind. Most of her angry shouts, however, were lost beneath the sound of rushing water . . . and Bates's scream. Those few extra moments on the weakened bank, those few extra stomps from the animal's hooves was all it took. The forelegs went down first. Instinctively, Bates jerked backwards. The next instant, a blur of rocks and mud and swirling water took down the horse and rider.

"Get off—*quick!*" Merrick yelled needlessly, for at the same moment Caroline gripped his shoulders for support and swung her leg behind. She tumbled painfully to the rocks. It was an awkward dismount but the fastest way she knew. Bruises, sprains, or broken bones could heal. There was no time to waste—it it wasn't already too late—to save Peter.

Turning Ghebellino directly for the river, Merrick crossed the width of rocky terrain to the turbulent edge and swung off the horse.

"No—Merrick! You'll get swept away." Her plea went unanswered as she watched him jerk the boots from his feet, then jump into the murky ice water. In precious seconds, he approached the thrashing Bates. Caroline watched as the drowning man kicked Merrick away in panic.

Keeping her eyes riveted on the two men, she ran along the shore, stumbling over and over. Then she saw the countess, who'd just reached the gaping hole where Bates had last stood. The woman jumped down from her horse and squatted on the edge, straining to reach something.

It must be Peter, Caroline thought, her hopes soaring.

In the swirling water, Merrick blocked out the bone-chilling cold as he repeatedly dove in search of his son. With Peter's life at stake, he'd left Bates to fend for himself. Yet whenever he surfaced near the panic-stricken man, Bates hollered, "Get away! You'll drown me!"

The current swept them farther downstream, despite their best efforts. Merrick swam hard, while Bates appeared to have given up. He glanced back at the drowning man, then readied for another dive. A woman's scream upriver brought his head around. Elena had somehow fallen in. Stroking wildly with only one arm, her head and shoulders bobbed haphazardly. She was coming fast—straight toward him. His limbs ached from the cold and exhaustion, but still he fought.

Before she was within twenty feet of Merrick, the countess pleaded, "Take him!" It was then he saw that her other arm clutched Peter's tightly bound body to her shoulder, barely high enough to keep his face out of the water. As the two came up even with him, Merrick finally heard his son's frightened squawls.

"Hang on to him!" he yelled. "I'll bring you in!"

"No! You won't make it with both of us. I'll weigh you down!" She shoved the baby over to him.

Merrick was faced with no choice.

Caroline batted away the relentless tears that misted her vision. "Mer-rick!" Her legs couldn't keep up with the swift-flowing water. All of them were out of sight now, gone beyond the bend in the river.

"MER-RICK!"

It seemed like she'd run for miles but she knew that wasn't possible. Minutes had passed. But she didn't know how many.

When do you stop searching?

Never! her heart screamed.

Choking sobs overcame her as she forced her tired limbs to go just a little more. Then she heard it. A baby's fitful cry.

Her feet were suddenly quicker, her legs lighter. As she ran, the gasping, angry wails grew louder. When her burdensome skirt caught on a bramble bush, the sound was so close she knew Peter was just on the other side. Without missing a step, she gave a solid yank and let it rip.

She rounded the bushes and came upon on a grassy bank that sloped gradually into the water. At its edge Merrick lay

still, with his arms and legs splayed out. Even the loud cries
of the bundled baby next to him didn't rouse him.

Caroline rushed over and knelt at his side, uncertain who
to tend first. "Shh—Peter," she comforted, then turned her
attention and begged, "Merrick, wake up. Dear God, please
wake him up . . . Peter, it's okay now. Shh—"

She laid her ear to the front of Merrick's wet shirt. Despite
the baby's continuous squawls, she could hear a faint heartbeat. "Oh, Merrick—please, open your eyes."

Her hand smoothed across his cheek and the shadow of a
beard grazed her palm. Tears ran freely down her cheeks.
She sniffled, then spoke with unrestrained emotion. "Don't
leave me, Merrick . . . not now . . . not when I finally
know that . . . I love you . . . I—I probably always
have . . ." Her fingers toyed with a lock of his wet ebony
hair that curled over his forehead.

"Did you hear me?" she asked with more boldness, stifling
the tears. "I said that I *love* you."

Merrick drifted through a strange dream. Crying. A baby.
Peter? Yes . . . no, a woman. The crying formed words.
love you . . . always have . . . I love you. It was Caroline's
voice calling him back. He had to go. He *wanted* to go.

His eyelids were like lead. He struggled to open them. It
was such an effort. He was so tired. He'd never felt so
drained. Why?

Flashes of memory returned. The horse went down. The
man . . . Bates went under. The woman . . . the countess
. . . gone.

Open your eyes, he heard Caroline say. But he was trying!
Something touched him gently on his forehead. Her hands
. . . no, her fingertips . . . they were like a butterfly's
wings. In his drifting mind, he saw them float over ivory
keys. Music. Her voice was soft and lilting—like a sweet
melody.

Be strong, his spirit commanded as a light fragrance of
lavender and pine permeated his dream.

"Be strong," she repeated as if by rote, "Come back to me, my love."

His eyelids slowly blinked until he focused on Caroline's moss-green eyes. How he longed to see them light up with laughter and sparkle like emeralds.

Chapter 14

The night sky was clear and bright. Like the turbulent waters of the swollen Rhine, the thunderclouds had swept on, leaving behind an incandescent ring around the full moon that told of more rain to come.

"We should wait and get an early start," Merrick said wearily as he came into the cabin with his retrieved valise. "We might make the farmhouse before the storm. But after we've had a chance to wash and rest up, we'll no doubt get caught in it when we leave."

Back beside the river Caroline had made him rest before they'd gathered the three remaining horses and headed back up the long trail. A blouse and sweater among the countess's few belongings had served to bundle Peter once again. To stay his hunger, Caroline had found the leather pouch of goat's milk in the countess's supplies, as well as some tea biscuits which she'd dissolved and fed him. After the scant meal, the baby had calmed considerably and finally fallen into exhausted sleep.

It had grown increasingly dark on the trail as the twilight

had settled in. Because they were climbing the mountain, the setting sun had stayed with them with each successive leg of the trail. Only beneath the thick canopy of evergreen, had it become difficult to see. When they had emerged on top, the sky still glowed deep red-orange while in the east early stars glittered.

Inside the cabin, Merrick worked hard to make the small room comfortable, starting a fire from the embers. When Caroline took the sleeping baby through the shadowed room to the crate, Merrick moved with surprising speed. He dragged it over near the weak light of the still-small flames and thoroughly inspected it, extracting the single rusty nail that had nearly taken his son's life. Placing the wooden box safely out of range of flying sparks, he let Caroline finish putting Peter down and went on with his business.

The legs of the bed scraped noiselessly along the hard-packed floor until he drew it almost to the rock hearth, then turned it on its side. The thin mattress flopped over, leaving the rope webbing to cast a strange grid pattern from the growing light of the fire.

As Caroline sat back on her heels, resting her palm on Peter's chest, she silently watched Merrick plod around the room. In his own tired manner, he was driven like a man with a mission. From the assorted collection of items they'd brought back, he came up with enough blankets to drape one over the upended frame, as well as a few to form a bed on either side.

Studying him, she lowered her head and laid her cheek on her raised knees. "What, may I ask, are you doing?"

He looked up, then silently walked over to her. Without a word, he took her hand and let her stand, then led her back to the now-cozy fire. When he cupped his hands around her shoulders, she glanced down at them and tingled under their familiar warmth.

Turning her gaze back, she was met with his dark, mid-night-blue eyes. They remained that way for what seemed a long time. Seconds or hours, days or years—it no longer mattered. It didn't matter that he'd come into her world six short months ago. Only when that blade pressed to her throat, when Peter vanished in that wall of mud, when Merrick was swept from sight did she truly understand the value of time . . . the value of life.

She trembled beneath his touch, anticipating the kiss she longed to share.

Yet Merrick spoke only with concern. "You've been in those wet clothes too long, little one. I've set this up for your privacy, so, while I keep to the other side, you may hang your things on the legs of the bed and be assured I'll not wander over in the night."

He touched his lips to her forehead and a wall of confusion tumbled down upon her. He had but to ask—no, not even ask. He need only take her in his arms and she would not refuse him again. But how was she to behave when he kissed her tenderly like a father to a child? Her churning feelings were not that of a daughter, yet how could she convey such without putting question to her innocence?

Merrick released his hold on her shoulders, but to Caroline he still held her soul captive. Her heart was lost to him forever.

Suddenly his words came back to her *I'm afraid my heart has already been claimed . . . if my heart hasn't been claimed, I've surely lost it forever.*

As he turned to walk around the barrier he'd constructed, she reached out at the last moment and took his hand. He looked down, then followed her slender arm until their eyes met once again, his filled with question.

"I—" she faltered, her voice betraying her anxious anticipation. "I'd . . . like you to stay."

Solemnly, his midnight-blue eyes searched her face, "Are you sure, Carrie. I never expected . . . after what I did—"

Her hand went up to his chin, resting her fingers over his lips. "But you didn't. You couldn't hurt me, despite the hatred you had for what I'd done to you. My deception was unforgivable. You saved my life once, yet I plotted against you. You saved me a second time and I could no longer believe all those things Ilse said about you. I told you about my feigned pregnancy to wipe away all the deceit and trickery I'd brought onto you. You had every right to be angry, especially when I would have stolen your son from you. That night your rage had chosen to punish me. But in leaving my bed, you imposed the true humiliation—shunning me as though I were not fit to be taken."

"That's the farthest from the truth," he said sadly, shaking his head. He took her hand and pressed a kiss into her palm. "You have formed a very twisted vision of your beauty, little one. You didn't deserve to be taken in vengeful rage like the spoils of battle. You deserve to be cherished with care and tenderness like the most precious gift." He stroked the soft angle of her jaw with the back of his fingers and her lids fluttered closed. Her thick lashes of deep, rich brown lay still against her flushed cheeks. "I've hurt you so deeply with my anger and self-pity."

Her eyes then opened, revealing the glistening shimmer of emeralds. "It's time to turn our backs to the pain. I don't want to feel pain anymore, Merrick. Teach me what it's like to be thrown into a world of ecstasy."

He fingered her damp curls at her neck and smiled. "I see you've read Ilse's diary thoroughly." She dropped her gaze, and opened her mouth to speak, then hesitated. But he placed his finger beneath her chin and gently brought it back up. "Don't ever be afraid to speak to me with your eyes. Now . . . what were you about to say?"

"Ilse wrote that . . . you taught her the beauty of making love. Do you . . . think . . . you could teach me?"

This time, it was Merrick who opened his mouth without the words to speak. "I—don't know how to answer you. But," he quickly added when her face flushed with misunderstanding, "it's not because you wrongly asked. I don't know how to answer you because I want you to know in your heart that you are ready."

"I am," she offered.

"Ilse thought she was ready, too, but she wanted the physical pleasure . . . not the eternal unity of one soul to another. Carrie, never in my life have I ever completely understood what I'm about to tell you . . . not until now, that is—at this very moment. I pray that you will not take as long as I have to fully realize its meaning."

Caroline stared at him seriously, her trust in Merrick filling him with a warmth he'd not known existed. He took her hands and lowered her down to sit upon the blankets. The screened barrier held in the heat, warming them though their clothes were still damp. Once settled, he fixed his gaze upon Caroline's as she waited patiently for his words of wisdom.

"All of us—every one of us—has experienced that deep longing to be with someone, to feel the heat of their touch, to know them intimately." He watched her blush once more. "You're not alone, Carrie. It's natural. It's part of who we are. But that's only one side—the physical side of it. As important—perhaps even more so—is the spiritual side of it. To some, like to Ilse, it was like a double-edged blade. She thought crossing over to the other side would sever her lifeblood—her identity.

"To become one in body with a man, Carrie, takes little effort. To become one in spirit sometimes takes more than a person wants to give. It's frightening yet exciting to make that kind of commitment, to share with one another your entire being—your mind, heart, spirit, body," he said, his own heart now pounding with that same fear and excitement. "When you give yourself the first time, you truly give an irrevocable gift. It can't be taken back and given again to someone new. What I'm speaking of is not your physical chastity, but the spiritual innocence of joining as one."

Merrick faltered, wondering if she could even remotely grasp what he was so desperately trying to convey. He wanted to commit his entire being to her. Yet was she certain? Would she wake up one morning as his wife and suddenly realize that she no longer felt her soul interlocked with his?

"Merrick?" Her voice drew him back. "I know that I seem . . . that I've not had the chance to learn as much as you. But if I told you that I believe I am ready to make that commitment, would you think I was old enough to know the responsibility involved?"

He looked somewhat startled. "Would I think you were old enough to *know* the responsibility or old enough to *accept* it?"

She was dead serious. "Both."

"Yes."

"Then I do."

" 'I do'?" Merrick parroted, then broke into a smile and Caroline returned it. "We sound as if we just spoke vows."

She shrugged, embarrassed.

Merrick craned his head around, surveying the dingy, shadowy interior of the cabin. "It doesn't look like the proper place to say vows." Then he turned to her and his smile faded into a solemn, searching look. "But I can't think of a better place to propose. Carrie, I love you with every part of my soul. Please say you'll marry me."

Caroline's eyes misted and her throat tightened. It was all she could do to nod even though she wanted so desperately to tell him in her own words as beautifully as he'd just done. Finally, with her voice still caught, she half-sniffed, half-chuckled and threw her arms around his neck.

"Yes," she managed to whisper. "When I thought I'd lost you today, I thought I'd lost my soul, my spirit, everything."

He slowly pulled her away. "And you're ready to make the commitment?"

She nodded as her fingers caressed the black curls at the nape of his neck. "I'm ready right now," she offered.

"Right now?" His dark brows arched at the two-edged meaning.

"Now."

"Carrie, I love you and that's why I think you would regret not waiting until the ceremon—" Her soft lips pressed against his with insistence, igniting the smoldering fire deep in his loins.

She released him and sat back on her heels, keeping her eyes locked with his as she unbuttoned her blouse and peeled off the soiled, damp cloth, unveiling the creamy skin of her long, slender arms.

Each article of clothing that her trembling fingers removed, revealed more and more of her exquisite beauty, until she stood before him, slipping the final garment over her toes. The blazing fire danced in the hearth behind her, sending flickering light across her flawless skin, silhouetting her curves with tantalizing clarity.

Merrick was almost undressed when he froze, mesmerized by the woman before him, the woman who would soon be his wife. Though tonight they could not celebrate the sacramental ceremony, they would celebrate the union of their bodies and spirits. Merrick rose to his feet in reverent silence and faced Caroline. After a brief moment, he offered his hand to her. When she touched his palm, he held tight and each took that first step to the other.

Merrick gathered her into his arms with painstaking gentleness, wanting her to trust him and not be frightened. His mouth brushed hers fleetingly. But when she leaned into him for more, her firm flat belly pressed against his arousal. A pleasured groan escaped his lips as he crushed his mouth to hers with an urgency that couldn't be restrained. He curved his hands under her bottom and pulled her closer. Her deep-throated moan overwhelmed his senses.

He lowered her down to the warmth of the blanket, melting under her gaze of complete trust, complete love. As he lay down next to her and propped up on one elbow, his eyes roamed down the length of her golden fire-lit skin. Her large round breasts whet his desire. When her hands came up to cover herself, he glanced up confused, then saw the look of self-conscious embarrassment.

"You have nothing to be ashamed of, Carrie," Merrick soothed reassuringly. He moved her hand aside and cupped her full breast under his palm and lowered his lips to pepper light kisses around in a circling spiral until he reached the dark nipples. Caroline's gasps as he suckled her drove him wild.

As she reveled in her newfound delight, his hand roved from her breast and across her belly. Her breath caught as he followed along her thigh, purposely avoiding her center of awaiting need, prolonging the heavenly agony. His fingers stroked the inside of her silken thighs, parting them a bit each time that he brought his touch closer and closer to the soft curls of her womanhood.

Her back arched ever so slightly with growing anticipation. He felt her hands move, tentatively at first, then she brought them up and ran her fingers through his hair as he teased her other nipple erect.

Caroline's mind swirled. Each sensation forced her beyond what she felt possible, yet still not far enough. Then his first touch within her moist, intimate folds brought a flash fire licking at every inch of her body. Her hips lifted and a guttural moan emerged from deep within, urging Merrick to quicken his tantalizing caresses. The ecstasy increased until her body responded of its own accord. Blindly reaching out, she slid her fingers to Merrick's broad shoulders and down his arm, gripping his muscles with the tense pleasure quaking through her.

Merrick trailed his kisses up to the hollow of her shoulder, then to her neck, still petting her, bringing her to the very edge before he would slip his weight onto her for the consummation of their passion. Beneath his gaze, Caroline's eyelids closed tight, her mouth dropped open as she drew in gasps of air.

He nibbled on her earlobe, then kissed it and whispered, "Are you sure, little one?"

Her fingers tightened around his arm, her soft brown lashes lifted slowly, revealing a smoldering yet pleading look in her emerald eyes. She could only nod.

He lowered his mouth to hers, slipped his tongue in to seek her response until she followed his lead, sharing the gift of oneness, taking him in a way that was a sample of their coupling soon to come. When their kiss grew feverish, he knew it was time.

Moving onto her, his manhood easily found her moist entrance while she moaned amid the distracting kiss. As he hungrily pressed his lips tighter, his mind begged . . .

Forgive me, Carrie.

He thrust his hardened manhood fast and deep. Her startled scream was muffled to a cry that only the two of them could hear. Merrick held her tight, not moving until her pain could subside. He dropped his head down and kissed her shoulder as her sobs shook him to the core.

"The worst is over, little one. I promise you."

The tearful crying continued as her hands slid over his back and held him close. He then knew that she didn't hate him for what he'd done.

"Let it out. Let out all the pain," he said, fighting back his own with no luck. All of the emotion he'd held back—the anger, the sadness, the bitterness—choked him until he could stand it no longer. He wanted—no, he *needed* to pour out his soul inside her, to feel wrapped in her nurturing womb.

As if she felt his need, Caroline's sobs slackened and her body relaxed. Merrick lifted his head and met her tear-filled gaze. Slowly he moved inside her, watching her fearful eyes for any sign of renewed pain. But with each successive thrust her lids fluttered a bit more, her hips tilted slightly to meet his. Gradually he built her back up, step by step, pulsing a rhythm until her hands pulled his chest down to her.

The soft warmth of her breasts next to him sent an added frenzy to his loins. He buried his face in her lavender-scented hair and pushed harder and deeper. Caroline's legs curled around his waist and tightened in her moment of fulfillment.

Her body's response triggered the culmination of his own blinding ecstasy. His deep groans mingled with hers as the pressure within him released, spilling into her, filling her with promise and pleasure—for them and for the little one soon to grow within her womb.

As he started to lift his heavy weight from her, she roused only enough to slide her hands to his hips and hold him. "Don't go . . . not yet," she begged, her eyes opened only slightly and she smiled contentedly. "I never want this feeling to end. I wish you could stay inside me forever."

He relaxed enough to quell her fear of losing him but held his weight off her so he wouldn't burden her breathing. Kissing the uptilted corner of her mouth, he answered, "I'd like to stay inside you forever, too, little—" He cut off his own words. "I think it's time to stop calling you that. I guess it was my way of denying what my heart knew all along—that you're not a little girl anymore."

"But I like the name now."

"Then you'll like it even more when I start calling our baby 'little one.'" Caroline closed her eyes and stretched her sated body beneath him, too caught up in the afterglow of their lovemaking to fully understand his meaning.

By all rights Merrick should have fallen asleep long ago, exhausted from his battle to save Peter's life. Yet at that moment, he had never felt more awake and alive.

Several minutes later, Merrick lay on his side, once again propped up on his elbow, staring down at Caroline. Her breathing was yet uneven, her breasts lifting with each shallow intake. His eyes took in the deep red flush of her nipples, still aroused from their passion. He looked down at her belly and a wave of joy washed over him. Now his seed was moving within her and his child would begin growing in a mother who would nurture him—and Peter.

He reached up and smoothed his hand over her tummy, her satin skin soft beneath his touch. Her eyes fluttered open and she gifted him with another sweetly satisfied smile.

"How do you feel?" he asked, his midnight-blue eyes swallowing her.

"Tender." Caroline reached down and covered his hand with hers, reveling in the warmth of his touch, which seemed to penetrate into her womb and flutter to life.

"I'm sorry," he offered, looking slightly miserable.

"I know."

"Are you sorry you gave yourself to me?"

"No—never." She smiled—something she decided she might never stop doing. His hand gently rubbed her belly in an intoxicating caress and she let her eyes drift closed once again, imagining herself rounded out with his baby.

"Merrick?"

"Mm—?" He nuzzled her ear, renewing her inner fire.

"Would it anger you if I were to conceive this night?"

His kisses fluttered across her neck. "I fully plan on it." Tired of the talk, he sprinkled more kisses down to her breast, nipping and sucking on her nipple until Caroline squirmed beneath his touch. As he slid his legs over hers, his manly desire was evident.

She tensed. "Wait, Merrick."

He lowered his weight onto her, leaning on his forearms. His loins ached to join their bodies once again. "What is it, Carrie?" If she denied him until their betrothal, he'd surely lose control. Already the rich dew of her womanhood moistened the tip of his throbbing, erect shaft, poised to enter and be sheathed by her.

Caroline stammered. "Is—"

"Are you afraid it will hurt again?" he asked. When she

nodded, he thought of another fear that could lie dormant ready to tear apart all they now had—the fear that she would suffer the same fate as Ilse in childbirth.

"Are you afraid to carry my child?"

She shook her head in silence. He looked upon the child he'd taken into womanhood only moments earlier—the fearless girl who'd stood against all odds—and he felt his need for her grow.

"Be strong, little one. I promised you that it wouldn't hurt again . . . and it won't," he said gently.

As he slowly slid into her, Caroline tilted her head back and gasped from the rapturous sensation that expanded through her body. He lowered his lips to hers, kissed her once, then twice, each one accompanied by slow, even strokes into the feminine depths of her being. Her initial introduction to this wonderful, delirious world had been filled with anxious frenzy; this time, however, Merrick seemed to sense her need to take it with less urgency as she learned the nuances of her response to his body and his spirit.

His voice was raw with emotion as he dropped his face to her hair and spoke intimately into her ear. "I died a thousand deaths when I thought you carried another man's child. I wanted it to be mine. I told myself it *should* be mine. Now that we're together, I can only think of filling you again and again."

"Then I'll never deny you that joy," she breathed to his rhythmic thrusts, meeting him with equal fervor until they climbed once more in union of body and soul, making their love spiral upward into joyous heights.

"Merrick?" Caroline whispered, her head lying on his shoulder as the dawn crept into the room.

"Hmmm?"

"I understand what 'making love' means."

He chuckled silently to himself. "I hope so."

She playfully swatted his chest.

"Okay—what do you understand?"

"Making love means more than the coupling of two people. I think it means that each time we join together, we bind together all that we are, building our love one step at a time, creating something—a link between us that gets stronger and stronger until absolutely nothing can break it."

With his eyes still closed, Merrick grinned. "I like that."

She nestled closer, content with herself for pleasing Merrick, as well as for coming closer to understanding spiritual fulfillment.

"If couples bring their individual strength into their commitment of love to one another," she pondered aloud, "imagine the potential for our relationship with our gifts of the mind."

Merrick answered her musing. "Let's look at it as an added bonus, a blessing."

Caroline leaned up and kissed his lips, then settled back down to sleep until Peter would wake.

But Merrick's eyes stayed open. Savoring the tender touch of her mouth against his, he began to feel his desire for her warm his loins.

A flash of lightning brightened the interior of the warm farmhouse, followed by a deafening roll of thunder. On a sofa in front of the oversized hearth, Lottie nervously put her book down on her lap. Hilde paused from her needlework and patted the young girl's hand, receiving a weak, but appreciative smile in return.

Merrick watched the exchange with warm approval of Lottie's decision to stay on as Hilde's companion. Then his attention fell to the freshly bathed baby who lay wriggling his fingers and toes happily in Merrick's lap. He offered each tiny fist a bent little finger, watching as Peter grabbed hold and used his chubby little arms to pull himself up—with his papa's help—to a sitting position.

Hilde said, cheerfully, "I'd swear that boy is the spitting image of you. More true now than ever." The ebony-haired baby giggled over some unknown musing, then looked into his father's eyes.

"Ja, Ich bin Ihrer Meinung. Das ist mein Sohn."—Yes, I agree with you. This is my son, Merrick confirmed aloud as well as in his heart. In deference to Lottie, they spoke in the tongue she understood.

"Was there any doubt?" Caroline emerged from the hall in a fresh traveling dress of deep burgundy that hugged her generous curves. She watched his admiring gaze and felt the ever-present flutter that Merrick's presence created deep within her.

His chuckle was joined by his son's. "Spoken like a true, defensive mother."

Lottie asked about their plans. "Will you be getting married before you board the ship?"

The couple looked at one another. Not only was Caroline mildly taken aback by the blunt inquiry, but she didn't think that their intentions were so evident. She was at a loss to answer. If she had conceived last night as he'd planned, it would have to be soon. But waiting until reaching Sebula would be fine with her as well.

Hilde broke the silence. "I don't think the baron would like to draw attention to his new wife by having their marriage a matter of public record."

Merrick blinked and turned back to the older woman. "You're quite right. I—believe Caroline would like to marry in Sebula, though God knows it'll take heaven and earth to get her parents' blessing."

Unconsciously, Caroline smoothed her hands across her belly from habit, a gesture that did not pass unnoticed by Hilde. Merrick followed the woman's gaze, then turned back to see it on him. She knew that he'd claimed more than Caroline's heart in that cabin. Did she also perceive what he hoped to be true, what he *knew* to be true? Her mouth curved up as she pointedly glanced at Peter, then Caroline, then back to Merrick.

"Do you have everything packed, Carrie?" Merrick finally asked, standing with Peter in his arms.

"I think so."

"Good. We should be leaving for the train station within the hour." Merrick again exchanged glances with Hilde.

"Lottie," the older woman said in German. "Would you like to take Peter in to dress him on *Tante*'s bed. I think she'd like to say her good-byes."

"Ja," she answered, happy to put down her studies and play with the baby.

As the lightning and thunder continued, Merrick started down to the animal stalls to ready the carriage and horses. Hilde guided Caroline back into her room to see to the final details of her baggage.

"What is your trunk doing here?" Caroline asked, regarding the old, yet decidedly familiar piece of luggage.

Hilde silently opened the lid, then turned to the wardrobe. "I have no plans to be leaving here, other than perhaps a move into smaller quarters in town. So I really have no need for it. Since the baron's hasty departure left him with no more than a valise and you do have Peter's things to worry about . . ." Her words trailed off.

Caroline watched her friend bring out the exquisite gowns the baron had purchased. "And since you have no use for maternity gowns hanging in your house, you thought I should have a means to cart them along with me in the event that I ever—"

"Have a social to attend in—say, six or seven months?"

The younger girl blushed bright red. She threw her hands to her face and whirled away in embarrassment. "Oh, Hilde, I didn't realize that I'd been so brazen about it. No wonder Lottie asked about our marriage. Is it any wonder that people will point fingers and stare at us when I travel unescorted with the baron?"

Her shoulders were gripped by her friend's two hands, turning her back around. "You haven't been brazen. As a matter of fact, you've been unduly quiet. No, child. It isn't that you've lain with the man you love that shows in your eyes. I believe that, as luck would have it, the baron has placed in you his next child. And from the twinkle in his eyes, he's not only sure that you'll need these gowns shortly, but my guess is that he's bursting his buttons inside."

"But——" Caroline looked down and splayed her fingers over her womb. "The fluttering . . . I thought it was just from him being near."

Hilde chuckled. "That could be, too. As you may remember, every woman carries a child differently. And every new mother has a glow about her when she is truly happy with her life's choice."

The younger girl's fingers touched her cheeks in awe. She turned to the small oval mirror inside the wardrobe. "You mean I'm glowing?"

"As radiantly as any woman I've ever seen."

Caroline spun around and hugged her older friend. "I really am happy, Hilde. Do you really think——? And Merrick thinks——?" Suddenly, her elation plummeted.

"What's wrong?"

"Merrick was right to doubt that my parents will bless our marriage—let alone any child I carry."

With smiling optimism, Hilde reached into the wardrobe. "That brings me to the second reason we're in here." She brought out the worn Bible and handed it to Caroline, explaining, "When I left you at the estate, I'd promised to try to learn more about the attempts on Peter, but that proved impossible. After you came to stay, I prayed that there might be another way in which I could be of help. Only last night, when I thought of your gowns and my trunk, did I think back on the conversations we had in our stateroom on the ship. You talked about the frivolous gowns and the riddle in your mother's Bible. Look inside the back cover."

Caroline flipped it open but there was nothing there.

"Feel along the edges. They're not smooth like inside the

front cover. It's been glued back down. I didn't dare try to steam it until I told you about it. I think your mother may have sealed something behind there that—"

"—answers the riddle. Of course!" Caroline exclaimed, then recited the poem from memory.

> *"Amid your battles you have fought,*
> *Stand armed with spiritual thought.*
> *While you walk this earthly ground,*
> *In this book your hopes are bound."*

During the time-consuming minutes that Caroline patiently held the Bible over the steaming kettle so that only the end paper was affected by the moist heat, Merrick came up to announce that he had only the last trunk to take down.

"What have we here?" he asked, stepping into the kitchen in his search for Caroline. After she briefly explained the riddle, he stood next to her, as caught up in the mystery as the women.

Finally, with book in hand, Caroline sat down at the table with Merrick standing close behind her right shoulder, his fingers resting casually on her collar bone. As Hilde sat alongside, she slid a knife under the loosened edge, sliding it carefully. Inch by inch, she peeled back the paper, lifting it high enough to peer beneath. A slip of writing paper lay folded in half, pressed against the hard backboard.

Caroline withdrew the note from its well-concealed hiding place and smoothed it open on the table. The tiny handwritten words had slightly blurred from the moist steam, making the message almost illegible.

"Dearest . . . Mother," Caroline began. "As I lie weak with Merrick's child, I know that I won't live through this trial—my punishment for tricking Merrick . . . and you. The deeper I sunk into this lie, the more wicked I felt, as though demon-possessed.

"I beg that you send Carrie so that I may see her one last time, that I may know that she can take this child that should have been hers. I promise I'll never tell her that I am not Father's child. Both of you have had to live with that pain, then I forced your silence by giving myself to Merrick, even though it is Carrie who is the intended first born of Father's line.

"Please let her come. If she doesn't know the true reason behind my request, and nothing transpires, then it wasn't meant to be. But if Merrick and she find in each other a unique, binding spirit shared only by them, then please bless their union.

"I wait anxiously for your response. Your loving daughter, Ilse."

Caroline felt Merrick's fingertips press gently into the hollow of her shoulder. Instinctively, she reached up to take his hand in hers. Fighting the quiver in her lower lip, she turned to Hilde, looking upon the woman who'd come to mean so much to her in so few months, who'd given strength and help in her quiet way. And now, she'd found the key that unlocked a barrier created by jealousy and lust, a barrier that had kept Merrick and Caroline apart—until last night.

" 'Thank you' somehow doesn't seem to be enough," Caroline said to Hilde, who rose to her feet and delivered a light kiss on both cheeks to each of them.

"Yes," Merrick added. "Thank you . . . for everything."

"I'm glad I was a part of your lives, for however brief a time it was." Her voice wavered. "I'm afraid I hear *Tante* calling. Go with my love. God be with you." The woman hurried from the warm kitchen before her tears should spill.

Merrick drew Caroline to her feet and looped his arms around her waist. "This puts things in a much different light."

Caroline looked up into his midnight-blue eyes and smiled. "So perhaps it was not such a dark covenant, after all."

"There are many covenants, little one. Like those of priceless valuables and aristocratic titles, I would still say that this covenant brought with it a lion's share of jealousy and greed . . . and death."

They were quiet a moment with remembrances of all the lost souls.

Caroline shook her head incredulously, "At least there was some good that came of all this—we now know that I was your intended from the beginning."

Merrick nuzzled her ear. "Ah. And you are the purest, spiritual side of that double-edged sword."

"And Ilse's confession now means that your father had not deceived you completely. He may have kept the truth about Louise from you. But he hadn't lied to you about the vision . . . the covenant. You were to marry the first born daughter of Ernst Hartmann. And I believe we *will* have a gifted child."

A flicker of renewed hope and trust danced in his gaze. "Still . . . it will take time for old wounds to heal," he said, more to himself than Caroline.

"But they will heal," she reassured him.

He drank in her luscious lavender scent, freshened from her recent bath. Her dark curls were pulled back as he liked, with a ribbon gathering the sides and letting the rest fall freely down her back. Her dark lashes framed the soft green of her eyes. Her inviting lips drew him closer until he tasted her, knowing that this kiss must suffice for the moment.

Caroline leaned into him, caressing the corded muscle of his neck as his mouth claimed hers with a hunger she welcomed. While cherishing this private moment, she longed for their journey to be over so that she'd not be taunted with the need to feel his intimate touch. His arousal strained against her as a memory of passion rushed back with vivid clarity, a memory of the moment she'd asked him to remain with her after all their strength had been spent. Looking back, she now knew why she'd clung to him.

The fluttering began again. Now aware of its new meaning, Caroline drew back with a somewhat startled gasp.

"Carrie?" Merrick's voice was etched with concern, then his gaze fell upon her hands tentatively touching her belly.

Her eyes met his. "Do you remember when I said that I never wanted the feeling to end? When I wanted you to stay inside me forever?"

"I'll never forget."

"I think—no, I *know* now that I needed you to share in the spiritual birth of our new life and our new child."

As his eyes misted, Merrick wrapped her in his arms and stroked her long curls. She pressed her cheek against his broad shoulder, and he whispered in her ear, "I love you, little one . . . and I love you, too, Carrie."

A lump caught in her throat at his touching welcome for that special, growing part of him that stirred within her womb. Tilting her head back as Merrick lowered his mouth to hers, she moaned quietly beneath the tender softness of his lips. The kiss quickly deepened, stirring desires that could not yet be fulfilled . . .

but therein lay a new promise . . .
A new covenant.

And they are gone; ay, ages long ago,
These lovers fled away into the storm.
Eve of St. Agnes
—Keats